TREKKING *To* TEEMA

Pieter-Dirk Uys

book

ROVOS RAIL
The Pride of Africa

THE MOST LUXURIOUS TRAIN IN THE WORLD

The publishers and the author, concerned about the escalating prices of new books in South Africa, agreed to include advertising that would subsidise, in part, the production costs of the book. We would like to thank the advertisers for seizing this unique opportunity.

Published by Book, an imprint of comPress, Unit 3.3 Hills Building, Buchanan Square, 160 Sir Lowry Road, Cape Town 8001, South Africa

ISBN 1-919833-10-2

Cover artwork by Radarboy
Cover lay-out by Audrey Botha
Typeset by User Friendly
Printed by CTP Book Printers, Parow

CHAPTER 1.

"But you can't even remember her surname!"

The small lines round her mouth seemed sharper.

Deli didn't get angry. She showed her irritation by creating lines on her face where lines had never seemed to be. Today there were many little lines round her mouth. Maybe she was tired, organising the party and the occasion of a fiftieth birthday. She'd done it all before so many times though. Parties couldn't be the reason for more lines.

"Well?"

She didn't look at him while brushing her hair, but he could see the idea of him leaving the next week on what she'd already called a wild goose chase to Africa, was not something she was just going to leave alone. Her brushing repeated itself as she stared at her mouth in the mirror.

"Damn all those little lines," she thought. "I mustn't let this thing get me down."

She put down the hairbrush. A bottle of perfume fell over and the amber liquid spurted onto the powder compact. She tried to straighten it and dropped her handlotion onto the carpet. It gurgled into a puddle of pinkness.

"Oh fuck it!" she spat and stared down at the squidgy mark on the design next to her chair.

"Deli, that's not the point!" he stated. "I know where she lived. I'll find her."

He tried to make it sound as if he was going to the local library to find a book on archery. Not all the way across the world to try and find an old black woman called Fatima. A servant whose surname he had never known. But he had loved her and she would remember him.

"She's probably dead." Deli looked back in the mirror and licked her lips. "How old was she when she bathed you?"

"I was seven," he said and smiled. "I was only seven."

"And she must have been in her twenties?"

"Maybe …" He found it difficult to even remember her face after all those years. "I don't know. Look, when you're seven everyone looks old. Twenty was old. Teema looked old when I was seven."

Deli sighed and closed her eyes. Rows of plates of food appeared in her mind and she shuddered. She was a vegetarian and here she was catering for meat eaters. His friends always ate meat, her friends always didn't. A great marriage.

He put a tie against his shirt and looked at the combination without noticing that he was already wearing a tie.

"If she was in her twenties, let's say 23, and I was 7, she'll only be 66 today. The Bowmans are 66 and they play squash."

As he heard what he said it sounded even sillier.

She groaned. "Angel, the Bowmans live in Los Angeles and are millionaires and can afford to be 66. And don't believe that squash story. I've never seen them play squash, have you?"

He hadn't, but he felt like an argument.

"Yes, actually I did," he lied.

"Your Fatima would be 66 in South Africa. A black doesn't play squash at the age of 66 in South Africa."

"No, but she might be alive and I might find her!"

"Why, David?' She turned to him and for the first time he saw fear in her eyes. "Why do you want to go all that way to find a 66-year-old black woman without a surname?"

He started knotting the tie round his neck.

"It was an idea. Look, forget it." He wanted to fight but he knew it wasn't worth it. Not yet. The fight would come later. "Help me with this, will you?"

She got up and walked across the room to her husband, took the tie from his hand and slowly pulled it off his neck.

"And you're going crazy too. You're already wearing a tie, dumpling."

She hadn't called him that since the night of their car smash, when he woke up in hospital with his arm in traction and she just winked and said: "Hello, dumpling." It had made him feel so alive.

"Is this a car smash?" he murmured, stroking her hair. "You only seem to call me that when I escape with my life."

"I don't want you to go to a country that looks like a video nasty!" she persisted. "It's Beirut all over. It's the Wild West. You put that behind you 31 years ago, David. No, look at me." She pulled his face round to meet her eyes. "We don't talk about that part of your life, remember? That was your rule, not mine. No mention of that part of David Clayton."

"Yes."

It sounded more like a sigh than an answer.

"So can we rather talk about tonight now? There are many names to remember and you'll have to make a speech."

"I know."

"But David, you won't remember all the names! You know how terrible you are with names."

She went back to the dressing table and sat down. She looked in the mirror at him staring down at the carpet in front of him.

"I didn't prepare a speech, Deli … maybe just a few thank you's?"

"That could take all night. They're all going to be here. You owe many people."

"I owe America." He looked up at her and smiled and his face was 26 again and she felt tears rush to her eyes. "And I owe you."

"No, you married me. That's a fair deal."

They looked at each other, while familiar pictures like those from a well-thumbed family album slid through their memories. Their first date; he was ill from too many oysters. She then dented a rented car. They'd giggled in bed and sex was impossible. A hangover. Her parents didn't like him because they sensed he was hiding something. He was hiding something, but so well that no one ever noticed.

"I really love you, Deli," he said softly.

She looked at his affection with horror.

"Oh Jesus, you've got cancer!" She leapt up and went to him, her arms round him, her cheek against his shoulder. "You've had terrible news from Dr Jeandro last week and now you want to go back to your roots to die!"

"I'm not going to die." He pulled her face gently away from him and kissed her on the mouth. The little lines were less.

"I'm not going to die."

"Promise?" She whispered, tears running through her carefully applied eye makeup.

"Yes, promise." David laughed, "I'm only turning 50."

The small package from South Africa lay on his desk for two days.

He wanted to open it, but then again knew that it would upset him. Herman Greef always managed to make him feel guilty, playing childish tricks on him by tearing the secure bandages off his past and making the cuts bleed again.

Herman would send him cuttings and cartoons usually from Afrikaans newspapers, and although David pretended not to understand or even try to make sense of his old dusty mother tongue, it was amazing how quickly the jumble of words reorganised themselves into a familiar hallelujah of those open vowels and guttural sounds that made Afrikaans so recognisable.

Herman would also send him *biltong* and *droëwors*, chips of dried meat tightly packed in a vacuum plastic holder, looking like prehistoric examples of dinosaur shit and sometimes tasting like it too. Occasionally Herman sent pressed flowers from the veld and bright yellow leaves from the trees of Kirstenbosch, the botanical gardens in Cape Town where they often went as small boys on school nature excursions.

Herman enjoyed the torture, and David fell for it each time. That darkened room of an African yesterday would for one brief second explode in a rainbow of colourful memories and smells and sounds, and he would have to try very hard to jam closed the door and move forward into his American life. And here it was again, another lethal gift from the land of his beginnings.

Only the stamps changed. They were once all uniformly floral, and the clumsy proteas and delicate disas and other truly strange artichoke-lookalike bulbs and buds passed from postbox to post office and then sometimes into stamp collections. Then there were the rash of political images, rows of former Afrikaner prime ministers, dour and brownly-tinted. "What a bad taste it could leave to have to lick their arses each time you want to send a letter!" Deli had smirked and dropped them into the box marked 'Stamps'. Then came the great concrete monuments to the state apparatus of the Boer empire: bridges and dams and power stations, and if you didn't know RSA stood for Republic of South Africa, you'd think the letter came from another grim socialist state in Central Europe.

David looked at the stamps on this package lying on his desk. There were many stamps disarranged in no particular order and they were varied, most new, all awful. A few posed sportsmen who all looked the same: white, blonde and winning something local. There were a few positioned animals, thin and bland. A transparent political smile here, a lumpy concrete monument there. Even a cluster of amoeba-like creatures.

"Looks like another incurable virus," David smirked.

He did eventually open the packet and kept the stamps which all went back into the box marked 'Stamps', which was next to the box marked 'Bills', which was next to the box marked 'Old Xmas Cards'. An ordered household, these Claytons. Close to a recycling plant.

4

The present contained a small business card, with Herman Greef's new address embossed in dark gold letters. Just his name and under it the word 'Publisher' in English and ... what was this? Zulu for publisher? No, Afrikaans: *uitgewer*? Herman had recently moved his office from Johannesburg down to Cape Town, back to the old roots, the old haunts, the old memories.

"Can't be healthy, my boy ..." David smirked as he flicked Herman's card into the small box marked 'Business Cards And Addresses: still to be Filed'.

He held a cassette in his hand. It had been recorded off something else, so didn't have a label identifying what was on it. Just Herman Greef's neat handwriting, its tongue deep in its cheek.

"Happy Birthday *ou ou OU* Pal!" curled round the edges of the sticker, and on the back: "Listen to this tape when you're alone and have a good ha ha ha on me ...!"

A funny tape? This was a new one from the master of the nudge-nudge joke. Probably the latest selection of Nelson Mandela jokes, or Winnie Mandela jokes or just any Mandela jokes. Herman Greef enjoyed his new democratic right to free speech and that gave him, he thought, the freedom to tell racist jokes under the guise of his human rights.

David slid the tape into his deck, picked up the earphones and slipped them on. He didn't want Deli to hear whatever was waiting for him on the thin band of surprise.

The soprano's voice was instantly recognisable. She'd sung so often on the radio with them as kids quietly clustered round it, either waiting to hear a beloved daily serial, or just quietly listening to what was being fed them by the State in the name of entertainment. The radio of the 50s had created his fertile imagination and that imagination had, in turn, given him a successful career here in the City of Dreams, finding other people's stories to turn into profitable films.

But Cape Town was so far from Los Angeles, and the rich voice of the Afrikaner opera singer, who also dabbled successfully in superb boerekitsch, sounded as if it was coming from a different planet.

He'd laughed at her songs all those years ago because she was so representative of that part of his background that he needed to despise in order to escape from it. She would sing of the gentle life of being Afrikaans, without having to look over the fence into the reality of the poverty beyond. Her subjects were the little white

5

children patiently waiting for a miracle from the angels and getting it, while small black babies just looked sweet and died with smiles on their faces. She sang of the thorn trees and the blue mountains and the lazy muddy rivers and the arid expanse of that Karoo that the 43c stamps couldn't capture. She didn't make it sound florid and operatic; she made it all smell real! But he'd never really listened, other than to laugh.

Not till now.

So this was his present from the joker!

Herman Greef knew that David would hear the first song on the tape and be prostrated with uncontrollable laughter. Herman Greef knew David would then be reminded of all the stupid sentiment and empty images that had built up their gallery of heroism in childhood. His old friend Dawid de Lange would at least turn fifty and have the best laugh of his life.

But David Clayton didn't have the best laugh of his 50 years. By the third song, the opera singer was still on an old farm, singing of gentle animals, vivid dreams and happy families. She'd pushed the edges of his imagination beyond the glossy postcard-confines of kitsch, and he found himself falling headlong into the picture with all its timeless detail.

When she sang of the sharp wind across the sun-browned veld and the flaming sunset on the Karoo and the glittering stars in a velvet sky specially spun over the promised land far down south, David was in tears. It was the first time he had allowed himself to cry for his country, to cry for his life and to cry for his inability to have cried for so long.

By the fourth song he had made the decision.

He would go back to this place he once called home and try and find it again.

When he looked out of the small porthole of the plane, the dawn had already escaped the coming of the sun. The red earth below, if it was indeed ground below and not a vast burnt chicken, was unmarked by roads, or buildings, or even low clouds.

David glanced up at the TV console against the ceiling where on a map of Africa the position of the plane was shown, a small white cockroach zigzagging across the screen from the top corner near Morocco, right across the former Congo and now slightly to the right of Angola, edging its way to the word 'Johannesburg'.

6

He was still dying to go for a pee, but put it out of his mind. "Think about something else and the pressure might move down to your ankles," he prayed. He'd wanted to pee since the movie ended four hours before. Not a movie he'd wanted to watch, but as David couldn't sleep on planes, he'd put on the earphones and pretended to follow the story. The plastic pieces bit into his head. The sound was woolly. The film was crap and he wanted to pee. He was jammed against the window because he'd asked for a seat there.

Deli had said to "sit on the aisle in case you want to pee, as always, and there are two fat people next to you."

"Oh no," he'd gurgled, always knowing best. So here he was, not on the aisle, yes with a pee and, yes yes, two huge fat black men sitting next to him and the relief of a toilet far down the plane.

Normally he would have said: "Excuse me, can I pass?", but somehow this being a South African Airways plane and those being blacks and him being white made the whole operation somewhat complicated. So he'd sat back four hours ago and tried to dry up the torrent in his loins.

It had been a monstrous flight. Twenty hours of discomfort. Plastic food. Air-conditioning that immediately set off his sinuses, so that he started blowing his nose an hour out of Los Angeles LAX airport, and now it was red and shiny and the constant sound of his snivelling set hackles up all around him.

"Sorry," he would mutter every time he took a breath and blew pieces of tissue snow all over the seat in front of him. First there was the five-hour flight to New York's JFK, then the wait for his connecting plane and the beginning of his trek to …?

David focused in on the one thought that froze in his mind: Where was he going?

A sense of panic gripped him. The area of his stomach not preoccupied with keeping him from wetting his pants contracted in a spasm of terror. What was he doing in this plane, flying over the burnt carcass called Africa, with a full bladder and an empty itinerary?

His life all seemed so far away and it was. Los Angeles, with the familiar smog and everyday race tension, and the office with its signed pictures of stars and producers and directors and the exhausting script conferences and the laborious meetings with inscrutable Japanese moneymen.

And then that recent birthday party for him. That's where it seemed to focus. The 50th birthday.

7

He'd made his speech and thanked everyone, and they all smiled happily and said: "Oh no, it's really nothing." He'd prayed he hadn't left out someone. The next milestone birthday was 60 and by then he wanted to be set up somewhere safely in retirement. Besides, most of them to thank properly would be dead by then!

Deli had excelled herself and the food was great and everyone seemed as impressed as they expected to be. His daughters both looked beautiful, their husbands stayed relatively sober and the kid slept through it all upstairs in Granny and Grandpa's bed. God, all he needed was to have a reminder of his uninvited grandfatherly status crawling around the floor .

"Don't look a day over 36, David!" said someone who could never get away with a barefaced lie, and even if he believed her, he knew he didn't look older that 43.

And it was at the end of his speech, milestoning his fiftieth year on earth and twenty-fifth in the City of Dreams – some called it the City of Angels, but it was only the devils that he seemed to meet – that he suddenly spoke about Fatima.

"I want to just end off by saying a thank you to someone who is far away. God, I hope she's not up there far away or down there far away ..." and he pointed down, "... and by that I don't mean downtown Sydney. She's somewhere in South Africa."

The little lines popped back round Deli's mouth. His agent muttered: "Oh fuck, wrong move ..." but David didn't care to hear the warning. Issie's rumpled face said it all, and his agent's often pained irritation at his impulses was always honey to his bee.

"Fatima was my ..." He paused to find the right word, then shrugged. "And I'm afraid there is no politically-correct way to say this; she was my nanny." Everyone smiled, but a little more set than before. "She was our maid."

Some women nodded, some men shook their heads. The hired waiters stood impassively and understood nothing, because they were from a Caribbean island that taught its people to go deaf when in service. Perfect waiters, hopeless maids.

"Anyway," David continued, "Fatima was our nanny ..." He stopped and knew he would say something for the first time in decades. "Oh by the way, I don't think many of you know this, but since I'm turning 50, I can let an old cat out of my bulletproof bag tonight. I was born in South Africa."

Did some of his huge circle of business acquaintances even look pleased at this news? Was that a "I knew the fucker came from some

8

colony" expression? Or was it just simply "Where is South Africa?" dashing through their busy ten-second attention-span brains?

"I was born there 50 years ago and left when I was 19, so really I'm an American now. Not an African-American. A real American!"

"Oh shit!" muttered his agent and Deli swallowed hard. Their black guests smiled correctly.

"It's a long story and I really don't want to get deeper into the soft brown pudding here, so just let me tell you that Teema looked after me from when I was six into my teens. Yes, she would bath me and my sister, not together of course, but separately. Then one day, Teema laughed and looked into the soapy bath water and said: 'Look, the little dove's getting feathers!'"

He laughed alone. The uncomfortable silence was only offset by a little giggle from one of his secretaries who was still hoping to meet this little dove her dashing boss was talking about.

Deli was covering her face with a hand and trying to show her bashfulness just not to look too appalled. But happily the night was well-oiled by now and everyone then smiled and again started talking about themselves, and the strange anecdote was more or less forgotten.

When was that? Just a week ago?

A mad seven days of requested documents, quick replacements, abrupt cancellations and repeated explanations, and yet there seemed to be no one who really understood what he meant when he said: "It's my roots, man. I'm going back to my roots!"

If he were black, it would've been applauded. Every wealthy black American, or 'African-American' who'd never been to Africa, was making publicised pilgrimages back to their roots, ending up in five-star hotels in the capitals of impoverished African states and giving in-depth interviews on prime-time TV.

"I'm just going back to find Teema," he explained to his fascinated daughters. They wanted to know more about this person so close to their father's heart. "Later," he then promised. "When I get back, there'll be a lot to tell you about where we all come from."

"You're an American!" said Deli, in a tone of voice as if she was accusing him of something underhand. "You've been an American for most of your life!"

"Yes, honey," he americanised, "But I want to know where it all started. My parents are dead. My sister is dead. The only one to know about my early days is Teema."

"But you don't even know her surname!" Deli nodded knowingly.

"Do you at least know her address?"

He didn't know anything other than her name. Then he started wondering if that was really what she was called. David looked back through the porthole into the eternal skies of Africa. Teema lived down there somewhere. He'd start in Cape Town, because that's where they had lived and the most clues were in his memory of those times. Herman Greef was also there, and a little comic relief would help. This time David would do the laughing.

He fastened his seatbelt, becoming painfully aware of the exploding bladder at his base, and just for the sake of survival turned to his sweating companion and said: "Excuse me, could I get through?"

The black man sighed and looked at him with a pained expression. "You want me to move? Oh, for God's sake man, can't you just piss in your pants?" Another American.

David smiled. "It's so cramped here that pissing in my pants will wet yours too."

While the air hostess vainly tried to create some order prior to the landing at Johannesburg, David disrupted row 41 and eventually got to the toilet, only to find it 'Occupied'. He panicked and put his head into the small kitchenette.

"God, if I don't find a lavatory, I'm in big trouble!" he rasped.

The blonde with the name tag that said 'Jeanette' looked up at him with big eyes and smiled. Her Afrikaans accent sent shivers of recognition down his spine. "No, man, that lavvy is okay. Just push. The lock's broken."

He was still peeing with blissfully closed eyes when the big silver plane touched down at Jan Smuts Airport on the scorched plains of the Transvaal.

'Welcome to The New South Africa!'

The neon sign glowed at Immigration. Even though it was 1993, the arrivals hall, like the rest of the airport, looked like something out of the mid-50s of an East European state.

David expected a big burly neanderthal official with red eyes so close together you couldn't even park a bullet between them. Instead he got a pretty coloured girl with a blonde streak in her dark hair. Her lips were painted bright red and glistened as she licked them slowly, paging through his passport and glancing at his entry form. "David Clayton?"

10

"That's me."

She looked at him with a surprising warmth. "I knew a Gillian Clayton once. She was a model in Durban."

"Oh?" replied David Clayton relaxing. "Maybe she's related to me?"

"I doubt it," said the beautiful coloured bureaucrat. "She was Indian."

A Clayton from New Delhi? Why not, here was a Clayton from Claremont, Cape Town. Originally ...

"You were born in South Africa I see, Mr Clayton," she purred as she paged back and forth, looking at the passport stamps from France and Iran and Japan and China and the old Soviet Union and the new Russia. "When did you leave?"

"I ..." There was no reason to stutter as he had prepared his speech. But he stuttered again. "I ... left when I was very young."

She flashed him another smile. "Before my time?" she asked. She couldn't have been more than 25.

"Yes," he sighed and felt a bit better. Not too bad so far.

"Okay, Bella, I'll take this now."

The gruff voice made him look up and behind the small prefab wall stood that neanderthal brute of his worst fantasy, red nose shining, piggy eyes flashing, moustache bristling and an X between the eyes where a bullet wouldn't even penetrate, let alone fit.

The beauty made way for the beast.

He pawed the passport. "Clayton. David Algernon." He rolled his rrr's. He made the name sound like a prescription for insect poison. He tickled the keys of his computer with fat fingers and watched the blue screen for the answer.

David could hear the man's thick breath force its way up his stuffed nasal passages into his phlegm-filled lungs, wheezing and suffering before being angrily expelled and launched into the air and onto innocent bystanders as a raspy cough. "What was the name you had when you left South Africa, Mr Clayton?"

An icy feeling pricked his spine.

This felt like a movie he'd once produced about South Africa at the height of the apartheid years, a film he was sure was still banned in this country, now in the process of shedding its totalitarian armour to expose a shocked and bleeding nation, reclining legs apart to take the rampart erection of a new democracy.

"My father was Bennie de Lange. But I took on the maiden name of my mother, Sandra Clayton, when I settled in America. Does this make any difference?" he added, regretting his question as soon as the bullmoose looked up and sniffed.

"You're a native, Mr Clayton. Do you know that? A native." He said it quite loudly and the other foreigners in the queue behind shuffled closer to hear the details.

Meanwhile along the wall of entry desks, true natives holding blue South African passports were waved past the desks with a smile and a greeting, mainly in Afrikaans.

"Welkom terug Dr Lategaan. Hoe gaan dit vandag?"

"Baie lekker dankie, Sarel."

Just examples of familiarity in the upper echelons of power, waning as fast as the rays of a new day after too many hours of hot work.

"I don't really understand ..." David heard his American accent clatter against the counter. It sounded so false here, as studied as it had been so many years ago.

"Native, man!" repeated the official. "Like in 'of these parts'. You're not American. You're African. Like me. I am an African!"

The big pink monster rose to his feet. His chest ballooned out from above his straining belt and for a moment he looked like a cartoon Superman ready to up, up and away. Then he let rip with another terrible cough and the grating sound sent the small insects running for the cover of dark and dank places under the desk.

"Sorry, man. I can't help this. I'm allergic to all this artificial air," he wheezed. "Give me the real air of Jo'burg any day."

He sat down again, seemed to shrink in size as another cough splattered across the eager foreign faces in front of him. He wiped the blue screen with his sleeve and clattered a few more keys on the national brain machine, answering his own questions cordially. "Here on holiday? Ja. Here for first time since emigration? Ja. Here with how much money?" Now he looked up and waited for something to happen.

"Shit!" thought David Clayton, once De Lange. "Must I bribe this creature? Will he take dollars? Is this already so Third World?" The experience of the casually broken toilet door in the plane seemed to confirm his fears.

He put his hand in his top pocket and brought out a handful of dollars. His Amex platinum card clattered onto the desk.

The asthmatic vulture pounced.

"Hey man, this is all we need. Better than *biltong*, more valuable than life." He stamped the passport with a flourish, while stroking the credit card with a sausagey finger. "Mr Clayton," he announced, "welcome to your roots." He looked up with another wheeze. "Just don't believe everything you read. Don't look at everything they show you. Don't expect anything you hope for. Don't panic. Don't run. Don't walk in the centre of Jo'burg with anything valuable in your pockets; don't go into black areas, and more than anything, don't be sorry you came!"

He handed the American passport back to David with a wide smile that seemed to hide his eyes behind red cheeks, while the two people behind him lightly applauded.

"Soos ons sê: jy's tuis ou maat, jy's tuis."

In the queue a translation was being whispered: "He said: welcome, friend, you're home!"

David Clayton from Los Angeles heard himself reply.

"Dankie Oom."

Thank you uncle?

Dawid de Lange was back.

CHAPTER 2.

"Had it always looked so American?" he thought, as he drove the small hired yellow Golf across the freeway system towards the City of Johannesburg clustered on the horizon. In the cleft of two hills rose the skyscrapers like a collection of shiny ballpoint pens stuck in the space like between two full breasts.

He'd never been to Johannesburg as a child and since this was his first visit back for over three decades, the first impression of what blacks called Egoli was one of the many Disneyland rides he was in for. Driving on the left was no problem, as he'd regularly done that in the United Kingdom and Australia. Somehow there seemed to be no specific left or right on these Transvaal roads, as cars and trucks roared past on both sides at high speed, often with a gesture of anger or, God forbid, even the cocking of a gun.

"Expect the worst!" they'd told him in Los Angeles, their knowledge built up on the look-bites from prime-time TV and the eternally dull and bloodsoaked documentary footage that seemed to flow from South Africa like a never-ending haemorrhage.

What was 'the worst'? Worse than Beirut at its worst? He'd been there with an ABC TV camera team at the height of the madness. Crouching behind a burnt-out Peugeot in what was once the fashionable centre of the Lebanese Paris, he knew what Berlin must've felt like in the horrendous final days of that war to end all wars.

Beirut was hot, sweaty, dirty and dusty. The smell was appalling, as if something long-dead had been trapped in the foetus of what was still unborn. Flies seemed desperate for something damp to latch onto and they energetically found that dampness in his neck or round his eyes.

For hours the film crew was trapped in the small pool of half-shade under the wreck of the car, waiting for something horrible to happen so that they could focus and later say 'Good shot!'

Against the shockingly blue sky, the pockmarked ruin of a tallish building held David's attention. He wondered what it had looked like in the days of its prime. Had there been a colour on the walls? Trees? Flowerboxes? People? Happiness?

He watched for signs of life and saw none. Then far up a door

14

opened. He noticed that because there were so few doors left. A woman came out onto her balcony, or what was left of it. The edges had been shot away and she could so easily have taken a large step to the left and fallen twelve floors. She then balanced a basket on her hip and against the torn concrete started hanging out small pieces of washing. Baby clothes. More than one child because the pink booties were tiny, but there were also blue clothes for a larger child. She was as unconcerned as you'd be in Milwaukee.

A marmalade cat jumped onto the edge of the balcony and rubbed itself against a jagged piece of steel that stuck out like a torn artery. A crumping explosion far off over the Green Line didn't even attract her attention. She waved the flies away from her face. Flies, on the twelfth floor? Did they wear little oxygen masks?

She went inside to the coolness of her ruined home and the cat stayed licking its paws, occasionally watching the gentle flapping of the little people's washing on the line, small flags of surrender high up the sky of a dying city. Could this Johannesburg with its urban skirmishes be worse than that?

David looked at the green trees and lavishly tended gardens of some of the suburban houses as he passed them by. Not much to see above the high walls. He'd heard about the barricades of the Witwatersrand. He'd expected to see Berlin Walls or Great Walls like in China. Most of them here were ugly prefab, dirty grey cement slabs set in monotonous rows and topped with glittering razorwire, like dangerous diamond necklaces round the throats of bulletproofed matrons.

It looked like Los Angeles!

In fact, everything about Johannesburg from the sunbaked safety of his car looked like Los Angeles, except that some of the black people seemed friendlier.

His expected ordeal through Customs had turned out to be a disappointment. He'd gone through the red to declare his camera and discman, because Herman Greef had given him that tip. It hadn't cost him anything. No one asked him if he had pornography jammed up his anus. He didn't, but somehow was looking forward to the experience of saying 'yes' to see what would happen.

"Don't try and be funny, David," Deli had pleaded on their traffic crawl to LAX.

"Funny? Deli, I'm not known for my sense of fun in tight spots!" he'd joked and nearly swerved into a battered Toyota filled with sweating Mexicans.

15

"I know you," she sniffed, the acid air making her nose itch.

"'Anything to declare?'! 'Yes, war!' or 'A bomb between my legs!'?"

"That's a thought …" he chuckled.

"That's a country where they don't laugh, David. They lock up and lose keys. They torture and burn people!"

He looked at his watch. He'd been in this country for three hours and all he'd seen was a relaxed friendly attitude with no fires, or flames, or fascists. "I've heard that the PR firm of Saatchi and Saatchi is backing De Klerk's new South Africa, but this is fucking ridiculous!" he called out to the passing traffic.

There were many old cars on the road, always a last sign of recession before it slid into depression. He noticed dozens of small square Japanese Toyotas and Euro-Volkswagens and some Amerasian Fords, minibuses crammed with black commuters, swerving in and out of lanes like toys, hooting at nothing in particular and stopping with a screech for anyone who stood at the side of the road and waved. These were the legendary taxis of the Reef. He'd been warned: 'Careful of the taxis!' He was.

Suddenly the traffic slowed down as the lanes narrowed from four to two. He found himself in a clutter of cars edging for the gap. Everyone seemed to have their radio onto a different station. A Tower of Babel of languages. Zulu pop songs, Xhosa adverts for cigarettes. Afrikaans request programmes. Clipped English recipes. Rap. Jazz. Elvis. Beatles. Township jive. The news. More murder most foul and frequent.

He glanced down at a copy of the only newspaper he could find in his rush through the airport concourse to the Avis car park. *The Citizen*'s front page was adorned with a list of numbers and percentages. 'One in 1000 South Africans was murdered last year and 1 in 70 was mugged …' "Lovely …" he sighed, and wound his window up, locking all the doors and feeling like a body on its way down into the fiery square hole of the crematorium.

Eventually the snakes of traffic reached the reason for the diversion. After hundreds of small red cones lined the lanes with official seriousness, David drove past a small manhole in the centre of the freeway, open and surrounded by a group of black men in denim overalls, eating sandwiches, sitting jumbled on their boxes and barricades, chatting to each other and waving at other waves from the cruising taxis. Once this narrowing of the bowel had cleared, it took no time for him to draw the yellow car up at the hotel in the city where he was to stay for a day.

His next connection was the Blue Train, leaving mid-morning the next day from Johannesburg Station and arriving in Cape Town twenty-four hours later. The idea of the luxury of this most unique mode of transport made him feel guilty. Deli had warned him. "Don't be flash. You know the dollar can buy the best for nothing. It's a country in a state of civil war. The Blue Train is bad taste."

So was his hotel.

Glossy plastic going as marble, edge-to-edge carpet with matching wall covering in the suite. Ashtrays everywhere in a No Smoking Room.

"Why?" he asked the housemaid who appeared three times during the first hour to replace his towels.

"Some guests can't read," she said slowly, "and if they do, they pretend they can't. But don't smoke if you can't read, and don't smoke if you can."

"I don't smoke," he said.

"Then don't smoke!" she droned without looking him in the face once.

So he didn't smoke, but wondered about the constant changing of the towels. He never found out, although the various housemaids, roomladies, 'suite comrades' or whatever they were now called, kept knocking softly at his door and saying "Room Service: Clean Towels." What did the other guests do with the towels in this suite that he was obviously not doing?

No one called him 'Master'. They said 'Sir', but mainly they said nothing. He also said as little as he could, suddenly terrified that his Afrikaner roots would show through his posh American accent and expose him to ridicule, loathing or contemptuous respect.

Most of the staff spoke various African languages. David had heard no Afrikaans, except on the car radio and that could've been a recording of a 50s programme, so affected and unruffled the sounds were, considering the high cliff on which the language was teetering. In fact, people tended to look round when they heard Afrikaans in the foyer; American was not a sound that seemed to faze anyone around him.

So it had happened here too. South Africa had become another silent partner to the American Dream.

While the States was inside, Nairobi thrived outside in the streets.

He'd showered, used as many towels as he thought indecent, did

17

not shave hoping to blend in more with the natural surroundings, put all his valuables in the safe downstairs where he hoped they'd remain and ventured outside into the heat of the City of Gold.

Egoli. Streets paved with gold. The gold of squashed bananas and bruised oranges. The gold of wrapping papers and cigarette box linings and yellowed newsprint bundled up into small eighty-sided balls. Streets paved with chewing gum blobs stuck to the cracked sidewalks. Traffic lights that flashed red to stop and then everyone walked and drove, green to start when everyone stopped and shouted at each other, and the brief orange in the middle seemed to be just another hue in the spectrum of this colourful Johannesburg.

The sun reflected gold in the gilt-mirrored buildings that housed the gold markets, and golden boardrooms of the bronzed businessmen playing fiscal roulette with a brassed-out economy that needed a soul transplant more than the relief of a final bullet.

Everyone was selling anything they could. Battered fruit and dusty vegetables, the same selection from one stall to the next, the prices high near the hotels and low down by the bottom of town where the goods inevitably were stolen, second-hand, or just rotten beyond price. Spiky hairbrushes, hairspray, hair gels, hair shampoo and hair were bundled together with used shoes and old-fashioned nylon stockings packed in ancient crumpled cellophane holders, covered in Arabic lettering and probably dating back to the days of a shah.

Bossy chickens were squawking in the open boot of a glossy new car. Bloody bits of animal carcasses lay carefully displayed on a spread square of ethnic material, itself so beautiful that David wondered if he shouldn't buy the whole banquet, throw away the meat, dryclean the cloth and take it back to Deli.

Zulu newspapers and glossy Xhosa magazines and English racing cards and portable radios, fizzy cooldrinks and soggy chips and melted icecream and dripping iced lollies. It was the ultimate African streetmarket and it went on block after busy block, street next to crowded alley.

In the store windows, the eurocentric shop dummies with their snotty expressions frozen in a fashionable Parisian spring, looked out glassily and pretended to be in Dusseldorf or Rome. Some of the whites walking to wherever whites still walked and didn't drive, had the same expression in their eyes, as if they were seeing better days when their delusions made sense, and not present tribulations that cost rands.

The sirens howled with the regularity of a New York on the cusp of chaos. Police cars cut corners and sent angry hawkers flying, while ambulances zigzagged through the madding crowd, red lights flashing, carrying someone from one death to another.

Black policemen in blue wondered around chatting. Brown policemen in khaki stood tensely and waited. White policemen in camouflage ran after fleeing suspects with drawn guns and occasionally shooting wildly in the hope of an arrest.

"Dear Deli, I've not seen anyone necklaced. Just a rumour. No tyres round anyone's neck. Just some stabbings, armed robberies, shootings, highspeed chases, mugging and what could become a massacre, and all this before midday on my first day here, but not a Goodyear tyre, not a Firestone tyre, not even a lit match did I see. So balls to all the rumours. Love David."

He posted a cluster of postcards of ethnic Marilyn Monroes in coy repose at the Main Post Office, which was filled with people just waiting for something. Black women wearing ornate cloth headdresses, patiently holding restless children in their arms, while on their heads balancing woven baskets filled with more fruits or other children.

The colours and the smells and the sounds were like a drug and David suddenly felt his head spin and he had to sit down on his haunches against a wall of the bustling hall for a moment.

"Probably jet lag," he though with closed eyes. He wished now he'd shaved.

"Master, you okay?" asked a soft voice and he looked at the boy next to him who was concerned and articulate.

"I'm fine." David said.

"Master looks very white."

"I am very white …" David said throwing away the pun and was delighted at the bell of laughter it elicited.

"Ja, and Master looks foreign also. With that jacket and those shoes. And the voice from the TV. Master is a cameraman from the TV?" The boy seemed to read his inner CV.

"No, I'm from Cape Town." David wondered if every cock on the block was sighing with the relief for not having to crow thrice.

"Cape Town is wild," said the boy. "Mad people live there. That mountain is like a gravestone. Makes you stop breathing. Jo'burg is best." His teeth were whiter than an ad and his large brown eyes remarkably clear. He glanced around the great lobby of the post office, not looking for someone in particular, but taking note of

19

anyone watching them. Then he turned to David and smiled again.

"You post your letters okay?" He whispered.

David whispered back. "Yes, I did."

"To America?"

"Yes …"

"Cape Town is now in America?" The boy laughed again, a trill of pure sound. His hands were never still, touching each finger one to the other, wringing round the fist, rubbing at the air. "So what you want, Master?" he asked, looking David in the eye.

David felt all his warning bells jingle and red lights flash. He tried to get to his feet, but the boy held his elbow down in a heavy hold.

"I just came in for some air …" David started.

"Hey man, I get you any drug," the boy murmured. "Any place you want, I can find you. You have hotel here? I go with you. You let me bath there. I fuck you."

The sunshine outside seemed to help burn away the echo of the words from David's mind. Now every black boy he passed in the street looked like a relative of his post office encounter. Why did they suddenly all look alike. And always smiling?

"Would Master like a nice pawpaw?"

Pawpaw was one of those special South Africa 'things', like Mrs Ball's Chutney and Peppermint Crisp Chocolates and Provita health rusks and squashes. How do you explain a squash to someone from the real world? Well, a squash is a squash is a … squash!

So to all they offered he just said yes with a vengeance. The fat black woman peeled a fat orange fruit and handed him a piece to taste.

Pawpaw. Soft and rude it felt in his mouth, sweet and naughty like something he wasn't allowed to suck, and yet had to to survive in this cul-de-sac.

Pawpaw. A silly name and also a repetition of familiar happy sounds. He bought the rest of it and wrapped it carefully in his piece of ethnic material, already stained with the blood of the animal bits he'd bought earlier on his voyage through the burst arteries in the heart of inner Jo'burg.

It was then, as the juice of the forgotten fruit cascaded down his neck into his shirt front, that he saw a name that shot out into his mind in three dimensional lettering, backed with golden lighting

20

and loud choral singing: Cyril Jonah Greenblow! A name to kill a parent for!

A Cyril Greenblow had been the sly bastard who organised that first big 'sports session' down at the changing-room on the rugby field at school. With Joanie Craig.

Everyone wanted to fuck Joanie Craig. And everyone eventually did. This first time round was still in the days before metrification brought in rands and cents, when shillings and pence exchanged grubby hands over games of marbles. Everyone, even juniors like Dawid de Lange, had to put in a 'guinea' to get a poke. That one-pound-one-shilling was a fortune in those days and no one really had the money, but they went to their busy parents' handbags, or wallets, and 'borrowed' the passion cash. So on that Friday afternoon after cadet practice on the rugby field, there were at least 12 horny boys waiting for that eventual chance to poke blonde Joanie. Dawid had been at the end of the line, not because he was the last, but because he was the smallest. He was also the youngest and by comparisons to what he'd seen in the boy's showers, he was also the worst blessed cockwise. Herman Greef as always, was the first to come and last to go.

And here Cyril's name was on a poster for … what? A local movie? Yes, some karate film starring a 'star' from 'America' and produced by this same Greenblow. It had to be him! Only Cyril could produce a film called "Coming on Climax!"

"Oh please," giggled David, "nothing has changed!"

So he went into a café which sold everything from garish crystallised fruit to liquorice-tasting condoms, and phoned the new Telkom directory for the number of his old schoolchum Cyril Greenblow. It turned out to be another Disneyland funride.

"Hello? Is that Enquiries?"

A flat accent to kill plastic flowers answered him. "Hold on, you're at Technical Services, can I help you?"

Then the phone went dead. He was sorry as he really wanted to ask Technical Services that three million dollar question: where was Cyril Greenblow?

David took out another 20c piece and tried again. "Hello? Is that Service Enquiries?"

"Hang on," said a funny voice, sounding as if they were deep in the water. "You're on hold …" And then it also went dead.

Two dead before his money ran out? He started again. Another 20c piece.

"Hello, is the ..." Dead. Another 20c.

The Portuguese café owner passed him a mug of real coffee. "On the house!" he said and sighed at the familiarity of it all. The coffee was rather good.

"Hello, I want a number please?"

"What number do you want?" The voice sounded digital.

"I want a number please ..." he pleaded.

"Ja, what number you want!" It was now a command.

"No, I want a number that I don't have!" David said in his best borrowed British accent.

"Do you want a number?" the disembodied voice demanded.

"Yes, I do!" he said in full-blooded American.

"What number, please?"

"The number of Mr Cyril Greenblow!" he spelt out like to a child.

"Do you have his number?" the child answered.

"No! This is the number I want!" David huffed.

"Who is the party you wish to contact." It wasn't even a question, just a matter of fact. "Mr Cyril Greenblow!" It was the first time David realised what a stupid sounding name that was.

"Hold please!" Suddenly the enemy also sounded American, like from the imported soaps from Burbank they all watched. He was subjected to terrible Richard Clayderman-type muzak. Tinkle tinkle chord vomit ...

"I have the party you request. Mrs Sarah Greenwood. Her number is ..."

David shouted and the cafe took note. "No, damn it! I want Mr Cyril Greenblow, the film producer!"

"Will you please let me finish ..." The thin voice at the other end was fighting for her right to speak. "Her number is ..."

"I want Cyril Greenblow, not Sarah Goldfish!" the American now roared.

"Sarah Greenwood! That's what you asked for, Sir." The voice was sweet and careful.

"No, I didn't. I asked for Cyril Green ... shit, what was his name? Greenfield? Greenhouse? Greenfinger?" This was not working out. He drew out his last tainted card. "I want the producer of 'Coming On Climax'!"

"Oh!!!" the person at the other end said happily. "Ou Cyril?? Hang on, doll."

Within minutes he was onto Cyril. Within more minutes he was again swopping bad jokes with his school acquaintance who never

22

liked him anyway, and within minutes David was invited to dinner.

"Seven thirty for eight!" Cyril said. "And don't arrive till nine. Bring a gun. Ring before you come."

So the tourist from Los Angeles rang the given number just before nine from his hotel room.

"Is Cyril there? This is David Clayton … de Lange …"

"Hang on," said the woman on the other end guardedly in a familiar local nasal whine. "Aren't you supposed to be here for dinner? Are you okay? You've not been mugged, or hijacked to a township, or shot at or something?"

"No," David said laughing at her wit. "I'm on my way. It's only just before nine."

"Ja, but you were expected at seven thirty. I don't know if there's any food left. You vegetarian?"

"No," he said, feeling angry at Cyril's advice to be late.

"Oh shit, then I really don't know what to feed you. Anyway, never mind, just come and we'll see what we can do. David who?"

"David de Lange."

"That's not American is it?" Her nasal accent echoed in his ear.

"No, it's …" But she'd put down her side and the line buzzed, happy to be free again.

So David quickly dressed, having showered again and used the newly delivered towels with abandon, took the lift down to the lobby and then the other lift down to the parking garage under the building. He passed three security checks. All they wanted to see was the residents' card he was given on booking in. Anyone could've flashed it. He drove his little yellow Golf up the narrow pipe towards the darkness of the night.

Johannesburg was empty. As full as it had been by day, it now looked like the world had ended and no one seemed to care. The mess was extraordinary. The decorations of trade that had brightened up the pavements were now lying thickly in the gutters. Everything looked black and white, and even the many-coloured neon lights ran greyly around their tracks in flickering circles.

The long blue-lit ribbon of Commissioner Street got thinner in the distance, where it swerved to avoid the sinister block of John Vorster Square, police headquarters and scene to many horror executions, where suspects slipped on the soap in the shower, or fell from the fourth floor.

The traffic lights, or 'robots', were red-eyed guards of honour along the edges of the road. Here and there the white taxi minibuses clustered at pick-up points like flies on a piece of dead meat, with people jumping in and out, accompanied by loud shouting and laughter. An empty wine bottle seemed to propel itself down the street and roll between the wheels of his car as he waited for the lights to change. The green wave started far away and by the time it had arrived at his robot, red was started again at the end of his rainbow.

He had no idea where to go, but the map on his lap, though complex, helped him manoeuvre his way round quiet suburbs and deserted shopping malls and eventually he drew up at the house in a Sixth Avenue.

The driveway was full of cars and the high steel barricades were closed. The security wall was also towering above him. All he could see through the gates was the reflection of his own headlamps in the reflectors of the Mercedes Benzes and BMWs inside. So he just parked his little yellow chariot on the edge of the street outside, checked the windows and doors, locked everything, left nothing behind to tantalise the passing disadvantaged and crossed his fingers.

The street was quiet. Pools of light were small islands of detail in the darkness. Very few cars were parked in the street. He rang the bell at the huge gate and waited. Inside a chorus of dogs set up a howl. He rang again.

A woman called at him from the stoep of the house. "Okay hang on, I'm coming, I'm coming. Oh, fuck off Nelson, wait now man!!!"

A blonde woman trippled down the path towards him followed by a huge dog that kept pushing his nose up her crotch. She was trying to find the right key on a bunch of many. "Nelson man, fuck off!" she snarled, with an edge of hysteria in her nasal voice and peered out at him.

"Are you David … thingieme?"

"Yes, hello, I'm sorry I'm late …"

"This damn gate doesn't open automatically any more. Some bloody bastard broke it again as always. So what's the point of all this press-button security, if you've got to go out and unlock the gate to see who's there to rape you! Come in … Careful the dog …!"

But Nelson was waiting for his chance to slip out and there he went, bounding down the road on his way to eat some small home-less person, or the two spoilt pekinese lapdogs in Fifth Avenue.

24

"Nelson! Come home!" She screamed down the road and a man appeared on the stoep behind her.

"Cynthia, what it is now!"

He joined them at the gate. David was still standing politely in the road.

"The dog! He's out. God knows where he's gone. I'm not schlepping around in the middle of the night looking for him, you must be mad. Oh, this is my husband Bernard. This is Cyril's friend."

Bernard grinned and held out his hand. "Hi. You're the American. Thought you weren't coming. Leave the dog, Cynthia, he'll come back once he's fucked a few poodles down the road." He winked at David. "Dog's been neutered by the way, but my wife thinks anything that runs away from her is on his way to fuck something else. You can imagine what a performance it is when I have to explain to her I just want to go to the loo for a pee!"

They all laughed and went in through the gate, locked it, gave a last bellow for Nelson and went into the house.

"The dog is called after Mandela?" David tentatively enquired. They looked at him horrified.

"Winnie?" Cynthia bleated.

"Nelson ..." David volunteered.

"Oh, no, he's named after Lord Nelson, you know, the one in Trafalgar Square? The other dog is Emma as in Hamilton."

Cynthia mulled. "Nelson Mandela? Christ I never thought of that. Bernard, did you ever think of that? Maybe we should call Emma 'Winnie' and then we'll really be in the New South Africa."

They were in the house now and David saw Cyril in a deep producer's conversation with a young woman with big tits. He looked the same as ever, small and round and always busy down someone's front.

"So listen everybody, this is David and he's from America and Nelson's got out, and God knows where he is, and did you ever think he was called after Mandela? Isn't that clever? Drink David?" He just nodded and smiled at Cyril's wave. Cyril went on with his deep discussion. "Now sit down and I'll bring you something to eat. So what do you think of South Africa?"

The conversation all round stopped and everyone looked at him. Bernard handed him a drink. He took it to his lips and the ice burnt him slightly.

"I've just arrived ... it looks fine." They waited for more. "I've never been to Jo'burg before. Really, it's difficult to judge."

"But we're on the TV all the time in America surely?" Cynthia nodded as she spoke. "I mean with all the violence and chaos and lies and communists right here under our noses! You see it all on TV, don't you?"

Everyone leant forward excitedly to hear when last he'd seen their violence on his LA TV.

"Well, no, we see nothing any more. Now that apartheid is dead and De Klerk is steering the country away from …"

"Steering?" muttered someone and there was a laugh.

"… and anyway, the pictures are better from Bosnia and Somalia. Instant death in Sarajevo and a nice slow fade out from Mogadishu."

They all watched him, as if they didn't understand a word he was saying. "God, do these people know what I'm talking about?" he wondered, looking at the blankness in their eyes. "We do see bits and pieces every now and then, but nothing like ten years ago," he added, making them feel better. Bernard clapped his hands wryly.

"You see, didn't I say it? I said it over and over and no one listened. There it is, didn't I say it?"

Cynthia patted him on the arm. "Okay Bernard, I grant you that. You said it."

The others nodded and drank in agreement. David smiled and nodded along.

"I said it long before anyone even though it," Bernard muttered. This time he looked at David for a reply. David shrugged, nodded and smiled, and didn't know what the hell he was talking about.

"Yes well, there you are," he agreed and nodded along. His ice had melted.

"You're right," said Bernard gravely. "There you are."

They all drank.

"Yip," said David. "South Africa just isn't fashionable any more."

It was as if he'd announced the death of an only child. Cynthia put her glass down and stood up enraged. She turned on David, eyes flashing and hands on her bony hips.

"You know, that's such a typical American thing to say. You people are so shallow, if you don't mind me saying so. Look, I don't know you from Adam, and as far as I'm concerned you look like a very nice person, and we've known Cyril for years and anyone he likes we like, even if they are American and have opinions about this country after only being here for a few hours, mind you, but never mind. Fuck politics! We never talk politics in this house.

26

Come to the kitchen and let's see what the maids have left over. I'm sure we can find you something nice. You're a vegetarian, aren't you?"

David shook his head. "No …"

"Oh well, that's fine. We've got some lovely dips and there's still the icecream and fudgeblocks. Come David." By now they had squeezed past three uniformed maids and found themselves in the enormous kitchen. "Let me show you how we poor whites have to manage in this New Soviet RSA!"

CHAPTER 3.

It was a night to remember.

David wished he had a tape recorder running to recall the extraordinary things said, or rather not said but implied, or better not implied but suggested.

He scarcely said a word to Cyril who was getting deeper and sweatier into the actress's *décolletage*. Bernard and Cynthia moved in and out of the conversations round him, but the tone was similar throughout. A South African sense of being wronged, a feeling of being betrayed. These were people who say they had fought for the end of an evil system, only to see a new system exclude them from the rewards of their comfortable liberalism. David had to keep wiping a smile off his face, hoping that the words he heard were just a subtle form of sit-down comedy, in spite of the fact that no one had a sense of humour in that living-room.

Everyone was somehow remarkably on the brink of bankruptcy, as they all announced loudly at one stage or another. There was also soft talking about other places, other markets, other banks, other homes in mysterious refugee countries where they all threatened to go if so abused, and 'this place can go to the dogs for all we care'.

Nelson went to heaven too.

At some part of the night a screech of tyres outside and a large thud dispatched the sweet lumbering beast to a fairer place. All Cynthia did on hearing the sinister noise was to grope nervously for a panic button set in a wall-mosaic of 'Zulu Venus rising from the Sea'. The crimson button was set in her stomach, like a navel.

"Just some damn cowboys outside," muttered Bernard and Nelson was only found the next day. Never mind, his grieving owners quickly got another dog, this time a more vicious rottweiler and called him Winnie. After Churchill.

Winnie and Emma. Perfect for this new South Africa.

When it was time to go, they all got up and went. Cyril squeezed his arm and muttered something about tomorrow, and when David told him he was leaving for the Cape by Blue Train, Cyril said: "I'll come and see you off", which he didn't, and, with his fat hand firmly on the actress's pert behind, he propelled her out of the house into his bed and a brief career acting in crappy local karate films.

"Where's your car?" asked Bernard when all the glossy Mercs and chariots of the lesser gods had reversed out of the stables of safety into the road.

"Out there." David indicated into the darkness more or less where the dog was crumpled in the shadows of a shrub.

"Are you mad? Your car's probably stolen by now!" screeched Cynthia and hugged herself in horror.

"No, it's a hired car and …"

"Oh, that's okay then," she squealed with relief and kissed him on the cheek. "So nice that you came and told us all about America. Most of our friends are there now. San Diego, Atlanta. Bastards. Making money on the backs of our blacks and then running away as so-called refugees? My arse. My arse!" she bayed at the moon.

"Let me just check if the coast is clear …" said Bernard and out of nowhere a gun appeared in his hand and he peered out into the deserted street.

Cynthia nudged at David. "Listen doll, better take out your gun, you never know."

"I don't have a gun," David said. His hosts turned to him appalled, Bernard's pistol pointing straight at where his heart pretended not to be. David reversed a few steps. "Do you mind not pointing that …"

"You don't have a gun?" one of them said, or both whispered in unison.

"No, I don't have a gun."

Bernard came up close to him and his breath wasn't pleasant and the edge of the pistol pressed into David's arm wasn't either. "Who the fuck do you think you are?" he hissed at David.

"Pardon? Look, do you mind not …"

"Who the fuck do you think you are! Coming to this country and walking around without a gun!"

"You think we're paranoid or something?" Cynthia added her yap like a small lapdog.

"Shit!" spat her husband, "You think just because you're an American these savages will shine their torch in your face and say …" switching to a bad music hall version of a black accent, rolling eyes and all, "'no man, this guy's okay. He's American. We won't kill him!'"

This was becoming something similar. David was by now forced off the path into the ferns next to the wall.

"Look, I just arrived …"

"You think you're above all this, just because you're an American?" Bernard's face was pulled into a mask of grudge and envy. The gun was still sharply pressed into David's side. He swallowed uncomfortably.

"No, Bernard, I don't think I'm above it all. I hope it will never happen, but when it does, I don't want to be the one to shoot first."

God, that sounded like a line from daytime soap!

Bernard stood back. The breath seemed to squirt out between his pursed lips. He stroked his small pistol like a penis.

"No, you'd better get the fuck out of here. No really, I haven't got the time nor the energy for people like you who make us South Africans feel like we're a bunch of mad traumatised kaffir-killers!"

"What?" David couldn't believe his ears. Surely this was a joke.

"No," said Cynthia from the safety of the stoep. "He's right. You better go before we really lose our hospitality."

David walked through the gate and turned as they hummed shut behind him. "Thanks for the ..." The front door slammed. He was alone in the dark street without a gun. Suddenly he was very sorry not to have one.

When he got to his yellow car in the hotel garage the next morning, the small back window had been smashed, the flakes of glass giggling on the back seat like escaped diamonds, and the radio was ripped out.

If all the radios that were stolen from cars in Johannesburg were to find new owners, surely every man, woman and child on the Reef should have an FM aerial coming out of their ears!

As he handed the keys back to the car hire rep at the station, David asked her where to report the theft. The chubby woman smiled and shook her head, while automatically ticking things off on a list in front of her.

"No, it's okay, luvvie, all covered by the insurance. We sort of expect the worst every time a car goes out. Goodbye little car, we say. Really makes us happy to see it come back, even if it's in pieces."

David was pleased his Golf was relatively intact and swore the uniformed rep stroked the car gently, muttering sweet nothings into its useless aerial.

Platform 15 in the cement shell of Johannesburg Station was singled out by an uneven red carpet, which led from the out-of-order escalator to the middle of the platform, where a small desk stood, an island of smiling exclusivity surrounded by small straggly palms in green plastic pots, manned by smiling uniformed persons bent on taking the mind off the matter of the dingy surroundings.

The dirty concrete of the gloomy station made it all feel like an underground parking garage in a godforsaken building on the outskirts of Salt Lake City. The bowl of real yellow flowers on the welcoming desk was indeed a shock. They nearly looked too good to be true.

"Made in Taiwan?" David asked with a smile. He was given one to sniff and keep, so he slid it into his lapel. It still looked plastic. It smelt of detergent.

He booked himself in at the desk to broad smiles and good service, found his compartment on the plan and was sent down Platform 15 to where his coach-stop was marked with the letter G.

He looked at the glossy Blue Train brochure in his hand. Magnificent colour pictures of a shiny, unreal steel train bluely snaking its way through unnaturally green vineyards suddenly excited him again like a kid on a special outing.

"Aha," he muttered. "So The Blue Train starts its journey in Pretoria and is reputedly never late?"

It was late.

In fact, there was a bomb scare at Pretoria Station and the train only arrived Johannesburg after lunch, so that David was able to read through most of a discarded paperback he found in the dirtbin to his left. It was the steamy story of 'three loves, three studs and six bitches', and already by the second page one stud was dead and a bitch was very much on heat. He was so fascinated by the ins and outs of the plot that he only heard the third or fourth announcement: "There's been a slight technical hitch beyond our control," was the tinny excuse from the speaker above.

When the gleaming python eventually glided its way into the station and blurred blue in front of his eyes, the discomfort of waiting was forgotten. The fate of the studs and bitches would never be shared as the tome was tossed back into the bin on the left where it belonged, the author's quest for a readers' satisfaction unfulfilled.

He found his compartment to be a small bedroom with one bunk and a very large cinemascope window framing the view outside to resemble a glossy travelogue on TV. He took note of a small complimentary bottle of wine on the table. The excited babble of the German, French, British, Japanese and American fellow travellers in the passage outside made up his mind and he unpopped the gift and sipped the nectar.

Another train had pulled in next to theirs, an ordinary brown passenger express that would stop anywhere and everywhere to rid itself of travellers. There had been no attempt at creating that train as a 'non-racial, classless' object for tourists to photograph. Their comfort depended on class, and in most coaches, the colour of money. Third class was dark with black faces, second class peppered with poor whites who obviously couldn't waste any money on status, with so-called first class not looking much different, other than giving its crème *carte blanche* entry to the dining car.

The Blue Train's windows couldn't open because of the controlled air-conditioning. David sat back on his blue leather seat, sipped his expensive sweet white wine and looked through the clean glass at the face of the black woman sitting at the half-open window of the train next door.

She was looking out at him, but not seeing anything. It was the softness of her skin that struck him, as if the tinted glass of his window had filtered away all blemishes of a hard life. Soft skin. Sad eyes. Parted lips. Expressionless, like a small-town madonna. She looked like Deli when he'd met her twenty-something years ago, even though Deli was white and this woman a dark brown. He sipped again, then realised she was looking at him after all.

He smiled.

The woman stared in at the glass in his hand. He clinked the crystal against the window next to him. The sound was like a small gunshot.

Where would she find the money for another funeral? the dark-skinned woman thought, and leant her throbbing head against the grimy glass of the train window. The woolly clouds of breath appeared and vanished with the rhythm of her breathing.

A week before she had buried her sister, who'd been shot while standing at the side of the road in the township. A stolen car full of masked men had driven by and one of them opened fire at nothing in particular. Her sister wasn't that particular a target, just another ordinary mother waiting for her child to survive the hurdles of a school day.

She'd buried her sister and then yesterday her brother's youngest son was found mutilated next to the sandy road going to the church. He'd been so badly cut up the police just said it was a *muti* murder, blamed the local witchdoctors, and put his pieces in a box and handed it over to her to take to the undertaker. They'd buried him quickly because the pieces of the boy wouldn't keep in the heat.

She stared out of the window at the reflection of her brown train in the gold-tinted windows of the long, shiny coffin next door on the rails of Platform 15. What was this train? she thought, and wiped across the bottom part of the window with her hand.

A blue train? She looked carefully and eventually could make out the figure of a white man in the clean cabin. He was holding a glass and was smiling. He tapped the glass against the window. It sounded like the funny sound that happened before her sister died next to her in the street.

Where would she get the money? she sighed and sat back against the hard bench of third class. Both funerals had already taken place, there was the cost of the tent for the funeral feast, beer and a sheep had been slaughtered and served, and now she must find the money to pay, or else she'd be in trouble. They would telephone her employer in the suburbs of Johannesburg and she might lose her job.

No, she would lose her job!

She would find the money from somewhere! There was no one in the family who was prepared to pay for the funerals. Hers was a big family. There would be more funerals. Where would she get the money …?

With a shudder, her train started out of the station. She watched the silver-blue casket glide by, golden windows hiding golden people sipping golden liquid, and never having to bury their dead.

Where would she get the money to bury those still living …?

Poverty looked so romantic from the Blue Train.

Thin children wearing tatty rags waved happily at the lucky snake. David waved back, feeling good. While a light Mozart overture frolicked on the music channel above his head, the vast expanse of this cabbage-patch quilt called The Beloved Country unfurled itself as the silver beast gashed a steel scar across the land.

At first the dusty Transvaal countryside looked interesting, then just depressing through lack of variation. A mining community living in impersonal redbrick houses with red roofs and fenced with kitsch concrete wagonwheels would make way for grimy tin shacks and concentration camp blocks of single men's hostels, the living areas for the working people on the mines.

With forty-five per cent of the country jobless, whoever had work hung onto it in spite of bloody murder. Some of them were illegal aliens from a state to the north in an even more dire state of mind than this state of mines.

So many of the blacks lived underground, digging and burrowing into the earth that would eventually claim them as victims, while finding those golden chips to become the rings that shimmered on the fingers of the successful, and the golden fillings winking from the mouths of the sly.

But once the flat earth and brown mine dumps, teased by clumps of colourless bluegum trees, made way for the edge of the great savanna-lands of the central plain that was called the Great Karoo, David sat in awe as space made way for scenery.

The train hissed to a stop at the occasional station, all the platforms and buildings with their chequered awnings looking like film sets for a movie about Imperial India. The polite porters would distribute an afternoon paper, as if anyone sipping Pimm's in the lounge car was in the slightest bit interested in the banquet of death being offered as news. As the sun touched the jagged horizon, the Blue Train reached the town of Kimberley, centre to the various legends of diamond diggings and home of what was laughingly called 'the biggest man-made hole in the world'.

"A matter of opinion," laughed the French woman in the bar, sipping her champagne and not looking a day over forty. She was celebrating her seventieth birthday and had already entertained David through two provinces with her delightful tales of woe.

All her husbands had died like flies; her children were more crooked than a rubber pencil; she'd had everything that hung, cut off; anything that stood out, put right; blood transfused so many times, it had changed from the blue she'd been born with to the watery red with which she was now cursed.

She'd personally seen every war zone, and slept with every known politician who could spell her first husband's title without getting the 'sch' confused with the 'zs'. David felt he was being softly webbed by an old spider with great skill at spinning more than just a yarn, so he was sorry to excuse himself for a chance to walk on the platform at Kimberley. "Stretch my legs," he explained, enjoying every moment of his Boy's Own adventure.

If this was home, why had he been away for so long?

At this station the train was to change units. The barman gave one of his illustrative recitals and intensely explained that there were three types of electrical current used on the Pretoria/Johannesburg/Cape Town line, and so electrical units had to change from AC to DC, while somewhere in between the train became diesel-driven.

"That's nothing, man," said a retired police colonel on a holiday with another man who looked like his prisoner. "In the days of apartheid which of course, as you know, are dead, we had train apartheid … You know what that is?"

Everyone around nodded a bleak aye-aye-sir, but he still had to explain. South Africans seemed to love lingering on the details of their most appalling past.

"No well," he expounded, "in Jo'burg Station the whites-only part is in the front of the platform, okay? No fine. Then you come here to Kimberley and the whites-only part is at the back of the damn platform! So before we get to Kimberley, the train must stop somewhere in the veld at a special junction, and the front half must be taken off and dragged on the other line to join up with the back half, so that the whites don't get in first on the black side of the platform and the blacks not at the white part! That's okay from here through the Karoo and even Beaufort West, but when we get into the Boland of the Cape, then the train must again stop. Because you can't have whites coming last into Cape Town platform, because that's where the blacks-only part was, so the train must be swapped round again." He paused as the effect of his tale sank in to his sipping audience.

"Ja! Every passenger train going up and down this rail since 1948 till, ag man, recently, had to be swapped round upside-down, back to front, and back again – twice! Mad, hey?" He laughed heartily and patted his convict-lookalike companion on the thigh. "Of course I was never for that system, you know … 'apartheid'!" He actually dropped his voice for the word and only mouthed it with thin lips. "… Apartheid, man, never my cup of tea, nor my friend's here. But we had to obey orders."

The elderly German couple to his left sighed so deeply and horribly that the whole coach seemed to shudder.

They had only opened one train door to the platform, as in the recent past a scallywag had hopped on board and hidden himself

35

under the bed of a lady passenger and when she was preparing for bed, after popping her false teeth into a glass, the scallywag had stroked her ankle from under the bunk.

It was not a good experience for either of them.

She screamed and ran down the passage without her teeth and he was eventually bundled off the train at the next stop, still laughing. It was was the first time the Blue Train had halted at that small siding, but it caused no comment from the railway workers' houses as they were all deserted, their occupants having been retrenched by the new privatised railway conglomorate.

The lady tourist just slid her teeth back into her mouth, followed by a few tranquillisers and wrote in her diary how she'd been raped repeatedly on the second day of her South African trip by four young black terrorists, who were very kind to her as she was a Scot and not responsible for apartheid like the English.

David took note of the twinkle in the eye of the porter who'd just told him this outrageous story in his delightful Cape Coloured accent. "You don't believe me, sir?" the man bleated looking happily hurt.

"No," said David quickly. "I'll believe anything nowadays. Will they announce when the train leaves?" He got off onto the platform.

The porter winked and laughed. "Don't worry, sir, you're a passenger. We don't leave our people here for the wolves."

David nodded and started a gentle saunter down the platform in the direction of the front of the train to watch the changing of the units. Every building had its windows covered by a crisscross of bars, either in a floral design, a paisley explosion of rounded circles, or just plain solid up and down steel. This he'd already noticed since he'd left Jan Smuts Airport the morning before. There wasn't a window in the whole province that hadn't been primed against robbery; now it seemed the country. And yet the robbers managed to slide through all precautions like a well-oiled virus.

"Teema!"

He suddenly spoke her name and stopped, staring at a large woman sitting on a bench, surrounded by battered cardboard boxes and full plastic bags. Small children hung around her skirts. Older teenagers lolled against the back of the bench, sharing a cooldrink.

David looked at her closely. Was he going to do this every time he saw a middle-aged black woman who could be his old nanny called Teema? That woman in the other train in Jo'burg station had for a moment so reminded him of her, or was it just her sad eyes? But then why should he remember sad eyes, if he'd only been a teenager when he'd last seen Teema?

The large woman who wasn't Teema looked up at him. Their eyes met. He smiled. She nodded. She looked so hot, so bothered, so fed up, that smiling was too much of an effort.

David went up to the small group of potato-eaters, as if they'd peeled off a Van Gogh sketch. They all watched him, whites of their eyes hot against the shadows of their skins. The smaller children stopped drinking from the tin. David glanced around their jumbled collection of belongings. "Lots of things?" he nodded at them and didn't have to try and look like a tourist. "Where are you going?"

There was no answer. The small ones cowered closer into the safety of the older girls. A teenage boy stood up slowly and seemed very tall among their huddled forms.

"We are going home." he said clearly, not blinking. Was he clenching his fist? David tried to look unaffected by his sudden feeling of panic. Why did he feel so guilty? He felt in his pocket for money, but maybe thank God, there was no change to buy himself out of this embarrassing moment.

"Ah," he said. "Cape Town?"

There was still no answer, just the open eyes of the children staring up at him, the sullen smirk on the face of the girls, his eyes narrowing as the boy-man looked David up and down. Then their mother spoke. Her voice was breathy and scarred. She repositioned her large body on the uncomfortable slats of bench under her.

"No, Master, we are going home to Transkei. That is where we are from. My husband works in Johannesburg. The children have been working there in Johannesburg. The little ones are new, and we want to show them our home in Transkei."

The boy snorted with what sounded like utter disgust. He started to say something, then just shook his head and looked away.

"Master is from overseas?" the earth-mother asked. David couldn't wait to nod over and over again.

"Yea," he confirmed. "Los Angeles. You know, Hollywood?"

It was a magic word. The sombre faces of the older kids seemed to freeze in a stare and then break out into a broad smile of recognition. There was a low mutter of explanation to the little ones to whom the name 'Hollywood' meant as little as owning a toy. Even the boy-man unclenched his fists. His head to one side, a slight frown between his eyes, he presented himself to David.

"So take me to Hollywood, Master," he challenged. "Take us all.

We can make a movie in Hollywood!" The children gave a delighted chorus of giggles.

David laughed and shrugged, wishing for the announcement for passengers to step aboard the spaceship next to him.

"Bill Cosby?" said a small voice at his feet. He looked down at the little girl and nodded.

"Rap man rap," said a girl with bedroom eyes and moved with extraordinary grace into a few rap steps. They all hugged one another, while the big woman clapped her hands with delight.

"Ah, Hollywood!" she understood. "No, we cannot go to that Hollywood. We must go home." She looked up at David. "Maybe you bring Hollywood here and then we can all work?"

"Yes," David nodded, "I'll tell them when I get back."

They looked at each other with nothing to say, the small faces of the children eager with the excitement of having an adventure here in the middle of an unfriendly world, and the youth calculating how much he could trust this stranger. He stepped out of the family group. David saw he was limping.

"I can sing," he confided urgently. "I can draw. I could also dance, but after the truck ran over my foot ..." He looked at his reflection in the train. "Does this cost a lot of money?" he whistled, trying to look in beyond the golden windows.

"Yes," said David, "but one day, maybe ..."

The young face turned to his with an expression of disbelief, starting in a smile and eventually laughing out loudly. "No, Master, you Americans are mad. One day maybe? Ja, one day pigs will fly back to Europe."

He limped back to his people, said something to them and they all broke eye contact with David and went back into their waiting neutrality. The large woman in their midst was the only one to still smile at him.

"Funny," he thought as he walked down the platform, relieved to get away. "She doesn't look like Teema at all."

The incredible journey recommenced and he ate and drank, and drank and ate.

He slept after lunch and when he woke up, had to drink again to get rid of the taste in his mouth. He put on a fresh shirt and a tie for dinner and then afterwards took off his tie in the bar. Over countless cocktails he spent till 3.00 a.m. talking American politics to a German who'd never been to South Africa before.

David didn't give himself away once; no, maybe just once. When he overheard an Afrikaans joke being told by the police official to his broken-nosed friend, he burst out laughing. David was quick to cough and ask for a translation which wasn't at all funny as the joke, but hysterical all the same, just listening to the mess they made of the story.

So he still remembered the Afrikaans language!

At least the dirty words hadn't faded away. Somewhere deep down in his memory were some small green men with grammar hammers, trying to straighten out thirty years of amnesia in preparation for his triumphant entry into the city of his birth.

The night passed by in sections of wakefulness and slumber, with the rocking of the motion leading to vivid dreams and the still breaks at the odd station rousing him with its silence, except for the tap-tapping of the steel bar on the wheels, as the engineer routinely checked for cracks and problems.

The closer they hummed towards Cape Town, the tighter the feeling in his gut. After breakfast he had a Bloody Mary and the vodka made him feel better.

"Bloody Winnie!" the police-pal gurgled into his beer, as David added salt and pepper. "Mary's not the problem here, it's that crazy woman. You know she commands an army of three million black kids who can't read and write? So what happens when she suddenly says: 'Okay, let's go for the nice houses of the whites and to hell with the consequences!'?"

"Pol Pot? Khmer Rouge?" suggested the Frenchwoman who'd changed her clothes and make-up three times since breakfast.

The barman just laughed. "Listen, anything is possible. There are no more rules and regulations. Just every man for himself. There's too much who have too much, and too many who have nothing."

The most glamorous train in the world, filled with blue chip aristocrats and blue blood exiles deeply distressed by the dismal state of mankind, slid down the steel rails to the southernmost tip of Africa.

CHAPTER 4.

Herman Greef looked exactly the same as he had all those years ago. The dusty silver in his hair had surely been there since school days? Those fine laughlines round his mouth? He always looked like someone's older brother and now that David felt his age, this bugger still looked like some kid's older brother, not ...

"How old are you now?" David asked, within minutes of shaking hands.

"Jesus Christ, De Lange, have you got a problem with age? I'm as old as you, man. Virtually to the day."

"Fifty ..."

"Forty-seven."

They both laughed and did a lot of backslapping.

"This all you got?" Greef asked, pointing down to the small suitcase in David's hand.

"Yes, I'm travelling light."

"Ah," replied the old joker, "Thought they'd mugged you at Jo'burg station and relieved you of the ten-piece, crocodile-skin set! Here, let me take it."

"No, it's okay ..."

"Kak man!"

Yip, the same Herman Greef. Bossy, short-tempered and so wonderfully local. David looked around the cavernous station concourse as they walked to the exit. Why did all these stations look like football stadiums just waiting for a *coup d'état*?

"I haven't heard much Afrikaans since I got here," he said, "and the word '*kak*' I haven't heard at all!"

"Well, *kak* is all you get around you, man, you don't have to be reminded of it. This fucking country is really up to shit! Makes me so sick!"

His voice seemed to carry and some people peered round. An old black man sitting on his haunches squinted up at them as they passed and skillfully spat just where David was to put his foot. For a moment it looked as if Greef would kick at the crouched bundle of rags. "Fucking country ..." he spat back as they walked on.

It was grey and misty outside. David looked round to see the mountain, but there was just cotton wool cloud and monochrome chill.

"God, I'm sorry Table Mountain is covered," he moaned.

"Is it?" Herman Greef looked, screwing his face up against the drizzle. "Fucking mountain. Come, the car's on a yellow line." There was a pink ticket fluttering on the window. Greef tore it off and scrunched it up in a little ball. He flicked the rose-tinted missile into the wetness. "Fucking town," he declared.

In the murkiness of the fine rain, Cape Town looked like nothing and everything. There was now no specific landmark to assure David that this was not some town in Ohio, or the Free State, or outside Manchester.

There were roads everywhere. Incomplete concrete flyovers with bridges leading to nowhere, clusters of robots, rings within rings of traffic circles and so few cars.

"Where are all the cars?" he asked.

"Probably all stolen and being resprayed in the townships. Fucking bastards!" Herman Greef shouted suddenly at a minibus taxi full of blacks that had swerved into his lane and just stopped to let off a passenger. "God, man, sometimes I wished I had a laser-gun in the front of the car, you know, like in *Star Wars*. Then you just focus, push the button and pow! Gone! Shit, I'd use it all the time."

"Don't they have one of those already called the AK47?" David tried to joke and watched people and pigeons bedraggled on the pavement in the rain, waiting for something to change; either the robots, their lives, or the weather.

"Oh, a tasteless joke from the American tourist?" Herman Greef jeered, not in the mood for anything light. "Wait till you go to a restaurant with your wife on a Saturday night and some black fuckers run in with AK47s or sawn-off shotguns, and force you to lie on the floor, usually with a soggy chip up your nostril. And then they nearly cut the fucking rings off her fingers and take your wallet and the credit cards and just for good measure, or because they're so pissed off that you don't carry the family fortune in your pocket, they rape a few customers. Fuck them, De Lange! They deserve to die. And I'm not shy to say I'll be just too happy to oblige! Hey! *Fok off, man!*" He bellowed through his closed window at another passing motorist who gave him a two-finger and swerved into their lane to force them to slow down.

By the time they skidded round the corner into the driveway of Greef's cottage in the leafy suburb of Rosebank, David was carsick and very happy to be alive.

There was a young man working in the small garden. Herman Greef called to him immediately. "Hey! Shit, I can never remember his name … Remember to do the pool before you go, okay, boy?"

"Yes, Master."

No 'sir' down here in the Cape, just old habits that died hard. David stared at the dark-skinned mixed-race 'boy' half his age cutting at a small bush. Their eyes met. David quickly greeted him with a warm smile.

"Hi. I'm David. From Hollywood."

The gardener shrugged and went back to his bush. Maybe the magic password down here wasn't 'Hollywood'.

"You're in the guest-room at the back," Herman Greef shouted from the kitchen, where he was mixing some cocktails. "Got a door leading out to the pool. Don't leave it open, hey. And always keep the safety door locked as well. They cut through steel with their arrogance nowadays. Fucking democracy!"

An unfriendly large dog was watching him from the small back terrace through the glass door as David opened his suitcase and hung up his few things. The rain against the window drummed unevenly and suddenly he had to sit down. This felt like home, this sound, this smell of wetness.

He was back in Cape Town!

"Cheers, De Lange!" Herman Greef lifted his glass of whisky and they toasted the world without pointing it out. "How's Deli?"

"Fine. She doesn't know you, but says she's sure you'll keep me out of trouble."

"Ja, man, no steakhouses on a Saturday night for you. And your kids?"

"The girls are both married. Bette's at Universal Studios, doing art display, you know, with all the tours and things, and Helena's got a little son, Marcos."

"You're a fucking grandpa?"

They looked at each other for a moment as sounds from the past echoed through their heads. The cheering at sports day, barked orders at the cadet pass-out parade, the exhaustion of rugby finals, boredom at cricket practice, sing-alongs round a roaring campfire, dirty laughter in the boys' toilets. Their lives were now more gone than coming.

"Oupa?" nodded David. "Yip. It feels great."

The feeble laugh qualified the lie. He hated being called a grandfather. He hated the name Marcos. He didn't really like Helena's husband either. And it was not because he was Mexican.

"So what's with this Marcos?" Herman Greef insinuated. "He a Mexican? I mean, the father?"

"Eh … yes, I believe so. Not that it matters."

"Bloody old liar, De Lange. Once a boer always a boer!" He cracked his glass against David's with a tinkle of ice.

"*Vrystaat!*"

They sat and talked through the afternoon, into the evening and until morning. The empty bottles of red wine replaced the empty bottles of white wine. There were liqueurs, and even a few cans of beer. Tears were shed at one stage when they realised how many of their mutual friends had died. Two middle-aged men tend to look old and tired, especially after the amount they drank, and that didn't add to their sagging confidence in a long and happy life ahead.

When the clatter in the kitchen announced the arrival of Greef's trusted and seemingly immortal coloured maid Frieda, the two buddies had been sitting and staring through the window at the feeble new sunshine for some minutes.

"When did that happen?" muttered Herman Greef at a sunbeam on his sleeve and got up unsteadily, shaking it off like an insect. "*Jisis*, I've got to piss." He lurched out into the passage, calling, "Morning Frieda?"

"Morning, Master Herman!" came the disapproving voice from the kitchen.

David stared again at the photograph on the table in front of him, now with its glass covered in greasy fingermarks, as the face in the frame had been under close examination through this night of long-nosed stories.

Joanie Craig.

The girl they'd all queued up to bang in the sports-shed. Didn't look like Joanie Craig. She used to be quite plump. She had dark hair. She had rosy cheeks. Big tits. This Joanie Craig was blonde and elegant, and there was nothing rosy about her face.

"She chewed me up from the balls to the wallet. Jesus, what a cocksucker!" Herman Greef had sighed, after the stormy story of his life with Joanie had spilled out onto the table in front of them, among the littered mess of snapshots and old school albums and tarnished rugby trophies. And ex-fiancées.

"She was number three, purely because I always went to her for comfort and a bit of a fuck when Number One had a nervous breakdown and tried to kill herself and Number Two ran off with a hockey player from the university team, half her age, arsehole. Being with Joanie Craig was like being with one of the boys ..." he chuckled, "... until we got into the old in-and-out. I think she was the first girl I fucked." He thought, then shrugged nonchalantly. "Maybe not, but she's the first girl who sucked my cock, that I remember."

"Ja, I remember that."

"You watched?"

"Cost me a few guineas in pocket money. Oh come on, Greef, we all watched! There was nothing to see! I remember someone saying: 'Joanie's sewing on a button and biting through the thread!'" They laughed and coughed and pawed the face of the woman who as a girl had helped them pretend to be men.

"Shit, and so I gave her a ring and she gave me hell."

"Did she sleep around?" David slurred, hoping she did and that there were some juicy stories coming up. "I mean, why didn't the relationship work out?"

"I don't know." Herman Greef leant back in his chair and wiped his face with a damp paper napkin. "I don't know what she did when I tried to get away from her. I just hated having a mirror in my life, who remembered every pimple I'd squeezed since I was 12. Anyway, De Lange, it didn't last that long. She walked out one day and then sent a grown-up daughter to collect 'her things'! My fucking things! Then when I moved to this smaller house, I gave her the big car. Oh fuck it, serves her right! The more shit she's got on her plate with this new government coming, the more shit she'll have to dish out in taxes. The have's and the have-not's, *ou* De Lange, you've heard of them, haven't you?"

They drank to the have-not's. Herman Greef chewed drunkenly at his bottom lip and felt nothing.

"It's funny, you know, De Lange? You dream about your life when you're a kid, and there's nothing to stop you from getting to the top of the ladder! Unless you fuck up with booze, or get lazy, or get killed. But generally, if you roll up your sleeves, you can get there. And I did, man. I knew what I wanted, and now here I am, maybe not the top publisher in the town, but certainly the most success-ful ..."

"Congratulations."

"Thanks. Big deal. Who's reading? No one can predict a future market. Burning the books to keep warm in winter maybe? But the ladder, that's the bitch, the fucking ladder suddenly ends halfway and there's nothing you can do to find an extension. No amount of experience, no knowledge, no flair, no fuck all, if you're not black here and now. That's a joke hey, De Lange. It's still whites only. But those are the ones that get left behind." He poured another round of red wine carelessly. Spots of red stained the faces of the happy boys in the black and white snaps. "Fuck it all, man! Anyway, soon the space men will come back to this smallholding called Earth and see what a balls-up we've made, and probably eat us for dinner."

"Suck us up through a straw?"

"Hot dogs?"

Joanie Craig's face seemed to smile now as the day broke and the wetness of a Cape squall steamed away. The grass twinkled in the sunshine.

Frieda stomped into the living-room and stood arms folded, surveying the damage of the night before, till her beady eyes rested on a bleary David Clayton.

"I see," she snorted. "Drunken party in the middle of the week?"

"I'm David ... de Lange, Frieda. Herman Greef and I were at school together," he explained sweetly.

"Ja?" Frieda narrowed her eyes at him. "And what's changed?"

He looked at the mess on the floor, the soggy chips crumbed into the carpet, wine stains on the wooden table top. Like a midnight feast in 1955 ...

David Clayton, now starting to dissolve into a stranger once called Dawid de Lange, spent his first few days in the Cape driving around the place of his beginnings in a daze.

If it weren't for the huge overpowering rock-mass of Table Mountain anchoring his memories, and the occasional glimpse of the past on a white beach with the blue sea crashing ashore in froth, he wouldn't have known where he was.

All the old landmarks of his childhood were gone.

It was as if there'd been a virus that had dissolved anything older than half a century. The charm of the colonial houses, the flat-roofed, white-washed, small-stoeped Malay dwellings that featured so colourfully on many calendars and promotional packages selling the quaintness of this Cape had made way for concrete blocks that housed bureaucrats. Here and there some madman had spent a fortune restoring his old heritage, but doing it so well that the shiny clean and new old building with its 'broekielace' balconies looked rather more like a recently constructed kitsch salute to a New Orleans past so far away.

Whereas Johannesburg was a chaotic street-market, Cape Town seemed more demurely mercantile and better controlled. Countless small stalls filled the now pedestrianised city streets that teemed with the slow to move, quick to laugh and legendary laid-back citizens.

Again David was struck by the lack of real concern with the fast-forward blur of violent change happening in the north. Maybe it wasn't amnesia, but more the refusal to lie down in submission to the fearful horsemen of the coming apocalypse.

Occasionally he would find himself standing next to himself at the age of six, and like that small white person wearing a baseball cap with the Malcolm X on it, stare with awe up at a huge aeroplane flying over the city, giving the tourists a view of this womb with a view, this cradle of now nearly redundant white civilisation.

It all had started here on a day in April 1652, when three small Dutch vessels bearing gifts of death by musket and measles, sailed into Table Bay. April 6 was still celebrated as a public holiday even now, but with less and fewer mention of those champions of the white dream. Founders' Day it was now called, but celebrating which founders?

The statue of Jan van Riebeeck stood forlornly on the city fore-shore, a block away from the plinth bearing his plump wife, Maria, both monuments now home-base to the pigeons of the Cape who knew two losers when they shat on them.

The embryo of European standards grew and gave birth to a carbon distortion of life 'back home', with a Little London and Kleine Amsterdam and Schone Frankfurt taking root in African soil. Three hundred-odd years of foreign peoples' way of doing things had fossilised the true locals either into forgotten cadavers lining the foundations of the land, or as a mute serving class. It was 'Master' here and 'Madam' there, but somehow between the bows and the scrapes of the Cape Coloured people, David could detect a very healthily erect centre finger. "Fuck off whitey!" was the most exhilarating phrase he heard during his three days on the Cape Peninsula.

He was passing the umpteenth beggar on the street in the city centre with no intention of giving any more alms. The words floated up to him, as he nearly stepped on the neat square of cloth spread out on the sidewalk, next to a rough handwritten sign:

I'M BLIND DEAR MA'AM
DON'T EVEN KNOW WHAT COLOUR I AM
BUY A SOUVERNIR

The man was not white. David stopped and took a step back. "What did you say?" he asked.

"Ah, you're also blind, but not hard of hearing. I can smell a cheapskate when they pass. Maybe I was wrong with you?"

The accent bounced lightly on top of an obvious education. David fished some coins out of his pocket and dropped them among others in the blind man's cup waving for attention.

"Sorry. My mistake. Generous too? I heard a 20c, a 50c, a big Rand coin and then something foreign." David glanced down and saw an American quarter between the local coins.

"American quarter. Sorry," he said and made to fish it out.

The blind man covered his tin cup with a newspaper. "Please. An American quarter is worth more than the whole cup of cash put together. I'll stick it with my other pesetas, lira, francs, pfennigs and drachmas. Soon I'll be a rich man."

"What the hell is the story here?" David thought, looking down at the seated figure. It was as if the blind man also read minds.

"Don't be sorry for me now. You've got much bigger problems walking around with your eyes open. You're going to be late for your appointment."

"How did you know I've got an appointment?" David asked.

The man snorted and gave a gurgle for a laugh. "Second sight, you old American *poephol*!" he said and waved David on with his newspaper.

Like that old blind man who sat in front of the OK Bazaars in the old days, David remembered. The one who sold shoe laces. He was black. The way he sat so forlornly, he looked as if he only had one leg. Then late one afternoon, young Dawid de Lange was coming from a film at the old Metro Cinema, and he saw the poor blind man get up, stretch both legs, fold up his white stick and get into the back of a large American car that glided to the edge of the pavement. He even waved at Dawid as he drove by. The next time Dawid walked by this rich beggar giving his pathetic performance, he pointedly looked the other way.

"I've always looked the other way," he thought at his reflection in the mirror of the lift. The smart image of David Clayton grinned back. "American *poephol*!" Yip, there's a perfect description for David Clayton. "Arsehole!"

Joanie Craig was not in her office when he knocked on the door and opened it. It was five minutes before one. He was early. He looked around the passage, then knocked again at the door with the sign 'Cosmetics Consultant: J. Craig CCL.'

"Hello? Joanie? It's me. David!" he called round the door.

There was no one in the office. The soft scent of her perfume couldn't hide the evidence of a heavy smoker. Glossy blow-ups of pretty models proving the success of the products they were paid to push, stared icily at him from the walls. He sat on the chair near the window and looked out onto the city. From here it looked like those postcards he still had up on the wall of his LA office. The height seemed to blot out the damage done on ground level by progress. Seagulls milled about the space between the skyscrapers and glided back and forth, mouths open, honking away and watching for food on the ground. A man was sitting at a desk in the office across the block typing away at a console. He looked out of his window and saw David watching him. His mouth clearly formed the traditional South African greeting: "Fuck off!"

The door open and Joanie walked in carrying some parcels. Her hair was darker than in Greef's much-pawed trophy photo. She was also pregnant. David got up quickly. "Let me help you with those," he said and took two of the carrier bags.

The girl who looked like Joanie Craig smiled and looked at him gratefully. "I'm finished! Thank God the age of chivalry is not dead after all. Just put them there. Are you in a meeting?" she asked, nodding towards a closed door with her head.

"I've got a lunch date. At one. I'm David … Dawid de Lange."

She nodded and held out her hand. "Hi. Joanie's in the office behind that door. I gather you mean Joanie Craig." But this was Joanie Craig! "I'm her daughter."

"You look just like your mother!" David gasped. "Spitting image."

"Really?" The girl frowned and pulled a face. "Well, I don't know when last you saw my mother."

"At school," he shrugged and smiled. "Before you were born."

"I should hope so …"

The door opened and a woman came into the room. David was immediately struck by the hardness in her face and that she had no resemblance at all to her daughter.

"Judy, shit doll, you're late … David?"

Then he saw the old Joanie Craig in her eyes. She opened her arms and he returned the hug. He could feel her heart beating against his chest.

"Dawid de Lange?" Judy repeated, now leaning against the desk and stroking her pregnant tummy. "You never spoke about him."

"No." Joanie Craig stood back a step and studied David's face keenly. "Dawid de Lange ran away and left us to get rich and infamous. Where did you go?"

"Everywhere."

"And the circle ends here?"

"I suppose you could say that, yes."

A seagull screamed so close it could've been in the room with them.

Joanie Craig broke the spell. "Well, Judy's going to man the office while we go off for lunch. Messages, doll. No 'phone back later' shit. We need all the consulting work we can find!" Judy saluted and sat at the desk, pulling the phone into the centre. "And don't have the baby while you're here."

"Only if you take a three-week liquid lunch, mummy!" She winked at David and he felt himself blush.

Just like her mother.

"Come on, Dawid de Lange," said the mature stranger to his left. "Lunch can be on your Gold Card. Mine's been stolen."

They had to wait in a small line for a table squeezed into the corner of an Italian eatery. Joanie had just lit a fresh cigarette when the first of a series of cocktails appeared out of habit. He got one too, but then later switched to a glass of wine.

"She looks just like you. I thought I'd gone back in time," he said once they'd settled into a salad, after a long, uncomfortable monologue from her about that 'cunt Herman Greef'.

"Wasn't I prettier?" She wasn't joking. "I had nicer hair and bigger tits. Did you ever …?"

"No!" He looked around, sure everyone knew what she was talking about. "But you watched the other boys doing it? I remember you, Dawid de Lange. Always the little innocent, the little goody-goody one. The boring one who inevitably split on us when the teacher asked."

"They would've expelled me."

"They did expel me. Remember? I just went to another school, learnt how to speak English properly. Stopped giving it away in the

49

sports-shed!" An old familiar wink reappeared and made him feel better. "I became the headmaster's mistress …" His face made her finish loudly. "… Once I'd left school, of course! He was a great man. Taught me a lot about boring things. Took me to Europe for the first time."

"And Judy?"

He didn't want to ask if she was a child from an early marriage or not. Had they speculated about it the other night over bottles?

"Not that cunt Herman Greef's child for sure!" she announced.

Joanie talked solidly throughout the lunch, darting from one subject to the next, asking countless questions and then answering them with a selection of possible answers. David just nodded and shrugged, somewhat relieved not to have to do the hard work, often appalled at the obvious paranoia that had entrapped Joanie's spirit.

There was the usual hymn to 'the fucking government' and to 'those bastards in the ANC'! She loathed the 'capitalist thugs' who ran the 'so-called free press that sucks!' And occasionally balanced the politics with a passionate 'the shits stole my Gold Card!'

"You know one thousand women get raped in the country every day!" she spat out. "And those are only the one's one hears about! Every time I get into the lift with a man I feel raped!" She glared at two obviously gay men at the table next to theirs, then realised her mistake and smiled dazzlingly. They looked pleased, then giggled at each other and said something mean about her.

"Give me queens any day," she sighed and took his hand. "And your marriage is okay, you say?"

"I didn't have a chance to say," he laughed, but she held onto his hand and eventually he told her all about Deli and the girls and his 25-year-old marriage. "And yes, I suppose my marriage is okay."

"Doesn't sound like it from your story." She patted his hand and lit a cigarette.

"Really? Maybe I didn't tell it all that well."

"Oh no, you made it very clear."

The waiter brought their second round of strong coffee. Suddenly there was nothing left to say. The two young men left and soon they were the only two customers in the restaurant. Joanie's house cocktails continued arriving. She caught his look as she picked up a fresh glass.

"Got a problem with my cooldrinks?" she asked. "I'll put them on tick if you like. God knows I don't want to waste your precious dollars!" She drained the glass and tapped against it for a refill.

"Don't be silly …" he started, then gave up, looking down at his fingers tearing silver paper from her cigarette box into small strips. "Do you remember our maid, Fatima?"

Joanie was looking at him, but was far away. She did not answer him, but asked: "Judy is prettier than I was?" There were tears in her eyes. He put his hand over hers. It suddenly felt small and cold. And old.

"Well, if she has a little girl, you'll just Xerox yourself into another generation."

"Don't make me cry, De Lange! I hope that fucking baby strangles itself with its own umbilical cord, so hear me God, wherever She is!" She suddenly got up and jammed the table sharply into his stomach trapping him against the wall. She leant over towards him and whispered loudly. "Don't tell a soul, but if you do I'll deny it. My daughter isn't even married!" She waited for a reaction, but he just smiled. "Big deal? Is that what I read in your wise LA eyes? Everyone has babies without getting married? Maybe, but I was determined my kid wouldn't hurt herself like I did, and here she goes doing things worse than I ever could imagine. Worse!"

And with that she turned and barged out between the tables, dislodging chairs and slammed the door behind her.

"Will Master want the bill?" asked the Italian waiter in his Cape Coloured accent.

The blind man was still sitting on his perch when he passed by on his way to the parking garage. He stopped and dropped another handful of coins in the cup.

"It's me again," he said. "No Russian kopeks. Sorry."

"How was the lunch with the lady?" asked the sightless man.

"Hard going." David crouched down next to him. Their backs were against the same wall that housed one of biggest banks in the country. "I haven't seen her for many years. She's got problems."

"Mmmm." The brown man nodded at a passerby as a coin clinked into his cup. "Sounds very normal. You got no problems?"

David could from his position see under the parked cars in the street in front of them. A bedraggled black cat sat crouched under a Mercedes, ears flat against the head, yellow eyes snarling out at him. He nodded. "Yes, I suppose I do. I'm trying to find someone and I don't know where to start."

"Mmmm." They sat watching the busy pairs of feet shuffle by on their way to something important. "Where did you see her last?"

"How do you know it's a her?"

"Men usually know where to find each other. Men aren't so imaginative about hiding away. Women have reasons to hide."

David tried to remember where last he'd seen Teema. He still couldn't remember her face, or her surname. He was 15, she must've been 25. They were at home, she in the kitchen, he was doing homework. "At my house," he recalled.

"Mmmm." The dark man sat touching the tips of his fingers against each other, two slim elegant hands. "If it's your mother, you should be ashamed of yourself for losing her. If it's your sister, maybe she doesn't want to be disturbed. I think it's your nanny."

He moved his body from its crouch and looked at David's face. For the first time the sightless eyes looked into his. The blind man laughed, obviously seeing something funny.

"You've come back to find your nanny!" he hooted. "You feel guilty because for all those years you expected her to call you 'Master' and you were only 12 and she was 48?"

"She was 25."

"You've got a big sorry to say. How do you know she'll want to see you again?"

"She was a great friend of the family. We loved her."

"And if you've got her surname, you should be able to trace her, so that means …"

"I can't remember her surname."

The sightless eyes didn't blink.

"Well, friend, start at the beginning. Go home. Find her name scratched out on the toilet wall. I love … Beauty?"

"Fatima."

"Even easier. A Malay woman? A coloured woman?"

"No, she was black."

"Like me?"

David looked at the brown man's skin. Thin, transparent. Not white.

"Not as light."

"Do me a favour!" he gasped. "Light? You mean I've been under the wrong impression all these years? But, tell me, do I look Jewish?"

"What?" David felt his mouth dry in panic.

"A joke, man! Jesus, you're fucked, hey? Listen, take a deep breath and start again. You've come home? So, go home!"

"I don't know if that will help …" David got to his feet painfully, his back hurting, his knees cracking, his age telling.

His blind friend chuckled. "And you better hurry up. By the sounds of you, old Fatima doesn't have much time."

As David walked away, he realised that he didn't even know the beggar's name.

Old habits died hard.

CHAPTER 5.

At first he couldn't find the road that went to the suburb where he was born. Everything seemed to lead to freeways that led to other freeways that led back to square one. So he got himself onto the old Main Road where the trolleybuses used to run – no longer, of course – and followed his instinct till he came to the street name that had featured so clearly on his exercise books at school.

St Andrew's Road.

He didn't remember so many trees.

"There were trees ... but not these trees. He leant against the bonnet of his hired blue car and studied the geography around him. Over there was the house where those people from England had lived. There was the house where the Gallimores stayed. ... The Galloways? ... The Gallimeads? ... Whatever. So his house must've been there. He walked towards the high hedge and looked over the wooden gate. The garden was overgrown, not untidy but in charge. The small crazypaved pathway snaked up to the front door. The house was no longer thatched, but otherwise it looked exactly as he'd imagined.

"Exactly ..." he whispered and opened the gate. It squeaked. He shuddered and looked down at the rusty hinges. "Exactly."

He slowly approached the house, expecting barking dogs, or an angry shout from the windows, or even a shot. Then when he peered into the sitting room he realised the house was empty.

"Hey!" called an elderly man with a red face wearing a cloth cap peering over the fence from next door. "You here to see the house?"

"No," called David, then changed his mind. "Yes, actually I am." The cloth-capped neighbour waved and disappeared.

David was looking back into the empty room, when the cloth-cap reappeared at the front gate and bustled up to him waving a pamphlet.

"Here's the address of the agent. Asked me to keep an eye. They've moved their offices, so the number on the sign is no good." There was no sign. "Oh bugger, the kids must've taken it off again. Well, it's quite nice, isn't it?"

They looked at the cottage, more suited for an English countryside than the oakshaded confines of Claremont.

54

"I actually ..." David was going to say "grew up here", but didn't. "Actually I just wanted to have a look around."

"American!" rejoiced the cloth-cap. "I can make out that accent quite easily now. Well ..." The neighbour looked quite conspiratorial. "You could buy this house for 49 dollars 22 cents."

"Really?"

"Rate of exchange." The pink face creased in laughter and he rubbed his hands. "I'd buy the place myself if I knew I'd be staying."

"You're going somewhere?"

"Maybe over to Canada. Never been, but all the kids are there. The grandchildren, you know. It's very far for them to come every Christmas to see us."

David was listening with one ear, aware of the twittering of birds and the humming of bees and, was that the sound of a horse clopping on the tarred road?

"This is absurd," he cried and ran to the gate as a policeman on horseback cantered past. "On horseback?"

"Yes, the new neighbourhood watch."

Birds, bees and the horse on the tar.

He could've been twelve!

He'd bunked school again. Hated school. Wanted to listen to the radio. All his favourite serials were on between 10 and 1.00. His mother wasn't very sympathetic.

"You want me to call the Doctor, Dawid?"

"No Ma, but I think I should stay in bed ..."

The sad little wail he and his sister always used when they were 'sick' sounded so effective to him and so transparent to his mother, who read him like a book. "Alright," she sighed. "In bed. No fancy cooldrinks. No radio ..."

"No radio?"

"How can you have a radio on and be sick at the same time?"

So once again he would wait for his parents to leave for work and his sister to go to school, she fed-up that he'd got away with staying at home and her having to leave. Then in his striped pyjamas, he would slink downstairs to the kitchen where Teema was preparing to work on the sitting-room furniture with her bottle of oil and soft rag. The big radio stood on the table like a giant bird cage, waiting to expel its imprisoned sounds.

"No, my child, you're sick. You must be sick. So go upstairs and be sick!" she commanded without looking at him once.

"Look at me, Teema … please?"

"I'm not looking. I see those eyes and I have to give in. I won't give in. I'm not looking …"

But she did look and her serious shiny face opened up into a broad smile and she opened her arms and he ran to her and she held him tight against her body. She smelt of Sunlight soap.

"I know you make up stories so that you can stay here with me, not so?" she cooed

"Yes of course, Teema!"

"You lying little white worm!" she laughed and switched on the radio. "Okay, you let this out and get me into trouble, I put the *tokolosh* on you, and he will turn you into a big, red cockroach! And go put on your slippers! No bare feet down here!"

So he ran upstairs and put on his slippers.

It was then that the warm sunbeam on his back made him look up at the open window, into the garden, the tall poplars near the hedge not moving a leaf, the bees humming round the honeysuckle creeper under the window, the doves gossiping in the oak trees and a horse pulling the bread cart slowly down the road. He waved at the bread-man and ran downstairs. It was time for his first serial. Teema would fill him in on the weeks he had missed since his last 'illness'.

"'Forbidden Love'!" he said nearly 40 years later.

The neighbour looked at him with raised eyebrows. "Really?"

"No, I was just thinking of a radio serial I once listened to …" It made even less sense. He thanked the man and went back to his car. There were fresh horse droppings on the tar.

"Exactly!"

He sat in the car for about an hour with all the windows open, listening, remembering, even smelling the past as the aroma of freshly tilled soil and cut grass filtered through his imagination.

Teema's room was at the back of the house with its own little toilet. On sunny days he would sit with her while she packed countless small objects into cardboard boxes to send back home, to him an exotic rural kingdom of wild chiefs and bloodthirsty warriors.

"But this is your home, Teema," he would say.

"Ja, this is my home, but my family lives in Transkei. I must keep them healthy and send them food."

He remembered unwrapping an object and looking at the egg.

"You're sending them eggs?"

Teema would smile. "Nice eggs. Boiled. They should keep."

David would never eat an egg and not give Teema a thought after that.

"Where the fuck is she?" he snapped and hit the steering wheel. The hooter's blast made him jump, and he looked round for some reaction in the street, but suburban life purred on in St Andrew's Road. He tried to get his list of clues straight.

"Teema lived here and I lived here. Then I left here to go to England and where would she have gone?" Transkei!

"Transkei? Are you out of your Mickey Mouse mind?"

Herman Greef laughed and threw the afternoon paper with its headlines of turmoil at him. "Rather go to Sarajevo, man. You can't get into the damn Transkei. There's an army blockade from our side and chaos on theirs. Don't you get any news in LA?"

Herman seemed to enjoy flaunting history's small print and then accusing David of knowing nothing.

"Sure we get news. Your violence is very familiar to us," he said.

"You Los Angelians have taken some good lessons from us on that score. Crazy country you chose to run to. From Martin Luther King to Rodney King in one breath."

David rushed to the defence of his adopted madness. "I suppose if most police beatings were videotaped like his was, we'd all have Rodney Kings in our lives!"

Herman Greef snorted and folded the sportspage into a holdable square. "You keep your bleeding blacks, old friend. We've more than we can mop up. Bugger it! Western Province lost the match."

David took his coffee cup to the kitchen. Frieda was tidying up an already tidy space.

"You're here late, Frieda?' he asked.

"I'm finished long ago, Master Dawid. I'm just waiting for Master Herman to drive me home."

David then remembered the headline on page one. Stone-throwing on the Cape Flats.

"Where do you live, Frieda?"

"Out on the Flats. Manenberg. The buses are so dear, and the taxis so full. There's always some trouble somewhere." She sighed. "Master Herman tells me you went to America when you was small?"

"Yes. I was 19."

"Is it nice there? Like we see on the TV?"

"What do you see on the TV?" Images of the brutal beating of Rodney King at the hands of the police came to mind.

"Like the serials on the TV! *The Bold and the Beautiful*! *Loving*! *As The World Turns*! Shame, American people are so nicely dressed, even though they got terrible problems with drugs and children and all that. No man, Master Dawid. You must now come home! Here's a place that makes sense to you, hey?"

"Was that a question?" he thought, then answered. "I'm here to find an old friend, Frieda."

What the hell, cards on the table.

So he told her about Teema. Frieda stood against the stove, her arms folded, eyes narrowing and widening as the story of his childhood unfolded.

"What's her surname?" she asked logically and he cringed.

"I don't know."

"No, but those natives have civilised names when they work for you whites. It's what they call her at home, there in that Transkei. You know, her native name!" The coloured woman's lips curled in distaste. "No, Master Dawid, those kaffirs make me very nervous."

"Those kaffirs?" He couldn't believe his ears.

"Sorry. Master Herman is also touchy about the word you people made up. Those 'blacks'. Call them what you like, but those kaffirs still make me nervous." She put a scarf round her head and tied a firm knot. "Well, your native girl maybe had friends there where you lived? Other nannies, or chars? They don't all die young, hey? Go find out."

Teema's friends ...

"And, ag please man, Master Dawid, tell Master Herman I'm ready. I've already missed one of my soaps. I don't want to wreck my night's viewing."

David went along for the ride. It was his first excursion into the soft underbelly of the Mother City, the coloured areas wrinkled with poverty and sagging through overcrowding. Herman drove his car quickly, his knuckles white on the wheel. Dawid sat at the back, although he nearly lost the battle, when Frieda refused to sit in front because she insisted it was against the law.

"Not any more, Frieda, damn it woman, get in or you can walk!"

So Frieda got in, rather break a law than walk home, and sat on the front seat pressed up against her door as far from the white driver as she could. She knew this was not right. How can such

58

things suddenly change? "Miss Dorothy's girl always sits in the back, Master Herman. It's the law."

"No, Frieda, Miss Dorothy's girl sits at the back because Miss Dorothy's dog sits in the front. It's got nothing to do with the law."

The coloured townships looked relatively neat and already quite middle class, with extraordinarily large mansions squashed onto some postage stamp properties.

"Indians." sniffed Frieda. "They got no damn taste."

They dropped her at a small gate that led to a rickety corrugated iron house already skewed by the vicious south-easter winds of the last decades.

"Thanks Master Herman. Master Dawid, you can come and sit in front now, hey?"

"No, never!" hissed Herman. "I refuse to have an American on the seat next to me. Leave him in the back, Frieda." And then he said something in Afrikaans that made Frieda laugh loudly and run into her home.

"What did you say there?"

Herman drove off into the traffic without so much as looking. A car hooted and squealed towards another lane behind him.

"If you're that interested, relearn the language!"

While eating dinner that evening, David broached a touchy subject.

"But she's black! I mean, if you're not white, you're black and Frieda's not white," he said, trying to make sense of the nonsense of black-on-black prejudice.

"You tell her that. She's whiter than my mother."

"You mean your mother was coloured? What are you saying, Greef?"

"I'm trying to lighten what intends to become a very heavy, very boring conversation. De Lange, Frieda is a coloured."

"I know, Herman …"

"There are some coloureds who are proudly black and some who are hopefully white. Frieda is a racist, it's as simple as that. You don't need to be white to be a racist."

They drank the wine and tasted the food Frieda had prepared before she'd left for her side of the blanket.

"She calls blacks 'kaffirs'." David tried to lighten that with a smirk, but it sounded like a condemnation.

Herman Greef sighed and leant back in his beautiful chair. "You fight all your life to defuse a word like that and never use it and really come down on people who do, and then it's found alive and well and in your home. Kaffir. What can you do?"

"She says you don't like it either."

"Never use the k-word myself," Herman stated, exploring his teeth with a toothpick.

"Not unless you're driving," David thought, but swallowed that argument quickly.

"De Lange, I've given up. Some months ago she came back one afternoon after walking Valkyrie ..." David had yet to find enough courage to make friends with Herman's Alsatian. He'd watched Frieda take the dog for a walk on the nearby common and she seemed to manage quite well. "My child" she would call the huge beast and be licked for her love.

"Well, she came back looking like hell, you know how Frieda carries her heart on her face. 'There's a kaffir down the road!' she said. God man, at first I wanted to explode, but then knowing what a successful neighbourhood watch she was, I mean whenever she just sees a loitering person of colour in the street she phones the police, I didn't explode. I said: 'Frieda, okay. What do you think he's up to? Robbery? Assault? Murder? What's this "kaffir" doing down the road?' 'He's just bought the house.' she said." Herman Greef nearly choked with laughter. "Fucking New South Africa! Don't you think that's funny?"

David felt chilled to the heart. "Yes ... very funny."

So David spent the next three days watching 'kaffirs in the road'.

St Andrew's Road.

He'd started by knocking at doors and pressing security bells, but no one would open when he said: "I'm looking for someone who might have known our maid ..."

Some of the black girls he watched were either walking to the shop, or just sitting in clusters on the grassy surrounds to the pavement. They all looked too young. There was an old black man who walked by with difficulty, but he wasn't a local garden boy. He was the Anglican Priest.

"I'm terribly sorry, Father," David stuttered. "I thought ...'

"Of course, you thought I was an important politician living here in a former white area, but I'm not. I'm just a humble servant of God, as opposed to a servant of the Devil. That's a rather nasty joke at your expense, I'm sorry. You look lost?"

"If you mean religion, I ... eh ... yes ... well, it's ..."

"It's hard having to admit that the most beautiful room in your spiritual home has been boarded up for too long. Don't be shy of that. That is the story of our lives here in this extraordinary land. The secret is how to open that darkened room without everything in it falling to dust at the first taste of fresh air."

So David told Reverend Nkotse about Teema. The old wise face didn't crease with laughter when he said: "And I don't even know her surname."

"Do you think she's still alive, Mr De Lange?"

David thought for a moment, more about being called that for the first time in so many years. "Yes. I'm sure she is. I know it."

The old priest stood in the middle of the road, his hands placed flatly together in a gesture of prayer. He looked up and down the street a few times. "Yes. I think you'll be wise to try up at No 34. The lady who works there is of a certain age and a specific generation. Even I am frightened of her. Good luck and beware of the dog."

David tried to find the hidden meaning in those wise words. "The dog? You mean the devil?"

"No, my son, the terrifying rottweiler at No 34!" Reverend Nkotse waved and walked on.

David stood at the steel gates of No 34 for nearly twenty minutes, pressing the button which he heard ring somewhere inside the house and stepping back smartly as the hungry rottweiler lunged at him at regular intervals.

Eventually a small voice bleated an accent from the intercom to his left. "What is it, Master? I can't control that dog. I'm locked up in the living room because he will now also bite me."

"You mean you can't come to the gate?"

"No, Master, now I can't go anywhere. I'm not very good friends with Nero." Nero was not good friends with anyone it seemed. He lunged again and specks of dogfoam splattered David's face.

"Look, it's very simple. I'm looking for someone called Fatima who worked here in 1955 ... 56 till early 1960. Are you there?"

"Yes Master, I am here. I was here from 1961. Fatima, you say?"

"Yes, and I don't know her surname!"

"No, but I remember a Fatima ... wait now, this is a long time ago. It was in that house that had the grass roof?"

"Yes!" Nero snarled again and leapt at his face, clattering against the gate with a crash. "That's the house. Fatima ... come on, you must try and remember."

"Master, it was ... Kgositsile or Mzaidume ... there was a Kgositsile in that house ... her family was in Langa. They worked at the meat market."

"Fatima?"

"I don't know that name, Master. I can't remember, Master. Please, if you go away and the dog can calm down, I can come out of the sitting room and go to the toilet. You are making my life very uncomfortable, Master."

"I'm sorry ... thank you ..." But the intercom was dead.

He looked at Nero, then made a small movement towards him. The dog went crazy and threw himself against the gate.

"Fuck you, dog!" laughed the white man and walked towards his car, with the black dog racing along on the inside of his side of the wall. David could hear him gurgle and growl.

"Oh shit, I must write down those names ..."

But when he got to the car he couldn't remember either. Meat market? Would that mean butcher?

He phoned all the butchers he found in the phonebook in the black suburb of Langa. There were not many, but the lines were mostly engaged. It took him a day of waiting at phones and trying again and again. "Are you the cops?" asked a man, after David had for the umpteenth time spelt out his mission.

"No, I'm from the States," he explained inanely. This seemed to occasionally appease suspicion.

No one had heard of Fatima. No one repeated the sounds that were like those two names, the one with the Ks and the other with an M. Most of the butchers hadn't been there in the late 1950s.

"We bought meat from the back of cars then," explained a deep-voiced woman at his last resort. "In the townships there was no such luxury as fridges, or storage, or even a buying structure. It was food. We had to take what we could get."

"And you don't remember a black woman who worked in St Andrew's Road?"

"Darling?" the voice mewed at him down the line. "Don't be such a tourist. Everyone worked in a St Andrew's Road. Maybe you should put something in the paper?"

God, he hadn't thought of that. "What would I say?" he asked.

"Looking for Fatima. Come back home. All is forgiven. Sign it 'Master'. Millions will bang at your door. Forgive me, darling, I have trade. Good luck hey?"

"Thanks. No, I mean it really ..."

But the customers in her meat market had called and she was gone.

> "Wanted. Information regarding Fatima who worked at
> 38 St Andrew's Rd Claremont in the late 50s for the De
> Lange family. Please contact Dawid de Lange ..."

He gave a box number at the newspaper office.

There was no reaction at all. A week went by.

He picked up some weight as Herman Greef introduced him to the fleshpots of the Cape. Seafood restaurants serving fresh crayfish, or juicy kabeljou barely out of the sea. His credit card took care of most of the festivities and Herman was happy to extend his hospitality indefinitely, it being such a good bargain.

David met a few other old school friends, all now divorced from their original mates, all now obsessed with the same issue.

"Listen De Lange, if I get you some bits of jewellery, will you take them back and keep them for us in the States?" was one. He even got a "Listen, Dave man, I can give you a few thousand travellers' cheques in your name. Hold them for us."

Such trust. Such desperation.

He nearly didn't meet Suzie Bernard.

It had been another exhausting weekend of a Saturday race meeting followed by squash, which he sat out for reasons of overindulgence. Then a cocktail party overlooking the new harbour structures, going on to a dinner at a wood and pink marble mansion that seemed to hang from the cliffs above the sea at Llandudno by its rivets.

"It's midnight, Greef, I really can't smile any more."

But Herman was happily involved with a blonde and didn't want to leave. "Then take the car," he said. "I'll find a way of getting home." The blonde nodded and closed her eyes. His right hand slid under her dress again.

"Keys?"

Herman looked up at him bashfully. "Sorry, no hands."

The car-keys were in his jacket pocket hanging over a chair. David took them and turned quickly wanting to get out as soon as possible. His elbow hit Suzie Bernard's glass right out of her hand.

"God, I'm sorry ..."

The drink splattered across the back of two heads in deep conversation. They didn't seem to notice.

Suzie giggled. "Gee, pray for rain and when it does, the plants don't even drink." She moved past David on her way to refill her glass. He watched her walk away, but she went into the dining-room before he could place the familiarity in her warmth. He went to the front door which was standing open. Outside the wooden deck stretched into infinity.

There was no land, no coastline, just a sea that went on and on, until it crashed against the shores of South America. Was there really a world out there? People bleeding and living? Other lavish diversions like the one he was part of? Did they have such parties in the hills above Beirut, Sarajevo, Maputo?

"It's like we're at the end of the world, and if you rock the deck, you'll fall down a bottomless pit and never touch sides."

Suzie Bernard stood next to him, quite close to him as she wasn't wearing more than a thin T-shirt.

"We are at the end of the world," he replied and felt her warmth again. He didn't look at her, but felt her eyes on his face.

"Dawid de Lange. I knew I'd see you again," she said and hooked her arm into his. He turned to her, covering her hand with his. It was also warm.

"I'm sorry, I don't remember you …"

"Suzie Bernard," she said.

"Yes, of course," he murmured. "Exactly the same."

He slept with her that night, picking up where he'd left off at the age of 19, when one early morning he sneaked out of her little room at the university residence and left the country.

"I still have that note," she said, snuggling up against him in the big white bed in a small whitewashed room with only a piece of seaweed blackly against a wall. "I've always used that note as the perfect example of utterly bad taste and appalling lack of sensitivity."

"Yes. I'm sorry."

"Rubbish. You never gave it a thought!" She sat up and the sheet draped around her. She looked so young, so unaffected by time. "Frankly, nor did I. You were quite a dull boy, you know, De Lange. We would've got married if you hadn't run away from the army like that and then by now we'd have been divorced and bitter and not here in bed together at our age."

She gave a piercing squeal of delight and covered them both with the sheet. It softly sagged down to edge the contours of their bodies.

"You don't have a condom?" she'd asked an hour before, or some-time early that morning, when they'd been entangled in each other at her small borrowed apartment, kissing and exploring flesh like two teenagers.

"No, I didn't think …"

"You didn't think you'd need one? Or you didn't think you'd be fucking? Or you didn't think it could happen to you?"

"All of them. I'm not a condom-carrier by nature."

She got up from the cluster of cushions on the carpet and went to the window, opened it wide and took a deep breath. David looked around the apartment.

"Minimalist?" he ventured.

"Recently cleaned out by a burglar and I love it, even though it's not mine," she said into the wind. "I have a flat in Johannesburg, so I just borrow when I'm down here." It was also that Suzie was always in a state of flux or movement, so she didn't believe in belongings.

She did, however, believe in safe sex.

"You mean just because you're 50, you think it'll take ten years before you die of AIDS, by which time they've either discovered a cure, or you'll be too old to care anyway? No plastic bag, no nooky. Sorry."

So they slept in their underwear, him pretending that his erection wasn't that uncomfortable in the small of her back and she pretending she wouldn't throw all caution to wind if he asked her to. He didn't ask for anything. It was one of the nicest nights he'd spent for many years. He told her.

"What does that say about your wife?"

"We have separate rooms."

"Is that very LA?"

"Very logical. My phone rings at all times of the night."

"Remind me to show you what an answering machine looks like!"

"Answering machines can't make decisions."

"Answering machines can save marriages."

"My marriage is fine."

"Good, then please remove your stiff pecker from my bruised hip." He rolled away from her, embarrassed, covering himself with a pillow.

"And go get some fucking FLs. I hate not getting it when it's so eager to be got!"

He went into a chemist later that day. It hadn't crossed his mind that he'd have a problem asking for contraceptives. He walked up to the counter. Someone was busy in the small alcove at the back.

"I'm coming," she called.

"Okay!" David looked around the shelves, filled with suntan-lotion and hair gels and all the strange things he'd never seen before. All for blacks.

"Suntan-lotion for blacks?" he whistled. "That's a new one."

"Only if you're white." He looked at the chemist. She smiled, perfect teeth glowing against ebony skin.

"You'll be surprised how sore it is to burn a black skin in the sun. What can I do for you?"

His mouth went dry. He suddenly felt thirteen years old again, standing at the counter of the chemist near school, his two-and-sixpenny silver coin clenched in his fist.

"What can I help you with, sonny?"

That squint chemist had looked so old, leering at him over the counter. Dawid de Lange's eyes blurred across the bottles in front of him. "My … eh … pa wants some … eh … of this." He pulled any bottle from the shelf and held it up to the chemist.

"That's for dogs," the man said with a laugh.

"Yes," said Dawid, heart pounding, "it's for the dog."

The hot coin in his fist burnt into his flesh. All he had to do was flick it in the air and slam it down on the counter when it fell. That was the universal secret sign for FLs the boys at school had told one another.

"Shall I put it on the bill, sonny?"

"Yes. The bill."

The chemist walked across the room to the counter where the big silver cash register stood. Dawid followed him, trying to manoeuvre the coin in his hand ready for action.

"Sir?" he asked and the chemist turned. Dawid flicked the halfcrown into the air with an energetic twitch. It went up and never came down, lodging itself instead up on the shelves that housed all those bundles of monthly things that women bought.

Oh shit, his money was lost!

The chemist looked up to where the coin had vanished.

"That's a good shot!" he said. "Do you win something?"

But Dawid de Lange was already out of the door and halfway down the street.

"Can I help you, Sir?" the pretty chemist asked again.

"Oh, sorry, I didn't expect such a young chemist."

"No, I'm not that young. Just proud of what I am."

"God," he thought, "coming from anyone in America that would sound so awful, but this girl …"

"I want some …" Oh shit! What were they called now? "For protection." He felt his face redden.

"Umbrellas?" she asked with a straight face, and before he could attempt again, she pointed to the left at a large display of what he at first thought were sachets of hair lotion.

"All the protection you could want, sir. Help yourself."

He looked from the one row of condoms to the next, even some flavoured with orange and lemon and mango. He turned round and looked at a young boy standing behind him, all of 15.

"Sorry …" said David as he made room for the boy, then looked down again to make sure. "Do you want something from here?"

"Ja, thanks, the ribbed ones on the top row. I can't reach."

David Clayton heard Dawid de Lange running out of the shop as silver coins rained from the roof. He leant across and took a set of three ribbed condoms. "Ribbed for extra enjoyment," it promised.

"Here," he said. "For your brother?"

The kid looked unamused. "No, me." And as he walked out he yelled to the back alcove. "Blanchy, put me down for 3 ribbed."

"Okay!" she called and came out from behind her screen.

"They're very confident," Blanchy smiled, looking older now. David laughed. "You can say that again … In my day …"

"In our day we didn't die for love. But I don't think the ribbed is your scene. Try these. Unflavoured but strong. Pay at the desk."

As he waited for his change, he glanced up to see where that coin could've landed. The shelf above was packed with baby accessories. She followed his eyes.

"Yes well, if these don't work, we have a whole range of nappies."

"That's not why we're … I'm …"

She pushed the packet towards him.

"It always pays to be careful. Tell your grandson he can come straight to me next time. I'm not shy."

When he arrived at Suzie's borrowed flat amid the cluster of Sea Point's beachfront highrises that evening, she was not home. They hadn't made an arrangement to meet, but with his newly acquired packet in his inner pocket, David was hoping on the off-chance …

When he got back to Herman Greef's, she'd already phoned from Johannesburg and left a message.

"What does this mean, business?" David asked, quite angry to be pushed into the background.

"She's a political animal, our Suzie, didn't you know? ANC and all that. At the beck and call of the comrades. She's probably having structural discussions about unstructured future plans, or whatever politicians pretend to do nowadays."

Strange, she'd never mentioned politics.

There was a bland American sitcom on TV that night, something not even immigrant Vietnamese would watch in the States. Herman Greef adored it.

"Great comedy this, man! Shit, I really would love to go to America again. Haven't been since the seventies. We know so much more about America now because of TV. Funny hey, all we see about our backyard is the death and the blood, and all we laugh at is the American Dream."

"No, Herman, believe me that is not an example of the American Dream. The one thing I've always loved about being there are the choices I'm allowed. I can choose any possible combination of facts and fiction. Opinions are made only to be changed, prejudices created immediately to be neutralised. The right to disagree, that's what American democracy has allowed me. What you see on TV here is some computer formula based on the lowest common denominator."

"Ja, and in an upside down society like ours, the lowest common denominator is on top. Oh fuck off, De Lange! Jesus, thanks for ruining my evening's entertainment!"

The nightly news bled slowly across the screen congealing in pictures of dead people. Herman changed channels to M-Net. A Vietnamese rainbow of war violence filled the picture.

"Seen it!" he muttered and switched it off. "I'm going to the Waterfront for a beer. Coming?"

"No, thanks. I'll read."

"Read?" Herman Greef the publisher looked at him as if he'd said something quite absurd. "What, for God's sake?"

"Alan Paton's *Cry the Beloved Country*. I got it at a second-hand bookshop today. I want to refresh my memory. Haven't read it since my twenties."

"Fuck the Beloved Country, man. Let's have a beer!"

"No, really."

Greef slammed his own front door as he went off on another wild goose chase, not so much after peace of mind than a whiff of pussy.

CHAPTER 6.

Two days later after countless futile attempts, David found Reverend Nkotse at his small parish church behind the newly erected supermarket.

"Not an easy man to find, Reverend?" David said, shaking hands with the tired cleric.

"Yes, I'm afraid I'm not a great help to my flock. I have been in Khayelitsha and other townships, assisting with the chaos there. The floods, revenge attacks, gangsters, poverty, disease ..." He sighed deeply. "I have seen more horror in the last few days than you could have witnessed on CNN in glorious colour." And then he started to cry. It tore out of his body like a coughing fit.

"I'm sorry ..."

David didn't know what to do. He looked around for help, but they were alone in the small walled garden off the vestry. The old man's body shook in spasms of grief. David put his hand on the bony shoulder, feeling the trembling emotion.

"Please, Reverend Nkotse, tell me what to do ..."

The priest gave a few shudders and then a deep breath. Slowly he looked up at David with tear-filled pained eyes, clouded red. "My heart is breaking ... forgive me, I must go into the church."

He turned and slowly walked towards the heavy door, but found it too hard to budge. David opened the door for them and they walked into the coolness of peace.

Reverend Nkotse shuffled to the altar and stood there for some time, staring up at the small stained-glass window. Then he turned to David and even tried a weak smile at his worried expression. "What can I do to help you, my son?"

David couldn't remember. This outburst had been so shocking, so moving that it was all he wanted to concentrate on.

"Would it help if you told me what has caused you so much pain?" he asked and gently took the old man's hands in his. They sat on a small wooden bench left there by the two elderly women who had come to do the flower arrangements in the morning.

Reverend Nkotse sighed. "Would it help whom? Me? I don't need help. I need anger. I need hatred. I need all the ammunition of revenge and then I'll be of use, but like this? Blubbering like an old fool in the safety of God's arms. This pathetic indulgence is of no help to anyone ..." He seemed to drift off and stared ahead fixedly.

"Help whom? Reverend?"

He blinked, looked at David. "Have you found your old nanny yet?"

"No. I'm still looking." David smiled and patted the priest on the arm. "Actually, that's why I came here today, to ask your advice."

"Ah, my advice." Reverend Nkotse took a deep breath and rocked himself back and forth on the small fragile bench. "Well, firstly don't go to into Khayelitsha looking for your old black nanny. Our people there unfortunately don't have time to be sentimental at the moment. Babies are dying untended because their mothers are already dead. Not murdered, just exhaustion. The lack of will to keep fighting! Houses are not houses, not shacks, not huts, but shrouds. There is no rule of law, or law to rule. There is just ... mess. Yes, that is the word: Mess! A mess ... I just don't know how to describe something so ... horrible. I have no words that paint pictures of such despair. My God-given alphabet is simply supposed to make you believe in goodness and hope. What I have seen makes me fear for the worst."

"A revolution?"

The old black man looked at David perplexed, then with a smile. "Oh no! No! There will be no revolution. The world is too small for that now. It costs too much to film a bloody revolution for the TV news; a massacre will suffice. No, I fear down to my soul that when I see so much unhappiness and inhumanity, I wonder what has happened to God?" He looked up at the altar, at the cross and the plastic man hanging.

They both stared at the stone floor, too moved to speak. Then the priest tightened his grip on David's hand. A small ladybird was scurrying across the grey slabstone, busily fluttering with her wispy wings, determined to get where she was going and fast! They watched the little world in its tiny red and black button move.

"Thank you, God," whispered the priest. "Thank you." He looked at David with a smile. "Look, God has answered me ..." He pointed down at the ladybird now disappearing into the shadows. "God still has time to help her with her shopping."

He started to laugh, and as the tears dripped down his wrinkled cheek, David embraced the old man as if he was the father he also couldn't remember.

It was just as the sun was struggling above the mists of the next morning that David picked Reverend Nkotse up at the steel security gates of his house in St Andrew's Road. The drive through the suburbs and onto the N2 freeway was against the traffic, so it didn't take them much time to get to the turn-off to Langa.

"Early morning is always the best time to visit certain areas," the priest assured David and patted his arm, as he nervously drove into the smoky gloom of the township. David had never been in a black 'location' before, an achievement he probably shared with the majority of white South Africans.

Reverend Nkotse was very much at home in Langa, knowing the small blocks of houses well, for many of his former congregation lived here. He'd been assigned to the diocese of the black ghetto for most of his life in the service of his church.

"I lived there in the 60s," he said, pointing across David to a small house backed by a huge palm tree that hung over it like a fat umbrella. "It was burnt down twice during the Sharpeville Riots. Do you remember those?"

Dawid de Lange had spent the Sharpeville Riots under his desk at school. There was much whispering and activity among the staff that day. The flagraising ceremony had abruptly been cancelled. A police car cruised into the school grounds and stayed there. Rumours of a march of blacks from Langa and the other mushrooming townships on the Cape Flats took over the imagination of the terrified Afrikaans children.

They'd all heard their parents talk of that Red Sea of anger aimed at the Houses of Parliament in Cape Town. The hated passbooks were at the centre of the controversy, but really people just wanted to get out and make a loud noise. "Look at us!" they wanted to scream. "We're also here!"

But Dawid de Lange never saw them. His eyes were tightly closed as he prayed to God to protect him and the school from the kaffirs.

"Oh yes," smiled the black priest. "I'm sure that word was used a lot in your day. Such ugly sounds together."

David wanted to mention Frieda's racial vocabulary, but thought it better left for another day and some other place.

"There was a police saracen parked in the schoolgrounds and we were shocked to see the headmaster had a gun tucked into his belt."

"Ah, the good old days?" murmured the priest clenching and unclenching his hands to stave off the pain of his chronic arthritis. "Turn left here …"

71

"It was like the end of the world for us that day. We were convinced we'd all be cut up into small pieces. But we weren't, and I believe the march ended peacefully and everyone went home?"

"Yes!" sighed the old man. "And apartheid grew stronger and my house was burnt down twice, maybe because they couldn't get to yours and burn that down!" They slowed down to swerve round a barricade of charred tyres and rusty drums. "I was part of that march you know, David? Right in front with the other churchmen. While you were in your Biology class praying to God to vanquish me, I was marching by, praying to the same God to help me. I wonder to whom He was listening! Stop here."

They stopped in front of an old school building, now partly used by the church as a creche and a clinic. There was an explosion of colourful graffiti on the dusty brick walls.

"That looks fun. What does it say?" David asked as they passed by. Reverend Nkotse peered through the bottom of his bifocals to read the writing on the wall.

"Nothing that you'll find funny, David. Let me see; this says 'One settler one bullet' and this one, roughly translated, 'fuck the boere!'"

Inside the building there was a surprising amount of activity. There were little black kids excitedly doing some interesting dance movements round a cassette machine playing an old Michael Jackson song. In another room, black and white women were busy with an aerobics class, some in fashionable leotards, others just with their workdresses tucked into their pants. The scent of exertion was strong, the energy catching. David's foot jigged out a rhythm on the wooden floor and he was nudged playfully by a beaming Reverend Nkotse. "Want to join them? You can. I do sometimes."

"Really?"

"How do you think I've lived this long, David? Just by divine intervention?"

They moved through the building, a rabbit warren of rooms and passages and each one was full of a newness, an exploration. A white matronly woman passed him carrying a steaming pot of soup. She greeted Reverend Nkotse and apologised in Afrikaans for rushing so, as she scurried past towards the other women waiting for her in the courtyard. They were loading a car with boxes of sandwiches and plastic mugs. David stopped and watched, trying to catch what they were saying.

Yes, it was Afrikaans. Afrikaans? Here?

Suddenly these women took him back to the days of his Sunday school. Every week, up early and dressed for Jesus, into the church hall and subjected to an hour of stories that no one believed anyway.

"Tell us about Christine Keeler!" shouted a naughty boy who got into trouble for even mentioning that name. David didn't know who she was and couldn't remember to ask at home. So instead of the Profumo Scandal, they heard about the wise man and the fool.

And then would follow the church service. Rows upon rows of women like those ones loading the car, with their purple or blonde hair, hard and big, teased and sprayed, never moving on its own accord, but conveying the signal of wealth and taste.

"God, it's like the 50s ..." David muttered looking again, even recognising their dress and shoes.

"No, it's a godsend. These are women from the Dutch Reformed Church across the golf course ..."

"Yes, like the ones I had to sit next to in *kerk* during the 1950s!" David gasped, even feeling guilty for not greeting them accordingly.

"No, the ones you sat next to in the 50s would never have risked their lives, and often their marriages, doing what these women do. They come twice a week, rain or shine, peace or unrest, and bring food to the homeless, the hungry, the unemployed. Sometimes there's not enough food for everyone and then someone gets nasty. That woman with the pink suit ...?" There she was, a figure from his childhood in a pink suit with a blonde beehive, sorting rolls in a large steel tray. "Last week she was hit in the face by a worker who hadn't found work and then didn't get any food. It was a bad day for him. It was a terrible experience for her."

"But she's back!"

David strained to hear the conversation at the car. From what he could make out, they could just as well have been busily organising the *kerkbasaar*.

"The churches are standing together and helping each other. Afrikaans and English and the black congregation and the Jews and the Muslims. It's not all the end of the world, you know David. It's also the beginning of something that as yet has no name."

The room at the back must've been a storeroom once, when this place had a purpose and not as now, a mission. The walls were stacked with boxes full of cardboard files.

"Millions of them!" David gasped.

"No, just a few hundred thousand. When the many structures of apartheid started unravelling and the pillars of control, like the passbooks and all that jazz ..." Reverend Nkotse said it with spite and malice, "... sagged into the mud of mundane corruption, and suddenly we didn't need to have our life in a book in order to live, these towers of paper remained as monuments to the terrible past." Thousands upon thousands of names, of lives, of fates, of dreams stacked up against a damp wall, forgotten. "We salvaged them from the rubbish heaps of history. Who knows, information like this could be important one day."

"You don't mean for me to look for Teema here?" David pointed at the mass of information and backed towards the door.

"Where else can you start? Every person had a file, every file had a name. And a surname!" He paused for that effect to sink in. David was ready to complain. "... And where they worked and for whom. If Teema is to be found, let us start between the covers of a department-mental file." He pulled one out of the first pile carefully. "Look, Gladys Bellow ..."

David took the name carefully, then laughed. "Gladys Bellow? Sounds like a British music hall character!"

"No, not her real name, but it was easier filing people under their white names. Now, I'd look for a De Lange. Fatima de Lange. I'll come and fetch you when I'm finished."

"Where are you going, Reverend Nkotse?" David didn't want to be left alone here, in this backroom full of yesterday's ghosts.

"I have a few people to see. Don't worry, I'll not leave the building. People get baptised here, taught here, trained here, counselled here and prepared here."

"Prepared for what?"

"Prepared for the grave. We have our own mortuary. If you'd rather give me a hand there ...?"

David took down the first cluster of files without more encouragement.

The sun had already hidden itself behind Table Mountain on its way to America, when Reverend Nkotse finished his day's work, having baptised two children and one adult, counselled a family about the trauma of moving house to a former white area, and finally preparing one of his oldest friends for her funeral. Mrs Dundi Petersen had died of old age a few days before, but only after she got him to promise ... no, to swear on the Bible, that he would make sure she was really dead, so that she wouldn't wake up underground. Dundi had seen all the wrong horror films. So he checked carefully. Dundi was as dead as dead could be.

He pushed open the door of the storeroom, expecting to find a bored David reading a church magazine. There was no one.

"David? Where are you?" he asked, faced with a jagged horizon of piles of files. A blackened white hand waved from behind them.

"Here, Reverend, don't touch anything, or I'll be crushed to death." David appeared from behind his paper barricade, waving a sheaf of documents in his hand. "Look! I should have worked for the KGB!" he said happily.

"You could just as well have worked for this government!" Reverend Nkotse murmured and leant over to take the files.

"Have a look! There's a possibility of four women. Hang on, I must crawl through a hole I made here ..." And David vanished again. The wall wobbled and swayed as he puffed his way through an opening on the ground, carefully extracted his legs and slowly stood up, holding out his hands in case the whole dereliction fell on top of him. "I'll come tomorrow and replace the files ..." he said, hoping the priest would just wave it away.

"Yes, good idea," agreed Reverend Nkotse. "Maybe you can get them in an alphabetical order?"

David had gone through generations of names. Some were just a cluster of consonants, many ks, many xs, many ws. Other names seemed to have lost all the consonants and were a gaggle of vowels. Some surnames made sense, most names meant nothing. There were Joneses and Smiths, there were Bothas and Van Wyks and De Langes. And yes, there were two De Langes and two Fatimas!

He clutched the files under his arm; their footsteps echoed as they walked through the empty building. "It's so late, I didn't realise ..." There was a weak light from the street lamp outside. "How was your day?" He glanced at the wizened profile of the old cleric.

"Never a dull moment," Reverend Nkotse replied. "Now I hope you're not a white man scared of driving through a black township at night? Are you?"

They stopped and David had to think about it. Yes, he was.

"No, I'm not," he said.

"Good," beamed Reverend Nkotse. "For I can't drive!"

They travelled back through Langa the way they'd come, with old Nkotse paging through the files and muttering information as he read it. David concentrated hard on the road ahead, not daring to wonder what would happen if something went wrong with the car.

When they left the main entrance to the ghetto behind them, and embraced the comforting yellow glow of the freeway lights, the Reverend suddenly gave a highpitched cackle of delight. He nudged David sharply. "You are a terrible liar and God will punish you!" he giggled. "You were weak with fear!"

"I was not!"

"You were too! You're pale as sin and have sweat all over your forehead."

"I'm hot!" snorted David, the icy terror in his stomach now making way for a cramp.

"Mmmm." Reverend Nkotse grunted innocently and looked out of his window. "Thank heavens Langa is the safest place on the Cape Flats," he added casually.

"Nonsense!" exploded David. "A woman was burnt to death there last week!"

"No, David," soothed the priest. "A woman was burnt about 4 kilometres down that way. About as far from Langa as Los Angeles Central and its riots are from where you live in Beverly Hills."

He didn't live in Beverly Hills, but never mind the argument. He was now quite angry and didn't hide it.

"You were teasing me, weren't you? You wanted to see what I would do!" The priest giggled. "God, I'm surprised you didn't suddenly go boo!" David seethed as he sped back to St Andrew's Road. He was not going to leave it at that. "I'm sorry to be such a tourist, Reverend," he said calmly. "I just don't understand all this fear and violence. Remember, I see it from a safe distance. Apartheid is gone; De Klerk seems to be a reasonable man; Mandela is a charismatic leader! All you need now is a democratic election. That's good! Europe should be so lucky! So what's all this chaos in aid of?"

Reverend Nkotse said nothing for quite a time. Faster cars sped past them, often on the inner lane, making David even more tense. Then once they turned off the freeway onto a relatively calm suburban road, the Reverend spoke.

"How do you get a square peg into a round hole, David?"

"You can't."

"No, I know you can't. But what do you do if you have to get a square peg into a round hole. Do you make the square peg round, or the round hole square?"

They turned into St Andrew's Road and stopped at his front gate. What is this riddle about? David then asked. "Pegs and holes? Too deep for me ..." he laughed.

Besides he didn't want to have to talk now, or worse, feel even more guilty. He wanted a shower. He wanted a drink. He could feel the old priest looking at him, but kept staring ahead at a woman walking her two small, fluffy white dogs round and round in the security of the light of the bright street lamp.

Reverend Nkotse opened the car door. "I'll study these files for you. I read the languages. I'll make notes and I'll phone you tomorrow. I hope you had a nice day, David." He pushed the door open and struggled out of the car. The door slammed shut. He turned from the sidewalk and knocked on the window. David leant over and with difficulty rolled it down.

"What is it, Reverend?" he sighed.

"David, my son, I forgot to say something very important to you." The serious face of the priest started to crease up. "Boo!"

Suzie Bernard phoned him from Johannesburg that night, very late. Herman Greef was out again, finding a "place to put it" as he said. David was on his bed watching CNN on the all night service of SATV. Carnage in former Yugoslavia, neo-nazi unrest in former East Germany, threatening civil war in the former Soviet Union.

"And how is the state of the nation, Suzie?" he asked, not without a trace of sarcasm.

"Ah, someone told you I was on the wrong side."

"Is there a right side? I've never been so confused in my life. A production meeting at a Hollywood studio is peanuts compared to trying to find a healthy political opinion in this town." A huge, covered truck on the TV screen opened up and vomited out a cluster of shell-shocked and bleeding women and children somewhere in Bosnia. Thirty seconds later the attention of the world focused on a starving stickperson in the Sudan. David's half-attention went along with it.

"Sorry I had to get out of your life again so soon, Dawid." She persisted in using his real name. "I never know where I have to be within the next 24 hours. I might be back in town over the week-end, but then I might not."

"Ah," he said as the camera's attention span briefly touched the Palestinians in crisis. "Then again, Suzie, I might be up there by the weekend too. Or I might not. I've found someone to help me find Teema."

"Good." Suzie was smiling on the other end and he could hear it in her tone. "I'll keep my eye open for you up here. I gather the ad in the paper didn't help?"

"Oh yes, it did," he lied. "Great response."

"Having to audition the masses now? To find your Teema of the Week?" The newscast grazed through other killing fields: an explosion in Colombia, a massacre in Sri Lanka, Mafia killings in Sicily, another child 'mistakenly' murdered by the IRA in Belfast.

"Dawid, are you still there?"

"Yes, sorry. Just the CNN News. One forgets there's a world falling to pieces outside as well."

"Forget the world. It's looking good up here," Suzie sighed, adding, "Any small progress is a huge jump ahead."

"What do you do for the ANC?"

"PR." He waited for more, but she gave none.

"Well then, give me a number, Suzie. Maybe I can see you up there sometime this week?"

"No, let me give you a friend's number. Leave a message or a fax."

"What about your work?"

She laughed. "Are you kidding? Phoning someone at the ANC Headquarters in Johannesburg? It's easier to get Yeltsin at the Kremlin. No man, leave a message. I'll find you."

He stifled a yawn.

"Go to bed now, you sound tired."

"Yes, I am. I spent the day in Langa."

"Brave tourist!" she teased. "Hope you saw something to tell the folks back home?"

"Yes," he said, a lightness in his tone now. "I saw a black woman smile. Bye for now."

The two De Lange files he'd found led to nowhere. The one Fatima was long since reported dead, while the other Fatima came from Transkei.

Transkei!

"That sounds more like it, Reverend!" he cheered, barely containing his excitement. He felt a bit bad telephoning the churchman and not taking the trouble to go in person, but it was so much easier this way. The old black man somehow made David feel as if he was treating him like a garden boy.

"Do you remember if she had a son?" the priest then asked. Teema's son?

David had often seen friends walking with her to the shops, laughing and jostling each other in the road, or shooing away a small barking dog, or often just sitting on the grass, their black legs stretched out, bodies resting back on strong arms. But a son?

"I don't think so," David murmured. "Was she married?"

"Oh yes," Reverend Nkotse was paging through the yellowed file. "She was happily married. It seems her husband worked in the Transvaal and they both sent money home to Transkei, where both their families lived. It says here she had a son called Henry."

"Henry!"

Across the years David heard his father calling: "Now where is that boy? Have you seen Henry, Dawid?"

"No, Pa."

"He's supposed to clear up all those oak leaves! He's been doing it all day. What do I pay him for!"

"I'll go and look, Pa."

"And when you find him, tell him to finish the job!"

David found Henry down at the end of the property, sitting on a log and smoking a cigarette butt, which he hid behind his back when David approached. Henry was slightly older than him.

"I saw that, Henry!" David said in his bossy white boy voice.

"Sorry, Master Dawid. I only have one a week, you know."

Henry was very black, strong and had Teema's sense of humour, meaning that he would always smile no matter what happened. That David found the most infuriating part of being white. He couldn't understand why blacks were always smiling!

"Pa says you must finish raking up the leaves!"

"I will."

The black boy took another puff, then handed the cigarette to David. The white boy shook his head. "I don't smoke," he said.

"You can have your own if you don't want to put your mouth where my mouth was." Henry smiled and handed David a whole cigarette. "Go on. It's time to be a man."

"Henry …" David Clayton breathed out the name from his childhood.

"You remember him, David?" asked the priest.

"God yes."

"Ah. We must thank Him for your recall?"

"Henry Henry Henry! Of course, he used to work for us in the garden. He'd rake the leaves and then I'd run across and kick them all over the lawn and he'd have to start again."

"Nasty little white boy you were."

"No, Reverend. It was an arrangement we had. You see, Henry got

79

paid only as long as he worked. Raking leaves was a short job. Now, if I behaved like a spoilt white boy and messed up his good work, he'd just have to take longer and get more pocket money."

"You bring tears to my eyes." The priest laughed.

"Henry taught me to smoke. How could I have forgotten him?"

"Well, now we have Henry and Fatima ..."

There was something David had to finally clear up.

"What surname is on the document, Reverend?"

"Masekela."

David had never heard her called that. Fatima Masekela.

"So where now?" he asked.

"Start looking for a Henry Masekela?"

Henry Masekela was packing his shirt into a light brown, leather suitcase when the front doorbell chimed. He glanced at his watch and hurried to the door. He called: "Ja, who is that?" No one just opened a front door in Soweto these days. It sounded like a white woman. He opened the door and Suzie Bernard stepped inside.

"Do you mind if I come out of the rain? You have a waterfall crashing down right in front of your door!" It was raining. Henry hadn't even heard the thunderclaps, or maybe he had and subconsciously filed them away as the usual unrest muzak. A spout of water poured down from the roof.

"No please, I'm sorry ..." He ushered her into the hallway.

"I've been meaning to put up some kind of stoep, but ... well, maybe next year?" he said and closed the door. The woman dripped Transvaal raindrops on his floor.

"I'm dripping on the floor. Shouldn't we go to the kitchen?"

"You want to drip there as well?" asked Henry straightfaced. She beamed. "Yes, then I'll go and drip in the lounge."

"Come."

He led her through the small house to the kitchen, a larger room than the rest and not as crowded with furniture. As they passed through the sitting-room, she noticed a huge settee and couch-set jammed against the wall. "We're still waiting to find the right house for us in a better suburb." Meaning a former white area, probably in the northern parts of Johannesburg. "So we keep stocking up on the right size furniture, but it makes living here a bit cramped."

She took off her coat and he hung it behind the kitchen door.

"What can I do for you, Miss ...?" She told him quickly. "... Miss

Bernard? I am in a bit of a hurry. I have to start my drive down to the Transkei, before the roads get too traffic-bound."

Suzie smoothed her hands along the cold linoleum tabletop.

"I'm not quite sure where to start. My good friend in Cape Town, Dawid de Lange …" She glanced up at his face, but he seemed not to recognise the name. "… he's looking for his old housekeeper, Fatima Masekela …"

"My mother is called Fatima Masekela." Then he added with a frown. "What did you say their name was?"

"De Lange." She drummed a rhythm out on the table softly.

Henry Masekela's round face was set for a moment, then a smile played over it like a ripple. "Dawid de Lange? In old St Andrew's Road? You mean those people still remember us?"

Suzie was relieved it had been so easy. "He's been living overseas for most of his life …"

"And I've been here in Soweto." cracked Henry.

"… he's looking for Teema."

Henry remembered the smell of raked oak leaves.

"He must be fifty now, fifty-one? Does he still have all his hair?"

She nodded. The pause was waiting for the next question: was Teema still alive?

"Yes, lots of hair," she said.

"Mine's not so lots. Does he have kids?"

"Yes, two daughters. Even a grandchild."

Henry Masekela pointed at a framed photograph on the full mantelpiece of two small boys standing on either side of a woman holding a baby. His late wife. His three children.

"I have a grandson on the way. Had three sons … now only two."

"Oh, I'm sorry …"

"No, it's long ago." He was happy to change the subject. "So is 'Master Dawid' coming up to see me?"

Suzie moved her palm along the warm tabletop to a cooler area. "Tell me first, your mother …?"

"She's been living in the Transkei." He didn't say more, but his concentrated looking at her seemed to be filled with information.

"That's what we thought." Suzie started. "And that's where you're going?"

"Yes," said Henry Masekela. "I've got to go to a funeral."

CHAPTER 7.

Suzie faxed the information down to Herman Greef's office and the next morning David took a plane from Cape Town to East London, landing in a hot dust storm which they say had never before happened on that coast. They blamed the ozone layer, the communists, the violence and the fact that South Africa's Springboks had lost a rugby test match against the New Zealand All Blacks. His hired red car was waiting at the airport.

"You're not going to the Transkei with this car, are you sir?" they asked.

"No," he said and drove off in the direction of the Transkei border.

When he reached the bridge crossing the river that had in the historical past seen bloody battles between boers and blacks, he was stopped by the South African Police on the South African side. They wanted to know where he was going.

"A funeral," he said.

They studied his American passport, looked at him carefully, searched the boot of his car and then refused to let him through unless he could furnish them with the right papers.

"What papers do I need?" he asked.

Someone mentioned a number and it sounded like a visa.

"Do I need a visa?" David asked again, aware of the other cars held up behind him, not yet daring to hoot, but fuming in the hot sun.

"No, you don't need a visa," the young policemen stuttered, "just a ..." and he repeated the number again.

"But where do I get that form?" David asked patiently, while carefully watching the obvious chaos around him.

No one knew where the form was to be found. Someone suggested he go back to East London, another pointed onwards to the capital of Umtata. The last resort of Pretoria was also muttered.

"Maybe if I just make a statement?" David asked helpfully. "I can tell you where I'm going, why I'm going there and whom I hope not to see buried?" This caused even more confusion, especially when he explained that Fatima Masekela was probably being buried that day, though he hoped it wouldn't be her.

"So you don't know who's dead, sir?" asked a thin cop, this one not white, but as confused.

"No, I don't. I'm just hoping it isn't Fatima Masekela," he replied.

"Then if it isn't this Masekela, why are you going to the funeral?" asked the officer in charge.

"Well, I'm going to the funeral to make sure that she's not dead." This was not getting better. "I will know who's dead once I get there," he smiled.

"And if it's not this Masekela who's dead?" asked another officer who had now joined the happy group of frowning uniforms round the car. "Do you promise to come back immediately?"

"Yes," said David Clayton. "I give you my word as an American citizen."

This was the worst thing he could've said. All the policemen, white, brown and black either watched *Loving* on TV themselves, or had a loved one who did, and they all knew that according to what happened on *Loving*, every American man was a liar, a rapist and probably a closet homosexual, when he wasn't cheating on his wife with her best friend. So David had to drive back to East London, find a hotel and start again the next morning. This time he arrived at the border with a fax from the American Consul in Cape Town.

"But now who's this?" asked the policeman at the border, waving the fax in the sharp breeze. "What has this Cape Town person got to do with what's happening on the Transkei border?" David explained and pointed out that the American Consul was a representative of the Ambassador, who in turn represented the American President, and that all of them, through this very fax, were saying that he, David Clayton, was okay and would not be smuggling arms into Transkei, or out of Transkei!

More policemen joined the severe grouping round the car and the black minibus-taxis heaped up behind the bureaucracy in limbo and waited. David could find no familiar faces from yesterday in uniform. Probably a new shift.

"What are you going to do here in the Transkei, sir?" asked a man carrying his rank with pomp. There was some onion on his teeth from his hamburger lunch.

"A funeral," said David, now wondering if the burial was not already a thing of yesterday. "My old nanny is dead and I'm coming to say goodbye."

This was a new one for the upholders of law and order. They

83

stared at David and one blue uniform even walked away in disgust.

"You come all this way to bury a kaffir woman?" asked a red-faced sergeant. "Shit! That's big of you, man. You Americans are also crazy, hey?" David nodded, hoping that this was the end of his interrogation. It was only the beginning. They let him start his car and drive on towards the Transkei cluster of officialdom. David smiled as he drove past the battered drums scattered on the road to make driving virtually impossible. Here was a Frankenstein, a creation of the South African Government, a so-called homeland republic swaggering around with all the trappings of independence, thriving on a fat packet from the South African taxpayer and then on top of it, thumbing its cosmetically structured nose at its master. He stopped at the chequered pole and rolled down his window.

"Sayibona!" he cheerfully greeted the Xhosa soldier in the Zulu language.

He was now beyond square one.

They ushered him out of his car, searched the vehicle with small mirrors on broomsticks which they held under the chassis to check for bombs. They photocopied all his documents, including his fax from the consul. They ate his packet of sweets. They didn't ask him why he was there and he wasn't going to tell them. Then someone realised he wasn't a South African.

"American?" beamed a fat soldier. "Clint Eastwood!"

David nodded hoping it was the right reaction, but also ready to shake his head if need be. He looked around at the faces looking at him. One smileless expression stood out from the row of similar stares. The young soldier's eyes slowly travelled down David's body, lingered on his dusty expensive shoes and rolled back up to his eyes. There was no interest here, no appraisal, just pure unadulterated hatred. The coldness of the glare made David shudder.

"Can I go through now?" he quietly asked the ranked uniform still paging through his passport as if it was the latest comic. "I'm late for …" he'd give the nanny story a miss here "… late for a meeting."

"You meet with the government?" asked the soldier handing back his passport.

"No … well, yes, sort of. It's confidential." David dropped his voice and everyone seemed to bend their heads closer to hear what he would say. He just put his finger to his lips and shrugged. Everyone understood and made space for him to get back into the car. As he started the engine, he felt the coldness of the singular glare on his face. He looked up and into a million years of unforgiven resentment. The weapon in the soldier's hands looked ready and even warm. He drove his car off, tearing the eye contact like tissue. Even through the back window he felt his inner soul was still being searched. For what? For being white? For being foreign? For being older than youth? For being here?

Once away from the cluster of official welcoming at the border, the Transkeian countryside settled into an uneasy repetition of desolation and stagnation.

It all looked washed out in a sepia monochrome, the grey stones making way for grey sand, and even the abandoned Coke tins looked dark-grey and light-grey as the bright reds in the logo bled its design into the thirsty dry earth.

Strange attempts had been made to fence off useless pieces of the land. Rusty poles stood in the middle of nothing, still holding onto a few strands of gnarled wire. The carcasses of cars seemed to lie in bundles together in the many jagged ravines, where once upon a millennium the rainwater had carved itself a pathway. The feeble suggestions of foliage were occasional, with nothing green, everything stark and carved out of silver foil and placed where one day, when God had the guts, He would come back to this abortion called Transkei and fill it with some discarded gifts of life.

It had been the curse of this tract of tribal land to be the grab-bag of nations. People came, saw, conquered and removed. The richness of former grazing land was trampled into dust by the fat ancestors of the thin spider-sheep now wobbling on stick legs and having wet dreams of a green leaf.

As he drove through the valleys and over the hills on the piece of tarred road which showed the only strong colour in its sharp white line down the middle, he tried to make the inevitable comparisons. Where had he seen all this before? America's Arizona Desert was red and golden, the sands of the Israeli West Bank were caramel, the dunes of the Kalahari soft as cottonwool. This looked more like a scene from a moon landing, although even the moon seemed blessed with light and shade, while here was nothing but glare.

He saw no one.

This was a relief, as everyone to whom he had said: "I'm going to the Transkei!" looked at him as if he'd suggested a holiday in the Balkans. People had died on these homeland roads, not just for lack of driving skills and the profusion of unlicensed township taxis, but often just because small angry black Davids flicked their lethal stones from slings at the invading Goliaths. There would be reports of rusty barbed wire dragged across lonely roads and when one stopped, a death by hacking would leave tourism in pieces and newspapers flush with the smell of blood.

No one passed him on the road; no one even seemed to be sheltering in the strips of shade, where the corrugated iron sheets hanging over the edge of the small mud huts offered the illusion of relief against the sun.

Did anyone live here?

He looked at his well-marked map regularly and mentally ticked off the combination of consonants that formed Xhosa names. He knew Teema's family's kraal wasn't that far into the Transkei once he'd crossed the border. The instructions Suzie had faxed him seemed simple when read in the controlled confines of so-called civilisation, but here in the wilds a hand-written letter looked as mysterious as a Dead Sea scroll.

He stopped the car at a turn-off to the left and checked his instructions. No, there was no pole to his right; no, there was no name. *Aikona*, there were no boulders wedged against each other like a cluster of rugby balls; no, there was no ... he had to check the paper again '... pyramid of rusty oil drums with the letter J painted on them'. He looked around the expanse of waste.

No, nothing was familiar.

Had he passed it? Should he drive on?

A sudden shot of reflected sunlight from the hilltop ahead attracted his attention. A new black car sped towards him, the sun playing madly off a crazypaving of chrome. The tyres were fat and bulging, there was a strip of colourful cloth flapping off the top of both the radio and cellular telephone aerials. The windows were tinted so darkly that there was no sign of life within the car. It all looked so much like a scene from one of the Mad Max films, that David watched the approaching landcraft with a childlike fascination.

The car skidded to a crunching halt on the other side of the road, facing him, the waves of heat curling the painted image on the bonnet into what looked like demented Chinese dragon. Silence.

Then a faint thumping rap-rhythm pulsated from within the closed machine. David knew he was being watched. He waved with what he hoped was seen as casual friendliness. There was no reaction. The windows remained closed. The multiple headlights glared towards him with a similar iciness which he'd felt earlier from the one border guard.

He thought of going across the road and asking the driver for directions, but that strange unnamed fingernail in the pit of his stomach scratched gently against his instinct and he decided: no, get the hell out of here as soon as possible! Suddenly David saw the situation from the outside and it made the small hairs on his arms curl with terror. There he was, a solitary white in a hired car in the midday madness of a banana republic, being watched by whoever drove around a semi-desert in a souped-up mafia Mercedes.

He got in behind the wheel and switched on.

The car didn't start. It was dead. His heart thumped in his throat. He tried again, then saw the anti-theft device dangling off the keyring. With a chuckled curse he slid the steel pin into the hole and tried again. His red car luckily responded and he edged forward. At that moment the black car seemed to reverse slightly, the front wheels turning out ready to attack.

It all seemed to happen in slow motion.

David put his foot down and the car slowly surged forward, like in those dreams he'd had in London after his sister had been killed by a hit-and-run driver, and he dreamt that he'd run after the car but never caught it. His feet were like concrete blocks on a slippery road, never moving but in terrible pain from all the running. He clutched his hot plastic steering wheel as the damp wet of fear embraced his chest. He saw the black monster start up and turn into the road behind him, purring in his slipstream, easily geared to overtake and win, but just hanging back enjoying the race. What race? What was happening here!

He saw his speedometer slide past the green into the orange and pant towards the red. His was a small hired car, for God's sake! These … whatever they were, killers? Soldiers? These blacks? … were in a newly stolen recently primed state of the art of war sedan and they wanted his white arse! Automatically he switched on the car radio and it was tuned to the Afrikaans service of Radio South Africa, now not called that, but tactfully referred to as Afrikaans Stereo. Another sly example of the national game of political Scrabble, through which the soiled Afrikaans past was being laundered to make the black future look second-hand.

"En ja-nee, hier het ons nou 'n interessante verskynsel …" the cheerful male voice burbled on about the history of a small town in

87

the Northern Transvaal and people were to telephone from all over the country, which they did, and share their reminiscences and experiences of days gone by. It was a programme in the chatty style of the early 50s here quite comfortably listened to in the nightmare nineties.

The warm sound of the Afrikaans small talk calmed him somewhat, taking him back to a comfortable time of numb happiness. He still understood every word, but it was those individual syncopations of communication that held him spellbound; the breath before a word, the pauses in the middle of a rhythm, the strange sounds of agreement and argument, the grunts, the mm's and the aahhh's, the guttural stops and the Germanic starts.

And while he was being bathed by the whitewash of his distant childhood and even found himself mouth the words from the radio last heard when he'd just started shaving, he kept his eye on the image in his rear-view mirror. There it was, the black panther, the shadow bullet, keeping pace with his haste, following in his every twist and turn, eating his energy like a new fuel.

This was like a movie chase through Manhattan – "Follow that cab!" – but not on a grid of roads and among a forest of buildings, but in a flat bomb-site where there were no corners and no angles, just a flowing road that came from nowhere and went to nothing. And somewhere along that pathway to Hades he would die. This he was now sure of. David Clayton formerly De Lange would meet his end at the hand of some …?

Where was his pen!

There was a Johannesburg number plate on the car! He squinted and tried to read backwards, but nearly ended up in a ditch. So he slowed down, hoping to make sense of the letters and numbers and write them down, so that at least the police would find something next to his battered and charred body. Maybe they were police? Maybe they were car salesmen trying to flog him a new model?

David had to laugh as he wrote down the registration number. "Ha, you bastards! I'm not a local yokel!" he bellowed at his mirror and felt like giving them a finger or two, but again the small fingernail scratched at the raw surface of his trusted instinct and he just gave gas and went like a bat out of hell into hell.

There was a coffin on the long table, held up by trestles borrowed from the church in the village about 14 miles away in the direction of Umtata. The coffin was of plain wood, but it shone because it had been rubbed and scrubbed and polished to look like a special texture, although it was just pine.

The dead woman in the coffin was also plain and shiny. Her plump black face looked like it was covered with a thin layer of plastic to protect that perfect skin against the ravages of death. Her eyes were closed, but not sewn together as with so many other funerals. They had closed by themselves before she had died. When she stopped breathing and, as she used to say, "went on to the next bus stop in the quest to find the God I so trusted and served all my life" her lids snapped shut permanently as the lights went out in her windows.

This room in which the laying out of the corpse was being attended was usually used as the schoolroom where she would teach the remaining children that life didn't come and go just because the sun set and then automatically rose. They needed an alphabet so that they could decide "when to cross a road or whether to stay and wait for traffic to pass".

Henry Masekela knew this room very well.

In childhood he had often begged to be taken back to the city with his mother after visits to his family here that seemed to drag on for years and eternity. He loved the city life and the activity in the township of Langa where he and Fatima lived. That wasn't her real name of course, but as white people called her that, the family called her that too. Her real name was Nomsato.

He looked around the room and at the members of the family, his uncles and their wives, his cousins and their sisters, his half-brothers and their children, all sitting around the side of the dusty schoolroom talking to each other, fiddling with their smart church outfits, some with enjoyment, most with discomfort. Henry was wearing the same dark suit he'd worn on so many of these similar dark occasions. Death and funerals happened more often now than joyous weddings and christenings. He'd bought this suit all those years ago after the 1976 children's revolution, when he'd buried his two oldest sons, only to wear it again when one of the sons returned from the dead to become his heaviest cross to bear. Henry smiled as he remembered the madness of that day and gently stroked the collar of his jacket, feeling the small tear in the fabric where the white carnation had been torn from its nesting place by the passion of their embraces. The lost son returns, slaughter the fattened calf!

He looked out of the open window towards the denseness of the midday glare. Even the flies hovered in the open window, contemplating a quick dash across the furnace into the nearest shade, but decided to stay and search for relief in Henry Masekela's eyes and mouth and nose. God, how he could remember the feeling of the tiny patter of fly-feet around his lips, as he slept in the shade of a cardboard shelter. He swore eating flies had been an unconscious reality in the life of any boy who had slept through a simmering Transkeian afternoon.

There were few cars parked in the area outside the cluster of huts that made up his family's kraal, perched proudly on the sun-scorched earth of a hill and giving it an untrammelled view of the surrounding barrenness. Some of his relatives swore that on a clear day one could see the sea over there to the east and even the skyscrapers of Johannesburg over there to the northwest. He'd just nod and agree, for to explain that the world was round and that Jo'burg was further from here than the sea was distant, was too complicated and anyway it sounded so bizarre that simple beliefs always carried the day.

He looked across the open coffin, could just see the tip of the nose of the remarkable woman the family had all called Mama. He'd been brought up by this woman, taught the rules of life and her precious alphabet of crossing the road. He was still alive thanks to her. Many of his cousins and brothers and friends were no longer around to argue about the distance between here and there.

He looked outside again, but there was no sign of Kendall.

"Kendall Masekela …" Henry whispered, as if only by mouthing the name aloud, he would understand whom he was talking about. Kendall was his middle son, also known now by a name that white people enjoyed and his family adopted; like Henry. His real name was also a combination of consonants and clicks that few people bothered to master. Plain Henry was so much simpler.

His sister Felicia joined him, sat beside him and took his hand in hers. "Kendall not back yet?" she asked and leant back against the stone wall, closing her eyes and feeling the iciness of the stones seep into her warm skin. "We've got to put the old girl in the ground before she starts going bad." Henry looked around quickly. Felicia always spoke too loudly. Even with her compulsion to always speak English, he noticed some of the older members of the clan stiffen and look away, as the very idea that the woman in the box would dissolve into the earth was repulsive to them all. "I can't believe she's gone. I wonder if she'd not just sleeping."

90

But the profile in the coffin didn't grin and the body didn't shake with laughter as always. That energy was gone and the world was a poorer place.

Henry started up, but Felicia pulled him back in his wooden chair. "I'm going to have a cigarette outside," he said and she got up with him and they went into the sunlight. He lit up and handed the cigarette to his sister.

"No, man, give me a break, Henry! I'm trying to come to terms with all this horrible fresh air. God, how I miss the smelly pollution of the big city."

Felicia lived outside the Eastern Province town of Port Elizabeth and always made the rest of the family laugh when she referred to her sleepy hollow as the centre of the world. Henry smiled and she nudged him. "Now don't be a snob about PE. More of us blacks die around my city than around yours!" She said it nearly bragging.

"Some standard of living you got down there," he smirked.

She pushed him away. "Well, I like it," she declared.

They both let their eyes scan the horizon. It was as if time had never moved since the twelfth century. Small puffs of grass fires discoloured the bleached sky. The heat waves broke up the edge of the world around them into multilayers of distance, sometimes overlapping, sometimes breaking apart completely to let some invisible plough through that left a dent in the circle of the earth.

"Why does Kendall bring that girl here?" Felicia shook her head and shaded her eyes against the sun. "You know how damn conservative our people are?"

"I think they were more impressed by his car than by her carriage," Henry chuckled and remembered to tell Tina that joke when they arrived. He liked Tina Swerdlow. He found her sweet and very sexy and surprisingly uncomplicated, especially for a white girl.

"A Jewish white girl!" she'd corrected him on their first meeting, sitting on their new sofa at home, her small white hand vanished in Kendall's big black mitt and a permanent twinkle of tease in her blue eyes. "Jews bring complications just by not being gentile. Because their mother is Jewish, your grandsons will be Jewish like me! Henry, do you mind?"

Kendall shrugged at his father and pressed her hand more firmly into his lap.

Henry thought for a moment. "Xhosa–Jewish or Jewish–Xhosa?" he asked.

"Does it matter?" she giggled. "Both are the chosen race!"

Felicia threw up her hands in desperation when Henry told her. "Jewish? Leave that alone, brother. We're here to bury Mama. The Jewish story will raise all the other dead too. One thing at a time."

Both of them saw the tornado stripe of dust at the same time.

"There he is ..." She pointed with a red-nailed finger. "Who's that with him?"

"I don't know. There was only one car when they left."

The two dots on the scorched plains forged across towards them, clouds of dust spurting out into the stillness and blotting out all light.

David was keeping his eye on his rear-view mirror, but it was impossible to see through the orange cloud of grit behind him. He just knew if he suddenly stopped, the car behind him would crash into him without even knowing what it had hit. Besides the fact that an AK47 bullet would put him out of his misery. Would they necklace him with the tyre of his hired car? What was the prize here? Surely not the small red sedan? Money? Travellers' cheques? Visa card? No firearms, he remembered with some regret.

The thoughts of a worst scenario kept repeating themselves in his mind and even though the radio was still on and the inane Afrikaans programme was making nonsense of his fears, David hung onto his steering-wheel for dear life.

"No blow-outs now, please God ..." he muttered, wondering why he always asked God so nicely when things were not going well. He'd done that when he was small too. "Please God make me well and I'll promise to do ..." And the list went on and on, but when he was happy he never thought of saying: "Thank you God, I promise I will ..."

"I promise I will ..." he repeated and swerved to avoid what looked like a rock in the road. He didn't even know where this road would lead him. He'd passed a pyramid of oil drums, but they were on the wrong side of the road.

So now he was going in the opposite direction! It had to lead to somewhere! And how come this black Merc hadn't passed him? A new Merc chasing a tired Golf? This sounded like one of those jokes he'd loved telling at school. The road dipped into a gully and shot up the other side towards what looked like a cluster of huts at the rim of the crown. Once up the hill, he turned and could see the hefty Merc take the dip in the gully with a crunch of tyres on gravel. The little Golf slowed down as it panted up the slope.

"Come on, you sweet German bitch!" he prayed and thumped his impatience on the wheel. Ahead he could see the reflection of the sun on other cars. "Oh thank God, thank God, thank you God …" he rambled as he shot his red go-kart into the area where the legionnaires of civilisation hopefully had parked their chariots.

He stopped and switched off his engine. As the dust settled he saw the Merc draw up across the space and the doors open. A young man and a young woman got out. Two blacks joined them from the building against the ridge. They spoke and pointed at him. He stayed put. "Please God, no pain …" he whispered.

Kendall Masekela looked across the rocky expanse to the dusty car with its driver sitting crouched over the steering wheel.

"Are you sure that's him, Dad?" he asked.

Henry wasn't that sure. "Well, he's here, isn't he?" he shrugged.

"He seemed to be speeding away from us," said the pretty girl at Kendall's side. "I'm quite suspicious."

"That's your Jewish background, Tina."

The girl giggled as Henry embraced her.

Felicia stepped aside coldly. "Don't make a performance here now, please. This is a very traditional gathering of very conservative people," she hissed. "Now, who is this man supposed to be?"

Henry sighed. "It's a very long story. In fact I don't even think it has a storyline. He and I once spent time in the same area." He smiled at Kendall. "I was their little garden boy."

"Oh Jesus," the younger man groaned, "the good old bad old days … I'll never understand you people. You keep moaning about what you went through under those whites, but you can't stop calling them Madam and Master and be grateful for feeling inferior. I just don't get it."

Tina went up to him and took his hand. "Never mind, 'Master', I'll explain what it's like to be superior. Remember as a white Jew I'm miles ahead of any of you. Now introduce me to the family." She put her arm in his and walked him off towards the hall. "Who did you say was dead? Your grandmother?"

Henry tried to make out the features of the boy from his past sitting in the car. He had no mind picture of what Dawid de Lange looked like. Maybe dark hair, maybe tall, maybe slim?

"He could be a security policeman, or a right-wing maniac ready to blast us to hell and gone," muttered Felicia, pulling her blouse from her body in an attempt to get cooler. "And anyway, what sort of protection do you have around here? Shouldn't the young and the brave be standing ready to protect us with their traditional cultural weapons?"

"They are." Henry gestured to the other side of the kraal where two of the young cousins were sharing the earphones of a walkman. "Come, I have a feeling our white man is more nervous than we are."

He started towards the car. Felicia stayed behind, arms folded. As Henry got closer to the car, he saw the man wind down the window giving him a clearer picture of a good-looking, middle-aged man, steely hair, sturdy features. A frightened face that stared up at him unblinkingly.

"Let me start by saying my name is Henry Masekela and I take it you're Dawid de Lange?"

David's face relaxed into a sigh of relief and he sat back in his seat, wiping his sweaty hands across his hot face. "Who the hell were those maniacs in the Merc? Some terrorists who hijacked the doctor's new car?"

"My son and his girl actually, and yes they took my car."

David looked up at the face of Teema's son. He didn't recognise any part of it, just a reminder of that perfect smile. "So you're still smiling, Henry?"

"Yes, but not for R5 an hour raking up dead leaves. Come, let me take you inside. I suppose you're here to see my mother." David's heart sank a few thuds lower. He'd found her too late.

Teema was dead.

From the open door he could see her lying in the coffin. She hadn't changed at all, still the same shiny face, the friendly wide cheeks, the high forehead. The strangely large hands folded on her chest. David felt hot tears burn down his cheeks. He tried to stop them by blinking, feeling in his pocket for his sunglasses, but they were in the car. Teema was gone. And with her went the story of his other life.

"Here." He took a tissue from the stern-looking woman who was Henry's sister, Felicia. "We don't usually cry for the dead; it's the living that deserve our tears."

"Shhh …" Henry gently led David towards the coffin. "I want you to meet …"

"No, please …" David pulled away and stood at a window looking outside at the grey land. "This was a mistake. I'm sorry to have intruded. I don't even know why I'm here …"

Henry put his arm around David's shoulder. "You're here to find your Teema? I know, Suzie Bernard told me."

"What did she tell you? She doesn't know anything …"

"That you've come back from America to find Teema. That Teema is the only one left who can tell about the boy you ran away from all those years ago? Am I right?"

David nodded. "Yes, sort of. But it was silly of me to have expected everything to go off as planned. How old was she?"

"She? The woman in the coffin? How old was your Teema?"

David had to make some calculations, while watching a cluster of vultures circle round a chosen spot down in the valley.

"Well, I was 15 and she must've been …"

"We're the same age, you and I."

David turned to Henry with renewed interest. "You don't look it at all," he said, amazed at the smoothness of the black man's face, the firmness of his flesh, the straight back and proud bearing.

"Nor do you."

David looked past him towards the coffin. "Teema looks the same. After all these years."

He now felt a need to go closer. He walked across the stone floor towards the trellis-table, feeling the eyes of the gathered family on him, aware of the sudden silence only broken by the jagged sputtering of the outside generator that coughed and revved. He stood at the side of the coffin looking down at the face of his youth.

"My Teema …"

"I'm not your Teema!" she would say as she sat in the sun of the backyard, plaiting her hair into small sausages that she then would weave into a pattern around her head. "I'm not yours nor anyone's. I belong to me and me alone."

"But where would you work if not here?" he asked, his voice still light and sunny.

"Oh come now, my child, there are hundreds of small boys who need a firm hand, not just you. I could work for anyone. I choose to work here because I like your mother, and your sister needs a granny."

"We have a granny." He meant his father's unfriendly mother living in the Transvaal.

"I mean a real granny who can spoil her."

"Then be my granny, Teema." He so wanted her to belong to him.

"I'll be very good. I won't treat you like a nanny."

"A nanny? You want a nanny, you can go next door and that girl can be your nanny. She's stupid and primitive and always grateful for scraps off a white man's table. She deserves to be a nanny. I am far beyond saying thank you for the breath I put in my lungs."

And now there was no more breath in her lungs.

He put out his finger and slowly moved his arm out towards her folded hands. When he touched the cold flesh, a tingle crept up his arm and down his spine. He pulled his hand away quickly. He wanted to bend over and kiss her goodbye, but all he saw was a spoilt white tourist from across the world making a pathetic public display of his sorrow at the death of a servant.

"I don't know what to say …" he whispered and swallowed hard, hoping that the emotion just under his control wouldn't burst out of his heart. "I'm so sorry, Teema …" He stepped back, looking up at some relatives moving closer to the coffin on the other side of the room.

Teema looked back at him with life.

She was standing there!

He looked down into the coffin at the peaceful corpse. She was dead, and yet she was alive! He felt Henry's hand on his arm, leading him around the coffin towards the apparition. There was no strength left in him to struggle, his dry mouth was the only reminder that he was there, living a nightmare. The Teema-ghost didn't smile.

She stood like always, her arms by her side, her hair plaited and woven round the crown of her head. Her ears were still pierced and the small golden earrings she wore had been given to her by his mother. He looked back into the coffin at the Teema-corpse and saw that she didn't have pierced ears.

"What is this?" he heard himself gasp.

"Dawid, here she is. Your Teema."

He stood in front of her, again as in the past overcome by the presence of someone he'd so loved and so easily forgotten.

"But …"

"That's her sister, Tansile. We called her Mama. She was a twin to Teema. She died of TB."

Tansile? Did he remember a twin sister called Mama? But then so many relatives were called brother and sister that Dawid de Lange had never taken much notice of Teema's relatives other than knowing that his father had said there were too many of them and none of them were allowed to stay with her in her room at the back, except little Henry when he came to work in the garden.

"Teema?"

He said her name softly, staring into her eyes, waiting for her to embrace him and stroke his head as she did when he wanted to be loved. But the elderly woman in front of him stared back at him over her dead sister's coffin with no expression of recognition or affection.

"Teema? It's me, Dawid … Dawid de Lange! I was going to marry you once, remember?"

What a terrible way for a mature white man to restart an old relationship with a former black menial!

"But you can't marry me, little boy!" she'd scoffed while drying his hair after the bath. "You're too young for me!" She patted him on the behind and her body shook with deep laughter. "I can't sit with a baby for a man? Wait till you get big; you'll find your own nanny among your own people." And when small Dawid de Lange had sat at table while they were all eating a solemn Sunday lunch, in honour of the stern visiting granny who didn't like cheeky maids, Teema was serving solemnly. She never gave away her sense of humour at tense times like this. It was here that he decided to ask his parents: "Why can't I marry Teema one day?"

No one seemed to hear what he said. So he said it again. His granny developed a twitch over her left eye. His mother kept spooning soft golden pumpkin into shiny white plates, next to bright green peas and rough-brown roast potatoes. His father suddenly narrowed his eyes, finding a spot on the wall at which he looked with intense interest. Dawid's younger sister Renate just fed her round face, unfazed by the impending explosion. Only Teema saw the lit fuse and made a small squeaky sound of dismay as she carried the soup-plates to the kitchen quickly.

Dawid looked expectantly from mother to father, then to granny. "It's not that I can't get bigger," he announced, "I can and I will! I know I'll be eight soon and then after ten years, I'll be eighteen and Teema will only be twenty!"

"No Dawid dear, we think Teema will be much too old for you," his mother muttered calmly and smiled automatically at her plate of food. "Besides she's already got a boyfriend," she added, not wanting to commit herself to names, ranks or numbers.

"I certainly hope not in her room, on our property!" his father hissed. "Dawid, eat your food and stop talking such nonsense!"

When his father put such a sharp accent on the word 'nonsense' and ended it with an upward inflection, it was time to change the subject.

Except for little Renate, who at barely five years old, had a sense of timing that would only let her down once, and that would be when she was run down by a car and killed for crossing the road blindly at a sharp corner some years later.

"You can't marry Teema, man. She's a kaffir!" she said slyly, licking her spoon.

The happy scene around the suburban dinner-table went into freeze-frame. Mother closed her eyes, while clasping the serving spoon so tightly that her knuckles turned blue; Father chewed at the air and swallowed air and burped loudly as a result; Granny sucked at her dentures, while Renate flicked her peas to the side of her plate reserved for hateful tastes. The horrible pumpkin was already there. Dawid's mind was racing. Kaffir? The garden boy was a kaffir! The man who worked on the drains was a kaffir! The drunks in town were kaffirs! But Teema? He kicked out at his sister with a vengeance and hit the leg of the table hard. Pain shot up his leg from a bruised foot. He gasped. The crockery shuddered and the top of the mustard jar fell into the butter.

"Rubbish!" Dawid snarled. "What do you know! You stupid … stupid …" He was not allowed to swear. In fact, he didn't know how to swear, because most of the words he heard at school didn't mean anything to him. So Dawid made up sounds that gave him a great sense of satisfaction. "You stupid heggle!"

"Heggle?" Renate fell into the trap with a wail. "Mummy, look what he called me!"

"Dawid! Enough!" ordered Father, not knowing what a heggle was, but suspecting the worst.

"Dawid? Say you're sorry," said his weary wife, somewhat relieved that the issue was a 'heggle', and not one of the many other fashionable words that could've forced an explanation from the grown-ups.

Dawid fought back tears of anger. "Teema is a lady," he said, controlling his urge to throw something at the smirking Renate. "I love Teema, and I will marry Teema one day, so you can all go and …" Images and words failed him again. "… you can all go and hop, skip and jump!"

He knew it was against the strict laws of Sunday lunch, but he leapt up from the table and ran outside to the garden, slamming the back door behind him while yelling: "Heggle! Heggle! Heggle!" He grabbed a cluster of sweetpea dozing in the sun, and crunched their purple and pink petals in his hand furiously. "Heggle … heggle … heggle …" he repeated, letting off steam and looking round for a stone with which to destroy that most hated of all heggles called Renate. He looked towards the house, but this time no one came out to take him indoors, like the many times he was in the wrong.

Exhausted by his heggle-onslaught, he walked round the side of the house, while kicking a flat stone along the dusty pathway, and sat on the small brick wall under the flapping washing that wobbled on the line, reflecting the sunlight at the whitewashed house.

He could see Teema in her kitchen, washing dishes in the sink. She was looking down at her work. Dawid studied her face carefully; her cheeks, her nose, her forehead, her hair. Her lips. Why did she suddenly look so different? Why did she suddenly look so much like a …

"A kaffir?" David whispered and felt tears in his eyes.

But now at this funeral in Transkei, her lips were thinner and her nose not so flat. Her hair was wispy and grey. Her eyes cold and accusing.

"It's me, Teema, Dawid de Lange …" he said again. Teema didn't take her eyes off his. She started speaking slowly in Xhosa to her son, but talking about David, who was surprised how much he seemed to understand.

"I don't remember all the Xhosa you taught me, Teema …" he butted in, but she spoke on, not blinking, not smiling. Then he realised she was using the English word 'birthday' among her Xhosa sounds. Another word was 'ashamed'.

Then she was finished, she turned round and walked away from them. David stared after her, but Henry held him back.

"Teema!"

"Leave her, David! Wait now, it's not that complicated."

"But why doesn't she talk to me? Why is she so hostile? I loved her! I was her child!" He felt disappointment make way for resentment. "She was never treated badly in our house!"

"We know. But you're wrong, David, you're not her child. I'm her child." Henry pushed him along the wall covered with children's drawings and pointed at a framed picture of an ornate Baby Jesus holding a woolly lamb. Their reflections in the glass bleated out at them. "Look there. I'm the the one with the kaffir face, not you."

"Why do you use that word!" David pulled away with distaste. Henry hooked his arm into the white man's as they walked.

"You people created that word," he said. "We just use it to make a point. We're not ashamed of it, David. You made it into a swear word; we just use it as ... as a traditional cultural weapon!"

They saw Teema vanish into a small hut on the edge of the kraal without looking back.

"Henry, what did I do wrong? Did I say something all those years ago? Did I call her names? Did we hurt her?" He turned to the black man urgently. "You've got to help me here, Henry! She's the only link I have with my roots. She was there when my parents died, when my sister was killed. I wasn't."

Kendall and his white pregnant wife were talking to other members of the family. It looked as if the men were less easily convinced of the wisdom of the relationship. The women on the other hand were giggling and enjoying Tina's bubbly uncomplicated conversation, while comparing fashion and make-up hints.

Henry laughed. "How little it has all changed. I remember when I brought my future wife here to meet the family, the men were all a bit reserved, probably jealous, but the women just wanted to finger the new fabrics and talk shopping."

David watched the hut across the kraal. His Teema was there, so near and yet so angry. "What was all that about a birthday?" he asked Henry.

Henry cackled with delight. "My brother, you will not believe me when I tell you that my wise mother, the backbone of our clan, is offended to the soul, because you forgot her birthday!"

"What? Which birthday?"

"Her birthday. Or should I say, birthdays? Teema says you owe her presents, and that is that!"

Teema's birthday! Such a performance that always was. Each year the family in St Andrew's Road dreaded that fourteenth day in August. She used that occasion to test their love and their loyalty, and that meant a decent individually-wrapped gift from each member of the family, and God forbid it should be soap, socks, handkerchiefs or writing paper.

"Look, my child," she'd explain to David, wagging a finger in his face. "Soap from a white means we blacks smell. Socks mean we don't know how to dress. Handkerchiefs just spread germs and kill us off, and writing paper? For what? I can't write!" David never knew what was meant to be funny, so often he wouldn't dare laugh. Then Teema would prod at his tummy with a sharp finger. "Let it out, boy, or else that crushed laugh will become a thorny cactus!" And he would laugh till tears burnt his eyes.

But his family wisely never tested the warning, so Teema was spared the soap, socks and handkerchiefs. Once Renate contemptuously handed over the writing paper she'd got from her granny in the Transvaal. Teema immediately posted it back to the old woman and suggested forcefully for a more suitable present for a four-year-old. So Renate got a doll and Teema an amused ticking-off from David's father.

"Birthday ..." David groaned. "Oh God, I don't believe it!"

"And a cheque won't do," smiled Henry. "She wants you to make up for all the birthdays you missed."

"Thirty-one birthdays?" David started laughing. The tension of the day, the silly chase by the black Merc, the wrong twin in the coffin, the rude reality of Teema's feelings, all suddenly became terribly funny. Henry enjoyed the laugh with him. "So what do I buy her?" David spluttered, "I don't even know her size, or taste, or what she already has!"

"Just no socks or handkerchiefs ..." Felicia added from the shade on the side of the building. "And no soap!"

"Or writing paper!"

Henry lit a cigarette. "Want one?" he offered.

"No, I stopped. You taught me how to smoke, do you remember?"

"Oh? What else did you learn from me?" Henry twinkled at him through the blue cigarette smoke.

"That smile," David laughed and shook his head remembering. "You taught me the use of that smile. That 'look-at-me-laughing-at-you-sucker smile. I use it all the time in my work."

"What do you do there in America?" Felicia asked, intrigued by this person so familiar to her family. "Make money?"

"Yes, that's what Americans pretend to do best. I work on the organisational side of movie-making, finding properties, negotiating contracts. That's where the smile comes in very handy. No matter what you think of the person on the other side of the desk, you smile and you survive!"

"Like when I was a kid," Henry remarked, spitting a small flake of tobacco off the tip of his tongue.

"That's what I remember about you, yes."

"No, David, I just smiled nicely because I had been brought up to be a gentleman by that woman in the hut. Remember her? The one you wanted to marry? Teema always said to me: 'My child, smile! Your shop-window is more impressive than your untidy store-room.'"

"God in heaven!" groaned Felicia dramatically, "what does that mean!" She pelted a large stone with small bits of gravel held in her one hand.

"I'm not sure," shrugged Henry, "but the smile never let me down, or did me any harm. Unlike you." His sister did not smile, just sighed and glared up at the flaming sun. Then she shrugged and went inside. "E … who gives a damn, my dear!" she said and closed the door.

Henry winked at David. "Doesn't smile much, but not a bad soul. So, what now?"

David shook his head, at a loss to know what to do. "Maybe you can make a list for me? Thirty-one possible presents for Teema Masekela?"

So he consulted with Henry and on occasion Felicia, then with Kendall and Tina. Between them they had made up an impressive catalogue of the many possibilities for Teema's gifts.

They laughed a lot, even though everyone felt bad making merry, with Mama resting in the box before the last hole swallowed her forever. They'd eaten from a large bowl of meat and drank a lot of beer. David tried to stick to warm Coke, but it made him feel just as lightheaded.

There was still so much he had wanted to ask of Henry, like the story of his life since their last brief conversation in the years when Hendrik Verwoerd was still Prime Minister, the Architect of Apartheid and the Son of the Boer God, not necessarily in that order.

There had been no mention of politics during the afternoon, not a hint of the fears and disappointments the last 40-odd years had stamped on these people. The lightness of their conversation was dictated by the delightful intransigence of an old woman who wouldn't be nice until someone repaid the debt of niceness to her.

Through the stories and the details, David gathered that Henry had another younger son back in Soweto, and that a third child had died some years before. Henry's wife was also long gone.

Kendall Masekela worked for an insurance company in Johannesburg and carried the blot of 'yuppie' with pride and creativity. Tina Swerdlow was the typical Jewish African Princess with a healing mission, which she took right into her relationship across the former colour bar, and her zany humour left the older members of the clan somewhat bemused, and the younger ones a little bit nervous.

The family offered David a place to sleep for the night, but as the sun started looking down beyond the horizon for the next dawn, he got back into his red car and with a lot of waving and hooting, went on his way back to the world. He'd not seen Teema again.

They'd all swapped addresses and phone numbers before David left. Kendall had a smartly printed business card with a fax number added in embossed letters. "Don't believe a word," Tina teased. "They use the fax machine to photocopy nudes from Playboy!"

As he drove bumpily off down the uneven slope towards the better roads, he waved at his newfound friends. Their Mama would lie in state till the next afternoon, and then they'd bury her in the little area where the graves of others littered the ridge with plastic flowers in tins, and wooden crosses in memoriam.

Was Teema watching him leave, a tight scowl round her mouth? David smiled, as he imagined her irritation. "Thirty years I waited every birthday to hear from that boy! I brought up that child! I bathed him and dried his hair! When he had the flu fever, I was the one to look in on him in the middle of the night! When he broke his leg at school, I was the one to phone for the doctor! Where would that boy be without me?" David called out of the window at the hot air skimming past his cheek. "In Los Angeles, Teema my dear! Far away from you and your birthday!"

It was on a birthday when he'd left for his great adventure. His nineteenth and his last in South Africa. He'd spent the night with Suzie Bernard in her small room at the strictest women's residence of the University of Cape Town, and if they'd been caught naked in her bed, she would've been expelled. But they'd been taking that chance so often, it seemed their relationship was blessed with good luck and much fun. They laughed a lot.

Their sex life was good. Suzie was full of experiments, not all of which worked. Occasionally Dawid de Lange would find himself entangled in some new harness made up of dogleash and rope, paralysed with laughter and naked on the floor while Suzie, in high heels and a hat, tried to work out what had gone wrong.

David by now knew that old methods worked the best, so it was always his idea to go to the drive-in movie theatre, where Suzie could sit on his lap in the back seat of the car and control the volume, both of the film and his passion.

His army call-up papers had been no surprise.

He was quite prepared to go and do what was expected of him and of everyone else his colour, sex and age. There were as yet no whispers of the impending dangers of this unofficial civil war that was creeping closer with every new wave of arrests and jailings.

"But that's their problem!" he'd insist when Suzie brought up the issue of arrest and imprisonment without trial; when she would mention strange names of those in jail; a Mandela and a Sisulu and a Sobukwe. "This bloody university is full of communists!" he would pant, as he unhooked her bra and cupped her breasts in his hands. "Fuck politics!"

"No," she'd hum, "me me me me."

And he would, as in those days it was safe to be unsafe. If a girl fell pregnant, everyone had heard of someone who knew of a person who could help. Suzie Bernard only found out she was expectant once the father of her baby had skipped the country and was in London. She never told Dawid de Lange she had once hoped for his child, never told him she'd had an abortion. He never asked her.

"So why did you leave my bed so suddenly?" she eventually wondered after they'd met again so many decades later.

"Well ..." David Clayton had to dust off the mental diary of Dawid de Lange and page back to 1962. "My parents wanted me to go to university: Stellenbosch, Afrikaans, Calvinist, etc, etc. I wanted to come to Cape Town, to be with you ..."

"You bring tears to my eyes!" she giggled and tweaked at his nose.

He pulled away. "Don't do that, Suzie?!"

"I love your nose!"

"Yes, but don't pull at it! You know I hate that!"

She stroked his furrowed brow, pushing the hair to one side.

"Who else did that to you? Your Deli?"

Deli never mentioned his nose; not her nose either, although that subject threatened to come up whenever they saw Michael Jackson on TV.

"God Deli, how come all the women in this town go to that boy's plastic surgeon?"

But when both his daughters grew up to have the same nose he'd

104

teased Deli for having bought, the joke lost its impact. Only Suzie Bernard was the one who went for his nose at the first chance.

"I love your nose, Dawid de Lange!"

His nose luckily led him away from the dangers that lay in wait. David had been casually approached by a school friend, not someone who was in the same class, but one above his; also not someone he knew that well, not even liked for that matter. Someone who was also friendly with Cyril Greenblow, now that he thought of it! It all had boiled down to this: his education would be paid for, if he reported on any suspicious activity among his fellow students on the university campus.

"Among whom?" he asked angrily.

The chap was vague and amused at his insistence on the names of suspected targets. "That's our line!" he said.

"A spy?" David exploded. "Fuck you!"

But it wasn't that simple. He didn't like Suzie's liberal friends at varsity. All their talk of overthrowing the 'fucking Afrikaners' made him irritatingly defensive about his background. But worse than that, he would've liked to have seen them get into trouble, these wealthy spoilt arrogant brats, who expected a well-paid future from a country they would sell to the highest bidder. He wasn't prepared to do the same, so when the contact made contact again, David told him to 'hop, skip and jump'!

He had inherited some money from his granny who had lived and then suddenly died in the Transvaal, although he'd never really understood her. Renate was not at all fazed that she'd been passed over in a will by a granny she'd never liked. In fact the day of the granny's burial, she buried the doll Teema had asked for in the garden.

Teema also had much to mutter about 'blood money', but David didn't hand his inheritance over to the Red Cross as Teema had suggested. He kept it in his bank and two days before his nineteenth birthday, when his crackly-new passport arrived from Pretoria, he withdrew his savings, bought a third class mailboat ticket and left Suzie Bernard's bedroom in jeans, shirt and a battered leather jacket that would be his uniform in the cold London winter for the next four months.

The heat of the Transkei hadn't lessened with the end of day. It was dark when he drove into the ornate gates of the hotel on the coastal road to Natal, garish neon announcing casino facilities, bars and golf. The drive from the kraal had gone so quickly, what with his head so full of old memories and forgotten conversations. He had a great need to talk to Suzie Bernard. So he phoned her from his cool hotel room and got her voice on the answering machine. It started in Xhosa, then went into Zulu and ended plummily in English.

"… And just in case you don't know what I've just said, wait for the bleep and leave your name and message, although I must tell you, what I said in Xhosa and Zulu is much more interesting! Ciao!"

"Hi Suzie. Dawid de Lange. Transkei. Wild Coast Holiday Inn. Lonely. Tired. Alive. Miss you. Have plastic, will travel. Don't return call as I'll be in Durban tomorrow. Royal Hotel. Found Teema. …" Bleep. The machine decided it had heard enough.

He sauntered across to the main hotel building, weaving in among small palm trees and skirting golf-course greens, passing swimming pools lit from below and surrounded with water-bars of countless fairylights and alcoholic delights. He had a quick fast-food snack, gulped the coffee down, paid the bill and wandered into the great golden hall, where fruit machines came to occasional orgasm, while generally devouring every coin dropped into their gullets.

David put a few rand coins into a friendly-looking machine, pulled the handle and lost them all. He tested his luck at a few others to no avail, but it was the people round him that fascinated more than the off-chance of a win.

He first stood next to a group of young black girls, dressed for a scene from the latest pop video, a mixture of grunge, hip-hop and white madam's throwaway. They were into the twentieth collective win, with plastic bags banging loudly filled with coins. They squealed with delight at more winnings vomiting from the pregnant machines. They amandla'd and fuck-me-man'd their way along the row of shiny robots, blowjobbing each with eager coins, until the rows of winning plums, or cherries, or pots of gold smiled out exhausted and post-coitally drained.

Then there was a family of traditional Afrikaners. The father flushed red with one beer too many, the mother crippled pale by one child too soon after the other. Children in shorts and sockless school shoes, standing on one side sullenly, twisting their thin arms together in contortions, balancing on the one leg, then the other, glaring up at David through little bushy eyebrows, pale lips set firm. The father was needing a shave, the mother was clutching a worn handbag and her mouth was moving as she seemingly sang along with the muzak song on the eternal infernal intercom.

David shuffled closer and heard something that was not a familiar pop song. The man was praying, as he fed his coins desperately into the hungry steel monster, pulling the erect arm and then watching the plastic artwork of fruits create one disappointment after the other. He was muttering away in Afrikaans, his wife echoing his words. Their children just stood and watched, waiting for a miracle to happen. The woman flickered a glance up at David, then nudged by her man, concentrated on the battle at the slit mouth of this devil's smile.

There was such an acrid scent of fear around those four pathetic humans, that David's first impulse was to get away from them, to find something bland and impersonal like a drink and a bowl of cocktail nuts. But he was mesmerised by the pale woman's hand, as it clawed one rand coin after the other out of her bag, handed it to her husband who fed it religiously into the machine, her eyes shut as she mouthed the prayer with him.

"Ons liewe Jesus, asseblief laat dit vir U Glorie werk, laat ons wen, laat ons wen … laat ons wen …"

After exhausting their hopes on one machine, they would stop and look around from one flashing altar to the next, maybe hoping for a clue that this one above all others would hold the big jackpot. They'd shuffle on to another position in front of an identical whirling mechanical fruit-salad and the routine would start again, while the kids just stared hatefully at happy blacks winning coins, and tipsy whites spending them.

"The great lifeblood of the Afrikaner nation?" David thought with a sneer in his mind, as he allowed his prejudice to overcome his interest. "White skins, empty heads, masses of kids, sympathetic God, cheap labour, protected employment: how could it have gone so wrong?" he smirked and walked on towards the outside bars, set in the gentle surroundings of this rolling lawn that went straight down to the Indian Ocean.

Suddenly he could be anywhere in the same world of neon and fruit machines and muzak and martinis. He heard American accents and Spanish words and Jewish inflections. He tried to make out who was black and white and brown, but under the garish red lights of Sodom and Gomorrah, everyone looked the same colour.

The night stayed neutral beyond the edge of the glowing

electrical compound of fun. There were no sounds of Africa outside, just the rhythmical hump and beat of fashionable Zulu aerobics booming from the disco speakers.

David didn't even feel slightly drunk, although he'd had a few. So when it was time to retire for the night, he signed the bar-check and walked back across the rolled lawns into the hotel. His room was situated along the wing that reached out towards the sea. The pathway from the main building took him along the green edges of one of the car-parks.

It was there he saw the pale woman from the arcade again. She was peering into a dirtbin and scratching around the garbage. She looked up and saw him, pulled her hand out quickly, even casually brushed the greasy hair from her face while attempting a smile. A streak of discarded pink icecream shone across her face. She wiped it off on her dress and stammered a greeting.

"I lose my sunglasses," she said in a bad attempt at English, looking aimlessly along the edges of the grassbank, obviously waiting for him to pass. There was a crude call from the parking area and she looked towards it wildly. David saw the uncouth father and the cross children waiting at an old car, the kids wrapped in blankets, the man wearing a tracksuit. He gestured to his wife to join them impatiently. She started crying.

David automatically put his hand on her shoulder, but she pulled away. His hand felt damp.

"Is something wrong?" he asked.

She spoke quickly, in bursts, not looking at him, not taking her eyes off her family, talking through the side of her mouth so that they could not see. "No man, I can't ask for something ... but we have nothing. We sleep in the car ... and maybe tomorrow we find something. We must find something! You please go away now ... I get a hit from my man. Go ... go!" She pushed David away with the terrible urgency in her voice.

"Can't I get you all a room?" he heard himself ask and was relieved she hadn't heard. The woman pushed herself across the grassbanks and onto the tarmac of the parking area. She wasn't wearing her shoes.

David turned and carried on towards his room, wiping the stickiness from his hand onto the back of his trousers. Then a woman gave a shrill scream and a child started crying. He turned and looked back, but there was no sign of anyone. He tried to locate where the car was standing, but there were no lights to help him.

The coloured man in the cap shook his head. "It's all this bleddy trauma, man. You know, doctors come from all over the world to study us as trauma cases!"

"Who told you that!" demanded the biker.

"It's all over the papers, man!" shouted the cap.

"Not the ones I read!" retorted the biker angrily. "Stop talking such *kak*, man! Go back to your coloured townships where you belong and leave us civilised people to get on with our lives!" He revved his powerful engine and drowned out the chorus of opinion from the now amassed crowd of onlookers.

David edged away from the centre of attention where he found himself, and walked back in the direction to his car. He heard some physical activity among the crowd behind him, some grunts and applause, and saw a few security guards peel off from the hotel entrance. He thankfully strapped himself into his car and made for the exit.

Which way now?

He turned right into the road to Durban and wound down his window. The hot sweet air hit him hard across the face and made his eyes water.

"He shot the kids through their teddy-bears?" The words boomed through his mind as he passed and ignored a cluster of hitch-hikers pointing in his direction. "You bring your family to the casino in the hope of making a fortune with God's help; you don't and so you kill them in the car-park? Fucker!" he yelled, and beat the steering wheel with his hands. "Fucker!"

CHAPTER 8.

"It's not good, David. Sit down."

He sat and got up again. "Let me see?" Mrs Peters held the telegram against her ample chest. "Let me see, Mrs Peters!" He took it from her. "It's addressed to me! Why did you open my telegram?"

"It's bad news. Telegrams are always bad news. I can help you accept it. So please, let me tell you what it says."

He wanted to unfold the form and read it, but somehow his landlady was insisting on helping so he handed it back to her. She sat down on the other chair in her front room with the three clashing styles of wallpaper.

"Telegrams to London don't get sent for birthdays and fun. It isn't your birthday, is it, David my dear?"

"No, but it was last month and I didn't get a telegram. In fact, my parents forgot my birthday." He talked quickly, not taking his eyes off the folded paper in her hands. "Just my sister Renate remembered and sent me socks, handkerchiefs and writing paper!" He gave a sudden laugh.

Mrs Peters tried to smile with him. "Shall I make you a nice cup of tea?" she asked, and got up, trying to herd him off his chair and out of the room to her cosy kitchen.

"No," he said. "Who's dead? It could only be my mother. She's been sick for some time. Or my father? I'm not unprepared you know, Mrs Peters. One learns to expect these things when you turn 25."

"I'm sure you do, my dear." She got up wearily and lifted the net curtains, looking out of the window into the misty London twilight. "Well, it's not yer Mum or Dad. It's yer little sister, David, I'm sorry." She turned to him with a grimace of pain and covered her mouth with her hand. "So sorry, my dear …"

David took the telegram from her shaking hand and smoothed it on his lap. It was short.

RENATE KILLED BY CAR PLEASE PHONE TONIGHT

"Why tonight?" he murmured. "They're still so scared of using the phone. My father always said the phone's only there to communicate news, not views." He got up suddenly and went upstairs to his room.

Mrs Peters followed him at a respectful distance. "You alright, luv?" she called.

"I'd like that cup of tea now, ta, Mrs Peters!" came out clearly and controlled, and she went to her kitchen, quite relieved that the poor boy had taken it so well. But in his room, David was lying on the carpet, clutching his stomach as the cramps nearly made him suffocate. "Renate ...!" was all he could croak.

Mrs Peters carried up the little tray with his tea and a nice warm roll with cheese. His door was open and she put her head round to see what he was doing. She saw him lie on the carpet in a foetal position, then a shudder tore through him, leaving him motionless.

"Are you alright, dear?" she whispered.

"Yes," came from the carpet. "Okay, I'm ... okay."

"Well, I'll leave your tea here, dear. Don't let it get too cold now, will you?"

As she went down the steep stairs, she heard the boy repeat the girl's name over and over. "Renate ... Renate ... Renate!" She always got the better of him.

"I'll be the youngest forever and ever and I'll always be the girl!" Renate would say to him, and stick out her tongue, and she was right. No matter what she said to irritate him, or did to his bike, or his rugby togs, or his room under the roof at home, their father always took her side. She was the greatest brat in the house and every time David tried to rise above her intrigues, she'd bring him down firmly to earth with a nice underhand trick. A perfect smaller sister she was, and when he left so suddenly, she was still plotting and planning another embarrassment at his expense, this one involving his love of the moment, 'that awful Suzie Bernard'.

His mother wrote to him in London eventually, once she'd come to terms with the fact that her son was halfway across the world, and had changed his name to Clayton, the surname she'd lost after marriage. Her husband was determined they should never speak to their son again, because he'd run away and become a traitor, as one of the newspapers had shrilly railed. David never received any letters from his father, although his mother would write in her small scrawl that 'Dad has mellowed and wishes you well'.

But it was the brat Renate who would send him wonderful home-made postcards and keep him up to date with what was happening at his home and her school. She was also growing up quickly, and soon she was out of the classroom and starting to study to be that physical education teacher she always dreamed about.

And now Renate was dead!

A car? Whose car? What car!

David did phone home that night, a first intercontinental call for him, and when he spoke to his aunt, her voice was as clear as if she was next door. She wasn't next door. If she was at their house in St Andrew's Road, that always was a sign of total emotional collapse in the family.

She was not very friendly. "Ja, Dawid, it was a hit and run. They haven't found the driver. Your parents are devastated. The funeral is tomorrow. Of course, you won't bother to come, because they'll arrest you for running away from the army!" The contempt in her voice bit into his numbed brain. "Hold on, someone wants to talk to you." And she handed the phone to Teema.

There was silence. David heard someone breathe. He knew who it was. "Teema? What must I do?" he whispered into the phone, holding the receiver so tightly he felt his fingers crack.

"Must I come back? She's dead! What can I do?"

Teema made a sound that he never forgot. It was the aching wail of a mother who'd lost her only remaining child. The hair on his neck stood up in shock. Once the terrible echo of the cry had died away on the phoneline, David heard her speak so softly he had to strain to understand her words.

"She was my baby … you were my boy … both are gone. I can have no more like you children … I'm not allowed to go to the funeral."

There was a horrible silence. He tried to understand what she'd just said. "Why? Why!"

"Because Teema is a kaffir!"

The telephone was abruptly replaced in Claremont, Cape Town, and buzzed its emptiness all the way to NW6 London. David tried to reconnect the call, but it stayed engaged.

So he sent a telegram and a wreath and many letters, pouring his pain and sorrow into carefully chosen words like 'so sorry', 'shattered', 'it will get better with time' and 'forgive me'.

He meant that the least.

So without incident David Clayton swapped one hotel room in Transkei for another in Durban, and found himself sitting at the window of his 12th floor suite, overlooking the sunset on the harbour.

He had a glass in his hand, the ice banging sides in the whisky. He couldn't stop thinking about those small dirty miserable kids, intertwining their thin arms, glaring at him, hating him, now dead and cold and already forgotten.

The phone buzzed and he nearly dropped his glass. "Hi. Suzie. Durban. Royal Hotel Foyer. Lonely. Tired. Alive. Come to see you. Over and out. Bleep!"

He didn't have to say anything, just took his jacket, drained the glass and went down to the foyer.

There she stood in her denim jacket, with her sling-bag full of papers, sunglasses perched jauntily above her hairline. She beamed at him and they embraced.

"Long time no see!" he said, and marvelled at the fact that she still looked 16. "What are you doing here?"

"Oh God, do we have all night? I hope we do. I'm starving! Do you like real Indian food?"

He nodded and she pulled him along the passage to a local curry restaurant, where they took a table in the corner and ordered drinks and food immediately.

Suzie didn't get a word in as David told her about the family at the hotel, about his feelings of guilt at not trying to save their lives. He made bitter sarcastic fun of his prejudice. "I thought they were scum, the flotsam of Afrikaner Nationalism, while actually they were just four desperate people in need of care, of love, of compassion! Christ, and I thought I'd learnt something from the Americans!"

Was this a joke? Suzie leant forward to help him. "Listen now, Dawid ..." she started, but he pulled his hand away from hers and bit into a spicy hot chutney. It made his eyes water and he was relieved to hide behind that. The innocent faces of those children were now becoming the familiar faces of his own.

"Stop being such a tourist!" Suzie snapped and he opened his burning eyes and looked at her through the wetness. "It's a terrible thing that happened, Dawid, but it was an isolated incident. In the rest of the country, families were also holding each other and caring for one another. Now you might call me a cold-hearted bitch, but I'd rather put my emotions to work helping the living, and let the dead get on with whatever happens when they die. That I can't improve, or understand."

"But ..."

"And as far as your so-called compassion is concerned, who cares if you didn't use your Gold Card to save four lives? People are in a state of depression here as a result of the officer-class of our society having left and taken the keys to the safe with them!"

"I left because I had no choice!"

"You left because you understood choice. Could you have got as far and financially as well here, as you did in the States?" She slipped at olive between her teeth and bit at it softly, her brown eyes burning out at him. He sipped some cold water.

"No, I don't suppose so," he said.

"And without officers with experience and background to lead, the foot-soldiers must make the decisions and so they fuck up! De Lange, the poor man in the street is not by nature a four-star general. The ordinary people take orders, don't give orders. Your little dead family found themselves out of their depth and they drowned."

The clink of knives on forks from the tables around them didn't mean people weren't listening.

"So I am to blame for it all?" David asked, not really wanting the argument to go on for much longer. "If I'd stayed here and not 'run away' as you say, the nation would've been a better one?"

Suzie Bernard shrugged and lifted her glass. "Who knows? Just don't feel you have to carry every cross you pick up lying in the road. Push it aside and drive on. Some of the crosses here look sturdy, but they're really made of Valium and tend to dissolve in the first tear."

They ate their delicious curry in silence, she using her hands a lot and him chewing carefully, discovering new tastes and smells.

"So why are you here in Durban, Suzie, besides to give me a fingerwag?" he eventually asked, trying to push his resentment aside, his irritation at the truth she'd so angrily splashed against his sparkling indignation. He would never allow himself to analyse his decision to leave South Africa, seeing it as a purely instinctive and natural progression in his development towards achieving success and independence.

Now this bossy woman had come back into his life and within minutes, ripped the old nurtured scabs off the secret wound. Like Herman Greef tried to do with his annual surprise package from the old country.

"Oh …" she shrugged and her eyes flitted about the room through habit, not recognising anyone. "Work, I suppose." And that was it, until the curry was well and warmly devoured and their plates

116

were stained yellow and dotted with the few remains of a rice base.

He tried again. "And why are you here, Miss Bernard, besides giving me a fingerwag!"

They were both exploring a litchi sorbet for afters, with Suzie licking her small spoon with abandon, as she had all those years ago. She still looked angry, but then gave a smile which made her suddenly look vulnerable, like on those afternoons after school in the local café.

"I must've been a hungry kitten in my previous life," she'd say then and lick her plate clean of chips and tomato ketchup with her pink tongue.

Now Suzie wiped her mouth with her fingers and licked them daintily. "Well," she eventually answered, "when I heard your pathetic little message on the machine, I thought I'd come and save you." She tried to beam at him and lighten the atmosphere. "You know, a bit of work, a lot of pleasure?"

"You booked into this hotel?"

"Are you?" Of course she knew he was.

"Yes …"

She leant across the table and kissed him on the nose. "Hello nose."

They skipped coffee and took the first lift to his room. This time David had come armed with the necessary plastic.

"You cold-hearted bastard!" Suzie squealed, when she saw them in the bathroom, tucked into his travel bag. "You're leading me on with promises of a better education and protection against the cruel world out there, while all you want to do is fuck me!" She started loud boo-hoo noises that brought him into the bathroom quickly.

"Stop that noise, Suzie, you'll …"

"Wake the neighbours? They ain't heard nothing yet. Here, Romeo, you carry the umbrellas!"

And so they went to bed and it was a disaster.

"I can't believe this is happening to me," David said twenty minutes later, after a fruitless attempt to thread a condom round a flaccid member. "God, this is damn teenage nonsense!"

Suzie had to cover her face with the sheet so he wouldn't see her laugh. She didn't want to hurt this dear, innocent, highly irritating man. She was still amazed how little he had changed in all those years. "Don't worry, De Lange," she said softly, "let the little thing make up its own mind. Come and lie down, and we'll tickle each others backs and fronts, and who knows?"

"I knows."

He got up and walked to the drawn curtains, pulled the drapes aside and the lights of the harbour lay there like shards of broken mirrors. The dark shape of a departing tanker blotted out parts of his vision like a tumour. Wherever he looked, he seemed to see the faces of the dead children, his daughters in a last expression of trust before he shot them through their teddy-bears.

Suzie joined him in the crack of the curtains and put her arms round his waist, her chin on his shoulder.

"We waited for all these years, Dawid. We can really just relax and have a good night's sleep? Okay?"

He turned in her arms. "I'm sorry, it's …"

"Yes, I know what it is. I'm sorry I was so abrupt, but it's not your fault." She went back to the large bed and opened his side of the covers. "Come now, beddy-bye."

They slept soundly and safely, with their arms sometimes entwined, sometimes holding hands, once or twice gently stroking whatever came to hand, not waking, not dreaming, not blaming.

The next morning David had a taste of what Suzie's work was all about. They had breakfast and at 10.00 a.m. went outside into West Street. There were people lining the boulevard, with a noticeable presence of uniformed men patrolling on either side.

"What's this?" he asked, as they crossed the road to the imposing lump of the City Hall. "A movie star in town?"

"You could say that," she smirked. "The leader of the parade was once in a big movie, playing his ancestor." She wouldn't tell him more.

They waited for an hour, sitting on a bench at a bus stop and watching the multicoloured crowd take their places on the edges of the street. While there were many Indians showing interest in the parade, when they heard what it entailed, they left the area quickly.

When David overheard two whites informing each other, he understood. "An Inkatha march? Zulus?" he asked Suzie.

"Is it safe to be here?" She gave him one of her wide-eyed no-comment looks. "But Suzie, if you're a visible member of the ANC, and they're obviously mainly Zulu-based anti-ANC, is this a good idea?" His voice became slightly pinched, as the urgency of not being found on the wrong side of the Rubicon, so to speak, became clear to him.

"I'll protect you, De Lange, don't panic now, man!" she muttered in the accent of youth.

They all stood watching the street vanish into a V of skyscrapers in the distance. It was empty, with the exception of people running from one sidewalk to the other while they still could, while others moved their parked vehicles to safer illegal parking. Some shopkeepers with experience of past marches covered their windows with protective boards. "They've all been bitten once, forever shy." Suzie had told him about the other demonstrations by unruly supporters of various black organisations which had ended in an orgy of looting and wanton destruction of property. "Got to hand it to those little buggers. They didn't just want pullovers from the display dummies; they wanted the right imported labels! Checked them first carefully before they grabbed. Inferior local product was left behind. Damn cheek." They had to laugh.

As he saw the shops close, David suddenly had a thought. He grabbed her arm. "God, the shops!"

"What is it?"

"I must buy Teema 32 birthday presents!" He looked so worried that she thought she must've misheard.

"You gotta do what?" she asked astonished.

He gave a sheepish grin. "I must still tell you; it's a long story. The mess at the casino somewhat distracted me. I met Teema in the Transkei."

Suzie hugged him with delight. "That's wonderful. That's what you came home for! I don't want to say thanks to me, but thanks to me, I found Henry Masekela and the funeral …" She stopped and stared at him. "Then Teema wasn't dead?"

"Yes and no." Not quite sure how to explain it all quickly, David looked around for something with which to distract her. Whereas before he'd seen Teema again, all black women looked like her. Now not one of them around him had any likeness to her at all. They looked much friendlier. "She has a twin sister who died."

"And did she hug you, and did you cry, De Lange? Come on, you can admit to crying. I love men who cry once in a while and ask for my handkerchief."

David became aware of a sudden silence around them, as if everyone was listening. He lowered his voice to a whisper.

"Why are you whispering?" she whispered back.

"No, Teema wouldn't even talk to me. It seems she's cross that I forgot her birthday."

"You mean it was her birthday, and she had to bury her sister?"

"No, the last 32 birthdays …"

That was too much for Suzie, who just had to sit on the pavement and bury her shaking head in her arms. It was so familiar to her, working with these wonderful serious women every day.

"The most underrated and abused hero in South Africa!" she'd call them and she was right. Overweight, ugly, tired and underpaid, they travelled on dangerous trains and taxis, while the dormant sun was still having a wet dream, and the morning dew would dampen their berets and their shawls. They would have to walk for most of their morning trek from their smoke-filled townships into the sleek and sleeping city where they worked, not just for a living, but often for a lifetime.

Usually they were the only members of the family to earn just enough to buy the bread, while their men, or husbands, or whatever they were called, queued up for work that never materialised, either because it wasn't there, or because it was easier to live without it.

Their children ran riot in the dusty streets, or were intimidated into regarding their parents as sell-outs and old-fashioned, but thanks to ugly old Mama, the pot was always filled. Ugly, because they had no time to make themselves beautiful; beautiful, because they allowed themselves to become ugly in the service of their loved ones.

Teema seemed so much like the many women who, in spite of the pain and the suffering and the anger, would stop everything to celebrate someone else's birthday, or expect a nice gift in return on hers.

"What do you think is so funny?" David couldn't understand what he'd said to make Suzie react so childishly. Even the people round them in the crowd started giggling, infected by Suzie's twinkling laughter. "I just want you to help me choose presents!" This set her off again and David decided to just leave her to her mirth and look at the passing parade.

Usually there were so many twitterings in the palm trees of this park opposite the hotel, where daily lunch-breaks were filled with people, taking in the sun and just being like the other local tropical birds of paradise, the loeries and mynah birds and small yellow chirping things. But suddenly they were all as still as a carving.

The people also had stopped muttering and buzzing, just Suzie Bernard gasped and snorted in the gutter as she had one of the best laughs of her year.

A new sound started filling the air, very softly at first, more like the rap rhythm coming from someone's radio. A whoa-oh-oh whoa-oh-oh, and as beat had become the anthem of this nation, David didn't give it much attention.

It was Suzie who suddenly stopped her mirth in mid-snort and slowly got to her feet. A strap on her right sandal snapped as she put pressure on it, but she didn't even look down. Her hand on his arm tightened.

"Listen."

"It's just someone's ghetto-blaster," he said and tried to unlock her vice hold on him, but it got tighter.

"No," she hissed. "They're coming."

The Zulus were coming!

"Like a slow motion flood," someone called it. "Black ants finding a way into the honeypot," another remarked. Half a million potential voters. Savages. Soldiers. Warriors. Kaffirs. Animals. Call them any name you like, their sticks and stones could break your bones!

They were a tribe all on their own, proud and headstrong, arrogant and ambitious. Their discipline sent shivers down the spines of adversaries. Their demands made grown men swallow hard. And today they were marching to the heart of the city from where they could be seen on every TV screen in the world.

"Look, CNN is here," said David, pointing to the cameraman, like an international tickbird on the flank of the enraged local bull. The lanky technician was reloading his equipment and checking it lovingly, his passport to a possible Pulitzer Prize.

The vultures of the media were waiting, some right in the line of fire, others safely on the first floor of buildings, where they clutched their trusted zoom lenses.

"Do they expect trouble?" David added.

Suzie let go of his arm. "Damn it!" she huffed, "we're too low down in the street. Come on, follow me!" With a hop, she pulled off her broken sandal and threw it with the other one in a refuse bin, sprinting barefoot down the pavement.

David had to run to keep up with her. "What's the rush ...?" he panted, but she wasn't within earshot. In his attempt to avoid people, he seemed to bump into everyone in front of him. "Excuse me ... excuse me ... pardon me ..." he breathlessly refrained, sounding more ridiculous each time, until eventually he just hunched his shoulders and barged through the standing people. "Mind there, arsehole!" he snarled, using his American accent. "Fuck off man!" became his rap and they listened and moved.

Three blocks further up the sound of the war-chant was loud and clear. He felt a tickle of terror start in his neckline and wiggle down his back. He remembered the film he'd seen somewhere on television recently, in which a major battle between the British troops, led by Michael Caine and Stanley Baker, were confronted by hordes of Zulu warriors.

That's where he'd heard that chant before, a slow hip-hop of impending doom. Even then he sat iced-up with fear, praying that it would never be his luck to hear a live performance. He couldn't see much as the crowd round him was getting bigger, but then he realised they were coming towards him, leading the procession; no, leaving the procession!

Whereas at first the morning seemed to have a sense of carnival, the citizens of the city now saw what the promised entertainment was and decided to go home quickly and watch it safely on TV.

By the time the first wave of warriors reached the block above them, there were only a few straggling observers, outnumbered by police, soldiers and peace-accord officials. The latter had large blue bands strapped across their chests, with the UN emblem on the back and the large word PEACE in various ethnic languages shouting out at any prospective executioner.

"Why are they doing this?" shouted David, pressed close to Suzie, wanting to protect her with his arms, but deciding not to. She'd just turn and move on, rejecting protection as always.

"It's just a show of force," she replied breathlessly, "you know, thumbing their collective nose at the authorities?"

"The government?"

"Whoever has the nerve to say 'Down Boy' to a Zulu."

There was a recent government ban on the carrying of so-called traditional cultural weapons, which in the case of Zulus were their spears and *knobkieries* and other symbols of their might and their history. Just because other blacks, i.e. not Zulus, carried AK47s as trophies, didn't mean the Zulus would lay down their cultural arms.

"And there he is," Suzie said with a tone of voice, as if she'd spied Rod Stewart leading a march of rock and rollers.

"Your movie star!"

At the head of the perfect wave of feathers and beads and denim and leather and shining steel, pranced their leader, the colourful Dark Prince of local politics, Chief Buthelezi, who had always evaded being pinned down either as an ANC-supporter yesterday when being one meant jail, or as a government stooge today when being one meant death. Floridly articulate to the point of babble, the leader of the Inkatha Freedom Party was leading his flock personally, dressed like them, but in his case a more designer style of leopard skin and fabric.

"Bet you no animal-rights activist will spray him with green paint for wearing endangered species," Suzie muttered with sarcasm. She was nervous. As a worker for the ANC, she'd never been to a rally or a meeting of this rival wing of the liberation movement. It was her job today to observe and to learn. "Look at the control of the men!" she said, and David saw the commitment and the energy in each of them as they approached.

The very ground seemed to shake.

The Chief was carrying a silver spear with inlayed beading on the handle. He was therefore the first to break the law against the carrying of traditional weapons and would rub the noses of those denying him his rights into the mud. "Catch me if you dare!" was written all over his grin.

Some whites were now joining the march, peeling off from the silent watchers and being swallowed up by the feathered and jostling mass.

David watched the Chief closely as he marched past, his face set in that broad smile, his eyes half-closed, his body muscular and fluid to the rhythm of the troupe. His expensive watch and signet ring glinted off his naked arm.

Suzie grabbed David's hand. "Come!" she urged and pulled him off the pavement into the boiling bubbling sea of blacks. For a moment she was swallowed up ahead of him and their hand contact was broken.

He'd lost her! He pushed into the crowd after Suzie and was immediately swept into the rhythm of the dance of war. "I'm here!" she cried and waved at him. He slowly bobbed his way towards her. Suzie was laughing and seemed to have rediscovered the joy of diving off a cliff into an uncharted pool of muddy water. "Isn't this wonderful?" she shouted, nearly drowned out by the chant. David noticed the men around them smiling with her and realised that they as whites were also welcome here. He nodded a greeting to the young man next to him.

"Morning!" he shouted. The young man gave him a dazzling smile and nodded back. "Not bad," David thought, "or else this is just good PR before they put us in the pot."

But there was no boiling pot ahead, nor a massacre. The only shop window broken was because the owner slammed his door so violently the glass shattered.

"Strange," David mused as they sat drinking a cold beer later that day, having mulled over the events: the handing over of a memorandum to the police on the steps of City Hall, the disappointed media mafia being cheated out of good bloody footage. "I recall so many pictures on TV of looting and the burning of cars."

"Skollies!" was Suzie's quick reply, using the Cape word that put everything lawless and 'alcoholically-motivated', i.e. legless and criminal, into a nutshell.

"None among the Zulus?" he asked.

She played with some sugar sachets on the table. Around them in the fashionable hotel coffee-shop, well-dressed whites and the occasional carefully-dressed non-white were deep in conversation about the state and politics and the state of their bank accounts.

"I don't know what to say to people when that comes up, and believe me, it crops up at every news-briefing. Why do all other liberation marches – not all, mind you, just the few that make the news – why do they seem to attract the lawless and the opportunists, the thief? I'm not saying our movement is free of that element ..." Her voice droned on in an official gear. Her whole face seemed to lose its lustre. Her eyes dulled and circled the tables round them, taking in secret thoughts, while her mouth gave David the party line. When she was finished, she didn't even expect an answer, but he gave one.

"You used the word education four times, Suzie. So then why is education always the flashpoint? Why do we always seem to get back to 1976, when the school kids lit the fuse because of bad education?" He was aware he'd used the word 'we', but she wasn't listening. "With all the money being poured into crap like the black homelands, which eventually have to be brought back into the mainstream anyway, why is education always on the back-burner? Teachers declared redundant, 70 pupils in a class, putting the lettered and unlettered together and hoping for the best? Does no one really want an educated society?"

"What does that mean, American tourist?" she snapped out of her lethargy. "Education and knowledge are the corner-stone of our democratic blueprint."

"Doesn't look like it. But then people without education don't ask questions, and people who don't ask questions easily say 'Yes Baas', or should I say 'Yes Comrade'?"

She glared at him, fuming, wanting to throw the sugerbowl into his face, but sachets weren't as effective as sugar dust. So she pushed back her chair and stood up.

"You've got so much to learn, Dawid de Lange, not just about us, but about yourself." And with that she flounced out of the coffee bar. Dog and cat. That's what they always were referred to as at school. Dawid *en* Suzie? *Hond en kat!*

CHAPTER 9.

"So, who are you taking to the matric dance?" Herman Greef asked sometime late in a sixties November, his tongue so deeply in his cheek it looked as if he'd been stung by a bee. Dawid de Lange wasn't exactly known as a man-about-town. Shy and not very good-looking, he wore glasses that didn't seem to fit his face, hanging lopsided from his over-large ears. His hair was also too short, but that was regulation. The combination of his father's discipline and his nervous personality meant he did what he was told.

"Joanie Craig?" Herman hooted. The other boys laughed and Dawid blushed. He'd thought about asking Joanie because he liked her, not for what she so often gave the other boys in the sports-shed, but because her sense of humour fascinated him. She used all the wrong words, swore like a sailor and somehow it never sounded vulgar. Just very funny. Her jokes made his glasses mist up.

"Joanie Craig's bringing her own *pomp* for the night!" one of the boys said, rubbing his finger through the circle of his hand and looking up to the sky in ecstacy.

It was after the last class that day that Dawid literally bumped into Suzie Bernard in the passage. He was coming out of his Afrikaans Literature class and she was on her way to her extra tuition in Maths, her arms full of books from the library and a lunchbox legendary for its delicious sandwiches packed by her extrovert mother, the opera singer. The gift of one of Suzie's sandwiches was seen as a great sign of acceptance. She was very popular because she could also do all the latest new dances.

She reeled back after colliding with him and collapsed in a heap of books on the stone floor of the passage. Her tin lunchbox clattered against a door and opened empty.

"What the hell do you think you're doing, owlface?" she spat and balled her fists, ready to leap at him. Dawid found his glasses hooked into his shirtfront and put them on. Suzie Bernard was flushed with embarrassment.

"Hell man, Suzie, I'm sorry. I really ... can I help you?" He bent down to pick up her books and their heads banged together loudly.

"Shit!" she said and held her forehead in her hands. "You damn maniac, fuck off before I kill you!"

No one other than Joanie Craig had ever used words like that other than in a joke, and Suzie was not joking. Dawid tried to apologise again, his own head hurting so badly he wanted to rub it too, but pretended it was nothing.

"I actually wanted to ask you, Suzie," he said, still in a state of semi-concussion. "Would you come with me to the matric dance?"

She looked as if she would explode. "You? You want me to go with you to the matric dance?" Her face opened up into a large laugh, just the sort of thing he was expecting, a good sarcastic ha-ha-ha from Suzie Bernard. "Alright."

He still heard the echo of her rejection in his head, when the word sank in. He took off his glasses and rubbed them, wondering if he could say: "Pardon?"

"Pardon?" he said.

"Yes, you damn fool, I'll come with you. Can you do the Twist?"

He couldn't, but at that moment trivialities like that didn't matter. "Are you down on the floor?" he said, and gave a small wiggle with his hips. He helped her to her feet, picked up each book and heaped them onto her arms.

She watched him closely, not liking what she saw. "Thanks for nothing. Get you eyes seen to before the dance. And those damn feet!" She looked down at his large shoes. "I don't want to be crippled." She walked on down the passage, stopped then turned slightly. "By the way, what's your name?"

"Dawid de Lange!" was all he could say. His joy was unbounded and he wanted to tell everyone that Suzie Bernard had said: "Okay!" When he told Herman Greef, the bigger boy didn't look pleased.

"You offer her money or something?" he growled, having himself been turned down by her earlier.

Before Dawid could defend himself, Joanie Craig came up to him and boxed him painfully on the arm. "You randy old *poep*, you could've asked me, you know?" He was surprised at her sincerity.

When Suzie Bernard told her friends she'd been asked to the matric dance by that Dawid de Lange and had accepted, she collected money from each one with a broad smile. She'd won her bet, that even the most boring boy in class would fall for her!

Thirty-odd years later the faithful dog went off again in search of the elusive cat!

When he got up to his hotel room, Suzie had left. There was a note on his pillow, scribbled on an ANC letterhead and saying nothing other than "Thanks for bed and breakfast. Phone me." He sat in a blue easy chair with a sigh. She hadn't changed at all, and yet nothing was the same. While his eyes focused far out of the window on a small boat drifting at anchor in the basin next to the harbour, his mind flipped casually through his Suzie Bernard file.

So they went to matric dance and he couldn't dance. She slapped him on the dance floor, or was it after he'd taken her home? Home! Suzie wouldn't waste a free ride with an impulsive gesture.

At the end of that year they left school and went their various ways: Herman Greef to the army to do his nine months' training, David to join a legal firm as their runner, a job his father had arranged and Suzie went to Europe for a year. Joanie had been expelled before the final exams and left with a big smile and even wore lipstick on her last day!

David and Suzie didn't write to each other. There was no need to. All he remembered when he thought about her was a searing weal on his cheek and a sense of anger and embarrassment.

Suzie's eyes were opened in Europe to the magic of history and the beauty of art. She wandered round museums in Rome and Paris, even Spain, although she pretended General Franco wasn't in power and it made her feel better. Thinking back to her reaction at such a young age, the older Suzie was always amazed at her early instinctive loathing of the strict control the state had on the people. She was only starting to realise that what she'd accepted as 'normal' at home was the exception to a rule sadly long since fallen in disuse. Man was not born to be free it seemed. So she decided to help man fight to become free. Armed with her passion for the art of the Renaissance, the awakening, the rebirth, Suzie returned to Cape Town and for the first time saw the wood for the trees. The oppression around her couldn't be hidden by her comfort and her convenient ignorance. She decided on a Fine Arts degree and enrolled at the University of Cape Town. Known for its liberal attitudes and curriculum, the university put her in touch with other young Afrikaners who also had heard about the writing on the wall, but didn't know how to read it.

She met Dawid de Lange again at the float-building party in her second year. As she staggered round the front of the truck on which the residence float was being built, her arms full of paper rolls from which the papier mâché was to be pulped, she ran straight into a young man who was looking over his shoulder. With a yelp and a crash, Suzie and her paper rolls landed in a entangled mess on the grass of the soccer field.

"Shit, man, can't you look where you're fucking going!" she bellowed and gave the startled boy a wildly aimed whack across the face. Her hand hit him flatly against the cheek and it sounded like a gunshot. It all set bells of memory ringing among the chimes of dizziness in Dawid's head, and he immediately knew who it was.

"Jesus, Suzie, can't you fall down like any normal person?" he winced, rubbing his face and relieved that his glasses were intact.

She looked up in the darkness at the figure, framed by the bright lights of the working area. "De Lange? Dawid de Lange! What are you doing here?" She got to her feet and peered at his face. This time she liked what she saw. "Christ, you've grown up. What is that?" She giggled pointing at his chin.

"A beard, if you don't mind," he said, very much on-guard as the slap had set all the stored-up emotions against this nearly-forgotten Amazon in motion.

Suzie Bernard came closer. She put out her hand to his face. He pulled away. "Don't be such a sissy, man, I'm not going to hurt you." She took off his glasses and he blinked at her suspiciously.

"What's it now, Suzie. Give back my glasses …"

"Hell man, De Lange, you're gorgeous!" She stepped forward, put her arms round his neck and kissed him on the lips. Dawid was so astonished by this that he kissed her back!

They went back to his small flat and made love. She taught him the little things she'd imported from Italy and France, and, he being a quick study, gave Suzie the first real orgasm she'd ever had.

The person David contacted first after arriving back in Cape Town from his Transkei–Natal crusade was Joanie Craig. "I need a big favour from you," he explained on the phone.

"You don't have to ask, Dawid. Hell, I think I owe you something you never got a chance to do." She gave a deep laugh and his passion that so deserted him in Durban surged back familiarly.

"It's not that interesting, actually. I need to buy a birthday present for a black woman."

There was a pause, and then Joanie asked slowly: "You want me to buy your mistress a gift?"

He laughed. "No, not my mistress, my old nanny!"

"You're having it off with your nanny … oh, *the* nanny? Don't tell me you've found her! Terry?"

"Teema. Yes, but I've some crow to eat before I can get an

129

audience with her. I don't know how to start."

"Goodness, David," she used his American name. "Go to the shop and buy her some soap, or what about …"

"Some handkerchiefs?" he added.

"Yes. Maybe some writing paper?"

They arranged to meet after work the next day and go shopping for Teema. Herman Greef was not very interested in his odyssey.

"Jesus, shit, Christ man, you could've fucking phoned. I was sitting here in a damn cold sweat for all the days that you were gallavanting around the warzones, poking old girlfriends and being the ugly American! It's not a tourist's paradise any more, old pal. People get killed just for being in the wrong place at the worst time!" He poured another stiff drink for himself. "I had visions of you lying in a pool of bubbling fat with a smouldering Goodyear round your neck, recognisable only because of the halo round your head. What would I say to Deli? Sorry Deli, your stupid husband's a dent in the tar?"

Herman Greef was not managing the tense times very well. "These fucking black bastards. Alright, we gave them a raw deal, and yes, if I was black I'd be cleaning my AK47 and shooting farmers in lonely spots, I know, I know, but there's a time and a place for revenge, and when you're trying to put the … what did your old priest call it, put a square pole in a round hole? Doesn't even make sense, but then religion was never my strong point. We just want to get on with our fucking lives, make a bit of fucking money, live happily to the ripe of old age of whatever …"

David left him ranting in the living-room, punctuated by the sound of the ice in his glass, and slipped into the kitchen. Frieda was preparing supper, as Herman was entertaining that evening.

"Who's coming?" David asked, wanting to lift the lid and sniff the pot, but remembering how Teema would hit him with a wooden spoon if he did.

"Business, Master David. Always business. Usually I find them draped across the settee with dried vomit on their imported suit jackets, but business is the name of the game. So how was your wild goose chase?"

He smiled and bit into a raw carrot. "Not so wild, the chase was fun, but alas, no gooses to be had."

"Shame. Did you find that kaffir girl you were looking for?"

David took a deep breath and tried to talk sensibly about an insensitive subject.

130

"Frieda, she's not a ... that k-word. How can you use that word, you of all people? That word has caused so much pain and anger, and it's time we stopped using words like ... kike, nigger and kike and ... " He couldn't think of any more words terrible enough to use. Most such words had become so part of the daily jargon that some successful products were even sold under those names.

"No, Master David, I hate words like that. I hear it on the TV all the time. 'Nigger', 'kike', no sis, those Americans swear terribly. No, I think you are right to call your black people ... what do they call themselves now?" Her face screwed up in distaste as she tried to remember what she'd heard in *LA Law*.

"African-Americans, Frieda."

"Ah, so your blacks all come from Africa?" She carried on cooking as if the small talk was only about blossoms and prices.

"No, most of them were born in America, but it goes to show how unhappy they are, and how badly they've been treated, that they now want to be called something that really doesn't exist." Thank God Deli wasn't hearing this.

"Ah, I see, Master David. They want apartheid." Frieda tasted something with a finger and smacked her lips, muttering happy noises. David watched her with narrowed eyes. What was this old crow getting at.

"No, it's not apartheid, Frieda, it's just asserting their right to be recognised as fully ... as genuine ..." He was getting deeper into unfamiliar area and it felt brown and smelt to hell and gone. "... Like real Americans. They were slaves, you know."

"Ja, we saw *Gone with the Wind* here on TV. Too long." She turned to him and leant against the dresser, folding her arms and looking at him with a slight smile on her face. Her eyes were ice cold. "My dear Master David, you really live in the skyscraper of your mind. Some of you imported whites think you're butter, but you're just bleddy margarine. Look at me. I'm coloured. I'm Christian. I speak Afrikaans. In fact, put Master Herman next to me and he's darker than I am. My mother was white, my father wasn't and throughout their marriage they had to live like his skin dictated. She was reclassified as a coloured. It was a real sad business, hey? But now its all over and even Master Herman brings cheeky coloured girls here to spend the night. I don't say anything, except I don't have to serve them, do I? But if the blacks take over this land, so different from me, I will be treated like a coloured by the kaffirs, because I'm not a kaffir!"

"But you're black!" he blurted out. "You're black, like they are?"

She looked at him while slowly drawing her breath in thinly between her clenched teeth. It made a sissing sound.

"They say that political convenience, you know, makes Indians and coloureds call themselves black. But I know what I am, and I know what they are, and call them what you will, Master David, a kaffir is a kaffir. Now, can I make you some nice coffee?"

When he told it to Joanie, she laughed till the tears came down her cheek in make-up streaks. David exploded.

"Damn it! Why do you South Africans laugh? Herman also thought it was the funniest thing he'd ever heard. Joanie, it's going to start all over again one day, because the same hatred and mistrust has been passed down from master to maid!"

"No, no, I'm not laughing because of that, although Jesus it's funny, I mean not funny ha-ha, but funny grotesque. Hang on, let's find a place to sit down, I'm dying for a coffee and I must confess something … well, very funny."

They'd already trekked around the shops and found a dozen varied gifts for Teema. Joanie was a genius at spotting just the right things. They sat at a small coffee-shop and ordered. He watched her as they waited. She needed her coffeebean fix before she could spill the beans. "Oh that's better. God, I die for my coffee." She sipped with closed eyes and shuddered slightly with delight as the coffee set her up for the next few hours, till the next one.

"What's the confession, Joanie? Something I don't know?"

Her eyes opened and she gurgled a laugh. "Little boys always remember the first tit they ever saw, don't they? How come you never got it up for me, Dawid de Lange. He didn't even answer. "Maybe I was just not your type."

"I was too small."

"Really? Well, that explains everything. By 'small' I take it you mean you didn't want to stand on a soapbox to reach the heavenly cave? When did your voice break? Late?"

"It seemed to have got stuck in the high notes till Standard Nine. I was always in shorts when the other boys were shaving."

"I remember, you had the cutest little legs."

"I had terrible legs!" He hated his body as child. "Sticks with ball-and-claw knees."

"Nonsense, you had sweet legs and an adorable little arse."

"Come on, Joanie, you can't remember." He licked the froth off his spoon, pleased that she did.

"A girl always remembers her first love."

He saw the old Joanie Craig in front of him, the sunny smile, the freckles, the untidy hair in plaits, always with bows untied, her full lips puckered in a permanent kiss, her white school shirt unbuttoned till the softness of her young bosom peeped out at the waiting world. The woman who'd taken her place, no, the woman into whom she'd grown, sat and twinkled at him here, so far in the future and yet so familiar.

"You're teasing me again, Joanie," he said.

"No, Dawid, I just didn't know how to tell you then. I was so upset when that Suzie Bernard tricked you into taking her to the matric dance. I'd so hoped you'd ask me ..."

"But I was such a nerd!"

"... So I was forced to ask my horrible cousin Benny, who wanted very much my tit for his tat!"

He remembered the heavily-built boy with a moustache dancing badly with Joanie at the dance.

"We thought he was your lover, your sugar-daddy!"

They laughed and her fingers touched his saucer. He didn't know what she wanted him to do, so he didn't do anything, just pulled the saucer towards him slowly.

"The reason I was laughing earlier at your Frieda story, was just that ... well, you've met my daughter. She's going to have a baby."

"You'll be a grandmother."

"No, that only happens to other older people. She's going to have a baby, and I think it'll be coloured." She pulled a face, a wide smile that made her look like a clown. There were tears in her eyes.

"I don't understand, Joanie. You told me she was engaged ..."

"No, she's not engaged, De Lange, she's pregnant. Oh, yes, she's been going out with a very nice boy from Newlands, but he's ... a boring twit who brings her flowers and opens doors for her! She needs a good fuck and when he didn't give it to her, she found this black dancer!" Joanie took a deep breath and waved at the waiter to refill her coffee. He did and she used the moment to pull herself together. "Well, I don't want to sound like Frieda, but it's a very new experience for me, being a white mother with a daughter in the arms of a k... of a black boy."

"Have you met him?" David asked with unnecessary sympathy.

"Yes, can you believe it, he came to clear my drains when they were blocked. A nice, well-spoken drain-cleaner who was, unknown to me, clearing my drains just to block my child's."

She laughed and he laughed and they held hands over the steaming coffees. "Not so long ago we'd hear the sirens of cop cars and scamper off to the abortionist, but Judy really wants this baby and I even think it will be her passport to a future. I don't know. I've been divorced for so long, I've forgotten what her father looked like, the drunk bastard, that it's good to know that she'll have someone with her, at least for a few years maybe."

"They'll get married?" David thought about his daughters and their clean American marriages. So simple, so dull, such a relief.

"They'll see. It depends on the future, whatever that means."

"That could mean life or death, Joanie …"

She pushed his hands away with sudden force and looked away with tightly closed eyes. "Don't talk politics, please Dawid. I can't listen to another word of politics. I won't read the newspaper, so if one of my favourite film stars died, don't tell me now, wait till the coffee's cold. I won't watch the TV. I won't listen, I won't think. I won't be involved." She unconsciously bent the teaspoon out into a strange Uri Geller design. "Oh shit, look what I've done!" She looked around guiltily and tried to bend it straight again and it snapped. "Oh no!" She started crying and the pieces of the spoon fell into her coffee. "This is so pathetic!"

She opened her bag and took out her tissues. She blew her nose. She put the tissues back and found her lipstick, rolled on a carpet of red, slid her lips together sexily, closed her eyes, and leant back against the wall of the coffee bar. The plastic scene of the Italian lake in the sun above her looked rainy.

"I don't know why I even told you about all this crap. I suppose I just want you to know that I hope you won't run away again. You're not still seeing that Suzie Bernard, are you?" He hadn't told her about their meetings, so he lied without blinking. "Good. She's a gold-digger."

"Suzie Bernard?" He couldn't think of a worse description of her.

Joanie sniffed with disapproval. "After all those husbands. Three? Four? Can't remember … never mind! Dawid, when the little brown grandchild slides out into my rigid arms, be there to catch me when I faint? Promise?"

He promised.

"Now cross your heart and hope to die!"

He crossed his fingers.

134

On that Sunday morning, he went back to church for the first time in over thirty years. He'd been to many churches since then, getting married, christening children and a grandchild, burying producers who'd died of heart attacks, paying careful respects to the deceased royalty of Hollywood that demanded mortals to pay court at the shrine, but he'd never been to church in the sense of listening and thinking and being. Reverend Nkotse saw him immediately and gave him a broad wink. His service was simple and full of familiarity with his subject, his listener and his God. He saw the positive in everything, while reminding his little, damp flock sheltering from the pouring rain outside, that for every piece of bad news, there are two bits of good.

"They say wise things and important things and we nod and we agree, but do we understand words like 'negotiate a settlement' or a 'democratic dispensation' or 'freedom'? If we are born free, why can we never become free? Or is it because we are looking in the wrong place for that security. Within your heart and your soul and your being, you are as free as you want to be. No one can enslave you if you have decided that the freedom of expressing yourself is your right. And if you decide to submit your will to that of another, that too is your right, but then don't complain. When you let others think for you, you will swing when they swing, you will fall when they fall and if they win, they very seldom take you along.

"Whatever is happening out there in the streets, and on your TV and in your newspapers, look first into your soul and realise that you are the only person in the world who can change the course of evil if you put your mind to it positively. Negative breeds negative; positive gives birth to dreams that come true.

"What do they say? Evil flourishes when men of good will do nothing? It might sound like something corny on a T-shirt, but then the corny words 'Free Mandela' on millions of T-shirts led to a revolution, and today we are on the way to a future. You decide. Do you want to come along, or do you want to stay behind?"

"Too political, as always," muttered the old ladies shuffling out of the church ahead of David. "Why always spoil a nice sermon with politics!" There was a lot of tut-tutting and clicking of dentures, but when they got to the doors, they greeted their pastor with great reverence and affection.

"A wonderful message, Reverend!" they gushed, and the gracious old Nkotse nodded and clasped their gnarled white hands with his thin black fingers.

135

When David looked down at the smiling face, he was so glad to see him, he just wanted to hug the priest, so he did. "Please forgive me for being so forward," he stuttered and blushed, standing back and straightening his tie.

The clergyman pulled David towards him by his tie and embraced him again. "That's what I pray for every day," he said. "Let's always be forward, David, and not get left behind. I'm glad you came this morning. You've been in my thoughts."

"And your prayers, I know. I felt protected on my amazing extraordinary journey." He quickly told Reverend Nkotse about the saga of the funeral and the farce about the gifts.

The priest laughed heartily and shook his head. "Sounds like my mother, and my aunts! Heaven forbid I forget a birthday. Or now even Mother's Day!"

They reached David's car parked on the pavement under the dripping oaks of Newlands. A pink parking ticket fluttered like an enemy's flag off the side window.

"The law never sleeps. They should go to church."

"Oh, they did," said the priest, squinting at the writing on the ticket. "Ah yes, metermaid Hellman was sitting at the back. I gave her my blessing first because she likes to slip out before the last prayer so that she can zap some of you felons with a ticket!" He took David's hand in his. The drizzle on his hair created a glow of small diamonds, reflecting the defused light and making him look younger and quite naughty. "So, David, did your Teema Rediscovered have anything to say about your childhood?"

"No," David felt drops leaking into his jacket and roll down his back. "But something strange has started to happen to me. I've started to say 'we' when talking about you fucked-up lot ..." He stopped, appalled at his carelessness. "I'm sorry, I mean you ..."

"No, my son, 'fucked-up' is a very good description of us all around here. So, can I now say: Welcome home, Dawid de Lange?" David Clayton smelt the rotting leaves under his feet and it was as if he'd never been away.

He flew to Johannesburg three days later with two suitcases carefully packed by Joanie. Each held tissue-encased and colourfully wrapped presents, tied with bows and ribbons and a small card fluttering off every one, carrying a different message from David, as well as the year of the birthday. It took them three days of work and imagination at Joanie's cottage not to repeat themselves in either the colour combination on the wrapping or the wording.

"I'm so scared the old girl will reject the whole thing as a bad show of appeasement," David said, pouring another drink for both of them and grabbing a cheese snack off the plate on the table. "Believe me, this is harder than submitting the treatment of a convoluted plot of a film to Warner Brothers!" Although they'd grown closer together over the days of the Great Wrapping, he and Joanie had so much to talk about that their friendship skidded past a threatened physical relationship and settled into a warm togetherness. He met her daughter Judy again, still pregnant, still looking like a xerox of her mother and with no hint of who the father of her baby was, so David said nothing either.

There was very little talk of politics during those three days. It was a great relief to realise that life was going on quite successfully all over the country, in spite of the constant constitutional rollercoaster that was taking everyone for such a bumpy ride.

He'd rung Suzie Bernard the night before, hoping to see her in the City of Gold, but she was out as usual, so he left another telegram message on her machine. Then he tried the Soweto number of Henry Masekela again, just in case it wasn't still engaged. It wasn't and Teema's son picked up the phone.

"Who's been on the phone, Henry? I've been trying all day." David shouted, believing that a public telephone line wasn't as clear as a private one.

"Your Teema!" Henry replied. "She's getting very involved with the old people and their problems in the township, and it's all done by phone. Instead of bothering with the 14-year-olds, the movement should look to their ancients for support. At least they can read and write and remember. David, why are you shouting?"

"Oh, can you hear me?"

"Yes, Soweto's always only a stone's throw from where you whites are. Listen, you coming to stay with us?"

David had planned to go to a hotel. The idea of spending a few days with Teema in Soweto was too good to be true. "I'd love to!" he said, speaking even louder. "You're sure it'll be okay with you-know-who?"

"Well, David, if she doesn't like your presents, you're out in the street anyway. You are bringing the presents?"

"Beware of white vessels bearing gifts. How do I get to you?"

"Kendall will pick you up at the airport. Give me your time of arrival."

A young black man in an elegant suit was waiting in the local arrival hall with a large sign: DAVID CLAYTON. "That's me!" David shook his hand. "Where's Kendall?"

"Outside in the official diplomatic parking. It saves a lot of time. Let me get a trolley."

Of course his bags were the last off the plane, so when they got to the shiny BMW, Kendall was in a heated discussion with two airport policemen, one white and one coloured.

"I know it says Diplomatic Corps, my brothers, but that's what we are. I am waiting for the Ambassador … and here he is. Good afternoon, Sir."

David was wearing some very casual clothes, and didn't quite understand what was being suggested.

"Kendall, the luggage …"

"All has been taken care of. You've met our new cultural attaché? Well, let's get back to the Embassy, Sir. These gentlemen have been so kind as to keep me company."

The uniformed men looked David up and down and shrugged. The new South Africa had no surprises left for them and they were used to seeing future presidents look like old garden boys, so an ambassador who looked like an old hippie was no big deal.

The big car roared out of the airport onto the freeway.

"So, how are things down in the Mother City?" Kendall lisped, lighting a cigarette with an exquisite thin gold lighter. The young man who had met David, who turned out to be a clerk from the office and Kendall's gofer, sat in the back and paged through a Penthouse magazine.

"Okay." David clipped his seatbelt into place, as Kendall put his foot down. "Bit rainy, but beautiful."

He watched the outskirts of Johannesburg blur by, with suburbs merging with the rubble of mine dumps.The concrete cluster of the city lay to the right against the skyline, again looking like any mid-western American town. They didn't turn into the jungle of sky-scrapers, but kept going along a wide freeway that eventually exploded into a jungle-gym of flyovers. And suddenly they were in Soweto.

CHAPTER 10.

The south-western townships of the Witwatersrand, internationally known as Soweto, is a city bigger than Johannesburg and yet till recently only recognised by Pretoria as a temporary squat for illegal aliens. Blacks. It didn't at first look like the war-zone David and the world had become familiar with through the television images of the past decade. Smoke-filled, debris-strewn, people-littered township roads, with soldiers firing into crowds of school-children; running figures splashing in all directions in search of safety; scores of shoes lying pointlessly on the uneven tar; a dazed woman sitting on the sidewalk with blood streaming from a wound in the head. There was none of that now, just countless minibus taxis bouncing over the bad roads and onto the sidewalks like white beetles. There was no breathless TV commentary covering the images of 'unprovoked attacks' and drawing attention to the 'critical levels of tension'.

"This is Soweto?" David asked, unconvinced, as they passed the umpteenth billboard advertising 'The Good Life'. He looked carefully for any sign of unrest. At last he saw a heap of stones scattered on the side of the road. "Oh yes, I see the stones ..." he added.

"What stones, my man?" asked Kendall, slowing down. "Oh no, that's for the rock-garden the kids built in memory of Comrade Chris Hani. Just after he was assassinated, they built it in the middle of the road, which was a bit of pain in the butt! So now it's just being moved to the park over there." Park? David looked at the square of mud and rusty pieces of motorcars arranged in a Stonehenge of remembrance. "That's called Gorky Park," Kendall explained cheerfully.

"Lenin Park," corrected the gofer in the back.

"Stalin Park, whatever," chuckled Kendall. "Great lack of imagination when it comes to the names we find for things of importance. Wasn't Marx one of the Marx Brothers?" he looked at David with a knowing smile.

"Not half as funny though," David nodded.

"Yea," drawled Kendall. "We watch the 'Three Stooges' and the 'Marx Brothers' and all that old crap on video. Tina's trying to educate me to the ways of the world. Can't say I'm a great fan of early American comedy. I'm more into Eddie Murphy and those other dudes."

"What other dudes, man?" came from the back. This was like an American TV-sitcom.

"Oh, hell man, you know, what's that cat's name?"

"Richard Pryor?" ventured the ancient white from the City of Angels.

"Right on, man. What a cool rapper!" Kendall whistled through his designer teeth. He slid some unrhythmical unpleasant noise into the car-stereo and he and his clerk clicked and mouth-boogied to the rap-crap, while the car ploughed through the humanity that lived in this international shrine to man's inhumanity to man.

David looked at the poverty and the squalor. "It's not much worse than what we have in the States," David heard himself mutter and was glad no one heard. He decided to keep his opinions about Soweto under lock and key.

They turned into narrow streets and drove up other wide roads. They passed shacks and small houses, some with little mono-chrome gardens with bleached vegetation struggling to assert itself in the grime and dust. Then they crossed another wide strip of tar and slid up an avenue of high walls and elegant houses peeping out above the bricks.

"We call this part of Soweto 'Beverly Hills'." Kendall waved out of the window at the passing scenery. "Just like home, hey? The best people live here. More millionaires than you can count on your fingers." Kendall held up his right hand. A finger was missing.

"God, what happened to your hand?" David felt his mouth go dry. Although he wasn't artistic enough to play the piano, the idea of losing a finger was second only to a rusty pin in an eye.

"I wore a ring and some dude wanted it, so they took the finger as well. Listen, I'm alive. I've still got nine other fingers. Can't play Duke Ellington in the movie though." The two suited dudes laughed loudly and whistled and shouted and the car wiggled across another road straight through a supposed stop sign.

David was trying to get used to Kendall's driving, but couldn't prevent his knuckles from showing white as he clutched onto the safety belt round his chest.

Kendall groped around the cubby-hole and produced a remote control which he pointed at a large gate to his left. The gate opened and the car glided into the paved driveway. There were two other cars parked against the ranch-style house. As they stopped, Tina came from the back of the house with a broad grin and a fluffy dog in her arms. "Welcome to Beirut!" she giggled and gave David a kiss. The little dog growled guardedly. "Don't take notice of the great watchdog." She said the words loudly for Kendall's amused benefit. "I asked for a rottweiler and His Majesty here brings me this little joke. He's a black man's dog, so he wants to bite whites, unlike our dogs who bite ..." She mouthed the word 'blacks' and rolled her eyes at Kendall. He rubbed her backside and nibbled her ear. The dog was delighted.

David looked around and nodded impressed. "Very nice, Kendall. Well, pity I didn't bring my camera."

"Never mind, brother, I've got the latest videocam inside. Take a cassette of how the other five per cent live in Soweto and send it to the little wife in the Big Apple."

"The Big Raspberry, actually. Los Angeles." It didn't seem to make much of a difference to the others where he came from, so he shrugged and followed them into the house.

It was certainly not that much different to back home, he thought, looking around the spacious living-room with designer furniture, designer art and the designer dog in Tina's arms. "Shall I get my bag?" he asked Kendall and started back to the door.

"No, leave the bags. I've just to check the fax and we'll be off."

"Off?" he asked Tina.

"Henry's house." She looked at David's confusion and then laughed. "No, David, you're not staying here with us unfortunately, darling. You're staying over in Dube with the Dad. Slightly more Inner City. You'll see what I mean."

Dube certainly was more LA Central than Bel Air!

Within a few blocks of the mini-palace on the ridge, they were back in the crossword-puzzle of the township, weaving between road barriers, and passing light yellow police vehicles on each block. The thick evening smoke from open fires in each home made David's eyes water. The tall poles with their spotlights far above the houses stood like sentries over the ghetto. The glare made the grey asbestos colour of the houses absorb a bluish tint.

They stopped in front of a smallish house with an ornate 11123 painted on the door. That was the number of the house. The house where Teema lived.

"I'll show you to your room," Kendall said, as he carried the suitcases into the house.

It smelt sharply of roses. The small living room was still full of furniture, with jars and vases of flowers on every surface. David smiled. Teema always loved roses and would often spend some of her own money on red and white roses for their house when his mother forgot, which was usual. They passed into the passage. David looked into a room to his right, but the door closed sharply in his face.

"That's Gogo. Granny?" Kendall called through the door, then shrugged. "Here you are."

David knew immediately that he was in Henry's room. There was a double bed and a dresser, a cupboard and a picture of Table Mountain on the wall. "Where's Henry sleeping?" he asked.

"Never you mind, man. Listen, Dad's very proud and he's made all the arrangements, so don't question. I offered a room at our place, but he wants you here. You be okay?"

"Of course!" David's good humour sounded forced. "Fine."

"Okay brother David, I'm off. Got to earn an honest living as well, you know." Kendall gave him a wink and left the room. David sat on the hard bed and looked at the picture of Table Mountain in front of him. It was a blow-up of a photograph taken many years before, not that Table Mountain had changed in a million centuries, but the city was smaller. Those terrible pepperpot blocks of flats had not yet been erected on the slopes of the great *berg*. There were still the smoke-stacks of the power station at the foot-end of the city now gone.

Did Henry have nostalgia for the city where he was treated like a kaffir? David saw his own reflection in the mirror on the cupboard. He looked long and hard at himself and wondered what his friends saw. Had he changed that much since he'd last seen them?

"Jesus man, you were 19 then," he hissed at his mature face. But Herman and Joanie and Suzie didn't look that much changed. Or was he just seeing the image of them he'd kept in his mind for so long, and not the reality of experience on their faces?

"What are you thinking, my child?" Her voice was the same as it had been all those times in the past, when she'd come into his room with the washing and seen him stare at nothing in particular. "What are you thinking so deep in the river of thought, my child?" she'd say and come and sit with him on the bed. He'd lean his head against her shoulder and smell the sharpness of the soap she used.

"What will I become one day, Teema? I want to be a teacher, and then again I'm not very good at studying, so I won't pass. Maybe I should go into the bank?"

"With your terrible adding and subtraction?" she'd laugh and ruffle his hair. "You're only eleven years old, my child. A lot can happen before you've got to make your mind up."

She wanted her son Henry to become a teacher. A teacher, said Teema, was the only respectable job in society. That and an undertaker. Preparation for life and death.

"So deep in the river of thought?" he now repeated, not taking his eyes away from his face in the mirror. He couldn't see her in the doorway, but could smell the soap as always. Did they still make Teema's brand of soap? he wondered.

"Well, I didn't become a teacher or an undertaker, but sometimes I'm not that sure, considering how many dreams I have buried."

"You bury dreams? What does this mean?" she asked softly from the open door.

"I have to choose ideas and projects for films and there's always more rejection than acceptance. Some people never recover when they're told: 'not good enough, thank you!'"

Did people hate the face of David Clayton he looked at in the mirror? All those young and hopeful energies that his job had to tame and send away bitter and angry? Then he turned his body on the bed and looked at the woman in the door. Teema had on a floral housecoat and her hair was still plaited and woven into an intricate crown round her head. She was wearing glasses with very thick lenses.

"Are you still cross with me, Teema?" he asked and felt tears prick his eyes. He swallowed quickly, certainly not wanting to restart their relationship on a tearful note.

She stayed in the doorway and shook her head. "How can I be cross with my child? I was sad for my sister going on without me. I wasn't expecting a ghost from the past to haunt me so quickly. You gave me a great shock."

"Have I changed that much?"

"You are a man now, Dawid. And I am an old woman, but no, we haven't changed at all. The world has changed. Come here." She held her arms open to him. His heart started skipping beats and he felt the flush colour his cheeks. He got up and carefully stepped over the suitcases on the floor. When he reached Teema in the doorway he was surprised to see how small she was. He put his arms round her and felt her hands join behind him, squeezing him against her. Before he could control himself, the dormant wave of emotion rolled out of his soul and he started sobbing.

She held him, like she'd held him when his pet squirrel was run over by a car, like when he cut his leg on his bicycle and needed stitches. But now no amount of medication could repair the wound of time. David Clayton wept for Dawid de Lange and his great dreams that had become so ordinary.

They were halfway though unpacking the suitcases of presents when Henry returned from the school up the road where he was the principal. He hugged David warmly.

"I hope you'll be comfortable here," he said, shrugging at the simplicity around him. "And don't worry about me, I'm fine on the couch in the lounge. It folds out and you can land a Boeing on it. And what's all this? Stolen goods, Gogo?"

Teema smoothed out the bedspread around her gifts with awe and disbelief. "Look what this child brought me? I've never had one of these things, what it is again, Dawid?"

"I'm not sure, let me see? Oh yes, a perfume atomiser. You spray perfume on yourself ..." He squeezed the small bulb and a fine cloud of smell burped into the air. Teema took it from him and repeated the action on herself. She laughed and hugged the small bottle to her bosom.

"It's just the thing to use against the *tsotsis* down at the station. When they want to steal my bag, I'll just spray them with my ... what is this called?"

"Chanel No 5," said David wryly. "Get yourself a cheaper spray for the thugs, Teema. This good they don't need to smell."

"Doom for them!" laughed Henry. "God, what a day I had again. I don't know what we're going to do. If I had a proper building that worked, maybe the kids would respect it, but there are no doors, there is no equipment and what we get is destroyed as revenge against the system. It's a vicious circle. What are the schools like in the States, David? Your children went to school there?"

David nodded gravely, not wanting to go into a description of the exclusive school where his daughters rubbed shoulders with the offspring of a Fonda, or a Sutherland or a Burton-Taylor. The expense of that luxury nearly crippled him, but his children avoided the birth by fire that many schools offered its pupils.

"It's tough out there for anyone, Henry. Thank God we're not starting over from the beginning now."

"Well, I still rake the leaves and my neighbours' kids come and kick the little pile into disarray. Nothing has really changed." They laughed at past moments.

David broke the moment of memory. "I'm here. I never thought I'd be here, with you. That's a change, isn't it?"

"No, you were welcome here always. Maybe it just never crossed your mind to visit, did it?"

He'd once driven to Langa with his mother to see why Teema hadn't come home to St Andrew's Road after a long weekend. The poverty and the cramped houses had shocked him and left a permanent impression on him. This would be like in hell one day, he was convinced, having to live three to a room, with no electricity or running water. When he asked his mother why the people in Langa had to live so poorly, she had no answer.

"That's what they're used to, Dawid," she said and changed the subject.

"No, it never did cross my mind. I suppose we were just separated by a fence, a train line and apartheid." Saying that word loudly chilled the atmosphere. David suddenly felt white and it made him uncomfortable. "Well, look if there's anything I can do to help around here."

Henry patted him on the shoulder. "Never mind, if the garden boy doesn't turn up tomorrow, you'll have your day full. Proceed with the next birthday. Where are you now?"

Teema put her hand into the suitcase and pulled out a present. She squinted at the tag through her glasses.

"1976."

Teema cooked her Dawid his favourite food that night. A cream of tomato soup that she specially brewed with fresh tomatoes, a crispy-browned chicken with pineapple chunks in a sweet sauce, cauliflower with cheese melted over it, golden carrots in a ginger dressing, and ending the meal with baked apples and cream. She and Henry delighted in his reactions and they did a lot of laughing, especially when Teema kept contradicting David's fond memories.

"Nonsense, my dear, you never ate fish. You hated those little bones and unless I took all the bones out you wouldn't eat it! You also didn't like pumpkin or squash! You wouldn't eat beans without tomato sauce! You wouldn't eat an egg if it still wobbled; it had to be fried to death, and you hated anything fresh like salad. Always chocolates before meals, always biscuits for breakfast, you and your sister."

It was the first mention of Renate. He suddenly went blank and couldn't think of anything to say. The clinking of knives and forks filled the space. Then David spoke.

"Henry, Kendall says he has a brother? Have I met him?"

Henry glanced at Teema quickly, then went on concentrating on his food. "No, I don't think you'll forget meeting Sizwe. He's … what shall we say …"

"Overt!" said Teema.

"How do you mean?" David asked. "Carrots are great, by the way."

"Thank you, my dear," nodded Teema. No one was seemingly prepared to answer the question, or talk about Sizwe Masekela.

More silence as they ate. Then Henry sighed and pushed his plate away. "No, let us not be polite. David is not a guest, he is family. All my life I've been aware that you are my mother's favourite child. You are my brother." Teema put her hand on David's wrist and gave it a squeeze.

"My child," she whispered and tears sparkled in her eyes behind those magnifying glasses. The small brooch was on her blouse, the fragile amethyst necklace round her throat. She smelt of Chanel No 5. She was wearing the blouse he'd brought her and the shoes that were slightly too big, but never mind. She wore the soft leather coat even though it was warm indoors. If he'd bought her a hat she would've worn it too. "My child," she sighed proudly.

Henry sat while gathering his thoughts, then leant back in his chair and folded his arms. "I don't talk about this, so let me get it over with quickly and then you can ask me questions, although I hope you won't." He got up from the table and stood next to his chair. "Forgive me for standing, but I can't talk about it sitting still. Pacing does help slightly."

So Henry paced the cramped space of the dining room, back and forth, rubbing his hands together as if in pain, looking at the carpet and not stopping once to see the effect his story had on David.

"1976, as you know, was the beginning of the end of the era of repression by the government, but it took us till today to make some sense of that, and it's not got safer for anyone. The revolution started in the schools, my school being one of them. The children had had enough of inferior education, they didn't want to have to take tuition in Afrikaans, oh there were many reasons, but none of

146

them enough to start a war. But there were also clever people around, who saw the great potential for a confrontation and it happened. A bloody battle that went on for years, till now and into tomorrow.

"My three sons were small. Sweetboy was my oldest and, well his name said it all. Then came Kendall and Sizwe. They were all involved in the excitement. For the first time they disobeyed my orders as a father. As a teacher I had given up long before then …" Teema said something in Xhosa, but Henry shook his head and carried on.

"Kendall and Sizwe vanished. One day they were gone and I didn't know where to look. I thought they were dead. We looked in the hospitals among the many young, bleeding and dying; the morgues where I recognised the children of my friends, but no sons of Masekela. That gave us hope. Maybe they were in hiding." David could see that Henry was forcing himself to find calm words to describe something wordless in its horror.

"Well, Kendall came back two years later, just suddenly one day. We never knew where he was. He never told us. He asked me to help him find a school outside the townships. We found a church-school in Lesotho and he completed his schooling there, went to college there and now is qualified. And as you can see, not shy to show everyone his credentials." Henry gave a wry smile and it lit up his sadness slightly. "But Sizwe was gone." He stopped talking, but kept pacing two steps up, two steps down, wringing his hands.

David looked at Teema, but she had her eyes closed. She rocked herself gently back and forth in her chair.

"And your eldest, Sweetboy?"

Henry just shook his head and kept pacing. Teema opened her eyes and took David's hand. Her hand was ice cold.

"Sweetboy was shot by the police one Monday afternoon just down the road from here," she said in a low voice. "We heard the shots. He went to help someone who was injured and lifted stones to make place for them to lie and die comfortably, and they shot him. They thought he was going to throw the stone. They shot him. Goliath shot David." She patted his hand and tried to smile, but her mouth trembled.

Henry had recovered slightly and could carry on. "So I was now suddenly with only one son, having had three one day and then no sons the next. And then Sizwe came home." Henry stopped walking and took a deep breath. He sat in his chair.

"Then one day Sizwe came home." David waited for more, but there was no more.

Teema started piling plates and Henry got up and carried them out to the kitchen. David started to help, but Teema kept him in his chair. "No, Dawid, leave it. We can do that much quicker. Years of experience." She shook her head. "I'm glad he was forced to talk about it. It's just on the surface, but still it's better than keeping the sadness inside so that it becomes a cancer. Do you ever talk about Renate?"

David gasped for his breath when she mentioned his sister. He shook his head and fiddled with the spoons. "No. There's nothing to say," he quickly muttered. "But tell me more about Sizwe?" he asked Henry coming back into the room.

"You'll meet him, David," he smiled, as he put the steaming apples in the middle of the table. "He comes and goes. If you don't hear him come in, he'll no doubt make himself known to you. He's basically a very confused boy … man. Cream?

Later that night, exhausted by talk at table, David couldn't get to sleep. Maybe the heavy meal kept him awake, but it was the sounds around him that made him sit up in bed every now and then, straining to hear what was happening. Sometimes he thought he heard shots, other times screams; sometimes voices in argument, occasionally in song.

Was that a real siren, or from a TV?

The neighbourhood dogs never stopped their barking and howling and whining, and at three in the morning he was groping around the curtains to peep out at the night sky. Was it full moon?

It was then he heard someone pass the window outside. He caught a glimpse of a man in a baseball cap, walking close to the house and brushing right past the pane without seeing him. He heard the front door open and close. Then Henry's voice raised in argument, then quiet again. A door closed. Was Sizwe home?

David now had to go to the lavatory. He opened the door to his bedroom and tiptoed down the passage. Suddenly the row of doors all looked alike and he couldn't remember where he'd gone earlier to pee. The third door? The second? He knew where Teema slept, that was the first door next to him. He decided on the third door and opened it slowly. It was the toilet, so quietly he went in, closed the door and switched on the light.

He stood with eyes closed at the bowl, relieved to be relieving himself when the door suddenly opened. David nearly wet himself, adjusted his position and expected Teema or Henry at the door.

A young man wearing a T-shirt and shorts walked into the bathroom. He took no notice of David standing uncomfortably at the toilet. Sizwe went to the basin and switched on the tap. He put his hand under the water and David saw blood wheel down into the drain.

"Are you okay?" he whispered, not wanting to wake the household. Sizwe took no notice of him, checked his hand closely and turned the tap off. He pulled a towel off the rack and wrapped his hand in it, turned his back on David and went out of the bathroom. His door closed with a snap. David was finished by now and hoped the flush of the toilet wouldn't wake anyone. There were still some drops of blood in the basin.

"Oh shit, what do I do now?" he said to himself in the mirror. He switched off the light, listened at Sizwe's door. He could hear the soft tones of a radio on inside. He went to his room and closed the door. A gunshot in the distance started the dogs up again and he didn't sleep a wink till the sun shone into his room at 6.30 a.m.

When he came out of his room at eight o'clock, Teema was setting breakfast for him on the table. There was no sign of Henry or Sizwe.

"They are both out, Henry to school and Sizwe to wherever he goes. That boy has got a demon in his heart, it makes me so sad. Eggs like you want?"

The eggs were the best he'd had since the last set she'd made for him in the late sixties. She sat opposite him and watched him eat with a smile.

"That's good, my child. You must eat."

"God, Teema, you sound like a Jewish mother!" he said with a full mouth.

"I am everything. Jewish, Christian, Muslim. I am black and I am white, I am man and I am woman." He stopped eating and looked at her, amazed at her words.

"No, that is what is in a poem I was reading to some friends the other day. I do a lot of reading to people who cannot read. I like that. It gives me a chance to find out about others."

He laughed. "And I always thought you couldn't read!"

"How you always believed anything I told you!" she teased.

"But what do you do around here usually, Teema? Do you have great-grandchildren?"

"Not yet, but I think Tina will soon have a boy. Kendall needs a child to keep him at home, he is such a show-off. I work a lot with the old people around here. I have a dream, Dawid, that old people can also be of use in this new society."

She spoke for nearly an hour, mesmerising him with her articulate descriptions and passionate conclusions. As always education was her subject, but in the age of the breakdown of communication, she spoke about highly original ways of informing the children of the positive things in life.

"If next to every old-age home, we had a pre-school, a nursery school, just think how many children would have grannies there to love them and talk to them and tell them stories? Our old people are being forgotten and our small children are being misplaced. But sometimes it is even more terrible than just finding love for those without love. I must help put the tears back into the eyes of the little ones …" She sighed and shook her head. "What do you do when you see five-year-olds who have seen death so often, they cannot cry when their parents are chopped up in front of their eyes? What do we do with a generation of children who have no tears?"

He noticed that she had pain in her hands. She rubbed the joints of her forefinger and grimaced. "The weather's changing," she winced. "I always felt it in my finger, especially down there in St Andrew's Road. That's why I knew when to do the washing, or when to argue with your mother about waiting for a day or two."

"Did we treat you well, Teema?" he asked, pushing his plate aside and leaning his face on his hands, his elbows on the table.

"Elbows on the table, Dawid, what would your father say?"

He nearly took them off but didn't, still feeling slightly guilty and even expecting to hear his father sternly remind him: "People who put their elbows on tables, put their feet on couches and their contempt on your values," he would say. It was all nonsense, of course. David had watched Robert de Niro in Elaine's with his elbows on the table, and George Bush in the White House on television with his feet up on the edge of a couch.

"I was very happy with your family," Teema continued. "I loved being with you children, specially when you were growing up and could talk to me. I earned well and could put my child through school." She smiled. "I am proud of my Henry." David nodded. He liked Henry a lot. "But when you left, Dawid, it all changed." She looked him straight in the eyes. He wanted to look away, but forced himself to look back at her. This was a look of accusation.

150

"I had to go, Teema. I would've been forced into the army and end up shooting your son in the township!" he said, his throat dry.

"Instead you left to go to England and some other white boy in uniform shot at my son in the township! If you'd been there, you could've maybe stopped those sons of other white women from enjoying the shooting as much as they did?" He covered his face with his hands. Her tone changed. "No, I don't want you to feel guilty. You were young and it was your life. You always had dreams, my child ..."

"Stupid dreams that sound so silly now," he muttered.

"Dreams that came true. You wanted a family and a home and a job? You've got all that now, haven't you?"

"Yes, Teema. I have a wife called Deli and two daughters and even a little grandchild. So often I would wish you to be there in LA with us and hold the baby and be there for her."

"I've stopped being a maid, Dawid," she said softly.

He looked at her in horror. "That's not what I meant! I was lucky to have you there to guide me through those years when my parents were just being what they could under the circumstances ..."

"Your parents were good people," she started, but he stopped her and got up and started pacing like Henry had the night before.

"Yes, of course they were, but they had no sense of ... of adventure. When I think back how restricted our conversations were, just talking carefully, respectfully within the small parameters of what was allowed." She looked confused. "No opinions ... no ... well, no fun! We had fun, you and me ..." He paused. "And Renate ..."

"I was just doing my job," Teema said flatly. "I don't want you to talk ill of those departed, Dawid. Your parents were very unhappy when you ran away." He tried to contradict her, but she held up a finger and gave him a look. He swallowed his words. "Your final note to them, to us; not very nice for a boy who had the best upbringing, a calm family life, much care and love."

"No love ..."

"Yes, love! My love! I was also there. You just ran off and we didn't know why."

"I told you, the army!"

"Everyone went to the army! A year! They survived. Sizwe spent his life in his army. If you want to see what that can do to dreams, meet my grandson and see for yourself." Teema was getting angry and she smoothed the tablecloth over and over with her shiny hands, gathering non-existent crumbs into a small heap and herding them into her hand, fluttering it in the air and then starting again. "I couldn't tell your mother why I thought you'd run away. I couldn't say to her: 'Madam, I think Master Dawid has gone to find himself in the world.' I was just a kaffir, Dawid. I stayed in my place." This was what he was dreading the most and hoped wouldn't happen, but she'd said the word and it was out on the table, like a broken corpse.

"Teema, if I ever called you that I'm sorry. If I also ever expected you to call me 'Master Dawid', I'm sorry."

She looked at him with a frown, her eyes huge behind the glasses. "You've come all the way to say 'sorry'? Is that why you spent so much time and money looking for me?"

He sat down again and covered her busy hands with his. "No, I came to find you, because … because I love you. You are my family, Teema. You're all that I have left. Only you can help me remember, only you can fill in the details. You're my family encyclopaedia."

She smirked. "Penny in the slot and pull my handle, my child? Like one of those fruit machines?" They sat and nodded at each other in silence. Outside a volley of shots shocked him into getting up and going to the window. "It's just games, don't look out," she called from the table. "Everyone has a gun and they play with their guns like you did with your little motor cars under the poplar trees."

She joined him at the window. Outside the smog of the early morning fires had started to lift and a bright blue sky could be seen through the tears in the mist.

"What does our old house look like down there in St Andrew's Road?" she asked.

"Exactly the same, a little more structured, the garden I mean. But it's all still there. It's for sale too."

"That's a sign, isn't it?"

"I don't know what you mean by 'sign', but yes, it's a coincidence."

"Would you come back here, Dawid?"

"I have a family over there, Teema. I would like to bring them here for a holiday and show them what I left behind."

"And trot me out like an exhibit at a murder trial? 'This is the Fatima who bathed me when I was a teenager!'"

"I was only seven!"

"Nonsense, you were a lazy teenager who loved having his back washed and his hair rinsed and his ears properly cleaned out. Does your Deli clean out your ears?"

The thought of Deli doing that made him laugh out loud. "I have them done by a doctor," he said. Yes, in Los Angeles everything Teema had done out of the goodness of her heart, now cost money; through massages and treatments and diets. Teema did it for free and only with love.

The street outside looked deserted. "Can one go out for a walk?" he asked her, his breath clouding up the window-pane.

"You want to go for a walk in Soweto? It's a bit crazy, but then let's see what happens. You can always hide behind my skirts if the big dogs want to bite you."

They walked round the block of small houses a few times, his arm hooked in hers, getting occasional stares from passing people and barked at by all the dogs, until Teema shut them up with a Xhosa word they seemed to understand.

As they left the house which Teema locked carefully, David smelt the sharp sooty air. He breathed it in a few times, enjoying it as it brought back memories of *braaivleis* and bush fires.

"Now tell me about Renate's accident."

Teema spared him the details of the pain and the shock, but he could read between the lines. The total horror of how her death destroyed his parents had never dawned on him until now.

"The driver of the car was a boy her age. He'd borrowed his father's car without permission to go and visit a friend, probably to show off, you know what kids are like. She was in a hurry to get to a class ... she was doing a study of physical training at the college and ran across the road. He was just coming faster than she thought. No one could really be blamed. She didn't use the white lines which were just half a block up, and he didn't have a licence. Ja, maybe they were both to blame. The boy came to the house and cried. Your parents sat and stared at him without saying a word. I gave him some cooldrink. He said: 'Tell them I'm sorry.' So now I tell you."

"What happened to him?" David asked hoarsely.

"I don't even remember his name. Your parents never talked about it. They closed Renate's room. Wouldn't even let me in to clean up. She was eating an apple before she left the house. That half-eaten apple stayed in the room till ... well, till I left St Andrew's Road, I suppose."

"You left before they ... before my mother died?" he asked, suddenly having so many questions to ask. Teema's weight felt heavy on his arm.

"No, I was still there when she died. Your father came to live with his brother in the Transvaal after she died. The house was sold. But then I was already gone."

"Yes," David remembered. "My aunt wrote to me that Pa was with them. I never spoke to him again you know. I once phoned my mother, just before she died it seems?"

"I remember that well. She was so happy to have heard that you were doing well. You'd just got a job in America?"

"Yes, I'd applied for a few and the New York job came through and I didn't have anyone to tell, so I phoned home and I hoped you'd pick up so I could tell you, but Ma did."

"Ja?" said the thin voice on the line. "Ja, hello?"

His skin rippled with recognition and he felt like sitting, but there was no stool around. He was phoning from the lobby of the boarding house in South Kensington. "Ma? It's me, Dawid."

She seemed to gasp at the other end of the three thousand mile link, a small sound that he always associated with his mother when she was taken by surprise. A small birdlike woman, she never allowed emotions to show, other than a smile or a slight shake of the head.

"Are you sick, my boy?" was her first question.

"No, Ma, I have good news."

"You're coming home?" she asked immediately.

"No, Ma, I'm going to America. I've got a fabulous job and I've met this lovely girl called Deli here in London and she's also going to come to New York with me and, who knows, we might even get married one day, I don't know." He spoke so quickly that he knew she'd lost his train of conversation down in Cape Town.

"That's nice, Dawid. Where are you now? America?"

"No, Ma, I'm in London, but I'm going to America."

"That's nice."

Then a horrible silence, punctuated only by the metallic click of the overseas line. Suddenly he panicked. There was so much to say and he yet couldn't think of anything. He just felt that he should say sorry.

"I'm sorry, Ma, about …"

He couldn't say Renate's name. His mother didn't let him.

"Just keep warm, Dawid. I'll tell your Pa you phoned. Bye bye, my boy."

"Ma …?" But she'd put down the phone.

He went to a pub and drank a lot, sad one moment, angry the next. Then he took a taxi to where Deli was lodging, knocked at her door till she opened and spoke to her about his life till early the next morning. Later she told him that it was then that she fell in love with him, that autumn night in London when he was at his most vulnerable.

"So you married your Deli when you moved to New York?" Teema asked, quite fascinated by all the details of his life she'd just imagined for so long. She had to look at maps to find out where England was and then America. Henry took great glee in handing her an upside-down atlas and watching her try and find London in Australia.

"No, we lived together for a few years on and off. Then she fell pregnant and we got married. It wasn't such a big deal in New York in those years; everyone was liberated. It was the era of sex, drugs and rock and roll. Before Aids."

Teema sighed. "That horrible word. Why don't they call it a name that doesn't make one expect help. Aid means assistance. There is a lot of that here among us, but still our men won't wear those condoms. They think its just another way of your white government controlling blacks."

They stopped in the street near a burnt-out car that was now a grimy playpen for small children.

"Did you always think these things, Teema? I never imagined you would be involved in the same areas here that my wife is involved with over there, you know, the aged, health-care …"

Teema thought for a moment, and seemed to choose her words carefully. There was no point in anger now, just patience.

"You know, my boy, when I worked for your family, I was earning a living to put my child through school. I had to pay my bills. I had to do something constructive. I wasn't acting out a lifelong ambition to be a maid and nanny. I had my opinions, even then. We spoke about you whites in your presence knowing you people never bothered to learn our language. When your Hendrik Verwoerd was assassinated, we danced and celebrated. You must stop looking at me through those old eyes, Dawid. While we were child and nanny then, we are now closer in middle age."

They started walking on slowly. He kept his eyes on the sandy ground, surprised at how small pieces of glass were reflecting the sun so that they were walking on a carpet of diamonds.

155

Teema shook her head as she spoke. "I wonder what our lives would've been like then if we were allowed to talk to each other, me and your mother, for example. You know, discuss politics, vote together. I could have helped her more. I tried, but your father accused me of interfering and that I must get back to the kitchen. So when she died, I gave my notice and left. I went back to my life as a black. As a …"

"Don't say it! Please, Teema, I hate that word!"

A young woman ran out of a small house and grabbed Teema's arm, rattling away in Xhosa and pointing into the open door frantically. Teema calmed her down and the woman ran back inside.

"A baby is being born!" she said.

"Shouldn't I phone for an ambulance?" David suggested, ready to sprint off to the house and make a call. Teema patted him on the cheek patiently.

"I am the ambulance, I am the stork, I am the teacher, I am the undertaker. I am Teema." She took his hand and held it against her bosom. He felt her warmth. "You see, in spite of everything, life does go on. You must believe, Dawid. Your dear mother was not really in control of her mind. She only committed suicide because she was ill, not because you left her. I'll talk to you later. Here's the key."

And with that she went into the house and left him alone in the streets of Soweto, shattered by news of his family he'd never ever imagined possible.

CHAPTER II.

"Dawid my boy, are you in there?" Teema's voice was soft, her fingers scratched at the closed door. "Are you alright, my child?"

He was still staring at the picture of Table Mountain on the wall in front of him. He had thought over and over of the times he'd been taken up the slopes of that great rock to walk along the contour paths with his mother and sister, his father leading the way wearing a nifty Tyrolean hat and carrying a walking stick, protection "against the snakes and other reptiles" he'd say. They'd marvel at the view and discuss how healthy walking was, but all he wanted to do was go home and listen to the hit parade on the radio.

"Dawid, there's a phone call for you."

He turned to the door, still deep in his contemplation. "Ma?" he said. "Is that you?"

The door opened and Teema came into the room with a glass of whisky in her hand. She came to him and handed it to him.

"Don't you want a drink? Dawid, you've even missed your dinner!"

Where had he been, sitting here in the darkened room for the last few hours? He was hungry, but he hadn't heard any call from the door. All he could think of was that his mother had killed herself and no one had told him. Worse, he'd just never thought that she was capable of something so personal, so definite, so final.

And it was his fault.

"It was my fault, Teema," he whispered and took a large mouthful of whisky. It burnt down his throat and made him cough.

"Your friend Suzie Bernard is on the phone. She wants to talk to you," she said.

"I don't want to talk to anyone, Teema. Tell her I'm in the bath."

"She said she's free tomorrow, in case you want to go out somewhere nice." He just shook his head. She stroked over his hair as she'd always done when he was sulky and irritable. "You didn't know about your mother? No one told you?" He shook his head. "Your aunt didn't tell you, write to you?" He looked up at her, his face set in a look of defeat. "You know we don't get on. I don't even know if she's still alive. Where does she live now? Not still in the north? I don't know …"

"I know. She's in your grandmother's house up in the Pietersburg district. She's not that far from here. In miles, that is; in attitude, light-years away …"

Henry came to the door. "There's a call for you, Dawid. Suzie Bernard." He sensed the heavy atmosphere. "Are you alright?"

Teema shooed her son back toward the door. "He's fine. Listen, Henry, tell Suzie to pick him up tomorrow at 8.00. They're going to Pietersburg for the day."

Henry rolled his eyes in sympathy and went back to the phone. "Hello Suzie, he's in the bath … well, no, he's just a bit upset I think. No, there was no violence out here, why, what have you heard? Really? We didn't see anything. No, pick him up tomorrow …"

Teema closed the door and leant against it. She looked over at the hunched figure of her only white child, as she always called him, sitting motionless on the bed, arms clasped on either side of his body, head down shaking slowly from side to side. She could only make out one or two words in his mumble of repetition: "My fault … just mine …"

The next morning Suzie had driven him past Johannesburg on the great cement freeway, the 'white road to Pretoria', before she stopped the small-talk about politics and the state of the world and asked him what she wanted to know.

"What happened yesterday? You're as subdued as if you'd been to a seance."

He watched the bleach-burnt vegetation of the Transvaal merge into new suburban developments. The many massive steel pylons straddling the countryside looked like alien warriors linked together by dozens of lifelines, electric cables like a multi-string guitar humming energy across the places where people lived.

"Can't be healthy, you know, all that electrical current so close to the houses. I'm still convinced the fact that we're losing our immune systems is because we're the first generation to have grown up under those magnetic fields, fed on microwave food, exposed to radiated vegetables. We're being fried alive from the inside."

Suzie knew he didn't want to talk about his pain, so she flipped back into the political chit-chat of the day. They passed through what was called Halfway House, but the enormous extension of Johannesburg's suburbs towards Pretoria would soon merge the two cities into one concrete fortress. They sped past the grey square of the Voortrekker Monument, erected as a symbol of the emerging nation that would rule the southern tip of Africa for 45 years of their proposed 1000-bylaw Reich. It had lost all its pomp and position in reality and just looked silly and an ideal venue for a future casino. Suzie laughed as she told him all the plans they in the ANC had for the great dead symbols of Afrikanerdom.

"You forget that you're disturbing my roots as well as your own, Suzie," he said quite enjoying his sudden sense of belonging to something so politically incorrect. "By the way, I didn't know you were married."

"Yes, I was."

"A few times too?"

"Indeed. I had to make sure that I didn't like marriage, so I tried it three times."

"What were they like, the husbands?"

"Not bad. Quite polite. Well-off. Boring but controllable. It was what happened to me that made it all go bad. I slid into the role of puppet with great ease, spending hours at the hairdresser, the masseur, the facials, doing the fashionable charity circuit, bathing black babies from the squatter camps after a storm. I even had a face-lift." She showed him behind her ear, but he didn't see any scar. "And then one day I thought: Jesus Christ, where is square one? What was it that made me look forward to waking up? I couldn't find it. I had to go to a psychiatrist. I tried hypnosis, and then one day I remembered that once upon a time I cared. So I dusted off my conscience and took my new car and drove around the country and it made me sick. I left the last husband and the new car, and when the African National Congress was legalised, it was the natural place to start putting something back into the future. I had dabbled in PR, so I offered my services free of charge. That's why they keep me on. I'm too old and too white, but I have a great mailing list and the people with money all owe me a meal. So I'm their best fundraiser, and learning the language fast."

"You speak Zulu and Xhosa?"

"Mainly, but there is one sentence I recommend everyone learn in all the black languages: 'I'm on your side!'" She laughed. "Just know which language to use when! Look, another army convoy …"

For the next few kilometres they passed one army vehicle after the next, crawling along the freeway in the slow lane. Each truck was full of white children, pink-faced boys wearing huge steel helmets and carrying monstrous rifles that dwarfed some by their size.

"What the hell is all this for?" he whistled as he counted them on passing. "Did someone declare war and forget to tell us?"

"Yes, back in 1976. We turn off here. It is to Pietersburg?"

He just nodded. "Will you maybe tell me why we're going? Just for fun, you know, would be nice to know. It is after all the heart of neo-nazi territory. I've heard of baking bagels at Bechtesgaten, but this could be even more ridiculous!"

And it was.

David worked out that his aunt and uncle lived in a small town beyond the thriving Northern Transvaal centre of Pietersburg, where the fiery rhetoric of neo-nazi fat men made lazy whites feel good, if not quite safe. Suzie was relieved they were not stopping in Pietersburg itself, as two of her ANC colleagues had already been viciously beaten up by some of the residents when they attended right-wing rallies as observers.

Endeldorp was also formerly a mining village that threatened to expand, but the mine ran out of riches too soon and it froze in its development. Recently many elderly couples had taken advantage of the cheap land around the town, and many retirement compounds had sprung up like potential slums, surrounded by high walls topped with razor wire and nasty bits of broken glass.

"Why was this land so cheap?" David asked, as they cruised into town at a slow pace, not wanting to enrich the town's coffers with a speeding fine.

"It's near a huge squatter community up there somewhere across the hill," Suzie volunteered, having read more than a fair share of newspaper comment about that 'trouble spot'.

Two years before squatters, or as they were now referred to as 'those with unofficial housing', had suddenly appeared on the farm of a Retief van Schoor, where they put up their iron and wood huts in a helter-skelter rash. The farmer-host was living in Holland where he'd secretly emigrated with his sons, leaving the farm to remain as a payment against debts left behind, so there was no one to stop the squatters.

"Those fucking kaffirs, excuse me lady," said the sweaty red-faced farmer at the petrol station, his huge stomach hanging over his trousers like a sack of grain. "I'm not a racist, man, shit, I've been getting on with my blacks for bleddy donkey's years, they respect me and I treats them like human beings. It's not fucking easy, sorry lady, but when those kaffirs just came from nowhere, even my own kaffirs was cross because these others were aliens, illegal aliens!" He savoured a new politically correct word picked up from CNN.

"We all thought, no man, this is now bleddy war. We got our guns, we sent the government a memorandum and said clean up Van Schoor's farm. Then man, you won't believe this!" David wouldn't miss it for anything in the world. Suzie wanted to go, but he pretended not to feel her tug at his arm.

"We got together and took a piece of paper and worked it out. Now a) If we shoot the bastards, there's all shit to pay. United Nations, America, all that *kak*. But b) if we bankrupt the bastards? So we get together and build a supermarket on the edge of the camp that is growing like a spider's bite on a baby's bum! Suddenly there's no war, there's business! Those kaffirs make us blankets and baskets and whatever they can, and we sell it! Man, my wife and daughter has just been over to the States where they sold a *fortuin* of this kaffirwork in dollars, not rand! So even the media doesn't any longer keep someone on standby at the Grand Hotel just in case of a massacre. We now live together in harmony!" He leant forward to Suzie and his stomach looked like it would burst like a condom full of hot oil. "But lady, let them just come with their communist *kak*. We'll flatten them before you can whistle God Save The Queen. You people from England?"

"No," explained David, vividly American in accent and pose. "From the States. Come to bring greetings to Dr and Mrs Groenewald. You know them?"

The blimp-boer led them to the Groenewald house on the outskirts of the town, his bakkie bouncing round corners as he cut across kerbs and gutters. He pointed out the neat house and waved at them as he carried on his way.

"I think I'm going to be sick," muttered Suzie, clenching the wheel of her car in revulsion. "Fucking racist pig ... what are you laughing at?"

David was doubled up with near hysteria, having to control it all during the blimp's monologue. "You South Africans are the limit, you know. That man is no worse than any redneck neanderthal in the Midwest, or brainless miner from Wales, or cappuccino-maker in Naples. Just scratch the surface, show them an alternative and they'll happily rule the world your way, so don't get your knickers in a twist."

"Balls!" she spat and pressed the hooter by mistake, making them both jump.

"Suzie, he's like my father's family! He's just like the old Nationalists were when I knew them. This man's just been left behind by the Great Leap Forward. De Klerk's now hijacked the old liberal seat and left his old constituency to find importance under third-rate banners. Come on, Bernard, these idiots are even too stupid to draw a swastika properly. "

Her mouth twisted with contempt. "The three biblical sevens, my eye!" She peered out at the house. "Do I have to come in?"

"No, you can wait here. Hoot three times when you see the storm-troopers advance, four times when the blacks come and once when you want to go to the loo!" He looked at her thunderous expression and kissed her on the nose. "I love teasing you. It's so easy."

David opened his door and looked at the gate to the house, an ornate wrought-iron design that merged an ox-wagon with a protea. He groaned. "Oh God, let this cup pass me by. I don't feel like it …"

He rang the bell three times and was just ready to turn and make a run for it when the door opened. A youngish woman looked out at him. "Ja?" That upward tilt of the voice at the end of in the sentence! She sounded like all his family had.

"Dr Groenewald?" he asked in his most polite Calvinist way.

"My man, ja?" she answered in Afrikaans, narrowing her eyes at him, then peered past at Suzie in the car. She started to close the door.

He spoke quickly. "My name is David Clayton, I'm from Los Angeles. I want to see your father."

She looked puzzled, but immediately more interested once she heard the accent that so entertained her in American soaps on her afternoon TV. "Oh, my father is dead. No, I am Mrs Groenewald. Come in, my husband is on his way back from the hospital." She opened the door wide for him.

From the car Suzie saw him put his hand behind his back and give her a cheeky thumbs up. "Fuck it!" she fumed.

The house inside reminded him of so many homes he'd been into as a child. It seemed nothing had changed in the tastes of the grassroots Afrikaner. Embroidered cushions lay on plastic covers of upholstered furniture. There was a jumble of small wooden ball-and-claw tables. Yellow lampshades with tasselled surrounds, balanced with clusters of crystal chandeliers tinkling from the white painted ceiling. The walls were decked with heavily gilt-framed pictures of prints of mountains and rivers, and the idealised landscape of this their beloved country.

On the piano that groaned under snapshots and standing photo albums, he saw a picture of his uncle and aunt. At least he was in the right house. He sat on a lumpy chair and crossed his legs. The woman stood around nervously and gestured towards to front door. "He should be here soon."

There seemed nothing to say. She stood and smiled at him and he recrossed his legs a few times. They both heard the car drive up to the front door and the door slam.

"This must be him." She looked immensely relieved.

The front door opened and a doctor walked in. David quickly recognised the walk, the clothes, the case, the paraphernalia of a successful private medicine man.

"This is my husband, Dr Groenewald ..." She said something softly in Afrikaans to the smiling man and his smile got broader.

"An American? This is a pleasant surprise. Come to see for yourself what it's like to still be fighting the Cold War?" David shook his hand, trying to work out what the words 'Cold War' referred to. Dr Groenewald gestured to the front door. "Doesn't your wife want to come in?" he asked.

"No, she's fine. It's not really a social visit. I should've phoned, but I didn't know your number. You remember Bennie de Lange?"

"Yes, of course, he stayed here with us when I was still a boy. A very sweet quiet man. My mother's brother."

Then it dawned on him. This was his cousin! Or second cousin, or whatever intricate linkage Afrikaners always seemed to find to satisfy their need of a closer relationship with all their fellow boers. Everyone in *Suid-Afrika* was related.

"Leon?" David said the Doctor's name carefully, not remembering what this cousin looked like. The man looked guarded and glanced at his wife.

"Ja, that's my name," he said.

"And do you remember Dawid de Lange?"

Leon Groenewald had never liked Dawid de Lange because he didn't like playing rugby.

"Yes. He was my uncle's child. He left South Africa so many years ago, I can't remember ..." He stopped and looked at David again, this time not just in a polite way, but with a piercing searching stare. "You're Dawid?" he asked.

"Yes."

David stood up waiting for a welcome-home embrace, but Leon stepped back and sat on the couch opposite him. The air in the

163

upholstery sighed as it was expelled, and the plastic covering gave a rude squeak. David sat again carefully.

"You ran from the army," Leon Groenewald stated, also recalling how envious he was at the time that someone had managed to get away. For this alone he would never forgive his cousin.

"Well, actually I wasn't in the army yet. It was a decision more about seeing the world than escaping my duty." The words sounded lame and David wondered why he was being so polite.

"So was it worth all the pain, Dawid?" Leon asked with a smile suddenly stuck onto his thin lips.

"No pain really. Hard work. Yes," he nodded, smiling back thinly too, "it was worth it." There was an empty space between them in which no communication could flourish. The doctor's wife sat on her chair, upright and excluded from the repartee.

"So now you come back like so many of the other vultures, ready to pick our bones clean?"

"Leon …" his wife bleated and he gave her a withering look.

"I'm in private practice, but even at the hospital we are seeing people return from their so-called exiles abroad, waving grand qualifications that no one has heard of and demanding the most influential posts. What will you be demanding, Dawid?"

"Courtesy?" David got up and the chair sighed with relief. The plastic cover quickly smoothed itself out and you'd never know that humans used it as a chair. "I'm not here to see you. I came to see your mother, my aunt."

Leon Groenewald nodded, not taking his eyes off David.

"Amanda, tell our guest where my mother is." He didn't look at his wife.

"She's down the road," said Amanda, even more pathetic now that she had a name.

"Well then, can I see her?"

"She didn't really like you, Dawid. She always said you were the reason why your mother took an overdose of pills." An icy wave of fury bubbled just below his control, but David knew the smile on his face was his only link with calm. "Well if you want to see her, by all means, pop in and say hello. My father's there too, and you'll probably recognise some other familiar names. Three blocks down, then left and second to the right. You can't miss it. It's our biggest retirement home. *Avondrus.*"

Evening Rest.

Leon also got to his feet, joined by his wife Amanda. David

walked to the front door and opened it. He turned to his cousin.

"I'm glad you're doing so well. Pity that there must be so many sick people around, but you've certainly chosen the right place. I'm sure around here a doctor's work is never done."

"My husband always does his work," bleated the poor Amanda from behind her lord and master. Leon Groenewald laughed and put his arm round her shoulder. She reacted as if she was being scorched by hot steam.

"America doesn't look so wonderful from what we see on TV," he said. "Violence and decay." He was really smiling now. David matched his smile sweetly.

"Yes, I'm sure you enjoy it all greatly. Thanks for your time, cousin." He turned and walked to the car, trying not to run, resisting the temptation to kick all the flowers in the garden off their stalks, or turn round and give the ghastly Groenewalds the two-finger. He doubted if they'd understand the gesture. "They'll probably just think I'm asking for tea for two," he fumed, as they drove through the neatly-manicured neighbourhood in search of *Avondrus*.

It wasn't difficult to find. The *Avondrus* cemetery stretched over a hill and seemed to link the town with the blue horizon.

"Bastards!" growled Suzie, as they got out of the car. The warm wind whistled around her ears.

"I should've known. How could they still be alive ..." David walked through the first rows of tombs, glancing at the inscriptions, reading some of them aloud. Suzie joined him and in silence they zigzagged through a section of the deserted burial ground of the local white gentry. They didn't find the graves of his aunt or uncle, and were just about to stop the compelling study of the head-stones, when Suzie gave a call.

"Come here, Dawid. I've found something."

He joined her in the pathway above his.

It was the grave of his father.

In the distance David heard the mournful wail of a steam engine. His father's grave. He stood looking down at the forgotten heap of stones and granite bricks. "There's a train coming, Pa ..." he whispered.

Suzie gave his arm a squeeze and moved away tactfully. David closed his eyes and felt nothing at first, just tried to remember what his father looked like.

He saw white gates closed and the pair of bright red lights framed by the two black circles, winking at him, first one then the other.

The sign BEWARE OF TRAINS was flaking away in the weather and some of the letters were gone. BE AR O RAIN was all young Dawid could make out and he read it aloud, as he did every Sunday when they stood here waiting for the express train to pass.

Dawid and Renate were always carefully dressed and brushed for church and usually his mother and sister were with them in the car, but this morning it was just Dawid and his father. That made them even more uncomfortable, as they never felt they had anything to say to each other. When Dawid spoke about his interests, his father made some cutting remark about how childish he was, so the boy said nothing.

Except when it came to trains.

Dawid de Lange loved trains and collected pictures of them with passion. His plastic do-it-yourself train kit at home was his prize possession. He'd always pray in church for the 'booms', as these gates were called, to be down for a long time so that he could watch the great steam-trains scream by.

The suburban lines had electric current, but the main line between Cape Town and Johannesburg still overwhelmingly used steam-engines. Some were the sleek thinly-snooted ones that sliced through air. Others, Dawid's favourite, were the fat flatnosed monsters that huffed asthmatically and ploughed through the morning sunbeams, the smoke from the stacks colouring the golden brightness a dark purple, and making Dawid take deep breaths every time it enveloped him.

He loved the smell of the smoke and the grit of soot. His father always instructed them to keep windows closed when the trains came by, but Dawid always pretended to forget so that the scent of the railways stayed on his clothes for hours afterwards.

Today his mother and sister were at home. Renate had a cold and Mrs De Lange decided to stay with her, as Teema had her annual week off to visit her family in the Transkei. Dawid sat quietly, straining his ears to hear an approaching train. He watched the mirror on the dashboard of the car which he knew always started shaking when a train was coming their way. He held his breath as the images in the mirror started shivering and strobing. He glanced at his father who was looking blankly ahead, disinterested and irritated by the delay.

"A train's coming, Pa."

"About time too," grunted his father.

The rumble got closer, the buzz in his legs came from the trembling chassis that picked up the energy from the tar, as the massive missile bore down on the crossing.

"It's a flatnose! Wow!" shouted Dawid at the black dinosaur lumbered by, pulling a dozen elegant sleeping-cars behind it and vomiting white smoke out into the still day. "Did you ever want to be a train-driver, Pa?" Dawid asked his father.

The older man started ahead, chewing at his bottom lip while he thought about the intrigues among the staff at his office. He was a senior accountant in the Provincial Administration and hated every moment of it.

"What did you say, Dawid?"

Dawid ordinarily wouldn't have bothered repeating his question, but his enthusiasm was fired by the fact that the booms stayed down in anticipation of another approaching train. "I want to be steam-train driver! Didn't you also dream about it?"

"No. Never."

Benny de Lange felt that his authority was being undermined at the office by a newly-appointed head of department, who just couldn't stand the sight of him and made it very obvious. It was a never-ending fight for survival, with petty politics on the one hand and strangling bureaucracy on the other.

"Train-driver?" he thought. He couldn't remember if he'd ever had any career in mind other than the one he was now trapped by.

A minute went by and another great iron locomotive thundered by, taking its baggage into the City of Cape Town. Then Benny de Lange suddenly smiled. "Ballroom dancing!" he said.

His son looked at him, not sure if he'd heard correctly. His father had a small smile playing on his lips.

"Hey?"

"Don't say 'hey', Dawid. Hay is what horses eat."

Dawid looked at the gates slowly lifting and his father started the car again and they crept across the railway lines. They drove in silence for a while, then Benny de Lange gave a little laugh. Again Dawid looked up at him in amazement.

"That's what I wanted to do when I grew up: a ballroom dancer!"

Dawid sat in silence, not being able to picture his father doing anything extrovert.

"Could you dance well when you were young, Pa?" he asked, the suspicion thick in his voice.

"Oh yes, I have a few cups I won, or had. I don't know what happened to them." He knew exactly where they were; in the bottom of his cupboard in a shoebox among the shoes. He would clean them once a year when no one was around.

"Wow, Pa!" said Dawid, shocked and delighted with this discovery. "That's fantastic!"

"Dawid, if you can't choose relevant words to describe your feelings, rather say nothing. The words 'wow' and 'fantastic' are not really sufficient, or linguistically appropriate."

"Sorry, Pa," said the boy and thought of his father doing the Twist. He smiled and shook his head. Wait till he told that cow Renate! "And Ma? Did she also do this ballroom dancing?" Visions of his parents in chiffon and tails flashed to mind. It made him very happy to imagine how human they were under it all.

"No," said Benny de Lange. "Your mother hates dancing. Says its primitive." They drove in silence, then he spoke again. "I'm sure she's right. Your mother is always right."

Somewhere on the road between Pietersburg and Pretoria, David asked Suzie to stop at a turn-off to the left, which had a few concrete tables and chairs. Small anaemic trees had once tried to pretend to give shade, but had by now given up and just leant into the wind. Luckily today there was just a breeze to cool the midday heat.

"Let's have the goodies we bought now. I'm quite hungry," he said, and they stopped and unpacked the various packets of dried meat and dried fruit and a bottle of fruit juice and some nuts. "A picnic, like old times," he beamed.

"I've never had a picnic next to a road," Suzie said, willing to try anything once, except marriage.

David grabbed her arm suddenly. "God, listen to that … that silence!"

She froze in her activity and listened. The silence actually hurt her ears it was so intense. Then slowly she got used to it and discovered an orchestra of sound. Birds and insects twittering and crisping, and far away the metallic click of an old windpump turning lazily in the breeze.

The road stretched straight out like a blue-black ribbon towards the one horizon and rushed towards them from the other. There were no cars around, just the flatness and the heat.

"This is what I used to dream about in America. Just like this. The silence, the sweet smell of the land, the heat, the dry air. And then from far, you could hear a car coming, and the sound would get louder and louder, and you'd look into the distance and see nothing, just the sound." He pursed his lips together and made like a child playing with cars. "Brrrr … Dgooooooooo … as it raced past! And we'd have cold Vienna sausages and soft potato salad that my mother made, and warm lemonade, and the old Ford would be ticking with heat, and then, whoooooooshhhh, another car would flash by and the sound would change key and become another song as it vanished into the foreverness. I dreamt about this, Suzie, and it's still here!"

Suzie nodded and chewed at the dried fruit, praying that her fillings would hold. The cement seat was cold and hard on her bottom. She kept having to wave flies away from her mouth. The sun above glared down at her and she wanted to go to the toilet.

"Listen!" David stood on the stone table and looked into the distance. "There comes that sound!" He closed his eyes and followed the approaching car with outstretched arms. It sped by and the exhaust fumes made Suzie cough. "There! Wasn't that fantastic?" he exclaimed, excited and rejuvenated.

"Traffic, Dawid. That's what we call it. Fucking traffic!" Neither of them saw the yellow police-van till it glided to a stop next to them. A hot and sweaty man in camouflage uniform peered at them through his open window, his fleshy arm overlapping onto the door of the vehicle. The driver next to him wore mirrored sunglasses. They both looked like actors in a bad American road movie.

"Excuse me, sir and lady, if I sound naive," said the policeman nearest to them, articulating each word so that they made little sense when strung together. "Forgive me if I sound stupid, but are you two actually having a picnic here next to a national highway?" He accented the word 'picnic' as if he was saying 'fucking'.

David and Suzie looked at each other and shrugged. Then David held out some dried sausage. "Delicious *droëwors* from the butcher in Pietersburg."

The policemen exchanged incredulous glances. Foreigners. "Let me not spoil your fun, sir and lady, but you are a few minutes away from a high-risk area."

"Cholera?" asked Suzie in her best British accent. "Or is it the Plague?"

"You could say that, lady. There are blacks across that piece of land who last night caused the death of two farmers and six of their own. You're playing with fire."

Suzie hated the police and would not even call them when she was burgled, which happened regularly.

"No, we're playing with food!" she said sweetly.

"Okay, be a wise guy, lady! You're the sort of tourists that go lying naked on a deserted beach, and then are surprised when you get raped and murdered. Just let me say my say and then you can make up your own mind. People are getting murdered for fifty cents. Their heads get bashed in for a piece of bread. Their fingers get cut off for a ring, or worse than that, you can be chopped into little pieces, or *braaied* with a tyre round your neck for no *fokking* reason at all, except that you're white! Now get the *fok* into your car and get back to a relatively civilised place, where at least we police can do our job and be blamed for it in the process. I've got the number of the car and I will make my report. You have been warned." The police-van gave a leap forward, then stopped. Suzie could see bloody finger marks all over the door at the back. The van then reversed to where they were sitting, now definitely off their food. The sweaty man gave them a fleshy smile. "Have a nice day!"

Back in Soweto, David told Henry and Teema about their nice day. Halfway through the description of the meeting with his long-lost cousin Leon Groenewald, Kendall and Tina arrived and joined them. The small lounge was full of people. Teema served tea and her special little cakes, which David devoured with relish.

"Sounds like you really found your roots today, my brother," drawled Kendall, sprawled out in his elegant three-piece suit.

"Pity we can't choose our relatives."

Teema gave a loud groan and gave David a pained look of suffering. "See what nonsense I have to listen to. This boy is inarticulate! He lives by the language of the hip and the hop and the rap ..."

"And the crap!" Tina gave a high-pitched giggle and buried her face in Kendall's shoulder. He gave her a bear hug and nearly squeezed the breath out of her.

"I love this spoilt white woman! Is it my punishment to love a spoilt white woman? Tell me Suzie, what do you dudes in the ANC think about up-front yuppies like me taking of the fruits of freedom?"

"Live and let live, Kendall my comrade, live and let live!" Suzie said with a twinkle.

"Tell me about your pa's grave," Teema interrupted. "Suzie said you found his tombstone in the cemetery?"

They all looked at David. He wiped the crumbs off his mouth and finished eating a biscuit. "There was still a dried rose in a vase on his grave. I wonder who put that there?"

"Maybe it's part of having been a member of the secret Afrikaner Broederbond!" joked Kendall. "They keep your grave pretty."

"I don't think my pa was a member. He was just too decent a person, maybe too conservative. Too unimportant. But I'm glad I saw the grave. It somehow ties a knot for me where things had been unresolved for so long."

He looked up and saw Sizwe Masekela in the doorway, wearing the same T-shirt, jeans and the Malcolm X cap. There weren't enough places to sit now, so David got up and made his chair available for the newcomer. Sizwe looked him in the face. David saw that only one of his eyes were working, the other eye was milked up and askew.

"We met last night. Is your hand okay?" David said quickly. Sizwe slouched into the free chair and pushed the cap out of his face. "Family indaba?" he said with a deep rich voice, filled with music and menace. "Who's dead, dying or asking for a good beating?" He looked up at David. "You're the white man who's got the hots for our granny?"

Henry shot to his feet furious and embarrassed. "Sizwe! David is a guest in my house! I won't have such talk here!"

"It's okay, Henry, he's just joking ..." David tried to calm the tensions. Suzie shook her head at him warningly, but he didn't notice. "Your granny is a good friend of mine, Sizwe. Maybe in time we can also be friends?"

Sizwe laughed, an infectious warm peal of enjoyment that seemed to boil out of his body, but his gaze stayed ice cold.

"I can't wait to be friends with you, American Tourist. But I don't have a car, or a house, or a bank account, or a Visa card, or a white fuck like my try-for-white brother over there!"

Kendall was also standing now, Tina heavily draped across his arm hoping it would prevent any violence. David looked at Teema and was amazed to see how calm she was. She gave him a surprise wink, which through her thick glasses looked like a wave.

"Isn't this fun?" she twittered. "I don't have to go all the way to

171

the zoo. It happens right here in my home. The monkeys fight, parakeets scream, snakes hiss. Very entertaining and sometimes very boring. Sit down Kendall. Henry, go and take a pill or you will have a stroke. Tina, sit properly like a woman and not some pet canary. Suzie? Dawid? Come with me to the kitchen. I want to try out some of the tastes on you I've prepared for supper."

She started for the kitchen, followed by David. Suzie stayed seated, feeling on the floor next to the couch for her bag.

"I really must go."

Teema turned at the door. "Nonsense, Suzie. It'll be suicide for a white woman to drive around Soweto at this time of the night! They'll kill you and then I'll feel terrible. You stay for dinner and we can plan how to smuggle you out later."

"But she's a member of the ANC!" crowed Sizwe. "'Don't shoot comrade, I'm on your side!'" he mimicked. "You people! Made of milk and sawdust! You make me sick!"

"Really?" Suzie needed to let off steam and this was more than a good moment. "Well, that's the nice thing about democracy. You have a right to disagree. If you don't like it, Sizwe, go somewhere else! If you don't know how it's done, watch me. I get up and I go." She joined Teema and David at the door. "Ready to taste the victuals, General." They left the room quiet. Sizwe glared at Kendall.

"Sell-out!" he spat.

"Bandit!" said the other son.

"Oh shut up!" sighed the white girl.

In the kitchen Teema lifted the lid off a cooking pot and stirred the contents with a large wooden spoon. "Those boys are like oil and water. One day the jokes we make to try and defuse the tension will lead to terrible tears."

"What's his problem, Teema? Doesn't he have a job?" David found Sizwe's arrogance infuriating and yet had no way of fighting it. Being white didn't help either.

"Suzie, hold this for me, my dear?" Teema poured the contents of the pot into the large strainer and it seeped into the bowl beneath, encouraged by her vigorous stirring. "Sizwe was nine when he disappeared after '76," she said. "He was dead and gone. We had a funeral service and put up a small gravestone, just to have a place to go and weep, to shout, to scream at God for taking away such a child. Seventeen years later he came back out of nowhere, two months ago. He is the oil, and Kendall is the water. Between them is a lit match."

172

"Oh Grannie! You make tears come to my eyes!" Sizwe stood in the door and slowly clapped hands. "Telling our guests, the tourists, all the dirty sad details of the lost generation? Don't waste your breath." He came close up to David and spoke to him softly and clearly. "I've been trained by the best. I can shoot to kill with my eyes closed, sorry, my eye closed; the other eye I lost in Angola. A lion attacked my comrades. The lion died. I trained at the best camps in Tanzania, in Zambia, in Zimbabwe. I fought shoulder to shoulder with the best in the world. I studied and I have a degree, oh yes, I'm better qualified than that baboon in there. I am a veteran. From the age of ten I have been a soldier. Now I come home and what do they call me? Come Gogo, what do you call me?" He pushed Teema sharply and she nearly stumbled.

David caught her in time. "Mind your grandmother, Sizwe!" he said in a sharp tone reserved for difficult producers. It worked.

Sizwe seemed to calm down. "They call me 'bandit'!" he said, still in the soft tones, the music in his voice mesmerising and beautiful. "I am the returning hero and these milkshakes call me a bandit? Here I am, David American Tourist, and I still have no vote, no say, no ownership of my own land. What do you say to that, with your great Bill of Rights and War of Independence and Martin Luther King and all that jazz?" Sizwe gave a little dance around the kitchen floor, his lithe body willowing to the rhythm.

Suzie was entranced by the strange beauty in this tormented man. Then Sizwe stopped and seemed to grow taller as he stretched himself to his full height. "So what therapy can you offer me? Miss Suzie ANC? Shall I go and teach the kids how to write a business letter? Should I help the doctors sew up a rotting womb in the hospital? Must I become a pop singer and make money sending out a message of love? Should I lie down and die?"

She knew he was talking at her, although his eyes were closed. He waited for her answer. She glanced at David, then Teema, not wanting to get drawn into another of Sizwe's games. The old woman had tears in her eyes.

"I'd say pull yourself together, Sizwe," Suzie said. "You're far better educated that the kids you left behind. It seems so anyway, if one is to believe all you say. You've got great … what is the word … charm." He opened his eye and lasered her with his look. "You could do anything you set your mind on."

"Could I get you to go out with me?" He watched her with a smile.

"I'm a bit old for you. But by all means, let's get together sometime and have a chat."

His body returned to its elastic form and he bowed down in front of her. "A chat!" he said in a mock English accent. "How nice!" He turned and went for the back door, shouting over his shoulder as he strode out into the night. "Don't wait up for me, darling. I'm off to do my MK aerobics!" And he was gone.

"MK what?" David whispered to Suzie.

"MK – the ANC army, Umkhonto weSizwe, but I don't think he's involved. God, but what a presence, what quality. If only he'd come down to earth …"

"Do you think he's on drugs, Teema?" David asked gently, realising how upset she was.

"I don't know what they call drugs any more. In our day it was two aspirins. Now they sniff glue and chew funny leaves, or pieces of chalk, or even human bones. Soup's ready. Plates are in the warming oven."

The atmosphere round the dining-room table was chilly. When dinner was over, even David wondered why even his favourite foods tasted so bland.

It was quite late. Suzie wanted to get back to the city. "How can we get you back, Suzie?" he asked, not wanting her to be forced into his bed because there was no one prepared to escort her back to Johannesburg.

Tina came to his rescue. "Kendall and I will drive in front of her. We can pop into that new club in Yeoville and take in some jazz. Or Kippies at the Market Theatre?"

"Why don't we all go? David? See how the real Jo'burg shakes its arse?" Kendall was already up and ready to boogie the night away. David shook his head. "Thanks, but no thanks. Not tonight. I've had quite a day what with lost cousins and dead fathers. I'll walk you to the car. Is that okay, Suzie?"

"Yea, sure." She took her bag and found her car keys. Her tension was palatable. "Bye all. Henry? Teema? Thanks." She followed Kendall and Tina out to the front of the house.

David got up. "Don't do the plates without me. I'll be back in a minute," he said and also went out of the front door.

Henry had been looking at Teema closely throughout the meal, working things out in his head. Now that everyone was gone and he was alone with his mother, he could ask her. "You once wanted me to find you the phone number of a florist up in Pietersburg. I did, and you said it was for some friend. Do you remember?"

Teema was studying her fingernails carefully. She grunted. "Ja, I remember."

"You didn't by any chance arrange to have a rose placed on the grave of your dead *baas*?"

She looked up at him and nodded. "On the anniversary of poor Renate's death, a red rose is placed on the grave of her father. It's a standing order, paid for in advance. It's the least I can do on Dawid's behalf."

"But he doesn't even know," Henry sighed.

"Yes, and that makes it so right. His mother would approve. Madam would say: 'Isn't that nice …'"

Suzie's damn answering-machine was on every time David rang her the next morning, but he didn't feel like leaving a message so he just hung up. What could he say to her? She seemed far more interested in the charming terrorist the night before and didn't even give him a hug or handshake, before speeding off into the night after Kendall's BMW.

David got to the airport hours early. He didn't want to spoil the gentle hospitality he felt from Henry and Teema, and knew that another confrontation with Sizwe would only lead to terrible things being said.

He sat in the business-class lounge, sipping lukewarm black coffee and looking at the morning newspaper without reading. That dried-up rose! He knew it was Teema. When he saw that bleached-out florist's card with the curled up corners and could just make out the words: "In Memory of Renate and love to Ma and Pa, Dawid", he knew immediately who his guardian angel was. It had all been too easy, her pointing him in the direction of the place where his roots lay buried.

Teema obviously wanted to stay out of it, so he said nothing. He just held her tightly a little bit longer, smelling the combination of her soap and his Chanel No 5 in her hair, her clothes, her embrace.

"God, I love you, Gogo Masekela!" he said, and she laughed and laughed till he was gone. And then she cried.

CHAPTER 12.

Herman Greef was waiting for him at the Cape Town side of the two-hour flight. He looked thunderous and David immediately apologised for getting him out of his office on a weekday morning.

"Fuck the office, any excuse to leave that! Just keep your cool, old pal. We're in a war-zone here. The little black bastards threw stones at me on the way out! Hey you!" He called a porter and imperiously waved him towards David's virtually empty suitcases.

"There's nothing in them!" David said and pulled them away from the man.

"Let the bugger do his job, man! Shit, Dawid, don't be such a bleeding heart."

They walked to Herman's car, parked in an ambulance zone. There were no officials around, so he didn't have a ticket or a sarcastic reception committee. They drew off into the cluster of cars. "Fasten your seatbelt and hold this newspaper on your lap. When I say 'shield', put it in front of your face."

David laughed. "What is this? Some game?"

"Ja man, it's called Saving Your Life!"

David glanced down at the newspaper headlines in his hand, which screamed news of the recent attacks on cars on the N2 freeway between the city and the airport. The squatter empires of shacks and hovels were now flush with the national road, like naked rotting sores exposed to the shocked eyes of the sheltered citizens, racing by their local Bosnia with crossed fingers.

The day before a young coloured woman had lost the sight in one eye after a stone was thrown at her car. It smashed the windscreen and gouged into her face. The fact that she was still alive to tell the tale was a miracle.

"They've got soldiers patrolling the bridges and keeping a look-out, but shit man, look at their faces when we pass."

Herman kept a steady stream of bitter rage going as they joined a steady stream of cars braving the unknown on their way back to their homes and hotels.

When they reached one of the bridges that would take them across the freeway to join it on the other side, David looked carefully at the face of the soldier standing by the side of the railings. The helmet was like a huge space dish covering most of his face. His weapon was nearly as high as he was, reaching his ankles. David saw the soldier's face and his heart missed a beat. It had the look of a terrified child. "He can't be more than 16!" he said in amazement. "What about the professionals? Or don't they take chances in the field?"

Herman grunted with disgust. "Now tell me, if a gang of youths suddenly march down on that kid, what will he do? He's been told not to shoot blacks because it will start a race war. He has been trained to shoot enemies to end a real war. His survival instinct tells him to run! What does the boy do?"

David sat in thought as they drove past the murky rubbish heap that was called Crossroads. He saw feeble fires in among the huts, dark figures against the glare of the flames, huddled together for warmth, if not safety. "I'm glad I skipped the army," he said, "I could never be exposed to this and come out sane."

"I was, and I'm sane," said the uptight man at the wheel who was growing more unbalanced by the day. "Anyway I've got my gun, so fuck them all. I'll take any little bastard with me who wants to cause me trauma. Move your arse, you pathetic yellow-bellied fucks!" He screamed out of the window and hooted wildly at the slow-moving line of cars ahead.

"Calm down, Herman! You'll pick on the wrong type one day and they'll kick dents into your door."

Herman laughed with anticipated enjoyment. "Can't wait. Let them come!"

They got to his house in one piece and flopped down in front of the open fire, each with a drink in hand. Suddenly David was struck by the difference in the homes of his best friend and his dearest friend. Teema and Henry lived cramped and frugally, but with great enjoyment of every item in their cluttered house. Herman, on the other hand, had expensive decorations purchased by the yard, and the books in his shelves looked untouched by human hands. There was so much space around.

"What are you looking at?" Herman asked, catching him study the edges of the room with renewed interest.

"So fascinating to compare lifestyles," David answered, but Herman was not in the mood for that sort of comment.

"Oh excuse me, we've been in the Beverly Hills of Soweto! We've had a Damascus conversion in a township pothole! Please forgive me for forcing you to slum it. Don't be such a prick, Dawid. When push comes to shove, they'll come and cut your throat while you're still dreaming about your designer democracy."

"Not Teema and Henry."

"Then that other mad s*kollie*, what's his name?"

"Sizwe."

"Ja. He's got your number, my friend. He's got your number!"

The phone buzzed loudly. "It's okay, the machine's on."

"No, maybe it's Suzie. I don't want her to hang up." David got up and sprinted into the passage. He picked up the phone.

"Hi Suzie?" he answered cheerfully.

"No," said the soft voice at the other end of the call. "It's not Suzie, you two-timing shit. You said you weren't seeing her!"

"Oh Joanie! No, I was expecting Suzie to call with some information about …"

"Lies, De Lange, all lies! You think I can't see, but I can hear it in your voice. You didn't get nookie from that uptight Mother Teresa, so now you want to keep your options open and smooth things over for the next dirty weekend?"

"Not at all like that, Joanie. I stayed with Teema and Henry."

Joanie gave a knowing laugh. "Yea, and I'm still a virgin. So what did the nanny say to the presents?"

David sat down on the small stool next to the phone, put his feet up on the pile of *GQ* and *Tatler* magazines on the floor, and told her about the delight as Teema had unwrapped each present in chronological order. "She wore everything new she could at supper: the blouse, the coat, the perfume. She loves the perfume spray. Wants to use it as a traditional cultural weapon against *tsotsis*!"

"And you're best friends now?" Joanie had been drinking and slurred the occasional extra letter in some words.

"Yes. The very best of friends. So how've you been?"

His old flame gave a deep sigh and he heard the ice clink in her glass. "Where can I start. Do you want it in a nutshell, Dawid de Lange?"

"Okay, that's a good place to start."

"I'm a grandmother!"

David gave a whoop of delight. "Congratulations!" He heard a strange sound on the line, then a gasp. "What's wrong?"

Joanie was crying into the phone. "No, man, shit!" she sniffed. "I'm a fucking granny! I'm an *ouma* and I have no *oupa*! There's this new small thing with huge ears and a tuft of black hair and I'm blonde and Judy's blonde! What does that tell you?"

David knew where this was leading to. He smiled. "I have no idea, Joanie. You do have nice ears though, don't you?"

Joanie Craig wasn't going to let modesty ruin her self-pity.

"I have nice fucking everything, including a beautiful pearly white ivory skin complexion that has driven men and ad agencies berserk!" She blew her nose loudly and seemed to drop something. "Oh fuck, there goes my damn glass ... oh bugger it, who needs to get pissed?" A deep resigned sigh. "So I'm a granny, David, what do you say?"

"Congratulations," he said with a straight face. "How's the little mother getting on?"

"That slut? She gave a little dainty push and the little slippery thing pops out like a cork! Not may I tell you in the strictest confidence in any way like the hours, the days of suffering I went through giving birth to her! Jesus, you'd think there was some fairness in these natural things? She deserved to suffer! I suffered." She blew her nose again.

"David, do you think I was a good mother? Do you?"

"I'm sure you were," he said gently. "Judy's a lovely girl."

"Thanks. From you that means a lot." What did she mean by that? He didn't think a question was going to be answered right now. "Well," she kept on, "aren't you going to ask about the baby?"

Here it comes, he thought. "Tell me about the baby."

"A girl," she sniffed. "Small, sweet, smiling, all the parts working." She paused and he appreciated her sense of drama. Her voice went down a few tones. "And pitch fucking black! Not even a toenail to remind me of my Danish forefathers! I've been ethnically eliminated!"

He started laughing, trying to keep it from her, but she heard his quick breath and muffled snorts. "You're laughing at me, you blooming shit! Anglo-Saxon, WASP, Aryan, All-American shit! Wait till your daughter comes home with a Negro!"

He exploded with laughter, enjoying the tears running down his cheeks. Herman came into the passage with a refilled glass of whisky which he handed David. "Jesus man, what's your problem?" Herman said, annoyed that fun was happening out of his reach and understanding. It just made David laugh more.

"That's exactly what happened! My eldest daughter came home one day with a black man, a divorced black man who was a doctor and knew more about anything than Deli and myself put together. So there, what do you say to that, old granny?"

There was a pause as Joanie tried to get herself together in order to take in this new information. The wind was now out of Joanie's torn sails. She straightened her emotional bow above the high-water mark of hysteria. "Okay Mister Big Deal American! It's all very good and well for you to be tolerant, but that sort of reality is very new here. I certainly didn't plan to be in the forefront of pioneers in the field of interracial breeding! Usually when this happened in the not-so-distant past, someone had the decency to commit suicide, or leave the country, or even bribe a department for new papers and reclassification! The father wants pictures in the paper and he will because he's a dancer with the ballet company!" David heard her shudder audibly. "Oh, De Lange, I just don't know if I can ever go to the supermarket with a black grandchild! Really ..." She started another dry pre-weep wail.

David snuffed it in the bud. "Please don't start that howling again, Joanie, or else I'll just hang up on you! It's very boring." She stopped the sob in mid-breath and seemed to calm down. David spoke slowly and seriously. "Now listen carefully. This is how you can solve that problem at the supermarket. Are you listening?"

"Yes, yes ..." She was keen to be helped out of this black hole.

"Okay," said David, as yet no tongue visible in his cheek. "You can just say the baby's your black madam's child and that you're its nanny!"

"What?"

"I'll talk to you tomorrow. Go to bed and watch the news. You'll feel better about Judy's daughter. Night."

He replaced the phone and roared with laughter. Herman Greef was distinctly peeved when David joined him in the lounge.

"What was all that about?" Herman asked.

"Sadly you of all people wouldn't understand. Let's just say there is a God somewhere up there, and He or She has quite a sense of humour. Especially when it comes to us people."

"Us people?" The sneer was back on Herman's mouth.

"Yes, us South Africans. See, I can say it without turning into a pillar of salt. Us. We the crazy. We the mad. We the grotesque, and we the bad!" Herman sat back in his chair and looked at David over the rim of his glass dourly. "Oh, come on Greef, loosen up! You look as if the world has fallen on your teddy-bear."

Suddenly the images of two dead children shot through their bloody teddy-bears filled David's mind. He shuddered, drained his glass and stood up to pour another.

180

"Someone walk over your grave too?" smirked Herman Greef from his chair.

David stood looking at the perfect oil painting of a perfectly abstract image in the ornate frame in front of him. He still didn't know what it was meant to represent, as it left him cold and devoid of imagination. "I never told you what happened in the Transkei hotel on the Wild Coast? It's a very short story, so you won't need a long attention span."

So he quickly told Herman the sequence of events that led to the moment in the car park that morning, when all that was left of the end of four lives was a shoe, a blanket, a picture magazine, a half-eaten bar of chocolate and two tattered, blood-soaked teddy-bears. When he was finished the story, still staring at the painting throughout, David suddenly saw some design and image in the mess of colours and direction. "Yes," he said to himself, "of course, it looks like bullet holes …"

Herman got up unsteadily and put his glass down with a crash. David wheeled round in fright.

"Very moving little tale, De Lange. Glad it caught your eager tourist's eye. For us locals though, it's just another sad hard-luck story about a sad hard-luck nation. Too late for tears, alas, too late for tears." He carefully walked to the door, trying not to look too drunk and in the process coming across very pissed. At the door he stopped and turned. "De Lange?"

"Ja?"

"I've made an important decision today."

"Good, Herman. Welcome to the human race."

"I've decided to skip."

"Skip?" David turned to him with a grin. "As in hop, skip and jump?"

"No, as in 'goodbye'. I've got a job in Australia. I'm getting the fuck out of this country before it eats me too. Here." He threw a cushion at David. "Don't forget your teddy-bear!"

Herman Greef had been gluing his escape plans together in secret for some time. It usually took months, if not years to apply for jobs in countries like Australia. David later found out that Herman had been over to Sydney for an interview the year before. Whether he'd also managed to get his money out of South Africa in the process was something David rather left unquestioned.

Herman was a wealthy man in spite of his frugal tastes, other than his car and his tailor. He was also a single man, and not even a gay man. His restless search for the perfect negative in a mate had meant that he'd by now exhausted the small pool of eligible young brainless society daughters and rich-bitch widows. Herman would need a nanny and a maid who was the right colour, had the proper education and no opinions, just blind devotion. Those went out with the gold standard.

David tried to bring up the subject but Herman was seldom at home, constantly on the move either to his upmarket gym, or out to dinner, or 'important meetings'. More than often he just would leave the house without any word. Since the Soweto episode, Herman seemed to exclude David from his life completely. It was now possibly time for the guest to reconsider his plans.

"Frieda, I really think I'm going to go to a hotel for a few days somewhere in the mountains, just to find my sense of direction," he said after breakfast one morning, his Soweto sojourn now a secret in his heart and not something he wanted to alienate Frieda with.

"Aren't you feeling happy here, Master David?" she asked, a frown replacing the blank expression of boredom that Frieda always wore around the house like an apron. She shook her head knowingly. "It's that naughty Master Herman Greef, isn't it? Oh yes, always running around town looking for something that he won't even recognise if he falls over it! Here, you want some fresh coffee?"

David did and sat at the small kitchen table, sipping and fishing. Frieda, the eyes and ears of Herman Greef's world, was in a chatty mood, and this would be the ideal moment to fill in many empty spaces. "So what will you do when he goes?" David asked, assuming that Herman had mentioned his plans to hit the owlrun to his housekeeper. Herman hadn't and, of course, wouldn't. Probably leave her a sentimental note and a few hundred rand in exchange for a life spent in his service.

"Ag, I don't know," she sniffed. "When Master Herman goes, I'll probably go too." She cackled with delight. "But my dear, wouldn't it be funny if heaven was for whites only and I had to go to the backdoor?" She thought David had meant life after death, while he meant Australia, which some would say was the final proof that there was death after life!

David wasn't thinking that clearly, or he wouldn't have pursued the issue, but he did. "No, Frieda, when he goes to Australia? Surely you won't want to leave your family and go there with him?"

Frieda carried on doing what she did every morning, cleaning, wiping, repacking, straightening, not skipping a beat. "He'll never go anywhere, my Master Herman. No, man, he loves this place too much. He even said that come the big election, we could go and vote together for the same party." She smiled and the thought of her voting for the very party that kept her in a second-class position all her life only made David laugh.

"You wouldn't vote for the Nats would you, Frieda?"

She wagged a crooked finger at him. "Hey! Voting is secret! I don't tell anyone who I vote for, or they come and burn down my house and kill me! But between us, Master David, I wouldn't vote for that ANC lot if you paid me. At least with the boere I know where I stand."

David was again amazed by the passion. "But you've always had to stand while they sat, Frieda!"

"Just my good manners, Master David. Yes-no, I have respect for them and they have respect for me." Her face creased in distaste. "But Australia? No *sis* man, that's a place that really makes me nervous. All they seem to do is …" She stopped and tried to recall what information she'd stored up on that place where kangaroos and Crocodile Dundee came from.

There seemed nothing of note in her mind. "… hell, whatever they do is so boring no one talks about it. It's not the place for us. No, if Master Herman does have to go …" and her voice dropped a few octaves and became gravely and soft, "… that's to say, if this country goes to the dogs, the communists, and everything's on fire and those with British passports go back home." She looked over her shoulder in case someone was listening. "You know, there is over a million people here with British passports? They're the ones who kept apartheid in place, ask anyone."

David listened with a broad smile and nodded his intention to do just that. He wondered what Joanie Craig would say about this, let alone Suzie Bernard.

Frieda went on with her doomsday scenario. "When Durban is burning, and the city here is cut off from the world by crazy squatters drinking the blood of white women? Then Master Herman and me will pack up and go to Florida."

"Look at the news, Frieda! That already happens in Florida on a very hot day!" he joked seriously.

She shook her head forcefully. "Not on my TV it don't. No, I love the look of Florida. It's warm and full of people like those Golden

Girls and I'd like to work for nice ladies like that any day. That house could do with a char."

"Well," thought David, as he went back to his room, "she's not in the picture about Herman's plans, that's for sure."

He took down his suitcase from the top of the narrow cupboard and threw some of his clothes into it while wondering what to do.

A hotel? But for what? Maybe he should go back to Johannesburg and see what he could do about his friendship with Suzie. He also had so many other things to ask Teema. His flight back to the States was an open return, but maybe the time had come to pop into the travel agent and plan an escape back to the real world.

"Florida! Frieda and the Golden Girls?" he scoffed and opened the drawers to collect socks and T-shirts. In the mirror on the wall he saw Frieda in the door. She was holding some carefully-folded washing she'd done for him the day before. He turned to her. "Thanks Frieda, I would've gone without that." He took the washing from her. She didn't go away, stood staring at him with the little frown on her face. "I want to give you something extra for all the things you did for me, Frieda," David added quickly, but Frieda wasn't there to wait for her extra bit of money.

"Australia you say, Master David?" she said slowly.

"Yes, Frieda. I wasn't sure if Herman had told you, but obviously you know." He glanced at her and she nodded and turned, shuffling back to the kitchen.

He packed quickly, scribbled a note to Herman – "Found more windmills to charge. Will phone. De Lange" – and left it on the door of Herman's bedroom down the passage. He looked around the living-room for anything he'd left behind. The cold perfection of the space hadn't changed since his first sight of it.

What will Herman take with him? Or will he just fax his fashion to Australia and reorder the same design in Sydney and life would go on without a hitch? he mused, looking hopefully for the last time at this magazine-page living-room. He went down the passage to the kitchen, a bundle of notes rolled in his fist to say goodbye to Frieda.

At first he thought she was out walking Valkyrie and was just going to leave the money under her favourite teapot on the dresser when he heard a strange sound from the small pantry off the kitchen. He looked into it, then switched on the light.

Frieda was crouched in the corner of the small shelved room, half hidden by polishers and brooms and an ironing board. David stared

184

down at her shocked. It looked as if someone or something had taken Frieda's arms and legs and spine and neck and pride, and twisted each off at the joint. She was crumpled together like a discarded glove-puppet, a flat bundle of apron and jersey and shrivelled brown skin. The sobs coming from the heap was the only sign of some life, some pain, some existence.

He knelt down and took her bony hands in his. They were cold and lifeless. "Dear God, what is it, Frieda? Are you ill? Did you fall?"

The small face like a dried prune stared out at him from the wisps of hair. The spotless white cap she always wore hung on her head like a piece of shroud. "What will I do?" she whispered. "I've been here all my life, first with his parents ... now with him ... and truly, Master Herman is my life and ..."

David patted the parchment claws in his hand. "Frieda, I really have no idea what Master Herman's plans are. Really, I was just talking in theory, just to make conversation. There's no need to worry ..."

God, he sounded so white, so wealthy, so like the heartless person Suzie Bernard said she once was and ran away from.

"No," Frieda droned. "I know he's going to leave me ... I now remember all the things I didn't understand ... messages from travel agents ... going to Australia last year." She suddenly smiled and her eyes lit up like small fires. "He brought me a small bear ... a panda, who are always drunk on those leaves?"

"Eucalyptus leaves," David helped.

She nodded, "Ja, those leaves. Please tell me it's not true, Master David. Please swear to me on the Bible that Master Herman is not going to leave me to the blacks!"

David needed to stand. He had a cramp in his calf and her nails were digging into his hand. He tried to smile comfortingly, patting her and trying to unclasp her hold on him at the same time. "I swear, Frieda! Really, there's nothing to worry about..."

She looked at him intently, reading his mind, cursing his lies, seeing far beyond his immediate transparent concern.

"Your native nanny was also left behind when you ran away, hey Master David?" she hissed.

"Well, I didn't run ..."

"... But she's okay, because those blacks know how to accept those things. They're not like us. Not so sensitive, not to similar." She squeezed his hands intensely. "Master David? Master Herman and me think the same! Believe in the same God! Eat the same food!

185

We are like one … we are like a …" She searched for something in the alphabet to help her claim Master Herman for herself. David wondered what she would say? Son and mother? Husband and wife? Frieda gave a shuddering, deep sigh. "We are like master and maid, till death us do part!"

It was then that the bottle of wine rolled out from under her folded limbs and bumped against David's knee. It was virtually empty and he stood up quickly so that the remaining red wine didn't stain his trousers. Frieda glanced at the damning evidence and gave him a skew smile. "Just medicine, Master David, to cure a broken heart."

He was relieved that the trauma was so easily explained, but knew it went far deeper than the bottom of a bottle of wine. He helped Frieda to her feet. She'd lost all her fire and the once straight posture had been pushed into a round-shouldered hunch of defeat.

"Come, let me help you …" he coaxed.

"No man, I'm okay …" she feebly slurred.

"Come Frieda, or I'll pick you up and carry you!"

She gave a little hiccup and a burp. "Oops. Sorry darling!" she muttered, and he led her haltingly down the passage to the guest-bedroom he'd just vacated. He steered her to the bed and manoeuvred her into position, so that all he needed to do was give a gentle push and she'd lie down. When she was flat on her back, her head framed by the airy feather-pillow, she opened her eyes.

"Master David?" she over-enunciated, punctuated by hollow hiccups. "I don't usually let this happen. I don't ever have a drink in the morning, or at work. Oh no, never! But you must understand, my heart is broken …"

Her eyes closed and her words evaporated into a rusty snore. Valkyrie whined and pawed at the outside door, wanting to be part of all the fun. David collected his suitcase and left the house. The young gardener was still there, pruning bushes, raking leaves and showing no interest in anything else.

As he drove into the city, the perfect blue of the day framing the mountain like a velvet surround, David smiled imagining Herman's face when he got home that afternoon, as he tiptoed into the guest room and looked down at what he expected to be David Clayton!

Dawid de Lange on the other hand was now a free spirit. His world was in a suitcase, and that was in the boot of a hired car. He stopped at a coffee-shop on the promenade of the Sea Point beachfront and sat in the sun at a small table, lazily watching the waves curl foamily round the rocks on front of him.

Where would he go? What would he do? "Take stock, De Lange," he heard himself say. "Time to take stock of all the pieces. Fill in the empty spaces."

An elegant old lady at the table next to him smiled at him and nodded wisely. "Always a good idea, young man. Better late than never!"

He drove into the city and left the car in a vast parking garage on what was called Floor J. It took him what felt like countless twirls round and round the merry-go-round of the concrete centre before he found an empty place. Many of the cars round him had cracked front windscreens, dents in their bodywork, or vicious scratches along the side. "What's happened to the cars on J deck?" he asked the attendant in the lift.

"J deck? All decks! Another rain of rocks on the freeways into town today. Safer to sleep on the job and avoid the war-zones."

"You sleep in your lift?" David questioned.

"Only in the day, sir. Ground floor."

He'd go to the travel agent first and find a flight back to Los Angeles, maybe in a week. But when he reached the entrance hall of the building which housed the agency, he stopped. He stared at the marble floor. "No, not now," he thought. "I can phone later."

So he retraced his steps and then diverted into Adderley Street on the way to Joanie Craig's office. He'd pop in to see her and tease her a bit, maybe even take her to lunch. He bought some poppies from a flower-seller in the small street closed to traffic.

"For your lady friend, sir?" cackled the round crone with open pink mouth, not a tooth in sight. She winked a small eye at him, hemmed in by hills of rosy cheek and a bushy eyebrow.

"Just a friend who's a lady," he answered and marvelled at the buzztrack of conversation around him. These Cape Coloured people had the knack of cheering up anyone with their energy and humour. They argued and shouted at each other about anything, then dropped the roughness and sharp language to smooth the brows of potential customers.

The flower-lady handed him the bunch of delicate red and yellow poppies. "Here, sir, very nice, but they don't last. I'd rather get some of these roses." She caressed a few perfect red blooms, each still with diamond drops of dew artistically scattered.

"How long will the poppies last?" David asked, now a bit irritated that he was buying flowers seemingly past their prime.

"Oh no, long enough to get your way, sir. By the time you leave tomorrow morning, the first petal will only just decide to give up the ghost."

He laughed and shook the bunch gently. The petals were still firmly attached to their stems, their ghosts alive and well. "That's about right, thank you." He waved at her, leaving her the change.

She beamed. "God bless you, sir, and God save America!"

David forgot about his accent so often that he was always surprised when the people heard it first and took for granted he was an American. "Well hell, I suppose I am an American!" he thought. "An American by name, a Capetonian by nature?" He was so busy glancing at his reflection in the shop windows that he nearly tripped over the man lying on the pavement. "Jesus! I'm sorry! Are you okay?" he stumbled, regained his balance and turned to the man.

"Why don't you just jump on my chest and kick in my teeth?" the voice floated up to him, as his blind beggar-buddy righted himself.

David crouched down and gave him a hand. "Sorry! It's me. Do you recognise my voice?"

"No," said the blind man. "I recognise your aftershave. You're the American in Paris?" The sightless eyes went straight for David's soul. The man smiled. "Still hunting for those better days, my friend?" He patted the ground round him. "Are all my priceless wares still in place, or have you kicked my living into the gutter?"

David checked the array of useless bric-à-brac. "No, all the crown jewels are here."

"So where are you going in such a hurry? Coming from the scene of a crime, or on your way to commit it?" The brown hands fluttered over the cloth on the pavement, fingertips straightening pencils and hairclips into perfect order.

David stayed crouched, leaning against the wall of the bank's building. The passing parade of humanity were suddenly just their feet and ankles and trousers, or stockinged legs.

"I've been all over the place," he said. "Spent a few nights with friends in Soweto …"

The beggar whistled tunefully. "I'm so impressed. You even lived to tell the tale?"

"… I was in the Transkei; and Durban during an Inkatha march."

"Hell man, what stories of Dark Africa to tell the folks back home.

But how's your sex life, my man?" David laughed. "Oh, I see, it's like that, hey?"

"I was going to book a flight back to the States, but … well, something just said: don't do it yet. What's in the air?"

The beggar made a show of sniffing around. "Life?" Then he turned his head and again David felt he was being searched.

"Those cheap Iceland poppies really give me terrible hayfever, pal. Do you mind holding them in the other hand?"

"Sorry …" David got up, holding the flowers as far as he could away from the sitting figure. "Well, I'm off to my friend Joanie. She's just become a grandmother."

The coloured man just shook his head sadly. "God, man, you sound more boring every time I hear you. Loosen those ropes and breathe! I hope the granny gives you what you want!" he laughed and added. "Maybe she's also allergic to cheap flowers? Have you thought of that?"

David hadn't. He said his goodbye and quickly made his way to the elegant building one block further up the street. He took the lift up to Joanie's floor. Two women started sneezing while they all stood in the small travelling-box looking up at the flashing lights.

Joanie Craig wasn't in the office. Her secretary, someone David had not yet met, said she'd take a message. He gave her the flowers and she didn't look very pleased. As he left the office he heard her sneeze.

"What's this?" His blind friend grimaced and pushed David's hand away.

"I bought you a hamburger." David brought the packet closer to the man's nose.

He sniffed and took it hungrily. "Just what the doctor ordered. You didn't pick up a nice cold beer while you were about it?"

"No, I don't think they sell beers there. Sorry."

The blind man laughed. "Just joking. Love to hear whites say that word 'sorry', even though you're American. Don't stand in the way of the merchandise, man, you're bad for business."

David flattened himself against the wall. Not one of the passing parade showed any interest in the display on the pavement. David watched the beggar carefully. He was staring ahead at nothing in particular. Was he really blind?

"What you staring at?" he asked and David looked away.

"Not staring, just … hey, how did you know?" He looked again, but the man was still focused on nothing in the distance.

"I feel it, man. Sixth sense. You see, God was in a hell of a hurry when He made the blacks. Look how He fucked up their hair? So He gave them rhythm as compensation. Us coloureds. He gave humour. Me the blind get a sixth sense. I still don't know where the fourth and fifth senses are, but the sixth one always knows when someone is staring. Okay?"

David nodded. "I see."

"Ja, you see and I don't. Maybe I see more than you?" The blind man's fingers ran up and down on the tar in front of him, like tickling the keys of a piano.

"What do they call you?" asked David, feeling the time had come to personalise this casual acquaintance.

"What do they call me?" mused the man. "Oh, they call me ... let me see ... 'bastard', 'beggar', 'piece of shit', 'hey you', 'fuck off'! Sometimes they say 'boy', other times '*hotnot*'. Once someone called me 'darling', but I don't think she meant it properly. But I call myself Phillip. Like the Prince. Prince Phillip of the Pavement! That's my title. And you?"

"I'm David," he said, wondering if a shaking of hands wasn't too absurd.

"David what?"

"Oh, David Clayton."

"Mmmm," Phillip rolled the hamburger wrapping into a small ball and held it in the air. "Thanks for the snack, David *ou* pal. Now if you'll just drop the litter into a bin on your way back to your wherever you're going ... where are you going?"

David sighed and took the greasy paper. "I'm not sure. Maybe I'll go back to Jo'burg. I have some unfinished business there."

"Sex?"

"I suppose that's part of it, yes."

"Well, don't waste time here in the Cape, man. Here you don't get much sex. Just sympathy. Ask me." He patted David on the shoe as he walked past him down towards the car-park. He stopped at the traffic light and turned to look back at the Prince of the Pavement.

Phillip was still playing his concerto on the tar.

CHAPTER 13.

After David had unravelled his sense of direction round the core of the garage from J deck to street level, he just let the car go whichever way it liked.

He turned up towards the mountain and sailed along Long Street with all the green lights in his favour, then up Kloof Street, to the right up a steep turn, and found himself going towards the dip between Table Mountain and Lion's Head, known as Kloof Nek.

He'd once been to a wild party in a house just on the ridge of the Nek. As he drove past the elegant and done-up houses, all now hiding behind high whitewashed walls with names like 'Cote'zur' and 'Cul-de-Sac' glimmering above their gates in plastic brass letters, he tried to remember which house it had been, but his memory failed and time had changed anything he would've recalled.

"I don't smoke," he'd said then, when someone passed him the soggy roach. The smell of *dagga* was sharp and unpleasant and he had immediately started the evening with a blocked-up nose. Dawid de Lange wasn't often invited to parties because he wasn't that much fun to be with. Always sniffling, or cleaning his glasses, or not understanding the jokes.

He only grew up once he'd met Suzie Bernard and she demanded from him more than he could ever imagine. She expected him to stand up for what he wanted. This he didn't mind at first; it was just he wasn't sure what he was standing up for.

David drove through many areas of memory that day, past the beaches of Clifton where he would join his pals on Saturday afternoons to watch the bikini girls, and then have a bragging session over a cold beer at the old Clifton Hotel, now no longer there, as were most monuments to his past. So much had vanished, and yet he still saw trees where they as kids had *braaivleis* and played their guitars.

As with so many exiles, David's mental clock had stopped on the day he'd left South Africa, and everything he looked at was first filtered through that timewarp. The faces of his friends probably looked quite different to those he saw. His constant amazement at the fact that they hadn't changed that much, was a reflection of his own hope that he, Dawid de Lange, didn't look like the David Clayton who'd celebrated his fiftieth birthday in the shadow of the Hollywood sign barely six weeks ago.

The letters from Deli and the postcard from his daughters were still unopened and unread in his pocket where he'd put them on his arrival from Johannesburg. He'd enjoy them when he had a moment, which couldn't be found on this impulsive tour of the Cape Peninsula.

The sun had already gone away from Claremont when he drove down St Andrew's Road, past his old home – a FOR SALE sign was still there – and stopped at the home of Reverend Nkotse. He rang the doorbell a few times before he saw a movement through the small stained-glass window. The door opened slightly, protected by necklaces of chains.

"Hello, I hope you don't mind ..." But it wasn't the old priest. "Oh, is Reverend Nkotse at home?"

A thin black woman peered through at him, looked him up and down and then closed the door. He heard the chains clatter and bunch up on the other side. She opened the door again, this time wider. She didn't smile, just nodded gravely and invited him in without words.

David followed her into the sitting room, its wooden ceilings and countless paintings and books giving it a feel of a small village library.

"Look, if it's inconvenient ..." David started.

"The Reverend is in hospital," the woman said and stood with hands clasped in front of her. David waited for her to give him more information, but she just stared at him.

"Why?" he said eventually. "I mean, what happened? Is he ill?"

"He didn't go to hospital because he wanted to. Are you that David Clayton?" she asked.

"Yes," he said, feeling like a captured felon. "Did he leave a message? Could you tell me what happened?"

"You have a car?"

"Yes, I do."

"It is visiting time. I was going to take a bus, but if you come with me, I will take you up to see him. They won't let you in without me, so you might as well."

Without so much as a smile, she led him out of the house again, waited for him to leave, locked the front door, hid the key under a large garden gnome with a huge smile and a fishing rod in his hand and followed him to his car.

During the drive to the Groote Schuur Hospital the woman said nothing. David tried to start a conversation, but it didn't lead anywhere. Eventually he drew the car up at a petrol station. The young black attendant beamed him a smile.

"Hi! Fill her up and check the works." David handed him the keys, then turned to the stern black woman at his side. "I want you to tell me what happened. I want to know your name. You're in my car. Don't be so damn rude!"

The woman turned to him shocked, tears in her eyes. She shook her head and took a handkerchief carefully from her sleeve, wiped her eyes a few times and blew her nose.

"I'm not rude. I'm his sister."

David sat back deep in his seat with despair. "Oh God, I'm sorry … I didn't know he had a sister …"

"Yes, and I am she."

The woman sniffed a few times and carefully replaced the handkerchief back in her sleeve. She looked out of the window to what was happening in the busy workshop of the garage, and didn't look towards David once while she told him what had happened.

"There is a clinic in Langa …" she started.

"Yes, I know. I went there with your brother …"

"There is a clinic in Langa," she said again, "where my brother works for most of his day. There was a petrol bomb attack yesterday. Someone threw a burning bottle into the room from a passing car."

She now gave him a chance to say something, so he did. "Who were they? Was it political?"

"They could be anyone. We think though they were maybe right-wingers."

"Oh come on, who would do something like that?"

"They could be anyone," she repeated in monotone. "We think they were right-wingers." She said it all as if he hadn't heard her the first time.

He leant his head back against the seat-rest and closed his eyes. "And your brother?"

"You'll see when we get there. I don't know more than that. He was burnt."

"Badly burnt?" David looked round at her carefully. She was still

193

watching men change a tyre. "You'll see when we get there. I don't know more than that. He was burnt." She turned and looked at him, repeating the word slowly, pointedly, horribly. "Burnt ..."

They weren't allowed to see Reverend Nkotse, as he was still in intensive care.

"The doctors are with him, sir," a young black nurse said softly, her voice warm with compassion. "He's had a bad shock, of course, but we've seen worse."

His sister gave a snort. "You've seen nothing. I have seen them necklace a child for going to school!" She didn't look at either David or the nurse as she spat her words out. Her eyes were in a corner where a young man was sitting listlessly in a wheelchair. "And what's wrong with that white boy?" she rasped.

The nurse patted her on the shoulder. "He's also a victim of unprovoked violence. Wait here, I'll see if Doctor is finished."

"'Unprovoked violence!' Tell me, Mr Clayton, is there any other?"

"What is your name?" David liked this brittle woman, sister to a man so gentle he would've given his life to anyone who asked. These thugs just didn't think to ask, maybe that's why the Reverend Nkotse was still alive.

"I am Miss Nkotse of course," she said.

"Of course. Well, please call me David." She didn't reply.

They sat in the hallway on an uncomfortable makeshift bench. There was the usual activity, but whereas general wards had much more noise and bustle, here the staff glided by on soft feet without much sound. The bleeps of the life-support machines in the ward round the corner punctuated the eerie stillness, like the start of a rap-rhythm. For years David had been very scared of such places, where the façade of survival was stripped down to the essentials of life and death.

Did his mother die at home? Did his father die in a hospital? Was his sister already dead in the street?

He felt Miss Nkotse look at him and turned to her.

"Do these places make you nervous, Mr Clayton?" she said.

David shrugged. "I'm glad I'm visiting and not resident."

She nodded and folded her arms, leaning back against the shiny green and white wall and closed her eyes. David expected more of a conversation from her, but she added nothing.

Maybe his mother died alone at home?

Pills? Did she drink poison?

What did his father die of? Heart? Broken heart? Did Renate think

194

of him before she died? Did he, her brother so far away, sense that moment of her death, or weren't they so close?

"No, we weren't close," he said, and Miss Nkotse opened her eyes and turned to him.

"He gave the impression that you were a special friend," she said. David looked at her confused. "Who said that?"

"My brother."

"Oh, yes! No, we got on well. I liked him very much."

She closed her eyes again. "He's not dead yet, Mr Clayton."

And he wasn't.

After a hour which felt like all night, Miss Nkotse was called to come and see her brother. David stood up as well.

"Sorry, sir, family only," the nurse whispered.

Miss Nkotse took David's hand casually. "He's family to my brother. To me he's my driver for the night." She led the way, holding David's hand tightly and pulling him after her. They went into the ward. It looked like a set in a space-age horror film, with tubes and small lights and sounds coming from all sides. Reverend Nkotse was in the furthest bed set along a wall.

There was nothing about him that looked familiar. His face was solidly wrapped with bandages. Cotton-wool covered his eyes. There was a green cloth cap tried round his head. Just his hands were free and undamaged, and lay dislocated on the blue blanket.

"That's him, I suppose," David remarked and pointed at the black hands. Miss Nkotse stood next to the bed looking intently at the bundled figure of the patient, as if she was listening for something. She went closer, put her ear near the head of the victim. She seemed to nod and straightened up again.

"He's going to get better." She looked down at the motionless man and touched his hand, stroking it gently with the tips of her fingers. "He knows you're here and he's glad." She leant in towards her brother and whispered something, then turned to David. "Come. Can we go now?"

He drove her back to the little cottage in St Andrew's Road.

"Will you come in?" she asked rather surprisingly, as he opened the car door for her to get out.

"It's rather late," he said. "Thanks anyway. I have to find a hotel for tonight."

"This is it," she said without a smile. "You'll stay in the guest-room. My brother wanted it like that. You have a bag?"

"Eh … in the back," he stuttered.

195

"Well then, don't dawdle. I'll put on water for tea." And she was gone, up the small pathway lined with shrubs and the odd ghastly, grinning garden statue.

When David put his case down in the narrow hallway, she came out of the living room with a bottle of jam. "Could you open this? My hands ..." He then noticed the badly scarred hands that she successfully managed to hide. He opened the jar easily and handed it to her. "Your room is just off there to your right. Clean sheets, towels, electric blanket and two cats. Are you allergic?"

"No, I like cats."

"Not that it matters. They live here; you don't. Tea will be ready in ten minutes. I'll make you a light meal. Have you eaten?"

"No, I haven't ..." he stammered.

"Doesn't matter, it'll be there anyway." And then she was gone, leaving David in monosyllabic confusion. Why did this woman make him behave like a naughty schoolboy?

The guest-room was small, warm and smelt of lavender, with a whiff of cat food. The two huge furry aunties were sprawled across the bed, chewing away at the memories of a dinner already enjoyed, licking their chops with long thin pink tongues. They opened an eye to check him out and then ignored him. "Sorry to wake you," he whispered and tiptoed out into the passage.

Miss Nkotse had laid a charming little feast on the narrow dining-table set in an alcove next to the kitchen. David suddenly felt very hungry, having last eaten that morning when he'd had his coffee with Frieda. The Reverend's stern sister watched him eat.

"You were hungry," she said.

"Yes," he laughed. "I'm always hungry. And I don't pick up weight either. The best and worst of both worlds."

She leant her face on her palms, her elbows on the table and smiled. Her face changed from its severity instantly to a beautiful expression of happiness. She looked years younger. David even stopped eating in his surprise. "I am glad to see that! You have a beautiful smile," he said politely.

She actually laughed. "Yes, that's why I keep it for only special occasions. In my work smiles don't help that much."

Miss Nkotse was a senior lecturer at a predominantly black college outside Johannesburg. She then told David how the structures of the education system were being softened and eventually dissolved by political currents and a jostling for power among students and teachers alike.

"What do you teach?" David eventually asked, pushing his plate aside.

"I'm in the philosophy department," she said, smiling again at his startled expression. "You look unnecessarily impressed, or don't you know many blacks who do things other than clean and sweep and pray?"

"No," David knew he deserved that. "I do have many black friends in the States who can teach me a thing or two."

"So can I."

They spent a timeless late night round that narrow table, sharing experiences in their work, in their countries and in their relationships with family and friends.

Eventually they both seemed to pause for breath. Miss Nkotse, who never told him her first name and he didn't ask, tapped against her cup lightly with the dainty teaspoon. The tea was cold now. It was time to call it a day.

"I've not have such a relaxed chat with anyone since arriving here," David eventually said. "Usually one's conversation is guarded and soaked with the inflammables of local politics."

"Funny you should say that, Mr Clayton. I do very little social intercourse, to coin a phrase. I am also hemmed in by what is becoming 'politically correct'." She shrugged. "It is hard to reinvent one's passions. All my life under apartheid I was 'politically incorrect' because the System was the target. Now ironically, as a teacher, I've become part of the System and find my mild criticism of the developing alternative hierarchy not a welcome democratic right. I don't know if I can cut my old foot to fit the new shoe."

He helped her carry the plates and teacups to the kitchen. "Leave them for the maid," she said, covering the heap of crockery with a dishcloth. He wasn't sure if she was joking, so he laughed and left the kitchen.

Outside the door of his room he stopped and turned to her. "I must ask you something … no, a few things, but there is no time. Did you always want to do what you're doing? I mean, where did you study? I mean …"

"You mean, how could I become what I am in this country?"

He nodded sheepishly. "Yes. I'm sorry, it's still so hard to find ordinary words to use in extraordinary questions. Yes, how could you become a senior lecturer in philosophy?"

She straightened a small painting on the wall, ran her finger along the top of the frame, glared at the dust on her finger and muttered: "That girl really doesn't do her job." So there was a maid! She turned to him. "Mr Clayton, it's not so complicated, you know. I always had an advantage on most because my parents were educated and sophisticated. They were exceptional people who didn't allow the degradation politics to cloud their horizons. My brother and I are products of that discipline. But I worked as a nanny for ten years before I could afford to go to a real college." She looked up at him from under her lids, a skew smile on her face, expecting him to answer.

"I can scarcely believe it!" he said, shaking his head.

"Oh yes, in the fifties. I still think back with great affection to those days, and to those children I taught to speak Xhosa, and the Afrikaans they taught me. I was part of their family."

"Do you still keep in touch?" he asked, fascinated by the images of another man's Teema.

"I don't have time to baby-sit anymore, but yes, I'm an honorary grandmother to all their children now. Christmas cards, birthday wishes, you know, the usual. I've even had the extraordinary request to educate them about future choices in an election, inform them of parties that are not predominantly white. So, maybe those years as a *kaffirmeidjie* didn't do any of us too much harm?"

David turned round in the passage, smacking his head with his hand. "Dear God, I'll never be able to make sense of this country! It should be so simple! First the good guys are in jail, the bad guys in power; now a good thing like democracy lies ahead and no one is separated by religious barriers like Israel, or … or …"

"Or ethnic chaos like Bosnia?" she added.

"I don't know. Who can compare anything nowadays? I just know that for every time I feel I understand what's developing here, something happens to make me have to start again from scratch."

"Good!" She held out her hand. "At least it shows we're not stagnating, wouldn't you say? Goodnight, Mr Clayton." He took her hand. The roughness of the skin made him look down. The scarred skin shone in the light. He pulled his hand away too quickly.

"Don't be scared, it's not catching," she said, looking at her right hand as if admiring a new ring. "It still works, still can write, still can open and close. I'm a lucky person."

"My God, what happened?" He'd forgotten about the hands he'd noticed earlier.

She took a deep breath, held it for a moment and let it out in a hiss. "About four years ago, I was woken late at night by one of my students. He told me there was a People's Court in progress, you know what that is?"

He nodded. "Kangaroo court."

"No, a 'kangaroo court' is what our people still call the official supposedly legitimate legal system. No, People's Courts are in concept very effective, but in reality utterly brutal. It seems that another senior student of mine was being tried for so-called 'crimes against the Struggle'."

"Being a collaborator?" David asked.

"You would call him that if you were a young black comrade without education. The boy was studying for a degree. That was his collaboration. I was too late."

David lifted a hand to stop her. "Wait a minute, too late for what? The verdict?"

"No, to save his life. They'd already had the trial that morning. He'd been found guilty of whatever it was he stood accused of. Condemned to death. His ... judges then let him go to his classes and make his farewells. And then they fetched him at midnight. And killed him ... executed him."

"Why didn't he go to the police?"

"And say what? 'Look after me, my own people are going to kill me?' Mr Clayton, there could be people queuing up a mile long at every police station with the same problem."

David took her hand again, this time gently holding it in his palm and studying the healed skin carefully. "This is a burn ..."

"Yes. He was necklaced. We're now exporting it to other flashpoints all over the world, I read." She turned to look at the painting on the wall, a peaceful landscape with what could have been Table Mountain far in the distance. "Let me just get the correct order of things ... they put a tyre round the boy's neck ... the tyre was filled with petrol. Then ... then they offered him a cigarette, you know, a final smoke, like in the films. He didn't smoke, but it was not an ordinary one. It was *dagga* ... marijuana ... He hoped it would ... help him. So he lit his own death warrant. The petrol exploded."

"Jesus!"

"That's when I rather impulsively intervened. I didn't think of pain; I tried to pull the tyre from the boy's neck ... but it had already melted into his body." She turned her hand in his and held him hard. "I now have a permanent reminder of my own frailty."

"What could you have done?"

"What could I have done? Well, I could've found and put on my glasses earlier so that I could see better where to run. I could've worn proper shoes so that I could've run faster than on bare feet. If I'd done those things, I would've got there in time. I could've saved his life!"

"They would've killed you too."

"No," she sighed. "I don't think so. You see when I got there, all I could hear them say were the words 'Dr Nkotse this' and 'Miss Nkotse that'. The same voices I hear in class, not the curses of murderers and terrorists. Just my boys misbehaving and saying to Teacher they didn't mean it …" She took her hand from his and turned, slowly walking away. "Good night, my friend."

And she was gone, up the passage and into another reality, leaving David with the lavender smell, the two purring cats and an icy terror in the pit of his gut.

Less than ten hours later he was in an aeroplane on his way to Johannesburg because of a sudden emergency. He'd been woken quite early by the two cats who ganged up during the night and both settled snugly on his chest, paws folded under their voluptuous bodies. When he opened his eyes to their combined purring, it was like being in the middle of a growling earthquake. He thought he'd had a stroke.

"Jesus, I can't move, I can't breathe … this weight on me …"

It wasn't until he opened an eye that he looked straight into the yellow fires of the two aunties.

"Meow?" said the grey one, not expecting an answer. The hefty marmalade gave a huge yawn and her bad breath nearly put David back into a coma. Carefully he wiggled out from under the cats, slipped on his clothes and tiptoed out of the room. Miss Nkotse was talking quietly on the phone. She waved at him and he waved back. When she finished her call, she smiled at him. "Good news, Mr Clayton. My devout brother's conscious and remembers us being there last night."

"How on earth would he know that?" David asked, pleased and impressed.

"Nothing to do with earth. His hotline to you-know-where!" the Reverend's sister irreverently suggested and vanished into the living-room.

"May I use the phone?" he called and she said something that sounded in agreement. He phoned Suzie Bernard, ready with his scathing message for her answering machine. But it was not a machine that spat down the phone at him.

"What the hell are you playing at!" she hissed.

"Hang on, can't we start with 'hello'?" he said, taken aback.

"No! I phone Herman Greef and all I get from him is a wild panic that you've gone mad, and that you left a strange note and probably committed suicide! He's frantic with worry. His servant says you drank a whole bottle of wine out in the morning and told her not to even make your bed."

"Frieda has a wild imagination and probably a huge, well-deserved hangover," he chuckled.

"I'm glad you think it's all so funny. What is it with you, De Lange? You keep leaving little notes to the people who love you and then run away. It's become a lifetime habit, it seems?"

"I didn't run away. I'm here with friends ..."

"Oh, well just warn them to keep their eyes open for your farewell note!"

An icy pause on the phone helped them both take a breath.

"Say hello, Suzie?" he said softly.

She gave a huff on the other side. "Hello, you shit."

He laughed. "That's the girl I've missed. What's happened to your infernal machine? On strike, or just a usual stayaway?"

"Don't make jokes, Dawid. I tried to get hold of you last night ..."

"I wasn't at Herman's last night ..."

"Jesus, you're telling me?" She flared up again. "That man's a basket-case. I've never known such delusions, such paranoia. Oh yes, he's going to emigrate to Australia, did he tell you?"

"Yes, but ...

"Fuck him!" She had never liked Herman Greef, right way back to the run-up to the matric dance when he took bets that he'd screw her before the term was over. He did, of course, and she resented that ever since. He never came back for seconds. "Dawid, are you listening?"

"Yes, Suzie, I'm listening!" His obviously raised voice had brought Miss Nkotse and a fascinated maid from the kitchen.

They stood watching him, wondering if anything was wrong. He shook his head at them and mouthed that it was 'nothing!' They went away.

"Are you there, De Lange?"

"Yes, I'm here. God, you don't need a phone, Suzie, we can all hear you easily. Calm down and don't shout!"

She dropped her volume so low he could now scarcely hear her. "Teema phoned me yesterday. Sizwe has vanished."

David closed his eyes and sighed. The least of his worries for sure. "And?"

"And she's desperate! She wants you to phone her."

"Suzie, Sizwe is a loose cannon! He's an unguided missile searching for a target! And what does Teema mean, vanished? Was he ever in that house for more than a few hours?" David resented Suzie's fascination with Henry's son.

"David, don't be such a …"

"A what? A racist?" he snapped back and felt his face warm with anger.

"No, not racist. I was going to say *poep*. Don't be such a *poep*."

If there was one word in the languages of all civilisation guaranteed to bring a smile to the face of the most unamused, it was that Afrikaans word '*poep*'. The English word 'fart' never raised a crease, but '*poep*' just made David burst out laughing wherever he was. He laughed.

"Good," she said happily. "I can see that smile. Teema said please ring her. It's not just Sizwe. It seems Henry's going to look for him."

"Oh God, Sizwe's a grown man!"

"Yes, and Henry's got a heart problem."

"Since when?" David asked, irritated that Suzie suddenly seemed to know all the personal details about his nanny's family. After all, Teema was *his* nanny!

"Since always. You don't know everything yet, 'Master Dawid'. Get on the line to the nanny and help her! She's upset!" He sighed, seeing his dreams of spending a day on the magnificent Stellenbosch wine route vanish like mist before the sun.

"Should I come up to Jo'burg, Suzie?" He suddenly knew he would.

"Does that mean another of your notes on the lavvy door for the friends who put you up last night?" she asked cattily.

"I'll get a plane as soon as I can," he said ignoring her sarcasm. "Where will you be?"

"I'll be where I'm always on a Thursday morning," she said in a matter-of-fact way.

"How do I get hold of you at that bloody organisation?"

"No, I'm not at work today, Dawid. I'll be at the …" He expected her to say meeting, press conference, Supreme Court, certainly not the "… hairdresser".

He had to listen carefully, thinking that he must've missed something. "Hairdresser? Who? You?"

Her sensible short curls defied any structure or style.

"Yes," she said enjoying her demureness. "I have a feeling an old flame might want to take me to dinner tonight?"

"You do, do you?" He felt a tug of excitement.

"He said he'll pick me up at my flat at 8.00."

"He did, did he?"

"Yes, but then he's not a *poep* like you." She hung up and David laughed again.

"That's nice. You should do that more often," Miss Nkotse said in the hallway, putting a scarf round her head as she prepared to leave.

"Laugh?" He nodded ruefully. "Yes, we all should ... where are you off to?"

"Church. I'd said I'd lend a hand. It's Thursday morning." David nodded, pretending to know the significance. "Stay as long as you like. Goodbye." And she was gone, leaving David awkwardly silent.

Only after she'd vanished up the street, did he think of all the admiring things he wanted to say to her. So he patted the cats, loaded his case and went off to the airport. And left a note for Miss Nkotse on the bathroom door.

CHAPTER 14.

"Teema? It's me!" He pushed the extra coins into the telephone so they wouldn't be cut off.

"Where are you, my boy?" She sounded flustered and out of breath.

"I've just got to Jo'burg Airport. I'm at the car-hire office."

"Dawid, can you come to me?" It was more like an order.

"How do I get to your house in that rabbit warren?" He had no idea where in Soweto Henry lived, or how to get there.

"Which hotel are you staying at?" she asked wearily. He wasn't, but Suzie's apartment was no place to start a wild goose chase after a terrorist with one eye.

"The Carlton." He chose obviously, knowing its ideal setting.

"I'll meet you there at midday. In the foyer. Please, Dawid, be there."

"I'll be there."

She was on time. He was reading the paper in the coffee-shop when he saw Teema come into the foyer from the street. She was wearing a hat and gloves, like a dowager on her way to an investiture. He went up to her and hugged her. She seemed to relax in his embrace. He noticed she was trembling.

"Want some coffee?" he asked.

"Yes. And some chocolate cake. It's good here."

The twinkle in her bloodshot eyes lifted the gloom slightly. He ordered from a waiter and they sat round a small table near to the window, which looked out over the inner courtyard and its waterfall. Teema wasted no time, not even to take off her gloves before she started.

"Let me put you in the picture. My son has a heart problem."

"I didn't know ..."

"No, that's one of the reasons he's still alive. He won't tolerate any pity, or compromise. He goes for check-ups and they say a pacemaker is the answer. Like mine. But he's stubborn and won't take off from school."

"You have a pacemaker?" he asked looking for any signs of illness.

"Yes, didn't you know? You broke my heart when you ran away. I needed a new engine." The coffee and her cake arrived and was elegantly set down. Teema immediately picked up her fork and carved off a large piece of cake. "Here. You like the icing." She held her hand under the full fork to catch any falling crumbs.

He looked around self-consciously. "I don't …"

"Come my boy, your mother's not here to see you."

Like way back then when she always kept him the bowl in which the chocolate icing had been, often just a thick crust around the top which he could glide off onto his finger. Now she watched him enjoy the cake as always.

"Nice?" she asked.

"Mmmmm," he mmm'd as always.

Teema took off her gloves and stroked them flat on the table. "Sizwe is … I don't know if there is a word. He's not crazy. He's not shell-shocked. He's just maybe too bright for that dull mantle of 'veteran' the Struggle has thrown over him." She seemed to settle into her chair with relief now that at last she could speak to someone about her grandson.

"He's a restless spirit, Teema. I could see it when I met him." David had so many other things he wanted to discuss with Teema. Now this irritating grandson came between them.

She shook her head. "You see, he's too old to join the youth gangs in the townships. He's from another generation. He feels he should be up there in Shell House with the other young leaders, not down on grassroots level. The kids don't understand what he's talking about. He calls himself a hero, a returning veteran from the war; they call him 'bandit'. They say he ran away, while they stayed and fought. That he can't understand …"

"Sounds a bit like the Vietnam War syndrome in the States."

She sat, prodding the piece of cake with her fork, looking for words. "I … I overhear things. I learnt many years ago to pretend to be deaf when other people talk."

"You mean at our house?" The scene around their dinner-table was clear in David's mind.

"I would serve the meal and your parents would be talking about me as if I wasn't there. At first I found it very frightening. I thought I was maybe transparent, but then I got used to it and quite enjoyed playing the maid."

"I know. I'd watch you."

"Yes, and because you were watching I gave a better show!" She patted his hand. "Anyway, Sizwe talks on the phone for hours. To … I don't know whom. There is talk of the Midlands, other places in Natal." She took a deep breath. "I think he's gone to Natal!"

205

Natal? David had to rack his brain to find the significance of Natal. To him Natal meant white beaches, hot sun and race tracks.

"There's a civil war going on in Natal, Dawid, in case you hadn't heard," Teema filled in his blank expression coldly.

"Yes, I have heard about the violence! I'm not that far behind! But there are also other things happening in Natal. Maybe he's found a job? Maybe he's found a girl?"

"Yes, I also said so to Henry, but my son is convinced Sizwe has become a mercenary in Natal. And he wants to go and fetch him. Like some great Hollywood hero. And his heart won't take it, Dawid, he'll …" Teema suddenly covered her face with her hands and started crying bitterly. The teaspoon clattered to the floor. This was not a soft weep of sorrow; this was a harsh wail of frustration. People sitting round them took note, but pretended not to notice.

David tried to comfort her. "Teema, don't cry. I hate it when you cry." He swallowed hard at the emotion in his throat. Teema sniffed and tried to control her tears. She wiped her cheeks, looking at him with waterlogged eyes.

"I never cried in those days …"

"Yes, you did. You cried. I heard you cry."

She looked down at her coffee and took a sip. "I don't remember crying. I was happy there." She said it without joy.

The waiter topped up their cups with fresh coffee. David leant over and picked chocolate crumbs off Teema's cake plate.

"So what do you want me to do, Teema?" he said.

She took his hand and held it tightly, her way of making him know how important it was to her. "You can't stop Henry from going. He won't even listen to me. He said he lost Sizwe once and he will not lose him again."

"Then what can I do, other than tie him up and lock the door?"

"Go with him."

David stopped picking crumbs and looked at her startled. "Me? Go into that Beirut situation? Me a white man, with a black man? With a Xhosa into Zulu country? In search of a psychopath! Teema, please, this is not fucking Disneyland!" He immediately regretted using bad language with her.

"Psychopath?" She breathed out the word slowly and closed her eyes. Spare tears rolled down her face. "That's the word I've been looking for. That's the word that describes Sizwe. It's not a good word, is it Dawid?"

He looked at her for a moment. "No, Teema, it's not a good word."

She leant towards him passionately. "All the more reason for you to go with Henry! It won't take long. Henry has a cousin there. Some good friends. Kendall will come too."

David groaned. "God, that's all I need. A *GQ* pin-up in Gucci camouflage and hair gel!"

"He loves his brother!" Suddenly the elderly woman in front of him seemed to tire. She sat, eyes tightly closed, fists clenched and breathing shallow gasps. It sounded as if she'd been running.

David leant forward. "What's wrong, Teema?"

She shook her head, but kept the strange rhythm of breathing, her large body moving with each gasp. David looked around for a waiter, wanting to get her a glass of water, but as always when one was needed, there were no waiters to be seen.

"Do you need some water?" he asked again.

She took a sharp intake of breath and opened her eyes. A sweet smile instantly plastered itself on her sallow expression. "I'm fine, my dear. Just a small unrest-related incident deep down inside my heart." She lifted her eyebrows at him. "And don't try and change the subject. My broken heart is all your fault! If you'd not just left us that note, Dawid, but phoned from the airport?"

"I went by boat, remember?"

"No, I didn't know that." She thought about it for a moment.

"Well, it would've been easier to phone from the boat. At least you're still on earth."

"In the sea, Teema."

"Ja ja, but not up in the air!"

The logic of it all defied him, but it all helped to divert his attention from her discomfort. The last person Teema wanted to frighten away was Dawid. No one knew about her heart condition, not even her son Henry whose heart was fine. Teema had never had much trouble fabricating a drama round a fragile storyline.

"One more thing, Dawid?"

He smiled knowing it wasn't just one. "Henry must not know that we met here today, or that I told you about his heart."

"You mean, it might kill him?" David teased her gently.

"Don't make jokes, my child. Henry is a proud man and if anyone knew about his heart, he would lose his job and his pension."

"And the house?"

"No, the house is ours." She looked deep into his smiling eyes. "Are you taking all this seriously?" she asked.

"Yes. I'll do whatever you say. I owe you one."

"No, Dawid, you help me only for one reason."

They looked at each. Then he spoke softly. "Because I love you."

She beamed, digging her nails deeper into the palms of her hands to avoid any sign of pain flashing across her face.

He rang Suzie's buzzer three times. There was no answer. He smiled at the security guard who watched him impassively. The huge black dog at his side didn't take his eyes off David either.

"I have a date ..." he said nervously. "Miss Bernard. We were at school together."

The security guard didn't understand a word he said. The man was an illegal alien in the country, working in a job that only needed experience. He'd spent his young adult life fighting in Mozambique. Now he brought his bush-war expertise into Johannesburg's premier suburb.

David pressed the buzzer once more.

Suzie's breathless voice filled the foyer. "Yes, De Lange! Shit, I'm sorry I was on the phone, I didn't hear ... come in. Seventh floor!" The door clicked open and David entered.

"Jesus!" was the first thing he said as Suzie opened the door. He scarcely recognised her. She'd changed her hairstyle. It was curled and fluffed and looked longer and thicker and ...

"You've dyed your hair!" he said. She just smiled and twirled round in the hallway. The soft silk of her colourful dress lifted gently in the turn. "That's great!" David said and clapped his hands. "What's happened, Suzie Bernard? Did you get a raise?"

She stopped in her tracks and pulled a face. "A raise? From the ANC? You could rather ask: did we 'demand donations' from the top couturier?"

"Did you?"

"Actually, yes." They laughed. She told him about a good friend who had gone into business with his sister and together had conquered the world of Johannesburg fashion. "This is one of his. It's really not the uniform I care to be seen in. Our look is more one of The People. Jeans and T-shirt."

"The right T-shirt!" he accentuated.

"No, the left T-shirt! Come, there's more."

She led him into her flat. It was in a modern building and there were many huge windows hidden by soft drapes. The floors were thickly carpeted, but it was the abundance of African art that gave

208

Suzie's home its atmosphere. Carvings and woven cloth, shiny black wooden totems and golden yellow figures in embrace. Mother with child, buck in motion, elephants caught in the stare of surprise. "It's a bit like a curio shop," she said half apologetically. It did and yet there was nothing contrived about it.

David whistled his appreciation. "Can I pick one up?" She nodded, pleased at his enjoyment of her great love. "Look at this expression ..." he murmured, studying the soft lines on the carved face of a young woman, eyes closed and head tilted to one side.

Suzie lifted what looked like a block of wood and held it out to him. He put the face down and looked down at what she held. In the core of the wood he saw a cluster of carefully carved and shaped figures, a family in repose. He saw each face, each expression. There was laughter and enjoyment and happiness.

"It's my absolute favourite ..." Then she added quickly, "... Today. Every piece gets its special attention."

David smiled and looked around the big living-room, feeling the warmth of the wood and Suzie's affection all around him.

"This must've taken a lifetime to collect," he said.

She shrugged. "Yes, well, isn't that what we've already had?"

He looked at her, trying to push the young Suzie out of his mind and focus on this mature woman in front of him, but they merged. "I still see the girl I loved. Do you have a portrait up in the attic that's a hundred years old now?"

She laughed, also remembering the *Portrait of Dorian Gray* by Oscar Wilde, which they were reading together to help her with her studies. "Yes. But it's in my passport!"

She led him into the dining-room. The curtains were drawn aside and the lights of Johannesburg lay like unclaimed gems in the velvet darkness. The room was only lit with a mass of small candles. The table was set for two.

"You cooked?" He couldn't believe his eyes. Suzie Bernard, the last of the great fast food junkies. She stood behind a chair awkwardly, nodding and looking at her handiwork.

"Yes, it's nothing special. Actually it's been delivered by the ...

"Don't tell me! I want to believe you did it all!"

"Like my hair and my dress and the make-up and the waxed legs and the condom next to the bed?"

"You did all that?"

She nodded. She was blushing. It delighted David even more.

"All that for me?" he asked.

She bit her bottom lip apologetically. "Oh no, I forgot to tell you. Nelson Mandela's coming to dinner!"

Happily he didn't. The two friends could spend their first real evening together, talking about trite and meaningless things like the incidents from their past they both recalled so clearly. They could indulge in that international hobby of all school friends, meeting after decades and wondering "whatever happened to whatsis name?" And this time there were no other people to take into account; no strangers, no aliens who hadn't shared in that blessed period of what in soft candlelight and with cold wine, seemed to be the most perfect childhood in the world.

"We were lucky, you know," Suzie eventually said, playing with her heavy crystal glass that reflected a million candles on each surface. "Growing up in the Cape with all that beauty, all the fresh air, all the best of a very private world."

"A very white private world," David added and was instantly sorry. Neither of them wanted to drag the barricade of politics over their daisy-lined pathway, but she nodded.

"Yes. That is terrible. And the fact that it took me so many years before I became aware of blacks as people and not just objects appals me. So I'm doing penance. It's a just punishment."

"Punishment? Don't you enjoy your work?"

She dipped her finger into the wine and then put it in her mouth, tasting the icy sharpness of the vineyard. "I enjoy doing what I do well. I enjoy doing something that is helping towards a future that just has to work, Dawid! If we fuck up on this gift of democracy, we'll never be able to dig it out from the smouldering ruins of society. But …" She picked up her glass. "… it doesn't help being white, or a woman. Our day is over, my boy. We've had the silver chalice for too long. It's time to pass it on to someone else."

"What will they do with our silver chalice?"

"If they're clever, they'll melt it down and buy a decent education. I'm just afraid they'll wipe it clean quickly, to get rid of all our bloody fingerprints and then just refill it with the nectar of absolute power. The King is dead; long live the King!"

They clinked their glasses together and the bell-like chime filled the room. The meal had been delicious. Whether she'd actually cooked it herself, he wasn't prepared to ask.

"Delicious meal. You'll make someone a very good …"

"A very good what? Nanny?"

"Yes." So they drank to nannies, past and future.

Kendall insisted on driving down to Natal in his car. Henry was sitting in front with his son. Kendall had a 'latest hits' rap cassette in his player and the inane rhythm from the rear speakers thudded into David's back through the seat.

Only three city blocks into the seven-hour trip, Henry turned to Kendall, exasperated.

"For God's sake, Kendall, switch that crap off!"

"It is the latest, Dad!" wailed the big baby and swerved to avoid a crowd of school-children getting off a bus. David just closed his eyes and pretended he was still with Suzie.

"Are you okay back there, my man?" called Kendall. David gave him a thumbs-up, keeping his eyes closed. Yes, it would be nice being back with Suzie Bernard.

"I haven't had sex for a long time …" she whispered into his ear.

"Me neither," he answered and they kissed again. He was careful not to weigh down on her, balancing his weight with his elbows. Her body was soft and warm under his. He felt her softness embrace his erection deep inside her.

"But you're married?"

"So were you …"

They left the past and concentrated on the present. The years had changed nothing in their enjoyment of each other. David now at last knew what to do with a woman in bed. Suzie, after three auditions, had found the right man to do it with.

They made love for a long time, losing themselves in passion and murmuring words at each other as they climaxed, separately and then together. They lay comfortably naked, uncovered by sheets and tracing along the details of their bodies with hands, with fingers, with tongues. Somewhere before the sun rose she got up and brought them each a mug of tea. They didn't say much, just sat together on the huge bed and felt the contentment of company.

"Not too sweet?" she asked.

"You or the tea?"

"Both."

She was sweet. He always knew that. It was the other Suzie he still had to get to know. Suzie Bernard, the hard-arsed survivor, the battle-scarred winner, the bitch. There was no sign of that creature around them that night.

"How long will you be gone?" she eventually asked.

"I hope not for more than a few days. How long can it take to find a missing person?"

She took the cup from him – it said 'Welcome to Disneyland' – and put it on the tray on the carpet. She snuggled back into his embrace. "I don't want to spoil your dreams, Dawid, but there are more than enough hospitals, mortuaries and police cells to search. It could take a few months."

"God, I hope not!" He'd not thought of that and was horrified at the idea. "He's just got to be alive!"

"That's nice positive thinking," she purred and kissed his chin. "What time must you meet them?"

David sighed, seeing his ideal night dissolve into a tense day. "Ten."

Suzie switched off the bedside lamp. "Then we'd better get on with it, De Lange. I don't want to have any 'what if' fantasies while you're playing Rambo in the bush. Now, is there anything you've always wanted to do, but never had the chance?" A few choice answers rushed to his mind.

"How do mean?" he said, his mouth dry with anticipation.

"I can't really put it into words. What I mean is something like this maybe?" He hadn't even thought of that!

"You've got a contented smile on your face, David!"

He opened his eyes with a shock and saw Henry Masekela lean across the back of his seat holding a packet of sweets out to him. "Hey? Where have you been? Anyone I know?"

David laughed and took a sweet. "No, I was just remembering something nice that happened …" He looked out of the window. "So where are we now?"

The Transvaal glided by like the painted backdrop in a silent film. The brown grainlands were dotted with clusters of tall lavishly green trees, usually sheltering a red-roofed farmhouse. Clusters of mud huts littered the landscape where blacks had lived for decades. Some were colourfully painted in tribal hues, often more for tourist attraction rather than by tradition. Massive prehistoric chromed dinosaurs roared past them, trucks hurtling down towards the coast.

"You know, man, most of the drivers of those things don't even have a valid licence!" Kendall shouted above the din. "All forged, and they're souped up to go up to 160 kays!"

Kendall himself wasn't averse to taking on a juggernaut, especially down the winding freeway from the high plateau to the forested regions of Natal.

Henry wasn't a great talker on this trip. There was so much he wanted to say, so many things he needed to know, but neither Kendall nor Dawid de Lange could be of much help. Henry'd taken a few days off school, something he hated even contemplating, but the need to go out and bring Sizwe home was stronger than his renowned self-discipline. Henry hadn't missed a day at his desk. This would be his first black mark. He smiled as he remembered how his mother had taught him that punctuality was the foundation stone to success.

"All this nonsense about 'African Time'?" she would now say. "It's just an excuse for bad organisation and worse manners!"

Sizwe's disappearance had caused more than just upset in the family. Certain shady figures had been around to Kendall's house demanding the substantial amounts of money owed them by his younger brother.

So Tina put her foot down. "I don't mind living here in New Beirut, my darling black man, but I'm not going to be a gangster's moll! I'm going to get us a place in the Fortress." That's what they called the northern suburbs of Johannesburg. And within a few days, Kendall and his white lady moved into a leafy street behind another huge wall. The house suited them well. The rental was surprisingly low and the landlords didn't mind black tenants. Nor, it seemed, did the nosy neighbour.

"The previous people just skipped to America, just after Chris Hani was killed! Left unpaid bills. A dead parrot! Real pigs and white too! Filth like you'd expect from …" she mouthed the b-word, "… blacks!" Her eyes were still for not a moment, checking out whatever they had brought from the 'location'. "Your husband?" she asked Tina. "What does he do?"

Tina was dying to say "Terrorist!", but showed no hint of sarcasm. "What do you think he does?" she asked, knowing the minds of these suburban battle-axes, her own mother being one.

"Carpenter? Plumber?" asked the neighbour hopefully.

"My dear, we should be so lucky. He's a mechanic." The neighbour nodded, delighted. "And he's a black belt …" The woman didn't know what that was and frowned. Tina played her card. "And what's more, shoots to kill."

The neighbour's eyes lit up. "Your husband should come and compare his gun with my husband's. Then we can talk our girl-talk."

Tina wondered what that entailed. She just couldn't resist a sigh. "Trouble is our dogs are from Soweto. They just bite whites!"

213

The neighbour eyed the growling Maltese poodle through the window. She shrugged. "So? Our dogs bite everyone!"

Kendall laughed as he told the story. "Tina can get on with anyone, man. I love that white doll!" He didn't refer to the midnight knocks of terror on the door of his Soweto home. Henry knew the tension and stress of the search for his lost son was also having a telling effect on his mother. She was still the most stubborn person he knew. Since her small heart attack the year before, the doctors had pleaded with him to convince Teema to have a pacemaker set into her chest, but she wouldn't hear of it.

"Nonsense, there is no such thing as a 'small operation'!" she huffed. "And besides, pacemakers? They keep you alive forever! I don't want to be alive forever!" And no amount of calm reasoning would have any effect on her argument. Teema would go on living only till God switched off her light, she'd say, and that was that.

"Is Teema okay?" David suddenly asked from the back seat.

Henry turned to him. "Why do you ask? Doesn't she look well?"

Then David remembered Teema's plea that Henry wasn't to know of their meeting in the Carlton coffee-shop. He now shook his head and looked back at the passing world. "No, I was just wondering how she was, considering she's been on her feet all her life."

Henry nodded and glanced at Kendall who now had his infernal rap booming straight into his brain via his small earphones. "No, Teema's Teema. It will help us all once Sizwe is back at home."

"And then, Henry?" David looked at the overloaded minibus taxi standing by the side of the road with a flat tyre, twenty-odd exhausted black passengers waiting patiently next to the road for someone to bring a spare wheel.

"We'll have to cross that bridge when we come to it."

"Cross that cheque more than likely."

Henry gave a dry chuckle. "Yes, you're probably right. But I'm not proud, David. If it takes money to keep Sizwe alive, then I'll give him money. After all, it's only money."

And it was money that gave them their first clue to Sizwe's whereabouts.

CHAPTER 15.

"ARMED ROBBERY AT UMLAZI!" the headlines screamed.

The grimy house on the outskirts of Durban was damp. Lavish banana trees and untidy ferns jostled for place in the overgrown garden. There was a smell of rotting leaves and somewhere a trickle of water broke the oppressive silence. A young girl had opened the scarred green front door for them smiling shyly at Henry, and then must've blushed when she saw Kendall, if blacks could go red with lovesickness. Kendall teased her and gave her a big kiss on her forehead and she fled into the house and they didn't see her again for some time.

There was no one else at home. Henry led them into a large room which seemed to be the sitting area. There were a few enormous unmatched chairs and sofas in an untidy disarrangement, carpets lay rolled up tightly against the wall and a ladder stood in the centre, draped with newspapers and paint splatterings.

"I don't fucking believe it!" Kendall gasped. "He's still painting this room. How long is that now?"

Henry dusted off a bulky chair with his handkerchief. "Two years something? That's a fast job as far as my cousin is concerned." He winked at David. "Family not always in the top drawers, organisationally speaking."

"Two years!" whistled Kendall and slouched around the room, hands in pockets, kicking at cardboard boxes filled with things, peering into packets, always on the look-out for something interesting, and in this case, if not fascinating, incriminating. He didn't trust this Natal cousin as far as he could throw him and he weighed 150 kilos.

"No wonder the furniture is so dented ..." David remarked and nearly disappeared into a voluptuous sofa. A cloud of dust rose and settled on him. He sniffed and knew sneezing would not be far away. The smell of paint was also sharp and unpleasant. He looked up at the ceiling with its few strokes of new colour. "Where is this Michelangelo?" he asked.

"No, not Michael, Rastar," corrected Kendall, busily twisting the cap off a jar to examine the contents.

David smiled and they waited. The damp from under the floor

seemed to have crept all the way into his head, when the front door suddenly burst open and a huge shadow fell across the wall from the passage.

A deep voice loud enough to shatter glass and peace vibrated into the house. "Beauty! Get the things in the car!" Then it called in a more friendly way: "Henry!"

Henry got up and dusted himself off. A dark cloud covered the doorway as a blimp of a man waddled into the room, having to squeeze through the opening sideways. His massive bulk was expensively upholstered in a pinstriped suit. He wore shoes large enough to sail in and on his head wobbled an elegant felt hat. The gold fillings in his front teeth glistened richly as he smiled expensively from crown to crown.

"Henry, my brother!" he bellowed, and opened his arms for an embrace. Henry who had suddenly seemed to have shrunk in comparison to his cousin, winced and steeled himself. He vanished into the hug of the striped bear. "God man, I'm so glad you're here! Why so long in coming? I just started redoing the house. If I'd known …" He shook with laughter and Henry shook with him. Rastar's eyes eventually peeled out from the layers of face fat and fell on Kendall who was watching the embrace open-mouthed.

"Kendall!" he boomed, "You fucking homo! Come and kiss me, you black stud!"

Kendall did what he was told and gave his uncle a peck on the cheek. The blubber-mountain released a creased Henry who then staggered back into his chair, relieved to be free. It was Kendall's turn to be hugged. Once enveloped by the huge arms, he was heard to say in a high-pitched gasp. "But Uncle Rastar, I've got a girl-friend. I'm not a ho …" But the bearhug pushed the "-mo" out soundlessly and Kendall decided that explanations were pointless. Rastar was known to pick up words and throw them around like lavish parties, for no reason and at the drop of a hat.

Then the Uhuru Bogart spied the fascinated face of a white man looking at him from out of the biggest chair. He dropped Kendall like a soggy roach and focused on David intently. "And this is the Afrikaans boy who kicked the leaves around when you'd raked them so nicely, Henry?"

David feared for his life and wished he was back thirty years ago to pick all the scattered leaves up one by one. He shrugged and gave a weak laugh, looking at Henry for help and expecting it. But Teema's son gave no hint of friendship. He solemnly nodded and

216

pointed at David. "That's him, Rastar. It's taken over thirty years to bring him to justice, but now we can have it!"

"Ha!" roared the Orson Welles and waved his arms.

"Have what?" croaked David.

"A People's Court?" suggested Henry, and if it wasn't for the twinkle forcing itself out of his eyes, David could've easily fainted from shock. Anything was possible in this crazy place!

Rastar roared with delight at his reaction and slapped his knees and set ripples of activity racing through every part of his tightly clothed girth.

"Hell man!" he wept delightedly, "I never laugh any more, man. Takes this damn teacher and his pansy son to make me really laugh. No, white boy, welcome to my humble house. If I had a garden out there and not a jungle, I'd force you to eat each leaf one by one, but unfortunately I don't have a green finger ..." He paused as a prompt, but David just nodded wide-eyed. "... I only have black fingers!" This time they all joined him in his enjoyment of his own joke.

The little black Beauty sidled in with a box of groceries and the afternoon paper balanced across the top. As she put it down on the rickety trellis table, the newspaper slid off onto the floor, falling open on page one. The headline immediately caught Kendall's eye. He picked up the paper and read.

"So where's Umlazi?" he asked. The little girl pointed out towards her right. Kendall ruffled her short hair and she ran out scalded by his attention. "Listen here, folks!" he said excitedly and read the report. A man had held up a bankteller in a small shopping mall at a favourite beach resort, not too far down the coast. There had been shots fired, but no reports of injury. Then two young white men were found slumped across the front seat of their car. Both had been shot in the head, in what police described as a classic example of execution-style murder. Henry followed every word with growing horror. "Do they link the two crimes?" he asked, his voice gravely and dry.

"Hang on Dad ..." Kendall skimmed the report, then carried on from where he'd left off.

Rastar listened with half-closed eyes, his rasping breath wheezing out of his throat. Henry got up and joined his son, reading over his shoulder. The report didn't mention names, but a description of a young man who seemed to only have one seeing eye, made them look at each other quickly. "What do you think?" he asked Kendall.

217

The young man shrugged and looked at his reflection in a dirty mirror skewly hanging against the wall. "I think every family around here has got one," he said lightly.

"A crook?" boomed forth from Rastar.

"No Uncle, someone with one eye!"

The room seemed to tilt as Rastar aimed his backside at a sofa and let his balance go. He crumpled into the seat and momentarily seemed blurred by the rising dust. The floor beneath them shook and tins of paint clanked together. Henry watched his cousin closely. "Rastar, did you see Sizwe for long?" he asked.

Rastar, still with his hat on, lay his head against the back of the sofa and sighed vastly. "Henry, take my word for it. He just arrived two days ago. I didn't even recognise him. Why should I? I don't know him! I also thought Sizwe Masekela, youngest son of Henry, was dead! Imagine my heart when this dangerous-looking man said: 'Hello Uncle!' Rastar tried to raise himself into a comfortable sitting position.

"What's the scene here, Henry brother? This boy of yours talks like some fancy student and he's much too old for that. Too much education, man! I don't understand what he wants."

"You said on the phone he asked you for guns?" Henry answered quietly. David felt his scalp prick with tension.

"Listen Henry, politics is death! Death for business! I have never mixed politics with pleasure. I do business with the best and if they're this or that, once they pay I couldn't care less. Sizwe wanted to meet the right people. I don't know right people, just wrong ones."

"But ..." But Henry had to go on hold while another volley of laughter tore through Rastar's body and spewed into the dampness of the room. When it had subsided and the great spent lungs had to wheezingly reclaim air by the cubic metre, Henry started again. "But if Sizwe wanted to become a mercenary in this Natal conflict, who would he go and see?"

David glanced at Kendall and whispered. "Mercenary?" Kendall nodded and rolled a wheel round his ear with his finger. "Sizwe is crazy, man. Must have fallen on his head off Mount Kilimanjaro!"

Henry looked up sharply at his son. "Don't say that! Sizwe is saner than most of the people I know! He's not crazy!" Kendall was shocked by the sudden sharpness and smiled sheepishly. "Joking, Daddy, joking ..." but knew he'd gone too far.

Rastar watched it all with faint detached amusement. "What is

218

the scene with this dead son that came back, Henry?" he asked, as if enquiring about a stray dog. David also turned to look at Henry's reaction with interest. This part of the story no one had been prepared to tell him. Henry sat back in his chair, looking as crushed as he felt. He traced across the grimy design on the armrest with his finger.

"I don't know much more than anyone else ..." he said in a half-sigh. "Sizwe was trained to fight since he was ten, when he ran away from home and school. He could shoot before he could add and subtract. He became an officer in MK before he was a man. He was burning with hatred ... the hatred he had packed in his heart when he fled his home on 19 June 1976." Rastar's eyes were closed as he listened, the rhythm of his breath rasping through his body. Henry stared at the pattern on the armrest. "Then it seems ... I don't know if the sequence is right ... they were told to prepare for war. They were going to fight the *boere* ... at last ..."

Kendall, by now perched on David's armrest, gave him a playful nudge, and whispered the controversial ANC Youth League slogan: "David, 'Kill the *boer*! Kill the farmer!'"

"Shhhh." David pulled away from him and looked towards Henry, who hadn't taken notice of the diversion.

Henry was measuring his words carefully, as a good teacher in a crisis would. "They were sent to Angola, but not to fight the *boere*. They were hired out to the MPLA forces against the rebel Unita army of Savimbi. I just know Sizwe lost most of his unit in that war ... and his eye." He glared at Kendall who was studying the gold ring on his finger. "Then the remains of what was once a proud fighting force, limped back to the training camp somewhere in Tanzania. There was an armed rebellion in the camp. The boys wanted to fight on their home ground, and not do other countries' dirty work for them. There were shootings ... I don't know what happened next, but it seems Sizwe got himself sent to Bulgaria."

"Bulgaria?" echoed David, trying to follow the geographical contortions of this story with as little ease as he did the facts.

"Yes, Sizwe went to the University of ... whatever the capital of Bulgaria is."

"Is there still a Bulgaria?" David murmured trying to picture a recent map of the New Europe, but the jigsaw-chaos of the Balkans and the former Soviet satellites all blurred into one cauldron. No one knew if it still was, or what its capital had been.

Henry shrugged. "Whatever it was called then, he studied there.

Then he went to East Germany, Leipzig, I think, to the local office of the …" He sighed and sat back, covering his face with his hands for a moment. "I don't know the details. There are so many subtitles and acronyms. And then when things suddenly changed there …"

"The Wall coming down?"

"The world coming down, David. The communist keepers of the purses suddenly vanished, often with their purses. Sizwe was stranded in a revolution not of his interest or making. He managed to pretend to be a refugee and got help back to the camps in Zambia. Then when he reported to his former MK commanding officer, he found they had changed the whole structure of command and he didn't belong anywhere."

Kendall butted in. "Mandela had just been released …" Henry nodded. "Most of the leaders were preparing to come back home, to move into big houses and drive big cars, while Sizwe just wanted to keep fighting till justice had been done." He looked at David with a defeated shrug. "To this day it seems …"

Rastar gave a deep snore. They looked at him and saw the huge runway of a chest rise and fall with the peace of sleep.

"The old fuck," muttered Kendall.

"No," said Henry, "he wouldn't understand all this. Rastar is an agent for the merchant, not the mercenary. So then when Sizwe was smuggled back in to South Africa …"

"Smuggled?" scoffed Kendall. "He could've taken a plane! Or hitched, but no, he has to get into camouflage and creep across the minefields on his stomach like Stallone?"

"Let me finish, Kendall," Henry said softly. "When Sizwe got back to what he thought was the front, the place which would benefit from his training and his hatred, he found a welcome-home party being given by the Soweto police force. One of the policemen who had shot at him all those years ago wanted to shake his hand."

"What did he do?" David asked, leaning in so that he could hear properly. Henry was talking quietly now as the pain of his loss became more acute with memory.

"He quoted from Julius Caesar and the Bible, while fingering the knife in his pocket. The policeman thought it was all Greek and laughed. So Sizwe came home and got drunk. He cried. He attacked Kendall. He insulted Teema. He accused me of being a collaborator. He threatened to kill us all. He was silent for a month. He disappeared and reappeared. He would have wounds, he would have burns, he would smell of whores. He would sleep for days. He

220

would eat nothing. He would read for hours. And one night ..." Henry swallowed hard, pausing for self-control. He glanced up at Kendall who looked back at him with compassion.

"It's okay, Dad," he said gently.

Henry gave a sudden laugh, his eyes filling with tears. "No, it's not anything terrible. It's just one night he opened my bedroom door. I must've been asleep, but woke up suddenly feeling a presence in the room. There was just some light reflected through the window. There he stood in the door, staring at me. I knew it was him; I could feel his eyes ... his eye on me. Then he came to the side of the bed and stood there. It was like when he was a little boy and my wife and I would be in our bed ... not a double bed in those days, but a single bed and boxes between it and the wall to give us room ... and Sizwe would come and stand at the bed and wait and we would open the blankets and let him in. So I opened the blankets and my warrior-child got into my bed and curled up against me like a baby, and I held him till he slept."

There was a pause, punctuated only by Rastar's snores and grunts. All of them were moved by the images in Henry's story. Henry took out his handkerchief and carefully dabbed his eyes. "The next morning, of course, he was gone. Maybe it was a dream."

Kendall went up to his father and crouched at the chair. "No, it wasn't a dream. He loves you, Dad. Really he does." Then he got up with a crackle of joints. "We'll find him! If Uncle Rastar doesn't know where to start, then I'll eat his hat!" He looked over at the beached whale in the sofa and nearly changed his mind. "Well, only with a nice dressing."

Henry needed the joke and the three laughed quietly, while at the door little Beauty watched with huge eyes. The bullet hole in her shoulder had healed by now, but her tongue that the vigilantes had cut out on one bloody night of violence two months before would never grow back again.

It was with a great sense of relief that David realised that they were going to stay at a small hotel off the beachfront in Durban. He'd asked earlier that day but Kendall was very vague and Henry didn't seem to mind where he stayed. David dreaded the thought of being put up by the flamboyant member of the Masekela family. Although he'd slept rough enough often in his life, even recently when on a camping trip with his daughters and their husbands in the Rocky

Mountains, a night on the tiles in the house that Rastar was still building would come under the heading of slumming it.

The Pendennis Hotel looked like the Ritz and the first thing he wanted was some good English tea. It tasted like dishwater and the teabag floated in the cup like a drowned mouse.

"Never mind, man," scoffed Kendall, "just pretend it's Earl Brown."

"Earl Grey," his father corrected.

Kendall didn't miss a beat. "Yes, Dad, I know, but the more fashionable one is Earl Brown." Henry winked at David and they sipped their punishment like good older people.

Rastar had at first balked at any suggestion that he involve himself in the search for Sizwe. He had a million complicated excuses, even blindly grabbing at Beauty as the reason for his sudden care. She was his only daughter, he sobbed, and what would become of her if he died?

David was sure he saw the girl pull up her nose at his words, but she was trapped in the big man's embrace and was forced to relax like some small kitten in the vice-like grip of a loving child. But then Henry played his trump card, which was vital information to Rastar about trading possibilities in the Transvaal. Henry had ideal contacts through his school and Rastar had no footholds in the North to sell whatever he traded in. A deal was made and they got out of the house as soon as they could. Beauty stood and waved at Kendall until the BMW vanished round the corner.

"What does Rastar sell?" David eventually asked, when they'd got to their hotel room and opened a window.

Kendall didn't know either. "This and that, man. You want an elephant, he can find you one."

Henry giggled. "You don't have to look far for an elephant when you see Rastar." He opened his notebook and looked at the names he'd squeezed out of the boulder that was his cousin. "I don't know where these places are," he said. "They sound like names of townships?" He handed the list to Kendall who got up from the chair where he'd been sitting, coddling a cold beer.

"I'll go down and check with reception," he said, enjoying his youthful leadership and looking forward to a late night on the dance floor of the local disco he spied off the foyer of the hotel.

When Kendall had left the room, David and Henry sat in silence for a few minutes. The nauseating smell of bad hotel cooking wafted into the room from the passage.

"Liver?" said David.

Henry sniffed. "Sausages?" he suggested and they both laughed.

"For the price we're paying, let's not be fussy."

David nodded and ruefully glanced at the three small single beds lined up in this special offer 'suite'. Not quite slumming it, but Ritz was not the word that came to mind. Then Henry got up suddenly. "Come let's go and look at the sea. This room gives me the creeps!"

The hotel was only two blocks away from the garish beachfront promenade that claimed so many fans for the city that called itself the perfect cosmopolitan holiday resort. Large blocks of luxury hotels loomed like space-age radios, dwarfing the palm trees and attracting parked cars like shiny ticks feeding off the parking meters lining the pavements. Rows of exotic black women in traditional costume sat on the pavements behind spread-out blankets on which they presented their wares to the tourists. Small black dolls strangled by coloured beads lay side by side with elephants, rhinos and protected species, carved and moulded and mass-produced. Crocheted doilies lay under yellow and red plastic snakes that writhed at the touch, and wind-up dogs hopped and barked mechanically in small circles.

"What a lot of crap," David muttered, as they past one similar exhibition after the next.

"That's what the people want," Henry remarked. "What should we buy our Teema?"

David had completely forgotten about Teema, sitting at her dining-room table in that small Soweto house, reading the newspaper with thick reading lenses like the ends of bottles over her eyes, searching for news of her beloved grandson.

The snow in the little plastic bubble fell softly on two plastic surfers covering the words 'Durban'. David shook it again and laughed. "Haven't seen one of these snowshakers for years …" He looked down at a smallish leather handbag, embossed with the fur of a buck and handstitched in bold hoops. "That looks quite nice," he said, so they bought it for Teema, and David thought he might as well buy one for Suzie and, as an afterthought, one for Joanie Craig.

"How many women do you need to bag?" asked Henry with a twinkle.

"No, just old friends," David said, as he counted out the idiotic new South African toyland-money into the hands of the smiling vendor. "Is that right?" he asked the woman and she nodded and closed her hands over the money in a grip.

"Yes, Baas," she said and her toothless gums winked at him. As they walked on, holding packets that weighed them down, Henry eventually remarked: "You paid her far too much, you know?"

"Yes, I know." David knew he'd confused his coins, but not that much. "What's a few rand extra here and there," he said with the casualness of a man with gold cards in his wallet.

"And those five pink notes?"

"Yes, five times ten rand."

Henry chuckled. "Five times fifty rand! You paid her with fifty-rand notes, not ten!"

David stopped and stared at Henry open-mouthed. "Why didn't you say something!"

"What's a few rand here and there?" Henry said sweetly. "And besides, in your American dollar that's scarcely the price of a hamburger."

So they stopped for hamburgers and David let Henry pay.

"What do we do now?" David asked, as they sat on the sand next to the sea eating. The sharp taste of the junk food was delicious and both men savoured each bite, each knowing how Teema would wag a practised finger in their direction. They felt like naughty school-boys eating forbidden food behind teachers' backs. Henry swallowed and wiped his mouth with his hand.

"I don't know. I can't believe Sizwe was involved in those killings in Umlazi."

"You think he robbed the bank?"

"Not impossible. He sees things like that as legitimate targets."

Wheeling round their heads and eyeing the buns in their hands with lust, a seagull cawed and shat tactlessly close to where they sat. "Fuck off!" shooed David and threw a handful of sand at the bird. The slight breeze suddenly gushed into a wind and the sand blew back onto them both, covering their hamburgers with crunchy Durban beach dust.

"Oh fuck!" groaned Henry and threw the hamburger some distance away, where the seagulls attacked it with a frenzy that made David happy not to be a hamburger. When Henry's offering was gone, David threw his towards the scavenger birds and it went the same way.

"Don't those birds have cholesterol?" Henry remarked and David suddenly thought of Teema's secret about Henry's heart problem and wondered if a hamburger had been the right thing for Henry to eat. He looked all right though. Henry turned to David.

224

"I don't know what to do, David. I feel we're wasting time. I know we're going to expose ourselves to danger, but he is my boy. You're still free to stay in the hotel and watch TV."

David smiled and put his hand on his friend's arm. "Thanks, but no thanks. I've seen all your latest TV programmes in the States five years ago."

Kendall had found out which name on the list belonged to what place in the area and they decided to start early the next morning. Henry and David spent a quiet evening watching an in-house video in silence. Kendall was out till very late and David vaguely heard him tiptoe into the room and get into bed.

They booked out of the hotel, once the breakfast they had eaten managed to settle down to an uneasy truce with their stomachs. They drove back and forth, crisscrossing the map of greater Durban and surrounding towns, from one contact name to the next, finding little help from anyone and no information about Sizwe.

"It's you, David man," said Kendall eventually, his ever manicured and coifed look now making way for the washed-out dampness that Durban's humidity cursed its citizens with, month in and month out.

"Why me?"

"You're white. No black is going to talk to two other blacks when there's a white in the party. You smell like the cops."

David looked at Henry, but Henry nodded sheepishly. "Do you mind staying in the car next time we go into a place?" he asked and David shook his head, not minding at all. The less he had to do in this wild goose chase, the more it suited him. He heard Suzie's laughter as she threw him a parting goodbye. "And remember, being white is not the answer to that question you're looking to find!" How right she was.

Without him shining like a beacon in a dark night, Henry and his son started making headway. They were directed to a small supermarket in a dusty rural area mainly inhabited by Zulu supporters of the ANC. It took much manoeuvring and imagination to find their way, but Kendall was never shy to roll down his window and ask the nearest person where to go. They always gave him a courteous reply, while David crouched down in the back seat, wishing for tinted windows and a frizzy hairstyle.

The dilapidated houses on either side of the gully-ridden gravel road soon made way for square grey-and-rust shanties, like on the edges of all the cities of the emerging new democratic state. Children could be seen everywhere, some dressed in neat colourful hand-me-downs, others in tatters, some even naked. There was, in spite of the poverty, a feeling of fun among the smallest kids and they could run after a scraggy chicken with as much enjoyment as city children would get out of a computer game.

"A Zulu-speaking ANC area?" echoed David, still trying to make sense of the sinister nonsense of this unofficial civil war in the untidy greenery of Natal. "Everybody looks alike. Who's to know who supports whom?"

Henry nodded. "That's exactly the problem. You've got to carry your heart on your sleeve, and God help you if it's the wrong sleeve." The car gave a lurch. "What's wrong?"

Kendall suddenly stopped the BMW on a steep incline. David felt himself slide to the left side of his seat and press against the door. Kendall whistled through his teeth, and rapped a warning.

"There's some shit ahead, could mean we're dead, what to do, when do we wake up, oh oh …"

"What is it, Kendall!" Henry gripped his son's arm and gave it an irritated squeeze.

Ahead in the track stood a group of youths, maybe thirty or more. They wore red bands around their heads, some were dressed in camouflage and denim, others in ordinary township gear, which was basically anything they had. The youths each carried sticks and some spears. The sun glinted on the blade of an axe. They stood across the road, blocking it, staring down at the car motionless at an angle lower down the sweeping hill. The fringing undergrowth seemed to bear down on the scene, bordering it in bright green.

David felt his mouth go dry and a pain shoot across his chest. "Who are they?" he asked, hoping the answer would be friendly.

"I don't know," Henry said slowly. "I just think we've maybe wandered into their territory …"

Kendall was clenching the steering-wheel with both hands, hissing a staccato rap-rhythm through his teeth as he watched the group stare back at them.

Henry wondered if they had the time to reverse the car down the hill, turn safely with deep gullies on either side and leave the area.

Kendall seemed to read his mind. "Can't go back now. The slope is too steep. Sorry, it's onwards or nowards."

They didn't move. It was like the scene had been put in freeze-frame mode. Just a colourful bird flapping out of the trees to their right attracted their attention briefly. Even the playing children seemed to have vanished, and the stray dogs and bouncing chickens were gone too.

"Oh fuck me mama, here they come," Kendall sighed and pulled his handbrake up firmly. The car secured itself on the slope, its powerful engine throbbing a bored purr.

Henry turned to David slowly, talking through the corner of his mouth. "Lie down on the floor, quickly!"

"No!" Kendall snapped. "They'll find him and kill him! Just sit and wait. They saw we were three in here. Just smile."

"Smile?" David wondered if anyone would be able to identify his charred body and tell Deli, once these creatures from hell bearing down on them had done their damnedest.

The gang moved towards them, divided into two groups and surrounded the car. David could now see how young they were. Not men, not youths, but boys. He knew the smile on his face looked like bright red lipstick drawn on the face of a crucified Christ.

Kendall took a deep breath and wound down his window evenly. The crowd moved closer and cut off the sunlight. The sudden odour of young, warm male bodies wafted into the car. Two of the leaders leant towards the window. David could hear their weapons clank on the roof of the car. No one returned the three idiotic smiles from the occupants of this imported car. David saw many pairs of eyes scan the interior of the vehicle and make inventories: watches, wallets, radio, jackets, briefcase. Lives.

"Howzit brothers?" said Kendall in a familiar tone. There was no reply, no reaction. The heat in the car was becoming tangible. David felt the sweat crease down his forehead. He realised that his smiling lips were stuck to his dry teeth and he had to part them with his tongue. In the process he pulled some skin off the inside of his mouth and tasted blood. "I think we're lost," said Kendall cheerfully, as if he'd been stopped by a bobby in London's picturesque Hampstead Village. "We're looking for the supermarket."

The leader of the pack stared intently at Kendall. The marked difference in their styles and appearances underlined the city-dwellers' obviousness and the rural cowboys' lack of imagination.

"Why?" the boy asked.

Kendall rolled down his window completely and leant out of it with one elbow. "You see this dude in the back?" he asked and everyone looked at David, rust-stained yellow of dark-brown eyes resting on his white face and the blue eyes and the steel-grey hair. "Ja, this is an American who's here on …" David crossed his fingers and prayed for Kendall's imagination not to let them down. "… with the National Peace Accord! You know, to check on violence and all that?" The boys nodded gravely as if violence was something that happened somewhere else. Henry cleared his throat casually and it sounded like a death rattle.

Kendall chatted on. "We need to visit the supermarket to talk to the man about the robbery."

The youths listened and translated quickly among themselves. Most of them now pressed against the windows on either side of David's, staring at him with renewed interest. He felt like a minor royal among major cub reporters.

The leaders leant into Kendall's window and spoke to David.

"You American?" David nodded and nearly waved. The sweat down his back made him stick to the seat.

"Roll down your window," said Kendall under his breath.

"What?" shot back David, this being the last thing in the world he wanted to do.

"Do it!" came from Henry and David slowly rolled down his windows, first the one, then the other. The kids on the block, for that is now what these warriors now looked like, peered at him as they would at an exotic animal in a cage. Then one smiled and his scowl was transformed into the laugh of a boy.

"You American?" he said and put his hand into the window. David looked down at it, as if wondering what it was. There were two fingers missing.

"Take it!" hissed Henry, and David took the hand and shook it tentatively. The boy laughed, a peal of enjoyment setting smiles on the faces of the other children. Suddenly the car was rocked from side to side as the boys scrambled to push their arms into the back windows for a handshake from the white American. David pressed the flesh and smiled, then laughed and then found himself asking for names and getting them. They touched his soaking wet shirt and his face and his hair. Their war-game ornaments on their wrists, crushed tins and bottle-tops and wire, scratched his skin and left red weals across his arms. Eventually the mass-greeting was over and the children stood back respectfully as their two leaders stood by David's window and looked in at him.

"The supermarket is not good," the tall one said, his eyes belying

228

his age with a hidden agenda of terrible experience. "The super-market is boycotted by the people. No one buys there."

"We're not going to buy," David drawled lusciously, grateful for the slur that his adopted land had given his original colonial English. "Just want to have a chat with the owner about the robbery."

This seemed to be the answer they wanted. The wild horde of overgrown schoolboys, gathered in front of the car, waving their spears and axes and sharpened sticks. The leader gestured that Kendall follow them and then they were off, like a collective Pied Piper, leading the car towards the top of the hill and down to the right where the supermarket nestled along a leafy ridge.

As the car edged forward, following in the steps of the comrade-gang, Henry and Kendall gave a shuddering sigh of relief. Henry turned to David with a smile drained of meaning. "Howdee partner!" he said and shook David's trembling hand. "Howdee!"

CHAPTER 16.

The supermarket was deserted. A makeshift amalgamation of small buildings and a rickety stoep held together with billboards advertising Coca-Cola and Camel cigarettes, this was where the locals could stock up on all the necessary victuals that made up their daily diet. Mealie meal, corn, samp, grain, and meat, as well as the utensils, knives, Coke and hair products that went with feeding.

The owner was an Indian man who had lived above his shop for the last 15 years. He now squinted out at them from behind a massive grid that protected his store from his customers.

"What you want?" he said, staring at the Masekelas with fear and only relaxed slightly when David got out of the car.

"Oh, are you the people who phoned from Durban?"

The arrivals looked at each other.

"No," said David, "we didn't phone …"

"Oh?" said the shopkeeper with a smile. "Never mind, someone phoned and said you'd be coming."

David looked at Henry as they both thought the same name. "Sizwe?" Kendall asked and shook his head. "How could he know?"

"Rastar," Henry muttered and sighed. This was going to be more of a rollercoaster than he had planned.

"Come in anyway." The Indian unbolted and unchained his steel drawbridge and they entered the stuffy, scented interior.

"Look!" said the owner, keen to show off his recent narrow escape. There were small holes behind the counter, among the tinned goods and the enamelware. "I was standing here," he said and positioned himself next to the evidence, "when that young man came here to buy cigarettes …"

"Sizwe doesn't smoke," said Kendall and seemed happy to have solved that problem.

"No," said the Indian, "but he pulled out of his pocket not money, but a pistol and shot, bang bang!" He pointed at the bullet holes again.

"What did he take?" asked David looking around at the debris of trade. Through the heavily barred window at the back he could see the expanse of the valley below, as it swept up to meet another crown of a hill on the horizon. Everywhere were small clusters of tribal huts, rusty shanties and spirals of smoke that indicated where people were living.

"Was anyone killed?" Henry asked.

The Indian smiled. "No," he said. "I'm still here!"

"But why are we here?" hissed David at Kendall. "This doesn't lead anywhere!"

"He took clothes!" the Indian said, stuttering over his haste to tell all. David couldn't see any clothes in the store and wondered what they were like. Overalls? Balaclavas?

"Describe the clothes." Kendall showed an immediate interest here and leant against the counter, his expensive finery making the faded poster of a forgotten pop star pale in sad comparison.

The Indian looked at his clothes with a happy nod. "Nice clothes. My clothes," he said. They looked at this scruffy man with the thin oily moustache, dressed in an old housecoat stained with various ancient liquids and paints.

"Your clothes?" David echoed.

"Yes, I was wearing my best clothes. I always do and my good customers like what they see and then I make them copies and sell. You see my brother is a tailor in Durban." He pulled a large scrapbook out from under the counter and showed them pages of Polaroid snaps of him wearing his best. He looked quite different. "The young man came in. He said: 'I like your clothes.' I said: 'Thank you!' He then asked me: 'What is your size?' I told him. He was pleased as we were the same size. And then he pulled a gun, shot it into the wall and stole my clothes!"

"Did you see his eyes?" asked Kendall.

"No, he was wearing shades. Ray-Bans!" nodded the victim enviously.

"What did he have on?" David asked. "I mean, when he came in."

The Indian shrugged. "Like any young man. Jeans. T-shirt."

"Any design on the T-shirt?" Henry asked, hoping it wouldn't be one he'd recognise.

"Very strange," the Indian murmured, trying to remember clearly. "It had a little mouse sitting on a chair and a big elephant ready to sit down on the mouse and the mouse was saying …"

"And the mouse saying …" added Henry.

" … 'Oh shit'?" finished Kendall.

"Yes. Funny T-shirt!"

Henry looked at David and nodded. "Sizwe." Kendall turned to the shopkeeper. "Did you describe the clothes he took to the police?"

"He took everything, man," the robbed fashion-plate whined.

"Even my underwear. Silk. I was naked."

"You were naked?" Kendall started laughing and had to move away from the counter into the racks of buckets and utensils. "Jesus, that brother of mine ..." he snorted.

David also felt a surge of laughter, but knew this was not the time to make light of Henry's concern. Henry was still wondering about the earlier call.

"The voice on the telephone? Was it the same voice?"

The smiling man stopped smiling and thought, as if he wasn't capable of doing both well at the same time. Then he smiled again. "Maybe. Maybe not," he said confidently.

Henry nodded and smiled back. "Thank you for your trouble. Come, you two, this is getting us nowhere." He turned to leave, but David stopped him with a question to the nervous shopkeeper.

"Why are you being boycotted?" he asked the Indian. The man's smile vanished immediately and a look of terror clouded his face. He glanced at the barred door and whispered. "I was just doing what anyone would do. I phoned the police."

"And?"

"And they came, but the young man was gone."

"And the boycott?" The Indian swallowed hard and hesitated. David tried again. "Why won't people support you any more, if you had such a good relationship with them?"

"Intimidation!" said the intimidated. "They will be killed. I will be killed. And I just phoned the police!" He gestured that they come closer. David and Henry leant across the counter and the man's faint smell of incense and spices assailed them. "This young man was a hero of the comrades. I nearly delivered him to the regime. I am now a collaborator. My days are numbered. Please, you must help me ..." His eyes filled with tears and he grabbed both Henry and David's hand and held on tightly, rubbing his cheek against them and weeping quietly. "Please ... please ..."

David pulled his hand free and gestured with his head that they leave. The Indian came to the gate still holding Henry's hand, tears running down his cheek before diffusing into his sideburns and moustache. "Could you unlock for us?" David asked and pointed at the gate.

The man fumbled with the locks and chains and quickly opened the barricade.

"Go! Go!" he hissed. "Quick. And don't talk to the papers. I am a dead man!" And with that he clanked the door of his new prison shut and merged into the shadows with his terrors.

The young group of comrade-fans was waiting round the car. "You see?" said the leader patronisingly. "That Indian is a dead man."

David looked into the eyes of this child-warrior. "Well, maybe you should all let yourselves cool down for a few days and then talk it over. Anyway, your comrade-hero got away. No damage done." The boy didn't seem convinced.

Then Henry came forward and held out his hand. "I am Henry Masekela. Sizwe is my son." This was a magic word and the boys crowded round him in awe. While nothing was said, there was a feeling of solidarity with them, as the three got back into the hot car and a shiny-faced Kendall started the engine.

David rolled down his window to get some air. "I hope all goes well for you … you men here," he said and some of the children giggled, but were frozen in their fun by a glare from their leader.

"The Struggle is all!" he intoned. "We demand freedom!"

The others joined him in scattered cries of "Amandla" and "Viva" and then someone said "Goodbye" and another even said "Totsiens". The sound of an Afrikaans word here was joltingly bizarre.

David watched the little group get smaller as the car roared up the hill and over the top, back to the real world of hot tarred roads and cold terrified people.

"Will that shopkeeper be okay?" David asked as he sat back, the air-conditioning now making him shiver.

"As long as he keeps his doors locked. They'll chop him up into small bits and hang him on the washing line for the crows to feed off," Henry answered, while watching the changing scenery as they sped towards the city.

They had to stop in order to wait for a truck to make a turning. A sea breeze was lifting the banana fronds listlessly. A hawker dozed under a makeshift cardboard canopy, while chatting schoolchildren in uniform were bunched up together on the other side of the burning tarmac.

It was Sizwe who found them.

After weeks of waiting around Soweto in limbo, aimlessly walking around the neighbourhood, being shunned by the people

233

he grew up with, viewed with suspicion by those he regarded as collaborators with the hated regime still in power, in spite of all that had happened to 'liberate the masses', Sizwe eventually heard that his dream had come true. Or, to put it bluntly, he got a job.

He gave Henry and Teema no hints of his plans, managing to carry on his lounging about as always, and when the chance came for a lift down to Natal, he left the home in Soweto with just his hands in his pockets. He had nothing and he wanted nothing.

There were two police roadblocks searching for illegal arms on the way down to Pietermaritzburg and luckily for them all, Sizwe's urbane friendliness got them through. No one seemed to think that a young black man who spoke a relatively unaccented English could be an enemy of the state. At least, that's what Sizwe thought. He would at last have a chance to prove himself and get rid of so much pent-up energy. No, boiling hatred was more the word.

He did not know much about the situation on the ground in Natal. This fourth province of the Republic of South Africa, once a glittering jewel in the crown of British imperialism, was now a patchwork of ANC and Inkatha strongholds. The spate of mindless massacres in the Midlands filling daily news reports with stomach-turning detail, showed that the seven-year-old war in the rural villages of Natal was far from over. A new generation of warrior was being recruited to fill the empty shoes of the dead fighters, and these were mainly the children. Some small boys had seen violent death so often that the drawings they made reflected bloodshed and horror. "What do we do with kids who have never played a normal game, who make guns out of planks at the age of four?" asked the soft-spoken man with the pale eyes into whose home Sizwe was ushered on arrival in the compound halfway between Pietermaritzburg and Durban.

Sizwe shrugged. It wasn't his problem. This elderly man was more of a puzzle to him, and he looked at him keenly. Sizwe had heard the legends surrounding this sly fox who looked so like anyone's favourite uncle, while having the reputation for being the most successful of the warlords in the region. While he looked as if he bounced small nephews on his knees, he was a general who gave orders only once and whose revenge for disobedience outstripped his cruelty in conquest. This was the man the press called 'Rommel', a backhanded tribute to another great warrior from a war foreign to most of the young blacks who made up his ragtag army of amabutho.

"You wish to be one of my amabutho?" Rommel asked Sizwe, having already decided where this cynical killing machine would find suitable use.

Sizwe nodded slightly, not wanting to show enthusiasm. "I've been trained by the best," he said and wondered how much this new employer knew about his CV.

"Six children were slaughtered last week," Rommel said and the benign smile over his face balanced the coldness in his eyes. "It has become a way of life to bury our children, our young men. Our future. The so-called leaders round the tables of negotiation in Johannesburg sit and talk and drink and give each other rewards and honorary doctorates, but here where the people are, there is nothing to look forward to except death."

Rommel ushered Sizwe out into the courtyard. Among the stolen cars being resprayed and expertly disguised, he saw a group of young men preparing various crates and loading them into a bakkie. "Your first introduction to working for me will be a party." Rommel smiled as Sizwe looked perplexed. "Never mind, you just go with them. And Sizwe?"

"Ja?"

"Do what you're told. There's no second chance here in anything, life or death."

The party he referred to was the funeral of the children. It was to be held across the valley at a place called Weeping Hill, where the graves of unnamed victims dotted the slopes. Six oxen were to be slaughtered for the mass funeral, one representing each child. From a round hut set under a massive gnarled tree with heavy green leaves, cups of traditional home-made beer were to be handed out to the many mourners with the compliments of their overlord. Corn-brewed lager was to be sold from the back of a laundry truck by an enterprising comrade who was called Tins.

No one seemed very interested in Sizwe, but he did what he was told and spent the day working hard not to attract too much attention. He started gathering information about those around him by watching and listening. Like him, most of them seemed to be dissident MK members, some returned exiles as he was, also impatient with the meagre fruits of ANC horse-trading that resulted from the arduous negotiation process in Johannesburg. These young rebels were bucking the official line, quite happy to be called extremist, as this was what they all were trained to become.

Sizwe had at last found other 'bandits', and that he was not the only one with a burning need to do something that would be remembered. He would eventually find out that the young men carrying and digging and on the lookout, were part of Rommel's well-trained group of soldiers, experienced in the use of automatic weapons and hand grenades.

Sizwe Masekela had joined one of the many death squads that made life hell for so many ordinary people in the valleys. An intense conflict had been raging across the densely vegetated gorge that separated the hostel where Sizwe was given a bunk and a gun, and the squatter settlements on the other side of the 'line', overcrowded with a ragtag bunch of frightened and confused people. Among them, of course, were the death squads from the other side, and, like in all small unpronounceable trouble spots world-wide, it was these young trigger-happy cowboys who amused themselves at the expense of the terrified settlers.

The funeral that followed hours of preparation was an excuse for a rally of blood-boiling rhetoric and the stoking of the ever-glowing embers of violence. While the six plain wooden coffins seemed to stand to one side, forgotten and forlorn covered by the strips of the ANC colours, green, black and gold, warriors queued up for pieces of meat that were being sliced off the slaughtered cows. They would take their meat, often at the ends of their spears, and dunk it into boiling water in the many black three-legged pots.

Sizwe didn't eat or drink. He sat and observed, weighing up the potential danger of each opponent, coming to the conclusion that while they all looked menacing in their designer battlerags, he had found himself among amateurs and poseurs. It wouldn't take long for him to work himself up to a position of power and respect, and then anything was possible.

The free-flowing beer contributed to a rowdy scene in which heavily-armed people swayed among the cows and roosters and mangy dogs. One of the coffins fell over off its base and the lid slid off. Sizwe was horrified to see the tightly embalmed corpse of a child spill to the ground, like a mummy that had fallen from the pyramids. It was quickly replaced and the coffin straightened so that the party could carry on unabated. Some of the youths gathered round the coffins and sang slogans of inspiration, while they mouthed threats of revenge.

"Who killed the children?" Sizwe casually asked a woman who came to sit next to him to remove a small stone from her shoe.

"Police!" she said firmly.

236

"Third force!" said another with conviction.

"Inkatha!" agreed a third, a fourth and a fifth.

When the coffins had been lowered into the ground and a volley of disjointed shots rang out a multi-bullet salute over the freshly packed mounds of soil, the gathered crowd stood in a sober semi-circle. Sizwe was pushed to the front on instructions of Rommel, who wanted him to carefully watch the procedure that was to follow.

One of the young commanders of Rommel's comrades stepped forward leading a goat by a rope. The local witchdoctor, sitting in all his sangoma finery and watching the gathered swaying mass, stepped forward holding a glinting blade with which he cut the throat of the beast. The goat seemed to give a gurgle of pleasure and shuddered into death. While all around him the watching crowd shouted and ululated and whistled, Sizwe watched the blood from the severed throat drip into a rusty bucket of water. Suddenly the crowd stopped voicing their encouragement. They parted at one side of the semi-circle and another young man was led forward.

Sizwe could feel the hostility around him. He heard words that he could still not understand. While his Xhosa was manageable, the local Zulu dialect made a fast delivery of sounds impossible to follow. He did pick up words like 'Inkatha' and 'peace'.

The two warriors faced each other like two wrestlers in an ancient arena of blood-sports. Their bodies shone with sweat and tautness. Then they lowered their hands, locked in a firm hand-shake into the bucket of water and the goat's blood. Encouraged by the local traditional healer who intoned chants above them, every-one was being witness to this symbolic ritual, as the two opposing leaders of Rommel's and the rival death squads, washed their hands of blood and so swore would never kill again. Everyone was relieved and no one believed a word. The killing would start again as soon as the blood on their arms was dry.

The drama of reconciliation was shattered an hour later when rival impis, sticks knocking against their shields, surged forward from the area under the trees where they had stood watching the ceremony sullenly. Fear gripped the crowd and people fled in all directions, spilling pots into the red soil and tripping over small children trapped on the ground among the stampeding adults. Rommel gave some curt orders and quickly a human chain was formed between the impis and the crowd of mourners. Another massacre had been averted.

As quickly as the violence had begun and ended, the party now recommenced. Sizwe gave a dry laugh and shook his head. Yes, he would bide his time and then soon this confusion would be something of the past.

He was given his first test immediately. The day after the introduction to his new environment, Sizwe was summonsed to the presence of his warlord and given his first assignment. "But I'm not a bank robber," he said charmingly and looked from the one lieutenant to the next, watching for a glimmer of humour, but there was none. "I'm a soldier in Umkhonto weSizwe. Besides, that is my name, Sizwe; not Al Capone." No one knew who Al Capone was. He realised that he would have to lose his education quickly if he was to keep his life. And also shut his mouth when he had something to say, especially if he thought it was witty.

So he did was he was told and robbed the small bank at Umlazi and got away with an insignificant amount of cash, which he immediately handed over to his cadre commander. It was only when he saw the report in the next day's paper that the death of the two men in the car nearby came to his attention.

He ran across the compound to Rommel's office, but was not allowed entry. He found his way round the outside of the building till he saw the figures through the closed windows. "What is this?" he cried, waving the newspaper in his hand and trying to attract Rommel's attention through the dirty panes from outside.

The elderly godfather opened the window and looked at him with a patronising smile. "You did a good job, Sizwe. We have other plans for you. You just have too much to say. And you say too many things that our boys have no knowledge of."

"You mean, I'm too much a man of the world?" Sizwe felt a sneer neutralise his polite smile.

"Oh no, we need men of the world. But not of the world of the white man. You need to go back to the roots that have given you strength and manhood." He started closing the window. Sizwe held up the newspaper. "What happened to these men? I had nothing to do with this!"

Rommel smiled again, his cold eyes flitting around the compound in search of someone lazy or something wrong, or some careless mistake. "Let's say it was an insurance policy on my part. I know you didn't do it. You know you didn't do it, but everyone else thinks you did do it. So as long as you do what you must do, no one will do anything to you. And we have a new name for you,

Sizwe Masekela. From now you are known as this Al Capone you seem to think is such a big deal."

Laughter came from the room as Rommel closed the window and referred himself to the conversation he was having before being interrupted.

Sizwe sat on a stone step in the sun. His head ached and his mind was full of confusing alternatives. He was now known as an assassin. He hadn't even pulled a trigger. Sooner than he thought, the reality of his new position dawned on him. He was trapped. It was then he phoned his uncle Rastar and heard about the visit of his father and his brother.

And the white man called David.

"I hate sitting in these concrete coffins," David protested looking out of the car window at the low grey ceiling of the parking garage,

Kendall and Henry got out. "It's safer for you to be here and safer for us not to have to explain who you are," Henry said. "We are to meet a contact on the top floor of the building. You would just look out of place there."

Kendall was getting impatient. He looked at his watch. "Come on, Dad, let's go."

David opened to door and half got out. "Wait! Who arranged this meeting?"

Henry stopped and turned. "A phone call."

"Someone you know?"

Henry shook his head. "No, but it sounded right."

"Are you going to meet Sizwe, Henry?" The black man stared back at him. "Did Sizwe set all this up? What's going on here!" David felt the bubble of anger rise in his chest. He didn't want to be used as a convenient means to an end and then dumped, just when the issues were coming to a head. "Trust me, David," Henry said and suddenly looked very tired and far older than his years.

And then they disappeared into the small door that was marked EXIT and David was alone in the dark.

He sat back in the car, irritated that he didn't have the keys to at least switch on the radio. The smell of petrol and oil made his sinuses cloud and he blew his nose. The sound echoed dully across the motor car mortuary. His back ached and he hadn't slept properly for the last three days. Since they'd left the grim luxury of the hideous Pendennis Hotel, they'd been staying in bleak boarding-houses, or any place that would allow two blacks and a white cheap accommodation without asking questions.

David had come to the end of his energy. He wanted to go home and have a bath, although he wasn't quite sure where that would in fact be. Anything better than the choices presently at his disposal. He also felt Sizwe was having the last laugh and wasting all their time.

He'd tried to ring the people on his mind, but everyone was out. Suzie's message-machine gobbled up his words and bleeped him out of existence halfway through his tender sentiment. He tried to make contact with Herman Greef, hoping there were no hard feelings about his abrupt departure, but also found Herman's machine opinionated and rude. Joanie Craig was out and her machine was not switched on, so the phone just rang. He even thought of putting a call through to Deli in LA, although they'd promised not to phone one another unless there was an emergency, which this wasn't.

Or was it?

The fact that he had given his wife so little thought during the last weeks of excitement and rediscovery worried David to the point that he started thinking he might have a marriage problem. The two letters he'd received from his wife had stayed in his pockets for days before he skimmed through them and then his only reaction had been a smile and a muttered "That's nice".

So he phoned Teema. He knew he could tell her nothing, but that she was the best at reading between the lines. It was up to him to suggest the things he wanted her to imagine.

"Any news, my child?" she asked quickly.

"Yes and no," he said. "We're on the trail, but we've not yet found the treasure." God, but he sounded like a twit! "Just want to know how you are," he added hoping she had a tale to tell.

"I dreamt about you all last night," Teema said and David knew she was terrified for their safety. "I dreamt you all were climbing a tree, like those big ones they have in that Natal, and then when you got to the top, the branches broke and you all fell into a fire." David felt a small explosion of dread detonate inside his stomach and gave a laugh, far too loudly. Teema heard it as a cry of pain. "What's the matter, my boy!"

"Nothing, Teema, I'm laughing. What an imagination you have. Listen, we've bought you something nice!" She said nothing. "Anyway, Henry and Kendall send love." She said nothing. "I'll tell them we talked." She said nothing. The pause of suspicion grew into a question mark. "I'm sorry I have no news really."

"No news is good news, isn't that so?" she said listlessly. "Your priest's wife phoned."

For a moment David was thrown and raced through his list of acquaintances. Priest? "Oh, Miss Nkotse? Oh God, is it bad news?"

"No, she said her husband was getting better. Since when do priests marry, David?"

"She's his sister, Teema. He's the man who helped me ..." He wanted to say "find you", but it made Teema sound like a lost possession.

"Take care, all my boys," she said and put down the phone.

Unknown to David, Teema then slowly sank to the cold floor of the hallway in a dead faint and lay there till late that night, when the cold of the Transvaal night forced her to regain her wits.

David suddenly thought he saw a movement out of the corner of his eye. He looked out of the windows of the parked car to his left and right and behind him, but the floor of the parking garage was as still as a tomb. The oppressively low ceiling seemed to inch down closer onto him and he shuddered.

"Like some Vincent Price movie," he muttered.

Then, in a flash, the door of the car was pulled open and a man jumped in virtually on top of him. David wheeled round and put his hands up to ward off any impending attack. He hit the man on the head with his fist and something hard landed sharply into his stomach, forcing him to double forward. He felt a stinging blow between his shoulder-blades.

"It's only me!" came the hissing words from behind his ear. David struggled to straighten himself. He turned his head, expecting more blows to follow and looked straight into the familiar scowl of Teema's youngest grandson. "It's me! See? The one-eyed terrorist!"

David's breathing came in short gasps as he weakly nodded recognition. He looked around for a weapon in Sizwe's hands but saw nothing. Sizwe had one fist balled, probably to hit him again if he struggled, while the other hand was hidden in his pocket, probably holding a gun. David gestured down at the telltale bulge in Sizwe's jacket.

"You don't have to shoot me," he rasped.

Sizwe pulled out his hand quickly, pointing something at David. "Bang-bang you're dead!" He held a roll of sweets in his hand. "It's only sweets, man. Want one?"

David looked at the familiar design on the wrapping and nodded with relief. He sat back in the seat and closed his eyes. A deep sigh escaped his tense body. "Jesus, Sizwe, you nearly gave me a fucking heart attack!" he said swallowing hard and feeling his heart beat a rumba in his chest. He had a great urge to hit the boy.

"Anyway, you've come to the wrong place. Your father's gone up to the top floor to meet you there, as I suspect you'd arranged?"

He looked at the smiling youth with undisguised irritation. Sizwe nodded and chewed his sweets. "No, that's right. I wanted to divert them. It's you I need to talk to."

David closed his eyes again. "Thanks. That's what I need like a hole in the head, to become your priest and confessor."

"Well, Dawid de Lange, if you want to stick your nose into other people's business, expect a drop of wet shit at the tip of it." Sizwe sat back on his side of the backseat and looked round the interior of the elegant car. "My brother certainly has expensive taste. Amazing what you can afford on an accountant's salary."

David nodded, thinking for the first time that he'd never taken much notice of the fact that Kendall worked in a minor capacity for a major insurance firm and yet seemed to have so much money at his disposal. A twinge of nagging suspicion forced itself out of the shadows of his mind. "Maybe he's got good investments," he said, not wanting to browse through the Masekelas' dirty washing at this time.

Sizwe gave an impressed exclamation. "Wow! That's it, for sure!" Then he seriously added, "He sells drugs to the kids in my father's school." Sizwe said it so matter of fact that David knew he didn't condone or condemn it, just mentioned it as fact. "You didn't know?"

David shook his head. "No."

"Did you know that my father is regarded by many of us in the Struggle as a collaborator with the System?"

David sighed and took another sweet from Sizwe's open hand. "What crap. Henry is a great supporter of rights for all, you included."

Sizwe smirked and nodded. "Yes, you're right. I don't suggest we comrades are always right. God knows where I sit now, I just see the wrongs we do." He looked at David. "Do you believe that I robbed that bank?"

"Didn't you?"

"Yes, it was part of my ..." He looked for a suitable word. "... Part of my brief."

"And those dead men in the car-park?"

"Do you think I killed them?"

"Didn't you?"

"That's for you to decide, De Lange. You must have some way of trusting your instinct. What does your prejudice tell you?"

David dug deep down in his traumatised conscience and knew that Sizwe could not have been involved with such cold-blooded murder. Not yet. "But if it was part of your … 'brief', you'd shoot to kill?" he said to the youth. "You just obey orders? Isn't that what your type of mass murderer always says?"

"Listen, De Lange, I don't expect you to understand anything. It's not relevant. You're not relevant."

"I was born here!"

"You ran away!"

"So did you!"

"Your System forced me out!"

"Crap! My 'System', as you call it, made life hell for millions, but they stayed and made the best of an impossible choice."

"Collaborate?"

Both men sat with white knuckles. The melting sweets helped them not to crack the enamel on their teeth, as they chewed grimly.

David spoke softly, but as clear as ice. "You sat safely in a far-off place, sponsored by bleeding hearts from Scandinavia and the UK and wherever you slammed down your begging bowl, and sent the most appalling signals back to the confused masses you'd left behind to fight your battle for you!"

Sizwe was looking at him with a smile while he listened.

David didn't care about the sarcasm glinting in his seeing eye. He needed to get a lot off his chest. "Liberation before Education?" he enunciated. "Isn't that what you called it? So the school kids ran wild and now we sit with a generation of men and women who can't read or write? While you, great conquering hero, come back with a Bulgarian degree, God help us all, and a repertoire of slick gigolo drawing-room patter?"

Sizwe slowly clapped his hands and nodded appreciatively.

"Good!" he said, "carry on, De Lange, your fascist roots are showing."

"And now you come back and confront those who kept the flame of freedom burning in their hearts, in the darkness so that you could find your way home; to these you give a fuck-you sign and swagger off into another sunset, not giving a damn about anything because that's what you want, isn't it, Comrade Masekela? You don't want anything!" David narrowed his eyes at the young man and waited for a reply.

Sizwe kept smiling as he thought and then he nodded. "You're right. I don't want anything. I came out a kid with nothing; I go back a man with nothing."

"Bullshit! That's not what I mean, noble savage! Divide and rule was always the cleverest part of that stupid system of apartheid that now lies beached on the shores of history. You've learnt well from your enemy. You don't want an educated mass of people asking questions because then you'll have to give answers! And none of you thought up any answers while sipping expensive whisky in five-star hotels overseas because you were too busy fabricating new reasons for your comfortable martyrdom. You don't want peace and prosperity, Sizwe, because that's not conducive to the type of criminal activity you all call the Struggle! You don't want democracy for the simple reason that no one in their right mind would vote thugs like you and your comrades into positions of power because you're too damn retarded to even run an election race according to the rules!"

David could swear he heard the car clock ticking in the deadly silence although there was no clock, just a digital time flash.

Sizwe was sitting comfortably. "Great, De Lange, I'm taking all this in!"

"Good. And you of all people, blessed with the talent to absorb and adapt information and communicate it in an intelligent, entertaining way, you could teach!" Sizwe gave a elongated groan. David turned the blade slowly. "You could help the others that your mindless Struggle has forced to their knees back on their feet and together with the many on the other side of the line, me included." Another groan from Sizwe. "Together we could start again and make a new world that made sense, and not just financial rands for those who exploited the pain of others to get rich!"

"Jesus, you should be in politics!"

"No!" snapped David, "I'm in Hollywood! Much more effective and the pay's great! God, you make me sick! There's Teema, slaving her fingers to the bone to put your father through an education, and him losing his health and his hopes trying to hold a school of dreams together in a storm of envy, and here you come and piss all over the picnic they've prepared for you as a homecoming party!"

David felt quite out of breath. He took out a tissue and blew his

244

nose. The smell of petrol and oil seemed stronger. The taste of raw anger was sharper.

Neither said anything for a time. A car hooted down the ramp and the echo bounced off the walls.

Sizwe fiddled with the creased wrapping paper that had held the sweets and spoke haltingly, although he knew exactly what to say. David's words had shaken him to the core with their unfashionable honesty. "As I said, before you went off on an Afrikaner tirade against us and what we stand for, you're not relevant, De Lange. I'm here because I care, not for you, but my family." It was David's time to groan. Sizwe started folding the paper into small sections as he spoke.

"Have you heard of umchina?" David shook his head. "It means I suppose, a gambling game. It's when we operatives re-enter South Africa legally or illegally to carry out a mission."

David smirked. "Ah. I'd call that more 'Hollywood' than 'Amandla', but carry on."

"I was just one of the many kids who got away in '76. In '77 I was being trained in Katenga, that's in Angola. It was there that I heard rumours that Henry Masekela was a police spy."

David turned to look at the youth, but Sizwe was intently concentrating on folding the paper in his hand. "They didn't know he was my father, so I said nothing. Then years went by and I was moved around." He stopped and seemed to remember things he couldn't talk about. "There was an uprising at the Quatro camp in Zambia, basically because the comrades were impatient. Food was bad, morale was low. The boer empire seemed invincible. I knew my family thought I was dead."

"You could've sent them a postcard," David edged in sharply.

"Yes, I wrote one and it got me into unbelievable shit. They saw the name Masekela. I was unmasked. They locked me up for a month in a metal freight container with no ventilation, no windows. It was dark all the time, day and night. I had lost my eye the year before. There was now just a hole in my face. When I had this crappy glass-eye fitted in East Germany later on, they had to cut open a socket to fit the marble. Much ado about nothing, hey?" David looked at Sizwe's face carefully. The strong jaw and the flared nostrils gave it a profile of arrogance and strength. The fingers were still bending and folding as Sizwe ploughed through the untended fields of his past.

"No blankets, no food, no medical help. The socket bled for

months. I looked like shit. I even developed an asthmatic condition because of the extremes of temperature."

"I also get that," David remarked.

Sizwe glanced at him with his eye. "No bullshit hey, De Lange?" He carried on talking as he looked down at his hands again. "Then I was transferred to Berlin."

"In Germany?"

"No, that was the name of a camp. No wire fences, just hungry lions prowling the perimeters, which was no incentive to make a run for it. I was now a suspect because of my father. I was given lice-infested clothes and put into a communal cell with fourteen others. We were allowed out for half an hour once a week. Party time! And then there was an exceptionally talented Matabele prison guard originally from Rhodesia. He would force us to lie on the floor, then kick us with his boots, beat us with coffee sticks and tell us to do the 'pompa'." Sizwe looked at David. "Do you know what that is?" David didn't. "Well, you blow out your cheeks and hold it there until the warders slap you to release it. Go on, try."

"No."

"Sissy boy."

David blew out his cheeks as far as he could. He felt the pressure on his inner ear and there was a stinging pain down his neck. Then suddenly Sizwe leant across and tapped him lightly on his cheeks. The pain was excruciating.

"Jesus!" David bend forward holding his aching face in his hands. "Fuck!"

"Ja, and that was just a love-tap, De Lange. Image that blow with the force of twenty-three years of hatred and envy behind it! It wasn't all bad though. Once I was forced by a warder to propose love to a tree and then to have sex with it in front of all the inmates. It was definitely a first for me."

David looked at Sizwe, tears of pain still in his eyes as he rubbed his face. "Did you do it?"

Sizwe looked at him and David could see Teema's twinkle in his smile. "Oh yes, make no mistake, when they say 'fuck the tree!', you fuck the tree! I had to do a lot of cheating to get my hand in the right place, but then I just closed my fist and my eye and thought of …" He stopped. "… Someone. But that was also dangerous. The warder said: 'Don't use your mind, do as you're told!'"

He opened the door and got out of the car to light a cigarette. The smell of tobacco smoke was quite a relief to David after the sourness of the fumes around him. He also got out on his side and leant on the roof of the car.

Sizwe was facing him from the other side. "Let me get to the point, De Lange. I was told that I could go free in exchange for volunteering for umchina. I said yes. So I was told … instructed to come back and kill a known collaborator." He blew smoke into the air and the grey blue cloud shimmered in the dullness of the neon light.

"Henry Masekela?" asked David.

"Yes."

"I still don't know why."

"At the time of the '76 uprisings he was one of the youngest school principals in Soweto. After the riots, he was left alone by the police, while all the others were arrested or questioned."

"Maybe he was doing his job properly?"

"Maybe. Anyway, then he was called as a state witness in the trail of some teachers who were accused of furthering the aims of the revolution. He refused to go, but the damage was done."

David shook his head and rested his chin on his folded hands. "But Sizwe, that was years ago surely. What's that got to do with your getting involved with mercenaries here in Natal?"

"Who told you that? Rastar the Fat?"

"Are we wrong?"

"It's not that simple."

"Then explain. I've got time."

"Well, I haven't. I don't want my father to find me here, so this is what you must do." Sizwe quickly told David how and what to tell Henry and Kendall.

David stopped him halfway. "Hang on, why can't you tell them all this yourself?"

"Because I don't want them to see me like this, and … well, I just can't talk to my father."

"He loves you."

"Isn't that a bit Hollywood?" Sizwe parried.

"He's got a heart problem," David replied.

"He's an old man …"

"Rubbish, he's my age!"

David's sudden affront made Sizwe laugh. "So you're also an old man! Fuck you, De Lange, I'm not going to kill my father!"

Another car came round the circular pillar and swept them with its headlights.

"Why should you kill your father! Sizwe, this is the 1990s; not some flaky boy scout camp in Central Africa!" Sizwe stood away from the car.

"Well, Dawid, as you said, I only obey orders. If I disappear no one will expect me to do what I was trained to do. So I just disappear. Tell Henry Masekela that in your opinion, his son Sizwe is stark raving mad and a lost cause."

"That won't stop him from searching."

"No, but it will send him home to Teema. I must get my life under control without my family getting in the way."

"Can't you get a job? You've got all the alphabet, Sizwe. My friend Suzie Bernard thinks you're very ... compelling. She works for the ANC ..."

Sizwe laughed and did a twirl on the stained cement tarmac.

"God man, you're such a *poephol*!" David automatically cackled at the word.

"Oh?" said Sizwe, "so you haven't forgotten everything?"

"Certainly not the word *poephol*. Well then, if I'm a *poephol*, Sizwe, you're an arsehole, and I'd rather be a *poephol*." The young man backed away from the car and seemed to wave.

"I depend on you to get my family home safely, De Lange. Make up any story. Convince them. Isn't that what you do best, you mindfuckers from Hollywood?"

And then he was gone, ducking behind the car next to the BMW and all David heard was the creak of a door and silence. He was left with the faint smell of cigarette and a perfectly folded paper dove balancing on the roof of the car.

CHAPTER 17.

The top floor of this modern city block in the centre of Durban seemed to comprise of one office suite after the next. David had walked up the steps from the basement garage to the ground floor. The foyer was deserted, although from somewhere he could hear the sounds of a radio. He took the lift up as far as it could go and then walked quickly along the shiny linoleum floor, peering through the mottled glass of reception rooms and hallways, checking the nameplates on the doors, from import companies to wholesale merchants.

He was aware that day had already changed to dusk behind his back while he'd been sitting in the car below life-level. The eeriness of the approaching night was compounded by the fact that all the lights in the building were on. Was this the crazy notion that it cost more to switch them on and off, than to leave them burning for no one's benefit?

But there were no doors leading off the passages to the living quarters of the black staff. What black staff would be living there anyway? he wondered. Probably doormen and lift attendants and cleaners and … God, once started, the list was endless. How would this country have managed for a day if magically all their unwanted blacks had vanished into thin air?

Then he came to the fire escape which carried a brash red EXIT sign over it, the neon behind it gasping uneven flashes. He opened the heavy steel door and the musty dampness of the concrete stairwell blasted him in the face. The smell of urine was overpowering and he coughed. He looked up and saw the stairs disappear onto yet another floor. Maybe this was it.

Looking carefully where he put his feet, he dodged the unpleasant mounds of soft-brown that seemed to dot the stairs and landings, and eventually came face to face with another steel door. "Push to open" it invited and he pushed and it didn't open. He rattled the bar and the door stayed unbudged and unfriendly.

"Oh fuck this," he muttered and gave the door a sharp heave with his shoulder. It suddenly gave way and David was propelled out of the building into another world.

It was dark already and the air outside was sticky and sweet. The smell of open fires invaded the areas of his sinuses where the sharpness of petrol and piss had numbed his senses. The door clanked shut behind him. David stood transfixed by what was staring up at him.

He looked again and a small white thing bleated and baa'ed. The small lamb seemed to do a little dance-step with its back hooves and shake its tail. "Baa!" it said and butted David's foot with a woolly forehead.

Sheep high up in the sky?

David looked up and, yes, he could see the lights of the city below him and around him, twinkling yellow and bronze and silver. He looked down again and did a double-take. The lamb had multiplied and now there were three cross-eyed creatures staring up at him, plus a stringy goat that watched this newcomer.

"What the hell is going on here?" he started to say to himself but also to his little audience, when a large figure loomed out from the shadows and grunted.

"What is it, Master?" it said.

David's strained control gave another lurch and he wanted to sit down as his knees gave notice. He stepped back and felt the cold iron of the firedoor brace his back.

A huge black man stepped forward into more light and David could see he was naked accept for a cloth round his waist. His head was shaven and in the murkiness of the Natal night, it was just the sharp whites of his eyes and teeth that seemed to claim a place in his face.

David cleared his throat and tried to sound casual. "I'm looking for Henry Masekela. Is this where he is?"

The man nodded and pointed to David's right, then said a few Zulu words and the small herd of lambs and goat trotted off into the shadows. David's eyes were getting used to the darkness around him. He could make out a large rounded shape silhouetted against the heavens and standing in the middle of the flatness of the skyscraper's roof. A fire was crackling in front of it. As he went closer, he could make out some figures crouched round the flames cooking food. The delicious smell of roasting meat invaded his jaded nose and made his mouth water.

He stepped forward into the light from the fire and the figures round it turned and looked at him.

There were two women and three men, a few small children clutching their mothers' bosoms and a large dog lying with its legs in the air, either playing dead or being dead. There was no sign of Henry or Kendall.

"I'm looking for two friends of mine ..." The man to whom he'd spoken earlier reappeared with Henry at his side. David was greatly relieved. "There you are, Henry! I was just saying ..."

Henry pulled him to one side and they stood up against the smoothness of woven thatch. David touched the roundness of the mound and realised that it was a traditional Zulu hut.

"David, I thought you'd stay in the car ..."

"My God, Henry, this is a kraal up here!" he said in awe and looked around. Suddenly it all fell into place: the lambs and the goats, the open fire and the huts. Not just the one they stood next to, but other smaller huts dotted about the vast expanse of barren concrete.

Henry nodded and pointed to the horizon. "These people all work here in some or other capacity, cleaning, servicing, security. They come from kraals over those hills and beyond. They were given terrible little rooms across near the lift shaft, but have rather built their own traditional living-quarters. So they keep goats, have a well in which a hosepipe dribbles fresh water, and even some trees growing in large tanks that were left here during some past renovation."

A ripe yellow moon had broken through the clouds over the sea and was spinning larger and wider into the night-sky above them. David looked up at the millions of stars that seemed to shine brighter over this bizarre timewarp, enhanced by the peace and tranquillity of a rural environment trapped in urban decay.

"And are they happy here?" he asked.

Henry gave a chuckle. "If I had a tradition to go back to, I'd run into its arms like a happy ending. But my tradition is your tradition, Dawid. Where do we go for the comfort of continuity?"

They thought for a moment and then both said simultaneously. "Teema!"

Kendall emerged from the shadows with two young men, who were hunched together, looking at something in their hands with great interest. Kendall gave a low hiss and they seemed to hide what they held and vanish back into the shadows of a hut. "What are you doing here, man?" Kendall asked and kicked a nosy goat away sharply with his imported boot.

"Yes, David," added Henry urgently, "we're still waiting for the person to arrive ..."

"He already has," David said quietly and looked around. "Can we talk somewhere?"

"Talk here!" said Kendall keen to find out what had happened.

"No, I'm sorry, this is just between Henry and myself. Come."

David led the way and Kendall stood in the shadows, watching his father and his white friend walk to the edge of the building. Their figures were sharply etched out against the garish shimmer of the dormant city.

David then spoke, gesturing and pointing with his finger, once even putting his hand on Henry's shoulder. Henry then turned away and shook his head. David had to again explain and pointed towards those faraway hills. Henry shook his head a few times, seemed to start off, as if trying to escape the onslaught of information, then slowly sat on something, covering his face with his hands.

Kendall watched David crouch down in front of his father and hold the man's hands in his, talking, explaining, telling him about his son, the son he so loved and the one that was now obviously as mad as a snake.

Kendall gave a sigh and even though he couldn't hear what was being said, sensed it was bad news about Sizwe and didn't really mind. He had other things to see to. He gave another sharp hiss through his designer dentures and the young men reappeared from the shadows. "Okay dudes, who's got the cash? Remember, those are just samples. There's a lot where that comes from, but nothing is free. Capish?"

The excited murmur from his potential buyers warmed his heart. This was an unexpected windfall. With a little bit a smooth talking, he could walk away with quite a packet tonight and these retards in their kraal in the sky would be able to have a rave-up that would crack their world in two. Kendall glanced up at the cut-outs of father and friend. They were now merged into one, as David held Henry in his arms and let him cry for the son that had died again, while in reality he still lived and breathed and killed.

David didn't feel like driving the six hours back to Johannesburg with Henry and Kendall, mainly because being with Henry was too painful. The black man had taken the strange news of Sizwe's defection very badly, not understanding how his son could just reject the love of family and exchange the security of home for the empty existence of 'the whore of war', as Henry called it. David had said nothing about the talk of Henry's supposed collaboration, and what it had demanded of Sizwe. He just allowed himself to be the simple bearer of bad news, and once that was done, wanted to go before he recanted and told Henry the truth, which was worse.

So they dropped him at the airport, having not questioned his excuse of a previous engagement in the City of Gold as a reason to fly. After buying a ticket and booking in, David took a chance and phoned Suzie Bernard, just to leave a cheeky message on her machine. She picked up the phone.

"I was just thinking about you," she said.

He was pleased. "I hope my clothes didn't get in the way," he said, waiting for her gurgle, but that old Suzie was still somewhere else between cold sheets. The voice he heard was the business-like Ms Bernard he still had to come to terms with.

"Bad news, David. I suppose it can wait till you get here ..."

"God no!" he exclaimed and felt his chest contract.

"It's Teema ..."

"Oh God, no ..."

"She's okay, David. She's had a heart attack. She's quite comfortable in hospital. I'm getting her the best medical care."

"But how ..."

"I'll pick you up at the airport. What time's the flight due?"

He told her and she hung up without saying goodbye. He sat on an uncomfortable plastic bucket-bench in the departure lounge. So Teema was the one with the heart problem, not Henry! God, how easily he always fell for her charming delusions. He should've known! He should've asked Henry! He should've ...!

Suzie didn't want a kiss from him when he met her at the arrivals hall of Jan Smuts Airport. "Come," she said, "I'm parked illegally."

When did anyone park legally around here, he wondered. The drive to the city was in relative silence, except for Suzie's concise description of the events that led to the present. "Teema's daughter from Port Elizabeth came up on a surprise visit to see someone on business, and luckily popped in to look her mother up. You've met her, I believe?" David tried to place the face of Felicia Masekela, but they all seemed to merge into one face and that was Teema's. He shook his head while confirming that they'd met at the funeral in Transkei.

"Well, she found Teema lying on her bed in a bad way. She didn't know what to do. Teema managed to say: phone Suzie at the ANC!

That's a miracle, because there are six of us Suzies and no one ever gets through to anyone there anyway. But they got me immediately and I went across to the Executive Suite and asked for strings to be pulled and the Secretary-General's office arranged for an ambulance and immediate acceptance at the Pine Lodge Clinic. I know it well; I had some surgery done there once."

He glanced at her driving the car, studied her pert profile. "Oh?" he asked. "Anything serious?"

"Yes. Age. I had a nip and tuck." She glanced at him and he saw a smile threaten. "You don't really think I'd look like this naturally after waiting for you to come back for thirty years? You shit! You made me old and withered and now you can go to hell!" Again he didn't know if she meant it, or if he should laugh.

The Pine Lodge Clinic in the fashionable fortress-suburb of Sandton didn't look like a place where people died. It was warm and spotlessly geared for the rich one-night-stand jet-setter. Soft sofas and chairs filled the foyer and gentle classical muzak wafted across the healthy palms. A trickling fountain calmed the fears and the general atmosphere was one of a laid-back gentility. The nursing staff looked like young aerobics instructors.

David's nanny was in a private room. Her daughter from Port Elizabeth was standing next to the bed, plaiting Teema's hair into small knots. He was amazed at the length of the hair now that he saw it loose for the first time. It was fine and grey and seemed to float round her head like a halo.

Teema was not wearing her thick-lensed glasses, but she immediately looked towards them as they tiptoed into the room.

"Is that you, my boy?" she called.

"Yes, it's me."

Teema held out a free arm to him. The drip was attached to her other wrist. He took her hand. It was warm.

"Why didn't you tell me you had a heart problem?" he said, not wanting to sound more than just a little stern.

"Because I don't have a problem!" she said firmly. "I have a sick heart. It must just get better. Otherwise my problems lie out of my body and you know that as well as I do."

Felicia flashed David a glance and plaited expertly. "Now we'll have none of this talking about family drama," she said, knowing exactly what her mother meant. "I'm in charge here and I say only small chats about bland things like love and laughter are permitted. No problems, Teema. Meneer De Lange?"

No one had called him that for thirty years. David felt the blush of embarrassment flush his face.

Suzie smirked and gave him a little bow of the head. "Can I get you a chair, meneer?" she asked hinting. He pulled one up for her and she sat. He stood next to the bed, holding Teema's hand. "How are you feeling, Mama Teema?" Suzie asked.

"As good as can be expected, Suzie my dear. Thank you for getting Nelson Mandela to personally book me into this place. I didn't know any of our people knew about palaces like this." She didn't show any sign of a tongue in her cheek.

Felicia laughed. "It doesn't take much to create a taste for cream, even though you've been brought up on sour milk!"

"Well, Teema, actually it wasn't Nelson Mandela personally."

Teema stopped her with a pointed look at the green bowl of flowers on the high table next to the bed. There was a small card balanced in the cascade of colours. Suzie turned her head sideways and read, then read again. She stared down at Teema with disbelief.

"Is this a joke?" she said, recognising the handwriting.

"No," said Teema with a straight face. "Flowers. Real ones."

"Our mother's work with the elderly in among the roots of Soweto's community has reached ears in the tops of the trees," said Felicia, suddenly very impressed.

The hour passed by gently and calmly, and Teema never gave a hint of the fear she carried in her diseased heart for the safety of her grandson. David found her looking at him intently at times, and while she didn't have the lenses to really see anything at that distance, he knew she was reading his mind.

Felicia had much to say and kept the small-talk down to the easy details of light-hearted stories. She asked Suzie what her job entailed.

"I raise money for the Movement," Suzie said, shrugging it away as if it were a mere routine.

"Do you ask from foreign companies too?" Felicia wanted to know.

Suzie pulled a face. "From the few still left here, yes."

"Well, let me tell you something you can keep for your next board meeting with some bigshot American conglomerate."

Teema's eyes closed, a slight smile of contentment on her face as she enjoyed the small movements of her daughter's fingers in her hair.

"During the bad years of oppression, when our township was full

255

of soldiers shooting to kill the children and getting gold stars in their books for it, and foreign companies were disinvesting with a haste that was, to say the least, obscene, a very well-known American concern announced the building of a fully-equipped Olympic swimming-pool in the township for the use of its many street children."

Suzie narrowed her eyes and nodded slowly. "I think I know this story."

"I don't," said David quickly. "I'd also like the name of the firm ..."

Felicia went on. "So they built it at a cost of millions. It looked good in the boardrooms of Wall Street. Everyone was so impressed. Civil rights leaders applauded. Stocks soared and everyone was happy."

"And the children?" asked Suzie, leading the story to its climax knowingly.

"Oh, the children? Good heavens, my dear, they weren't consulted. They couldn't swim. They hated water. They wanted a soccer field. Just a nice level piece of ground with some poles and a ball."

David laughed. "And I'd say a damn sight cheaper too."

"Oh yes," said Felicia, tucking Teema's little curls into a circle of braid on her head. "But a soccer field looks like nothing at a boardroom meeting."

"Well, the investment I'm talking about isn't all like that," sighed Suzie, hoping it could all be as simple.

"But it's not a sad story, Suzie," Felicia smiled. "The kids got their soccer field after all. Once the newsmen and TV cameramen and representatives of the philanthropic Americans went back to their triumphs, the water was drained, poles painted in the deep end and the shallow end, and now soccer is being played at the bottom of that Olympic pool every weekend since!"

David applauded the spirit softly. "Great!" he said.

"Soccer at an angle?" asked Suzie, indicating the slope of the pool.

"Minor snag," said Felicia. "Our little local team has won a national junior league cup. That's why I'm up here. I am their PRO. I must arrange for them to come up to Jo'burg and receive their prize." She patted Teema's hairstyle proudly.

"There you are, Mama. As good as Princess Diana!"

Teema beamed as she looked at her blurred self in the hand-mirror Felicia held up in front of her. "Tell the handsome men they can come in now, one by one," she murmured and David squeezed her hand. He ticked her off his worry list with relief.

His precious nanny would live to see another day.

Not everyone who knew Dawid de Lange was that lucky. Driving back from the hospital, David was wondering where he would stay and if Suzie was taking him to her flat, and what he could suggest if she wasn't. Suddenly she pulled the car onto the edge of a small suburban park and switched off the engine.

He looked at her with a smile. "Isn't this a little bit public for what I have in mind?" he said. Suzie had something else on her mind, and it showed in the tension on her face. David put his hand over hers, still on the steering wheel. "What is it, Suzie? Is it something I did that night ...?"

"Herman Greef is dead." He stared at her lips, seeing for the first time the same small lines that so irritated Deli about her mouth. Suzie spoke again. "Herman Greef is dead, Dawid." She bit her bottom lip and David saw her tongue play across it. Small fine lines that seemed to grow deeper as he watched them. A mouth like his wife Deli.

Dawid de Lange heard David Clayton ask: "How did it happen?"

"Someone shot him."

The numbing glass that seemed to have covered David's reactions like a helmet suddenly shattered and he took a painful gasp of air. He opened his door and got out, nearly being choked by the seatbelt. He fumbled with the catch and loosened it, leaving the door open, and stumbled across the pavement into the park.

The children's playground was colourful and miniature, and he seemed to tower over the swings and the slide. He lurched towards the roundabout and sat down on the small platform, held onto the poles on each side and propelled himself round with his feet.

Suzie stayed in the car and watched the sensitive boy from her childhood cry for his friend. She'd never liked Herman Greef and now that he was gone, couldn't pretend to care for him more. But to see Dawid de Lange so upset by the death of someone he hadn't seen for thirty years moved her and made her decide to leave her prejudice at the gate.

After about ten minutes, she got out of the car and slowly walked towards him, giving him ample warning of her approach in case he still wanted to be alone. But he looked up at her and held out his hand to her. "Come and sit on the merry-go-round," he said and smiled through his clouds. She sat next to him and kept her hand in his. They slowly moved in a circle, the trees and an interested mongrel who was watching them with his head to one side starting to blur as they sped up. Both used their feet to propel the little platform round and round and when Suzie closed her eyes, she was back on the funfair's Crazy Octopus, clutching her stick of candyfloss and screaming with delighted terror.

Then their energy waned and the circles got slower. Eventually the merry-go-round stopped and she saw how full of dust both their feet were from the red soil.

"So how did it happen?" David eventually asked. He bent over and picked up a thin stick with which he started drawing lines and circles in the soft soil. The little dog waited excitedly for the stick to become his.

"I mean, if he was shot … it wasn't suicide, was it?"

"No." Suzie then looked at him surprised. "Surely you never suspected that, did you? Of Herman Greef?"

"No," David shrugged. "But you never know what stress can do."

"Stress? Herman Greef?" Suzie said it with such a tone of disbelief, as if the brash chauvinist now being prepared for his funeral down in Cape Town could never have been considered that human.

"Did he surprise a burglar in the house?" David wondered, now suddenly thinking for no reason of the young gardener who was always impassively working on the same bush. Why would he think this man could be a killer?

Suzie shook her head and gave a dry laugh. "No. It happened in a traffic jam."

David looked at her with a frown. Why was she smiling? "Is that funny?" he asked.

"No," she said quickly. "But I suppose if you get impatient around other impatient people, things are bound to go wrong."

David let go her hand and got up, stepping with his feet onto the design of a big bird he had scratched out in the dust. He threw the stick to one side and the small dog pounced on it with vigour.

David put his hands in his pockets. "Herman was always hell in a car," he said. "The few times I was subjected to his driving added years to my life. He would lean on his hooter and scream bloody murder at anyone in his way. But to be shot for saying 'fuck off you black bastard'?"

"It was a white bastard."

"How do you know?"

Suzie also got up and with a flick of her wrist sent the merry-go-round spinning.

"Joanie Craig phoned me at the office. Did you tell her I worked there?" Suzie didn't care for Joanie Craig either, but didn't want to get into a discussion about her now.

David shrugged. "I might have … Joanie was with him?"

"No, it was in all the local papers. There was a traffic jam, some or other breakdown and all the cars were bunched up together … and it seems Herman let rip with his hooting and his screaming and his 'fuck-off-you-bastard' type of thing …"

She kicked at a clod of earth. The mongrel came closer to sniff at it and Suzie crouched down and held out her hand. Tentatively the stray dog crept closer, wary of human contact but dying for affection.

David stood at a tree, looking at the many love-carvings in its bark that announced forgotten and futile passions. Small hearts and arrows eternalising true love: H.S. LOVES F.P. He could imagine Herman, dressed in all the right gym gear, firmly gelled hair, carefully tended moustache, Ray-Ban shades, sharply scented aftershave. He'd give the traffic jam a minute of grace before starting his impatient hustle.

"What the fuck's going on here!" he'd mutter and drum on his steering wheel, turning the volume of his digital cassette player into the red, so the thudding beat of the technology dented the space of those round him. He'd wind down his window and put out his head and bellow. "Wake up, you fucking wankers!"

Some drivers and their passengers would hear and smile, still amused by such words. A woman of indeterminate age might see the strong profile and the thick head of hair and clench her thighs together for a moment of fantasy.

But this was not going to be Herman's lucky day.

In the car ahead of him, a second-hand car that was giving the owner no end of trouble, sat a man who had just come to the end of his tether. He was on his way to a final confrontation with the employer who had told him the week before that he had been declared redundant.

"I'm sorry, Belmar," the bored bureaucrat had boomed, "this is the way things are going. This is worse for me than for you. I like you and you work well. You are part of the business, the family …"

He droned on and it was when Belmar heard the same story recited to a young typist later that day, that he decided to walk out anyway.

But when he'd arrived home, feeling well rid of the burden of being a burden, his wife pointed out nervously that by resigning as he'd done, he'd also forfeited all his valued redundancy benefits.

Belmar had fallen into an old trap. He tried to reverse his actions and pleaded and made feeble jokes and suggestions, but it was too late. He was now out in the cold and without a warm glove, let alone a golden handshake.

So here he was, carefully dressed and rehearsed, on a last-ditch attempt to try and recover his lost investments, even if he only got back part of his redundancy packet. The boss would see him only for ten minutes. That was to be in five minutes' time. He would be late. This traffic snarl up would finish off all his chances.

And then there was this cunt in the shiny Merc behind him, edging towards him, hooting and shouting, with that disgusting nightclub-beat throbbing from his car, shouting and hooting, revving and … Herman bumped against the back of Belmar's car.

"Move out of the way, you fucking piece of junk!" he shouted and started laughing at the pale drawn face of the man in front of him. Belmar was looking back at Herman from out of his window with what looked like an apologetic smile. But it wasn't a smile, it was the grimace of madness.

Belmar got out of his old station-wagon, his large overcoat making him look even smaller and more fragile than he felt. He saw a dull scratch on the bumper of his car, certainly not caused by the rubber-embossed fender of Herman Greef's imported car, but it was enough to unleash Belmar's suppressed hatred of wealth and those with more than him. He stalked up to Herman's open window and looked at the face of the man who was a calling him names.

"Get back in your car, *poes*!" snarled Herman, now quite enjoying his performance. Occupants of adjoining cars wound down their windows and prepared to enjoy a good drama while they waited.

"What did you call me?" Belmar knew what names they called him at the office. *'Poes'* was one of them.

"I said …" repeated Herman Greef clearly for the benefit of his audience, "… get back in your *kak* old car, *poes*!"

As Herman laughed again, Belmar could see the gold-fillings in his mouth. The sharp onslaught of Herman's imported aftershave made him want to be sick. The heartbeat of modern muzak tore at his frayed self-control.

Then Belmar pulled out the pistol from his coat pocket and fired point-blank into the laughing face of the man in the smart car, who kept laughing even after the shot went off, mouth open, eyes half-shut with mirth, his head thrown back to allow the roar of amusement free passage through his throat. Now the new third eye in the middle of his forehead, dark-red and edged with sooty-black, didn't even spoil Herman Greef's good looks. So Belmar fired his pistol again, this time into the open mouth that had called him *'poes'* and Herman Greef's head exploded. David shuddered.

"What is it, Dawid?" Suzie asked, patting the dog whose eyes were now blissfully closed.

David turned to her. "I must get back to Cape Town. I didn't even say goodbye to him when I just left his house. I left a note ..."

Suzie didn't want to say what was on the tip of her tongue and David didn't want to hear it. She patted the dog on his head, got a quick warm lick across the chin and got back into the car. David glanced back at the tree trunk. J.S. LOVES R.M. ...

He wondered if his young heart was still visible, carved out on the tree in St Andrew's Road. D.d.L. LOVES S.B. Maybe Suzie would come down to Cape Town with him so he could show her. Once in the car he asked her. To his surprise she said: "Yes ... please?"

CHAPTER 18.

The silent gardener was still snipping away at a bush in Herman Greef's garden when David and Suzie pulled up in the driveway. Through the open door of the garage they could see Herman's ca parked. The sight of his dead friend's prize possession made David swallow hard.

There was another car drawn up against the stoep of the cottage. The boot was open and various boxes were standing around on the brick paving. The front door was open. The gardener gave no sign of recognition or interest as they passed him. David stopped in the door and knocked lightly.

"Frieda?" he called. There was no answer. He called again louder. "Frieda!"

A woman came out of the living-room, holding one of the large art books that Herman insisted on putting out for display on his coffee-table. David started as he looked into her eyes, for she was the split image of her murdered twin.

"You must be … Blanche?" he said, trying to remember if they'd ever met before. It had been interesting to all who knew Herman that he and his sister had nothing in common in spite of coming out of their mother's womb holding hands and locked in combat like the rivals they would become. Blanche Greef, now Tucker, looked at the couple in the door coldly. She wasn't expecting any of Herman's few friends, as she'd advised those who called not to come to the house, but to the church on the following afternoon. The woman in the door with the shortish hair looked her up and down without pretence. She returned the glare.

"Yes, I am Blanche Tucker. I'm sorry, the funeral is only tomorrow." She gave a flashed fabricated smile and turned to go up the passage, glancing down at the glorious colour reproductions of the paintings of Goya in her hands.

"I'm Dawid de Lange. I lived here."

Blanche Tucker stopped in her stroll and turned slightly. She had no recollection of the name or the face. Not that it mattered, for Herman's taste in friends usually left a lot to be desired.

"Really? I'd know that, surely. Were you a boarder? Did you rent a room? Were you and poor Herman room-mates?" She said it with such malice that David could feel Suzie stiffen with anger next to him.

"I was … Herman was my best friend," he said quietly.

Blanche looked him up and down with the same distaste as she had Suzie. "Really? He never mentioned you."

"Well, I don't imagine he did much talking to you, did he, Mrs Tucker?" Suzie's honeyed tones singed through the crispness of the atmosphere. Blanche returned with a practised parry.

"No, I didn't keep tabs on my brother. Well …" she closed the book sharply and the glossy pages met with a sharp slap, "… as you probably have heard, your friend is dead. I'm here to clear up. There are no souvenirs, I'm sorry."

"Jesus!" hissed Suzie and took a step into the passage, but David held her back.

"Herman was at school with us," he said with a careful smile. Blanche Tucker widened her eyes and gave a loud shrill laugh.

"Goodness, how sweet! That was so long ago, even I couldn't have been born then!" She loved the fact that she always looked ten years younger than her twin. "Mr …?"

"De Lange".

"Yes … Look, why don't you come to the funeral tomorrow, with your friend here. It will be such fun. All the old pals will be there. You can just wallow in the past and cry your eyes out. I certainly won't stand in your way."

A young blonde man came down the passage holding some of Herman's elegant suits in one hand, while dusting them off with the other. "Ma, they fit me like a dream! I didn't know Uncle Herman had such taste!" He stopped at the sight of David and Suzie. "Oh hello, are you people from the funeral parlour? Aren't you supposed to wear top hats or something?"

The fleshy cheeks wobbled as the man gave a studied dimpled smile. He winked at Suzie and swept into the living-room. "I'll put these on the chair, Ma. Now don't forget to take the CDs. I'm so bored having to listen to your Bizet's Favourite Hits! Uncle Herman's got the full opera of Carmen with Callas and that other American queen, what's his name?"

Suzie quickly glanced back to where the boxes stood at the car. She stepped towards them and looked down, seeing shoes and shirts and other of Herman's belongings carefully folded and packed, ready to be moved. She rejoined David outraged.

"These people are robbing him!" she said and pushed past into

263

the passage. She tried to take the book from Herman's sister but she held on firmly. Suzie let go and stepped into the living-room. Each chair was covered with items that Blanche and her son had collected from Herman's cupboards.

"What the hell do you think you are doing?" asked the limp-wristed man, his eyebrows reaching far into his carefully plucked hairline.

Suzie took the suits from him and put them over her arm. "Now which cupboard did these come from?" she asked and without waiting for an answer, forced Blanche to step aside and walked up the passage, hoping that the room she chose would be Herman's bedroom. It was, and she hung the clothes back into one of his cupboards. She caught sight of herself in a mirror and had to smile. The iciness of her demeanour was, in one word, magnificent. Herman would have been proud of her.

Blanche turned on David furiously. "How dare you walk in here and prevent us from doing our job? We are family! Bo? Phone the police!"

The blonde apple of his mother's eye stammered something, not feeling very brave as David stepped inside the house, pulled up to his imposing height and fixing the wimpish nephew with a glint in his eye.

Suzie joined them and the small hallway seemed very crowded. "No," she said firmly and in total control. "I will phone the police. I am a qualified lawyer, Miss Greef, and this can only be described in the simplest terms: theft! You!" Suzie clicked her fingers at the blonde in the living-room.

"Get those boxes back in here. Now!" The man his mother still called Bo squeezed past them and hastily started carrying the spoils back into the passage.

The carefully painted and presented Mrs Blanche Tucker stood frozen with affront, clutching the heavy book upside down against her renovated bosom, digging into the glossy cover picture with her sharp artificial nails. "You won't get away with this!" she snarled. "I have contacts and I have friends. As far as I know you could be anyone!"

"Well, we're not anyone," said Suzie. "We're Herman's past. We remember him from the best years of his life, and you're certainly not going get that from him, at least not until he is safely buried. Then you can rifle through what remains." She indicated into the house.

"Come, Ma," whispered her son from the stoep and Blanche scooped up her small clutchbag from the hallway table and huffed out of the door.

"Blanche?" called Suzie from inside. The woman stopped, her eyes tightly closed, her mouth set in a pursed line as she tried to control her rising hysteria.

"What … is … it … now!" she shot out staccato. Suzie came out onto the stoep with a smile. She stood in front of Blanche and indicated the book still in her arms.

"Mrs Tucker, you're taking Goya. Goya doesn't want to go. Free Goya!" With a slight tug she pulled the large book from Mrs Tucker's clamp and went inside.

David stood in the open door and watched Herman's family get into their car and drive out of his gate, the boot still open and the lid waving wildly as the car edged into the street and vanished round the hedge. The gardener didn't look round once.

Suzie wasn't in the passage or the lounge. "Suzie?" he called and looked into the kitchen, but it was empty. He passed the door to Herman's bedroom and saw her sitting on his bed, her face covered by her hands. He could hear her sobbing. David went into the room and sat next to her, putting his arms round her. Suzie's shoulders were sloped and her body felt so thin and fragile. "I don't believe that fucking bitch! Fuck that family! Jesus! What … vultures!" She sobbed and spat the words out at the same time, then gave a sniff and wiped her nose with her wrist. "I've seen a lot, De Lange, but that takes the cake! Herman's well rid of all of that!"

There was a tentative knock on a window somewhere inside and a small voice seemed to call the word "Master?"

"Frieda?" David jumped up and ran out of the room.

Frieda and Valkyrie were both outside the kitchen, standing in a flowerbed and peering through one of the barred windows. The dog with his paws up against the windows was taller than the maid.

"Frieda? What are you doing there … hang on!" David felt around for the kitchen door key on top of the breakfast cereals in the shelf, unlocked it and opened the door.

"Wait now, Valkyrie. Later, boy, later …"

Frieda stood in her green anorak, with a scarf round her head. She looked slightly tipsy. She wasn't wearing her false teeth. "Master David …" she lisped and took a step back when she saw Suzie join him, stepping onto Valkyrie's paw. The dog gave a surprised yelp and vanished back into the undergrowth.

"No, it's okay, Frieda, this is my friend Suzie. She's also Herman's friend. Come in."

Frieda shook her head violently and took another step back. "No, no, I won't come in as long as that bitch is there! As true as God, Master David, I just tried to get myself together after the terrible news of Master Herman ..." She started crying and her toothless mouth pulled itself into a grotesque pink half-moon. The sobs mingled with her words and made David's eyes fill with tears. "He was so mixed up, you know, Miss Suzie, so full of worries about what was going to happen and he always treated me so nice. I was his rock on which he could build ..." The sobs suddenly stopped and she replaced her sorrow with the shine of fanaticism. "Ja, I ran his house, I cooked his food, ask Master David here, isn't it so, Master David? Ja, I was part of the family and now they throw me out ..." She shrugged and pointed into the darkest part of the undergrowth as if she'd been banished there forever with the dog.

"They can't throw you out," David said gently, trying to coax the woman into the kitchen, but she shook her head and stepped back again, this time dangerously close to the edge of the swimming pool that filled the backyard like a small sea.

"Miss Blanche, she just walk in with that *moffie* son of hers and say: 'Get out you drunk' ... I can't repeat the word she used, but I tell you she's no lady. And you know, Master Herman said I could have the cupboard and the bed and the lounge-suite when he died. But I don't think the family will let me."

She looked up at him nodding away and muttering to herself. Suzie nudged David and he stepped out towards Frieda. "Listen now, Frieda. The funeral is tomorrow and after that I promise you I'll sort all that out, and you will not be forgotten or treated badly."

"You promise, Master David? Promise?" Frieda's eyes shone brightly and a small, shiny tear rolled out of her eye and down her cheek.

"Promise."

"Cross your heart and hope to die?"

David was just going to do that, when Suzie interrupted firmly. "Wait now, we've had enough of dying. Frieda? Do you have bus fare?" Frieda looked at Suzie as if she'd made an improper suggestion.

"What you think I am? A beggar?" She turned and shuffled towards the garden gate. "Hey Valkyrie? *Kom!*"

David called after her. "Oh Frieda, what about the gardener?"

Frieda stopped and half-turned her head as if the answer didn't warrant her full attention. "That garden boy?" she sneered. "*Sis*, I don't make casual conversation with that sort of cheeky kaffir." She gave a sharp whistle and the dog joined her through habit, off for another long walk which would take him to a new life in the ghetto. The gate edged closed behind them.

David had to sit on the step and Suzie joined him. "I give up," he said with a deep sigh.

"Okay," she said. "I have the key to a friend's flat on the beach at Clifton. You want to come and give up there?"

He kissed her, and as they left the house and locked the front door, he could swear he heard Herman Greef give one of his typically sarcastic snorts.

Once they reached Clifton, the sky had already disappeared behind a duvet of feathered cloud. They left the car halfway on the pavement of the narrow road that linked Sea Point with Camps Bay, carved out of the mountain rock from which hung great marble mansions.

"On another yellow line?" David remarked, as the wind slammed his door shut. Suzie shrugged and looked up at the angry sky. "It's going to rain!" she called, her words whipped away from her mouth by the erratic squalls. "We'd better get our bags in before it does."

David looked out across the sea. It was a purple dirty-brown colour as the stormy currents lashed it against the rocks below. The usually white expanse of the Clifton beaches of washed-out grey. Seagulls floated motionless above the waves, held into place by winds and will, cawing soundlessly and watching the unpleasantness below with interest.

"Leave the bags," David said suddenly and the first of the great football-drops of rain splashed against his cheek leaving a stinging burn. "Let's go down to the beach!"

"But we'll get wet!" Suzie wailed, touching her hair as if it would change his mind. But David was already down the first of dozens of cement steps leading to the snug coves of one of the most sought-after residential areas in the would. The luxury flats stood guard over the cluster of pre-war cottages hiding behind picket fences and under spreading palms. "Oh, fuck it!" was all David heard Suzie say.

It was so easy going down the steps. He remembered that from those old days, when they'd race to the beach, seeing who'd get there first. The one down last had to go up all the way to get some beers at the Clifton Hotel. He often found himself then wheezing up the uneven cement steps in the scorching sun, cursing the fact that he always politely waited for girls and their mothers to step down before him and so he always lost. "Polite twit!" he now shouted up at the seagulls and felt the solid unsteadiness of the sand under his feet.

He bent down to pick up a handful of the wetness and a sharp pain shot through the small of his back. "Ow shit!" he screamed and tried to straighten up, but it just got worse.

Suzie took her time getting down and when she saw David standing staring down at the sand, she stopped. "Don't tell me you found the ring you lost on my sixteenth birthday?" she called, but he didn't move. She heard him whimper and ran towards him. "What's wrong?" she said and took his arm.

"Careful!" he cried. "No pulling, no pushing, no nothing!"

She stood back. "What is it! Dawid!" she shouted at him, annoyed at his tone.

"It's my fucking back, man! Just help me to a rock or something. Once I sit a bit, it settles down." He waved out with his arm and she took it gingerly, looked around and saw a rounded mound.

"There's a rock, come …" she said and helped him move. It took forever, David shuffling one foot in front of the other, head held far down as if he was studying his feet and Suzie half at an angle under his weight. They got to the rock and very slowly she helped him sit, with much huffing and howling.

He carefully straightened his back and lifted his head. He could do it without pain and he smiled. "Thank heavens! What a relief."

At that, sheets of water cascaded down from the heavens. Suzie gave a shriek and hunched up against David, covering her head with her hands but it was useless. She then stood up and pulled off her jacket, letting the rain plaster her T-shirt against her body. The rain pelted them with marble drops and within seconds both were soaked to the skin.

"It's wonderful!" cried Suzie, wheeling round on the wet sand with her arms in the air. "I haven't done this since I was ten!"

"Wish I could join you, but I'll sit this tango out!" David called grimly from his rock and felt the icy water dribble down his neck.

Suzie leapt about in the rain until she sank to her knees, looking up to the dark clouds and laughing with open mouth and eyes. She turned to David with a laugh. "De Lange, remember how you tried to fuck me down here one night and passionately put your hand down on some broken glass? And that was the end of the sex?"

He nodded and looked down at the palm of his hand ruefully. He'd needed stitches and a tetanus injection and the subsequent attempts at sex with Suzie had just ended up in helpless giggles.

"It nearly wrecked a promising relationship," he said.

She sat next to him on the rock and leant her wet body against his soaked shoulder. "Dawid, we're probably going to catch our deaths and both be buried by Sunday. Then you can see Herman and ask him why he was such a grumpy bugger." She slipped her arm into his and kissed his cheek.

He stiffened at her touch. "I'd love to grab you, but …"

"Your back. Yes, I've heard of excuses but that one really gets the cup. How's the old back doing?" she asked.

"Old," he muttered and tested it carefully. "No, it's okay. I'll just take things easy."

"No fucking?" she asked innocently.

"I'll just stand and you can walk towards me." He turned and kissed her, missing her mouth and planting it squarely in her one eye. "This is good, Suzie. I'm sorry I should feel good when Herman is dead. I should feel terrible, but I don't. I'm glad to be with you."

"Me too. Tomorrow we can cry for Herman. Now let's cry for ourselves."

But she didn't want to cry. There was nothing sad about being their age and still feeling the youth of personality within. She saw the young 16-year-old girl of yesteryear walking along the sunny, white beach, holding hands with a tall boy. Her beach hat hid her face, but Suzie recognised the pert upturned nose and the gold chain round her neck. The boy looked like Dawid de Lange."

"Do you want to get married?" he asked her.

"Is that an offer?" she asked, glancing up at him with a twinkle.

"No, just asking," he said hurriedly.

"I will never marry!" she announced, convinced that this was the last statement of the subject. "Marriage is for fools and weaklings. I'm strong and I'm okay."

The boy seemed to nod his head slightly too enthusiastically. She stopped and pulled a small ring off her finger. "Here, De Lange, you keep this. If there'd be anyone whom I'd like to have with me forever, it's you. Put it on."

They tried to slip the ring on his fingers, but the ring was too

269

narrow, except for his pinkie. It slid on to the second joint and then stuck. She looked at it and shrugged.

"Maybe that's a new way of wearing them."

"Is this an offer? Suzie?" he asked, hoping she'd say yes.

"Don't be mad!" she frowned. "I told you: I'll never ever get married. Cross my heart!" Then she broke away from him and ran towards the huge rocks.

"And you went and lost my ring in the sand, remember?"

"Yes, I was very sorry. I still am." David watched the sea as he spoke. "The last postcard I got from Renate was one of Clifton, and mentioned the fact that she'd been down here for a *braaivleis* one summer night. She didn't often write, but as she grew up I think she forgave me for going."

She'd never said those words, but David had hoped they were between the lines of Renate's brief little messages to him.

"What did you come back for, Dawid?" Suzie suddenly asked.

"I came back to …" He stopped and thought of words to describe his odyssey, but they escaped him. "There were some things I had to sort out," he said. "Teema was the only one who could fill me in on my family, my childhood …"

"Did she?"

"No, what can you say in a few days, but there were things I found out."

"Are you glad you did?" He looked at her. "I mean, those few things, would they have been better left forgotten?"

David thought for a moment about Renate's death and his mother's suicide, his father's lonely last years.

"No, I'm glad I know about those things now. It's too late to say sorry, but it does tie up the loose ends. But finding you …" She pulled her arm out from his hold. "Why do you pull away?"

She got up. "Because I need a drink, a bath, a hairdryer, a towel, warm clothes and the idea of carrying you up those fucking stairs doesn't appeal to me at all. Let's start now, De Lange. I still want to get to the phone before the office closes in Jo'burg."

She helped him up carefully, him testing his back at each movement until he stood erect. She edged herself in under his arm. "Lean on me … not lie on me, De Lange! Lean! There we are. Now let's go."

From afar they looked like two cripples trying to find a lost crutch as they stumbled and swayed towards the steps, and very slowly, haltingly, painfully took them one at a time. Only if one got closer would one have heard the hysterical laughter as they made their way up towards the heaven of a warm shower.

Herman Greef's funeral was a nightmare. It was held in the Dutch Reformed Church at which he'd been confirmed, and to which he never returned, other than for the occasional wedding.

David hadn't been back into an Afrikaner church since his solemn confirmation at the age of 16. He knew that his sister had been buried out of this church, and probably his mother too. Did they realise she'd taken her own life? Would the Afrikaner God let her into his paradise, or would she have to spend eternity in the twilight zone outside the gates with all the other unclean, the blacks and Jews and Catholics, Brits and Communists?

He reminded Suzie to wear a hat to the service, and she laughed at him, so out of touch was he with the modern-day chosen religion. The car park was surprisingly full of imported cars and there were many younger people gathered in the entrance to the church.

The hearse stood to one side, the coffin visible under the few white wreaths and single flowers. David watched a pretty girl in a plain black dress place a rose with the others. She was racked with sobs and had to be led away and comforted.

"Well, that's someone who knew Herman like we didn't," Suzie remarked. They stayed to one side, feeling out of it and for the first time uncomfortably mature.

Suzie nudged him as Blanche Tucker appeared round the side of the church, supported by her two sons and followed by a cluster of Tucker lookalikes. "The family has landed!" she said dryly and David noticed Blanche wiping her eyes with a handkerchief and giving a superb performance as the last remaining heir of whatever Herman Greef had gathered through his lifetime.

"Dawid?" He turned round to see Joanie Craig standing behind them. She was wearing a hat. She looked at Suzie, recognising her immediately. "Christ, Suzie Bernard! You look exactly the same!" She shook hands with Suzie who in turn nodded her guarded appreciation of Joanie.

"You don't look bad yourself," she said and David was quite relieved to see the nice part of his old flame simmer pleasantly behind hooded eyes.

"I'm the only one with a hat on!" Joanie hissed furiously. "What's happened to the old *kerk*? It used to be all hats and gloves and dresses below the knees." Another girl in a floral minidress placed a flower on Herman's coffin. "Jesus, is that old Herman in there?" she asked and peered across the tarmac, trying to make out more through the tinted windows of the hearse. "Who's the glamorous widow?" she asked, pointing at Blanche.

"Herman's twin sister, the one that went to the private school?" Joanie nodded slowly. "So that's her? She looks so much …"

"Don't say the word 'younger', Joanie," muttered Suzie. "And go put your fucking hat in the car! You look like our mother!" That was all it took to propel Joanie back to her car.

She rejoined them looking relieved to have shed her disguise. "Can I sit with you? I haven't seen any of the old crowd, have you?"

They hadn't for the simple reason that no one could remember what the 'old crowd' looked like now that they were no longer the young crowd. But there were a few school pals there that afternoon and during the service, Suzie picked out some familiar profiles. She was shocked to see how puffy and tired her old classmates looked, how much smaller the men who'd been the rugby heroes were now; how much rounder the prettiest girls had become.

"I want to be sick," hissed Joanie into her ear. "I can't believe we look so shit! What's happened to these people?"

"Married!" was all Suzie said. "So what did you do with your ex-husband, Joanie?"

"I didn't kill him, although the temptation was great. He ran after a younger piece and had a heart attack. Good riddance." People turned round and shushed her, but some smiled as they heard every word.

David looked down at his hands and hoped they wouldn't lose control. Funerals always made him laugh because it was so close to crying. But then he'd missed the main burials in his family, so Herman's would have to make up for lost tears.

The service left them dry. It was recited by a man who hadn't know Herman Greef, who mispronounced his name twice as 'Hennie', who paid unnecessary tribute to the visibly grieving Blanche and her family, and who refused once to say a word in English. The gathered friends of the dead man, some of whom weren't fluent in Afrikaans, shifted around uncomfortably and everyone was relieved when the service was over.

Unnoticed by those who knew her, Frieda had tiptoed in through a side door with Valkyrie on a leash and stood quietly in the shadows weeping for her dead master, making sure to leave the church before the service ended. The dog stood quite still, giving only one small whine. They were nowhere to be seen when David eventually led Suzie and Joanie into the sunlight.

The parking area stood full of clusters of people talking in low tones, comparing memories or just swapping addresses.

"Well ..." sighed David, "that's that."

Joanie had been crying and put her sunglasses on. "I'm sorry to let the side down. Herman would've called me a stupid melodramatic bitch for crying, but I am. I loved him once, you know?"

"Really? At school?" Suzie looked at her with amazement.

"No, more recently. Anyway, that's all over now. Can't go to bed with a corpse or a photo." She broke away from them and walked to her car quickly, her high heels making a sharp sound on the tar.

Suzie nudged David. "No, she shouldn't be left alone now. Go ask her to come with us."

"Where are we going?"

"I don't know. I'll think of something. You've still got Herman's house keys, have you?"

"I was going to give them to his lawyer."

"Tomorrow. Let's go and talk there. Herman will enjoy it." So they went off in a small convoy to the cottage where Herman Greef had lived. The gardener was still there trimming the hedge.

"Good morning," David said and the man nodded. "You know about Mr Greef?" The man nodded.

"Come, open the door!" Suzie pushed David ahead and led Joanie along the small path.

The house was as they'd left if the day before.

"Is this a good idea?" said Joanie in the hallway, shivering as if a cold wind suddenly blew at her.

"Yes, it's a great idea," decided Suzie taking charge of the moment. "We'll go and sit in the kitchen, open a bottle of wine and get completely pissed."

"I've got to get back to the office ..." attempted Joanie, but Suzie just handed her the phone and she made a quick call.

Soon they were seated round the wooden table in the kitchen, with a selection of cheeses and biscuits laid out between them. David opened a bottle of red wine.

"It's a 1983 Pinotage," he said half apologetically.

"Pour!" ordered Suzie. "This is one wine we don't send back!"

She held up her glass and waited for the others to pick up theirs. "I want to drink a toast, obviously, to our absent host. I didn't know him that well and my memories of him aren't that happy ..." Joanie gave a raw sob and rubbed her nose with her hand. "Shut up, Joanie – crying makes you just look your age." Joanie took a deep breath and tried to banish her sadness with a forced laugh. Suzie stood solemnly, holding her glass in the air. The red wine glowed crimson against the light. "But more than for Herman who is now beyond all salutations, I drink a toast to us and our lives past, present and future. Let us remember what we discovered and forget what we destroyed; let us be friends always in spite of the loneliness that we've become so used to. Let us ..." She stopped and thought, and then gave a snort. "Fuck the speeches! Drink and don't *kots* on me. Right, who's first?"

They drank and David looked round at Joanie!

"First for what?" he asked.

"First with the secrets, first with the truth!" enunciated Suzie as if talking to idiots. "Come on, that's what a death in friendship is all about. Taking stock. Now's the time to get it all out of your systems. Okay, Joanie, you start."

Joanie looked startled at Suzie and David, now both leaning on their elbows, waiting for her to spew out the story of her life.

"Where should I start?" she stuttered.

"Herman Greef and you. That's a logical beginning ..."

CHAPTER 19.

He hit her. They'd both been drinking and Joanie's tongue tended to get looser the more she sipped, so she'd called him a name he wouldn't stand for.

"I was only joking, Herman! Jesus man, I just said 'mother-fucker'!" she gasped, holding her stinging cheek with her hand and backing away from him. "Haven't you seen any recent American movies? Everyone uses that name, even as a compliment!"

"Not with me, okay? I don't fuck mothers!" he snarled.

"I'm a mother!" she lashed out and dodged into the adjoining bathroom. Her reflection in the gilt-edged mirror blurred back at her. This was not a good idea, she thought as she splashed some cold water onto her face. She knew it the first moment she'd walked into the school hall and saw Herman Greef standing with their former school principal.

Their old school hall was decorated with colourful balloons and the same cheap tat that had hung limply from the wooden crossbars and PT ropes for their matric dance thirty years before. She knew going to such a class reunion was a bad idea.

"Isn't this nice?" she asked the principal who still filled her with dread. She looked around the walls for the shy flowers of her youth. Tired and angry eyes looked back at her, some women being the classmates who had rejected her as a loose girl, others being the wives of the boys, now men, who'd muttered her name in climax and refused to explain to their tearful spouses who 'Joanie' was.

"Fancy everybody being here again after all these years!" she said to no one in particular, and no one answered or even spoke to her. So she latched on to Herman Greef, who was table-hopping, not having brought a date. She hadn't seen him close up for years, and was pleased that his image on the social pages of the *Cape Times* didn't do justice to his looks.

"Want to refresh your memory, Joanie?" he whispered into her ear later that evening, after the last of the sticky puddings had been imploded by keen spoons and everyone felt old and full and silly, sitting around an empty school hall floor, or twisting and bopping self-consciously to forgotten hits.

"So we went back to his place ..." Joanie said on the day of his funeral, looking round the kitchen and nodding. "Yes, it could've even been this place. I don't remember the kitchen, but I don't think I got this far. Herman ripped off my dress in the hallway and had me on the carpet, banging my head against the floor like some bulldog with a rag doll. Rough bastard! No subtlety! Foreplay? Dear God, no! In out, biff bang, wham, come, out and go!"

She poured another full glass of wine and kicked off her remaining shoe. Her toes curled up on the chair opposite, warmly between David's legs. He didn't move his position again as it made no difference where or how he sat. Joanie Craig always got what she wanted.

"Don't speak ill of the dead," Suzie sighed and poured herself half a glass. The two already empty bottles stood proudly on the table and the snacks were gone. A pile of unshelled peanuts lay heaped in the middle and each time someone spoke, the flimsy reddish skins floated about the air.

"You're right," Joanie lifted her glass for the umpteenth time. "I'll drink to all the motherfuckers who've fucked this mother! May they rot in hell for all I care, present company excluded!"

"Don't look at me!" laughed Suzie. "I'm not that sort of a girl. Motherhood never sat well on my CV. Tell us about yours, David?"

David had stopped listening halfway through the tale of Herman's hitting Joanie. Somehow he didn't believe it, and besides, did it matter now? He'd been thinking about Herman, lying under six foot of damp soil and wondered what it felt like to be so finally and completely dead.

He looked up quickly when he heard his name. "My mother?" he asked, confused.

"No, darling," gushed Joanie, "the mother of your children? How come you're here so far away from your … what's her name?"

"Deli, like in 'catessen'," said Suzie helpfully.

"Like a salami?" gasped Joanie and clapped her hands.

David set some nuts in a row and played soldiers with others. He shook his head and sighed. "I don't know what to tell you. There's so much and yet so little. She's there, I'm here and I'll go back to her and that's that …" The silence after his words didn't seem to be justified. He looked from Suzie to Joanie. "Hey, come on, she's not dead too, you know."

Joanie lifted her glass and toasted his 'delicatessen' in LA, and then went on to discuss her daughter Judy's black lover, a favourite subject no doubt unleashed by the mention of salami.

David looked at his fingers flick the nuts at each other on the table. Was Deli dead to him? He couldn't imagine what he would say to her now, having been away for only a few weeks from her and his life of all those years, to have discovered his past to be stronger than the present he lived and was taking so for granted.

An argument about marriage brought him back into the conversation. Joanie was struggling with a fourth bottle of wine, having pushed the cork deep into the neck by mistake.

Suzie took it from her and handed it to David. "Last of the 1983s," she said and got up to go to the toilet. At the door she stopped and turned to them. "So there's me with three ex-marriages, Joanie with two ..."

"One!" she bellowed, "give a girl a chance!"

"Sorry, one, and our knight in shining armour still happily wed to a hardware store."

"Delicatessen, man!" Joanie slurred and they both laughed.

"Hey, Joanie, tell Romeo about your son-in-law's salami while I powder my nose," Suzie called as she went down the passage.

Joanie twitched her stockinged feet playfully into David's crotch. "Hi there, De Lange. Are you happy?" she twittered.

"As long as you keep doing that with your feet, yes," he smiled.

"No, man, I mean happy. With life. With love. With laughter!"

He sighed and poured them each a drink out of the new bottle. Bits of cork floated in their glasses like debris. "Yes, I think I'm happy, Joanie. I was happy till a few weeks ago. Can it change that quickly?" he asked.

Joanie nodded gravely and sipped from her wine. "Oh yes, De Lange, it just takes one look from the right person, or one thought at the wrong moment and you realise you've lived a lie! A lifetime cancelled out by one second. I seem to have those every day! That's why my life is such a zig-zag affair, or ex-affair should I say." She laughed into her glass and gurgled into the wine.

"Don't be sick now, Joanie," David warned, not feeling like a mid-afternoon pass-out on his hands.

"I'm okay," she said waving at him. Then she held the glass with both hands and looked at him intently, her eyes narrowed to focus, her mouth set in a determined line. She looked very pretty, albeit slightly shop-soiled. "Have you got that moment from Suzie Bernard"? she whispered.

"What moment? ... careful, you'll spill your wine ..." David straightened her glass and she pulled away.

"You know what I mean," she said. "I can see that look between you, that comfortable 'being together' feeling you have. I just want to know, has she given you that ...?" she waved around the air with the glass and splashed some wine on the table. The nuts shone soggily in the dull red puddle. "... That zap to cancel out a lifetime of limbo?"

Suzie entered and picked up the line. "Talking about Teema?"

"Yes," said David quickly.

"No!" shot back Joanie, determined to dig where her instinct smelt hidden treasure. "I want to know if you've found each other again, after all these years?"

"Does it look like it, Joanie?" Suzie asked leaning against the door frame, avoiding David's glance.

"Yes it does!" Joanie took a gulp from her glass and it went down the wrong way. She coughed violently and David had to slap her hard on her back.

"I think it's time the party was terminated," Suzie remarked from the door.

"No ..." Joanie coughed and spluttered. "No ... I'm fine! Shit, you haven't changed, have you, Miss Bernard? You don't approve of me, do you? Always giving me that 'I'm-better-than-you' look!"

"What the hell are you talking about, Joanie?" Suzie asked, not in the mood for a skirmish.

"Come, I'll drive you home. Dawid can follow in the other car."

"I'm fine ..." Joanie Craig stood up unsteadily and the chair fell over. She gasped and held her heart in fright, looked round slowly and then at Suzie wide-eyed. "What was that? A burglar?"

"No, you're throwing the furniture around. Come, come, come." Suzie stepped into the kitchen and put her arm round Joanie.

"I never approved of you, only because I didn't know you. Now I know you better."

Joanie looked at her suspiciously, not being able to focus on a face so close. "So you approve of me now?" she slurred.

"Yes, a little more than before." Suzie laughed at Joanie's expression and gave her a hug. "You're a tart with a golden heart and I'm jealous of your daughter."

"Jealous of the big black cock?" Joanie gasped.

"No, you drunk cow, jealous of that little baby!" She winked at David. "Never mind, Romeo, red wine makes me feel mumsy and uncommonly fecund. Trouble is I always seem to get remarried before I become sober again."

She helped Joanie out of the kitchen and they went down the passage in a drunken argument about men.

David tried to straighten the mess on the table, but then saw Blanche's face in front of him and left everything as it was. He looked at all the gadgets in the kitchen, the blender, the liquidiser, the coffee machine, the different types of tea and the touches of a bachelor's elegance that made his eyes cloud with tears.

Herman Greef might have been a chauvinist and an occasional hitter of lonely women, but for an Afrikaans boy from well below the line of society, he'd shown a great flair for style. Maybe not taste, but what money could buy, he had.

"Pity you couldn't take it with you," David murmured and walked through the empty house. He closed the door without looking back and locked it. The garden was strangely quiet, with no birds singing. Just the soft rustle of the water from the little fountain in the rockery.

Something was missing.

David looked about the garden and wondered if there'd been garden furniture that someone might have stolen while they were indoors. Then he realised how right he was: the gardener was gone!

He kept looking up as he climbed. He stretched out his arm and pulled himself up to the next bough, and from that higher and higher. Suzie was further up, and seemed to be getting away from him.

Although he felt the erratic tremor and dull thud of an axe in wood, he didn't look down until he heard Herman Greef give that laugh. He glanced to his side and saw his friend float by, arms folded as if reclining on an invisible chase. He waved at David and laughed, speaking in a strange tongue and then threw gold coins at them. Suzie tried to grab the coins and lost her balance. She gave a scream and fell out of the tree, the scent of her perfume slapping through David's face. He gasped and looked down as Suzie disappeared in the crackle of the fire below.

The entire tree was in flames from its base and yet in the centre of the inferno was a clear patch of green gas. On this stood Deli, an axe in hand. She waved up at him and started cutting at the trunk with great blows, encouraged by a cackling Herman floating on his invisible cloud, the new third eye in the centre of his forehead glowing like a warning light.

Dawid tried to climb higher to escape the inevitable, but soon with a chilling crack, the great tree wobbled and toppled over, hurling Dawid de Lange down, down, down … David sat up in bed with a gasp. His face was wet with perspiration and he felt iced with the empty fear that follows a nightmare. The reality of the dream was still tangible around him. He looked about to familiarise himself with his strange surroundings, but didn't know where he was. Not in LA. Not Herman Greef's cottage. Not St Andrew's Road. He was alone.

Then he heard the roar of the sea far below. He was in Suzie's friend's flat in Clifton. He kept hearing Herman's cackle in his ears and got up to get a glass of water from the kitchen.

Suzie was lying in the living-room, listening to some music through huge black earphones, which seemed to squash her small face between them. Her eyes were closed. David tiptoed past her and poured some water from a glass pitcher on the small bamboo bar. She opened her eyes and saw him, gave a little smile and conducted the orchestra in her head with her fingers.

"I had a nightmare," he said.

She nodded and shouted, thinking he too couldn't hear. "I just couldn't sleep!" He offered her drink and she shook her head. "No thanks!" she shouted again.

David turned to look out at the sea below, now calm and ordered with waves rolling in on designed cue covered in soft foam that looked sprayed on by an artist. There had been more to his dream than the burning tree. He tried to recall. There'd been something of the funeral and Blanche and …? God yes, there was also Teema trapped in some shanty in Natal!

"This country's driving me crazy," he muttered.

A police siren warbled across the water from somewhere to the right and he saw the flashing blue lights wobble round the edge of the coastal road and vanish again around some buildings.

They both had an early night. Maybe that's why they felt so grim. After dropping Joanie Craig at her cottage they had come back to their seaside flat. Joanie's daughter had been at the cottage with her baby and David introduced her to Suzie. Although it wasn't exactly the ideal moment to confront her mother with another problem, Judy announced that her baby would go into limbo and never see Jesus because she'd never been christened. This sent Joanie into floods of tears and Suzie helped her to her bedroom where she sat with her till she fell asleep.

"Why shouldn't your baby be christened, Judy?" asked David, not quite sure what the problem was. The fact that Judy and her young man aren't married didn't count as an obstacle any more. "Are you Catholic?" Judy shook her head and pouted. The baby gurgled and giggled at David, wiggling her little feet and giving him an eyeful of pink gums. "Anglican? Jewish?"

Judy looked tearful. "Nothing. I never thought of this! I mean, never having gone to church myself. And Hector is also not … well, he's American and his church is in Atlanta. Where do we go? I want my baby to go to heaven!" she sobbed and the baby giggled.

"Come on, woman!" growled Suzie in the doorway. "De Lange,what's your priest? Anglican?"

"Father Nkotse? Yes."

God! Father Nkotse! He'd completely forgotten to find out how he was doing! So when they got back to the Clifton flat, David rang the hospital and soon spoke to the cheerful sister in Ward D7. No, Reverend Nkotse was getting stronger every day, out of danger, looking good, very chatty, quite a handful, and if that sister of his came in once more to complain about the food, Sister would happily dispatch them both to the morgue! David asked when he could visit and was told the public's visiting time was from three to five the next day.

Slowly the monochrome of night lifted to allow the glow of daybreak. David just sat in the open window, lost in the smell of sea and the confusion of thought. He'd arranged to drop the key to Herman's house with the lawyer. Then the phone rang just after eight, snapping him out of his trance with the suggestion that they meet at the house itself at eleven.

David nodded and agreed to everything, still seeing the dawning day through a grid of exhaustion. Jesus, what had he eaten to make him feel so listless? Could it have been that vintage red? Was this Herman Greef's revenge on his friends for drinking the exquisite wine his twin sister would no doubt have used for cooking?

Suzie was not very talkative when she woke up in her sprawled position on the floor, wedged in between the large cushions with the earphones having slid down to her neck like two gloved hands prepared for a strangle. David was getting to know the signals of early morning moroseness and stayed out of her way.

She plonked a whole grapefruit on a plate and handed him the knife. "Please, De Lange, cut the fucker up and feed me. I think I'm suffering from 'Helbart's Syndrome'!"

"What's that!" he asked concerned.

"Whatever you can't explain, but won't go away. 'Helbart's Syndrome' puts it all in a nutshell."

"Any cure?"

Suzie gave him a bleary grimace. "Sex, drugs and rock 'n roll, I suppose, but certainly not at 8.30 in the morning. Do you need the car?"

He dropped her at the building on the City Foreshore where her meeting was to be held. It was yet another gathering of an unknown subcommittee looking into findings of a new unnamed commission of inquiry, but David gave up asking because he didn't understand and frankly he didn't care.

Like magic Suzie transformed herself from the hippie girl-woman with 'Helbart's Syndrome' to a dynamic PR with a love-conquers-all smile and a steely resolve to beat anyone at their own game.

"A remarkable woman," David thought, as he drove along the wide Eastern Boulevard across the bridges that spanned the city towards the suburbs and Herman's home. This was the road where the shooting had taken place. David didn't exactly know where, but the main traffic was going towards town in the opposite direction, so David had no sense of what it felt like to be trapped in a gridlock on one of the only two freeways into the Mother City.

A car was drawn into Herman's driveway, so David parked in the street and briskly walked through the gate. He wanted to do this quickly and get it over with. The gardener was back and David was quite relieved to hear the comforting staccato clip-clip of his hedge shears. Then what he saw stopped him dead in his tracks.

Deli stood on the stoep. She gave him a little wave as she always did when she surprised him with anything, something she enjoyed doing, often to his annoyance. The image he remembered of her wielding the axe in his dream was clearly imposed on her smiling face. He was relieved to see nothing in her hand.

"Well, David?" she said with a surprised inflection in her voice. "I know this is a bit out of the blue, but don't stand there looking at me as it I'm the worst news you've had all week!"

"You don't know how bad some of the news has been," he said.

They looked at each other, neither moving. The gardener had stopped his clipping and watched them impassively. Then David heard himself say what he'd dreaded from the moment he saw her. "Deli, is someone dead?"

The possibility of a death in his own immediate family had not crossed his mind, and yet now suddenly his daughters and their husbands and his grandchild lay in the open coffins produced by the richness of his paranoia.

"That's what I want to ask you, David! This gentleman here tells me 'the Master is dead'! Who is 'the Master'? And for one moment I must say I thought it might be you ..." Her face crumpled and she started crying into her hands. David broke out of his inertia and ran to her, putting his arms round her and holding her. Oh God, he thought, would she smell Suzie's perfume ...?

Herman's lawyer came round from the back of the house. "Oh hello, Mr De Lange, sorry, I was round the kitchen door. It seems someone tried to force it last night, and with the alarm not being set, we're lucky they didn't manage to break in."

"I ..." David toyed with the wisdom of informing him about the private wake for Herman with the 1983 Pinotages, but decided to let bygones be bygones. His hangover still throbbed in his head. "Here's the key. Sorry to have brought you out all the way."

"No problem. Mr Greef's sister is a persistent heir and wants to have an inventory done as soon as possible. She mentioned there was a vicious dog that she wants to have put down?"

David saw old Frieda in her shack on the Cape Flats, brushing Valkyrie while waiting for a non-existent pension from Herman's estate. "No," he said. "There was no dog." He glanced at the gardener. Did he detect a faint smile? The solicitor groped for his portable telephone in his briefcase. "You'll excuse me. Mrs De Lange?" He nodded at Deli and got into his car in the driveway.

"That's a name I've never been called. Is that who I'd be here at your grassroots level? Mrs De Lange?" she asked and took out her compact to repair her make-up.

David saw her suitcase on the stoep. "Is that yours?" he asked, going to pick it up.

"Yes. I had this address and took a taxi from the airport and found myself at a dead man's door ..." The unfortunate idiom froze on her mouth and she covered it with lipstick. As they got into the car, she asked. "What is that man's name?"

David couldn't remember. "Botha or Cilliers or something ..."

"No, the black man working in the garden. He looks very nice." She'd enjoyed her conversation with the young man who'd told her about his family and the house he was planning to build in the squatter camp 'once the violence was over'.

"Oh him? I've no idea. Never heard him say a word."

"Oh." They drove off and Deli half-turned to catch a glimpse of the youth with the gardening shears. He gave the American lady a small wave and allowed himself to smile.

David booked his wife into the best hotel. She admired the view of the massive mountain from her high perch above the city.

"You're not staying here then, David?" she said, peering down through the gold-tinted window at the toyland traffic down below.

"Eh … no, I'm with friends, but I'll go pick up my things and we can have a nice relaxed evening." He smiled.

"You mentioned your old girlfriend Suzie Bennett in one of your letters." He didn't correct her and just nodded, while rearranging the hotel stationery on the desk unnecessarily. "So how did it feel seeing old flames again after all those years?" she asked.

He smiled too broadly and shrugged too casually. "Oh, you know, life goes on." He kissed her quickly on the forehead. "I have to just pop in to see someone who's in hospital. I won't be long."

"Hang on, David, I'll come with you!" She picked up her bag and glanced in the mirror for a final check of her appearance. "Good, the jet lag hasn't pulled my face to pieces yet. Let's make hay while the sun shines."

They drove to the hospital, with David pointing out landmarks to her and filling her in on the details of this picture-postcard city, hanging onto the edge of a dark continent by its bloody fingernails. They drove past what looked like a great site ready for construction. "This expanse of open land in the centre of it all was once a Cape Coloured area," he explained. "It was ethnically cleansed by apartheid's laws and declared residential for whites only."

Deli looked at the empty space, pale green wispy grasses waving in the wind with the occasional church still standing to remind the interested passer-by that people who believed in God once lived there, till He looked the other way. "But there's nothing here now," she murmured and sensed the cries of the dispossessed, as they glided past District Six.

"It used to be a bustling area when I was a kid," he added, "although we were always terrified of it. We were told the devil lived there, and that drunks and *skollies* … thugs would get you if you ever went in."

"God, sounds like home!" she remarked dryly and he laughed. They talked about life back in Los Angeles, the well-being of their daughters and their marriages, the joy of the little grandchild who'd just recovered from whooping cough. "Do kids still get that?" David asked, amazed that his childhood ailments still seemed to haunt new generations of children.

Deli sighed. "I don't want to sound like a Cassandra and scream warnings from the rooftops, but it seems that legions of old diseases are making a comeback, well armoured against antibiotics and resistant to all drugs." She looked at David with a frown. "What is the talk here on the ground about issues like TB and Aids?"

He shrugged. "The ground is still too concerned about life to worry about death. Suzie says …" He paused only for a beat, then carried on, "… Suzie says Aids is a terrible shadow over the hopes of the future. About forty per cent of black babies born in Durban are HIV-positive."

"Christ!" spat Deli. "As if these people haven't had enough to contend with! I'd like to meet your friend Suzie. She sounds like quite a fighting spirit."

"Yes," David nodded, pleased with the image. "A fighting spirit is a good way of describing her. We'll get together in the next day or so."

"Ah," nodded Deli. "She's here in Cape Town?"

"Didn't I tell you?" Deli shook her head and moved the rear-view mirror towards her to check her lipstick. "Don't do that, Deli! There's a mirror in your sunguard!"

By the time they got to Ward D7, David had put her in the picture about his friendship with Reverend Nkotse. Deli warmed to the priest's personality immediately and looked forward to meeting him.

The old black shepherd was sitting in a wheelchair at the window when they walked into the ward. He was looking out at the green mountain slopes where one could see wild buck and antelope roam, although his face was still bandaged. He could see nothing. David was struck by his frailness.

"Hello?" he said softly, not knowing if the patient was asleep or not. Reverend Nkotse turned to the direction of the voice. A slit in the bandages made it possible for him to speak softly. David went closer to hear.

"David?" murmured the priest and took his arm eagerly. David was relieved to see the slim hands unscathed by the attack. "How are you?" he asked and squeezed his friend's hands affectionately.

Father Nkotse spoke in measured gasps. "I'm … fine … good that you came … I've been thinking of you and your little girlfriend …"

David's stomach gave a lurch and he couldn't believe his ears. "Girlfriends?" he stammered and smiled at Deli. "Which one, Father? There've been so many!" He gave Deli a wink.

"Teema!" came the reply.

David's relief was palpable. "Oh, Teema! No fine! Also been in hospital with a heart attack, but well and happy. Thanks to you."

"God … moves …"

"… in mysterious ways!" Ms Nkotse swept into the room and clapped her hands sharply. "Come now, don't tire him out, Mr De Lange. I've been talking to Sister Bruyns, Grenville, and she says the bandages will come off tomorrow. We must not spoil everything by overdoing it." She pointedly gave David a raised eyebrow.

Grenville? This priest was called Grenville? David wondered how a name like that had attached itself to a black baby, born in the wilds of Transkei 78 years ago.

"The seminary changed his name to something God would easily understand," his sister explained later. She never gave him her name and David didn't ask. Ms Nkotse dragged up two chairs for David and Deli and stood stiffly next to her brother, on guard against any excitement and filling in the spaces left by his difficulty in speaking. "It's … been … quite …" he started.

"… Quite a hectic time here in hospital, isn't that what you wanted to say, Grenville?" she asked.

"No!" he said, and was heard to chuckle behind his bandages. "I wanted … to say … it's been … quite a nice … few days!" He pointed in the direction of the sunshine outside on the mountain.

David leaned closer. "I want you to meet my wife, Father Nkotse. Deli, give him your hand."

The priest took her hand and stroked across it lightly. He nodded. "If this … was the hand of … a white …" he started.

"She is white!" hissed his sister.

"Shhh … a white woman living … here, I'd say: never washed a dish in her life …" Ms Nkotse nodded and gave David an accusing look. "But for an American … well-kept hands. Beautiful." He put his hands to his face and sniffed. "And smells … good."

Deli laughed and studied her hands. "You're not quite right about the dishes, but now everything is remote-control. It's the nails that go to hell if one isn't careful aiming for the button!"

"Deli surprised me with her visit," David said, hoping the conversation wouldn't be detailed around the activities of Suzie and Joanie. But then did Reverend Nkotse know about them? And then again, did it matter? Why was he behaving like a teenager? He added brightly. "I hope to introduce her to my old friends."

"I'm sorry about ... Herman." The priest shook his head slowly. "What a terrible waste ..."

They all sat in silence for a moment, the sun warming the chill left by the memory of Herman's murder. Then Ms Nkotse decided the conversation had taken a morbid turn and spent the rest of the visiting time telling them about everyone's ailments in the ward, the poor quality of the hospital food which she was convinced contained small pieces of ground glass, and the questionable morality of the night nurses. It was with quite a relief that David eventually detected the sparkle in her deadpan expression.

Reverend Nkotse seemed to enjoy her tirade and giggled regularly, hitting his knee with the palm of his hand and nodding in agreement with his sister's opinions, especially about the night nurses.

"My friend Joanie Craig's daughter has had her baby," David mentioned during a break in Ms Nkotse's monologue.

"Ah, the baby of the chocolate hue?" the priest chuckled.

David quickly explained the problem Judy and Hector were having finding a church in which to christen their child. Reverend Nkotse sat mulling over the problem, the tips of his fingers held together to form a cathedral. "How sad that this can happen ..."

"Typical," sniffed his sister.

"And how wonderful," her brother added, "that they have the courage to question and ask for help."

"And you're going to wheel yourself across town and baptise the baby?" Ms Nkotse asked with her skew smile.

"No, but ..." the priest thought for a moment, then chuckled. "But I can ... be wheeled down to the ... hospital chapel here and there we can ... baptise this ... new child of the Lord!

"David, ring Sister Bruyns tomorrow ... morning," slurred the priest, clearly showing signs of exhaustion, "and I'll make arrangements. We'll ... have to take whatever ... time they give us."

"Yes, of course," agreed David and patted his knee happily. They took their leave, Deli kissing the Reverend's hand which he then held against his face with enjoyment of her scent.

"Can you give me a lift into town?" Ms Nkotse suddenly asked, her handbag already under her arm and her scarf on its way round her head. "I have to make arrangements to get back to college by the end of next week. This old priest will be back in harness, and I must remount the bloody battlements of education."

It was in the car that she dropped the rather irritating but necessary façade of the stern sister and told David exactly how seriously hurt her brother had been by the petrol bomb attack. "They will have to do multi-transplants of skin to repair his face. He will not be the ideal person to send on evening visits to small children. They'll scream and it will break his heart. I just hope his eyes have not been affected, but only time will tell."

"Did they find the culprit?" Deli asked, appalled by the casualness with which violence was being discussed and, to a certain extent, accepted.

"My dear, we are all culprits. The only ones not guilty are the dead. Stop here, Mr De Lange." David pulled up at a corner and Ms Nkotse got out. She called into Deli's open window. "And enjoy your stay, Mrs De Lange. We're not all crazy, you know, just the ones who come back in search of something that never was." She pointed a mocking finger at David and went into the shop.

"That woman always leaves me tongue-tied," David said shaking his head. Someone hooted aggressively behind him.

"Where to now, Mr De Lange?" Deli asked, rubbing cream from a small tube on the back of her hands. So Mr De Lange drove Mrs De Lange to Clifton, taking the coastal route through the Mediterranean shimmer of the villas of Fresnaye and Bantry Bay, and round the edge of the mountain to see Clifton's beaches glow in the warmth of the sun. A few brave winter bathers were dotted around the spotless sand like beetles.

"Shall I come in?" Deli asked as he parked on a yellow line.

"No, I'm illegally parked," he said hastily, not wanting to confront Suzie Bernard with the surprise of a wife. "I'm not sure if she's there. Let me see first." Suzie wasn't at the flat. David quickly packed his bag and left her a quick note on the kitchen door, explaining little but saying all with a few words: "Delicatessen's here. At hotel with her. Will ring. Sorry."

Deli didn't say anything on the drive back to the hotel, which took them across the *Nek* that joined Lion's Head with Table Mountain. David could sense her discomfort and blamed himself for handling the day as badly as he had.

Once back in their hotel room, he rang for room service and when they both sat in comfortable chairs, each with a whisky in hand looking at the view of the sheer rock ahead of them, he decided to get it off his chest.

"I don't know where to start, Deli. This experience has been far more shattering than I thought. A search for an old nanny turned out to be the rediscovery of someone I'd forgotten ever existed." She looked at him intently over the edge of her glass. The ice nudged against itself and liquid. "There was a boy called Dawid de Lange who'd somehow got lost in the rush. But he's still living here." He smiled at her and looked a bit embarrassed by his emotion. She warmed to that forlorn look on his face she so loved. "It sounds so adolescent, doesn't it?"

"Yes," she said with a smile, "and isn't that nice? I envy you. There was once a girl called Deli Hepburn, but I'm afraid I can't even remember what she looked like." She got up and stood at the window. A bedraggled spotted grey dove sat on the ledge and glared up at her. "Your few letters were very revealing, David."

"Really? I don't think I said anything."

"That's what I mean. They were friendly and chatty and rushed and all the things one expects from someone so far away and so busy ..." She turned to him and took a sip of her drink. "They had everything, except a sense of belonging. Where do you belong, David?"

He scoffed. "My work is in LA ..."

"And your heart? Your ..." she searched for a word, "your adventure? Has this trek to Teema not opened a new frontier for you? And what is Teema? A woman or a land?"

He didn't know what she wanted him to say, so he just looked at her, thoughts tumbling through his mind in search of an answer. She turned back to the grumpy dove and spoke to it. "I wanted to come here and talk to you, not write a letter or leave you a note ..."

The note on the kitchen door of the flat in Clifton waved in the breeze of David's memory, one among the hundreds of other notes he'd once left on doors, on pillows, on desks, on pads, on tables. Slowly a single thought came to the fore of his mind and he followed Deli's shallow breathing through the rise and fall of her narrow shoulders.

"A note?" he echoed. "You would have left me a note? Saying what?"

She shrugged and ran her finger through her hair. "I don't know. That's why I came in person. How can you just leave a note after two daughters and a lifetime of marriage?" She turned and looked at him, biting her bottom lip and waiting for a reaction, but David just stared at her. She came and sat in her chair again, crossing her legs in a sigh of silk. "Do you get what I'm trying to say, David?"

He nodded slowly, the coldness of the glass against his chin numbing his mouth. "You're saying it very well, Deli. You're saying the marriage is over?" He couldn't believe hearing those words spoken so calmly in his voice. This only happened to other people.

"The marriage has been over for some time," she said softly, leaning back in the chair and watching the ice desperately skim around in the whisky to avoid being melted by the warmth of her hands. "Let's face it, David, we've been good friends and enjoyed each other's company but my career and your career don't leave much time for just being friends. Sex ended a long time ago; for me, that is," she added half apologetically. "And so it's as a friend that I came all this way to say to you: it's not too late."

He put down his glass and repositioned himself in this chair, leaning forward and clasping his hands. He was looking at her with narrowed eyes, a look Deli had come to know as a danger sign. "Too late for what?" he said, each word filling its own space and bringing with it a baggage of accusation. "Deli, you're my wife! I love you! I've come out here purely to find myself after all these years! Call it a midlife crisis, male menopause, whatever you like! I needed to come here! I didn't expect you to allow jealousy to ..."

"You misunderstand!" She put her glass down and slid to the carpet, sitting with her knees folded under her and taking his hands in hers passionately. "All I want to say is: you're here, David. You're now more a De Lange than a Clayton. If you've found something important here, then don't feel rushed to come back to me. I'll be fine. I'll be busy finding Deli Hepburn. I think I know where she's hiding. I won't be upset. I will understand ..."

There was a wild flapping on the window ledge and they both looked up to see the fat dove ward off an unwanted visitor with a beating of wings. Then the bird settled back into its crusted perch and closed a raddled eye.

David pulled himself out of the chair and brushed past her. He paced up and down in front of the window, the thick carpet fibres scrunching under the soles of his shoes. "You came all this way, halfway to Australia, to tell me that?"

"Actually no, I flew via Australia," she said. "I brought you a small koala bear from Sydney Airport." She hinted towards her luggage.

"A koala bear?" He stared down at her and ran his fingers through his hair bewildered. "Deli, couldn't you wait till I got back to LA?"

"No, that's the point, David! Then you'd be there and whatever

290

thread you'd found here would again be broken. Then you'd blame me, and I don't want you to blame me. I'm not leaving you! I'm just saying, if you want to pursue other adventures here, then you have my blessing."

"You mean if I find another woman?" he gasped, as if that was the most outrageous thing in the world.

"Well, if you set your sights that low, yes. I was actually meaning, if you found something here that needed your input. Our daughters have each got their own father figures sorted out now. You don't need to sit in on dreary Hollywood production meetings with uninterested people about ghastly films that you'd never go and see! You're a millionaire, David! You can afford to live out a few fantasies before …"

"Before I die?"

"No, don't take the easy way out. Before other people's dreams come true and edge yours out!" She indicated outside the window and the mountain seemed to edge closer and become clearer. "This place can't forever keep that boy Dawid de Lange's footprints in the sand of time. One day a wind of change will come and wipe the slate clean for the next generation of dreamers."

David just shook his head and wandered about the hotel room, muttering to himself.

"The woman's gone mad …"

"The woman's come a long way to show you how mad she's gone!" Deli stood up and came towards him.

He stepped back. "Don't try and patch up now, Deli, the damage is done."

"The damage? Look in the mirror, go on, turn." She pushed him round and their reflections stood watching them. "Who do you see?" David Clayton and his wife didn't smile back at them.

"Do you think we look happy?" Deli asked and slid her arm into his. He was so much taller than she was and yet the couple in the mirror didn't look that disparate in height. "Do they look like they've been together for nearly thirty years?" The Claytons stared back at them stonily. "Go on, ask them?" Mrs Clayton suddenly smiled at them and David found himself smiling back.

He turned to Deli. "What must I do? Must I fight with you? You want an argument?"

She shook her head. "No."

"You want a divorce?"

"No."

"Shall I get a separate room?"

"No."

"Then what must I do?"

She pushed him to the door gently. "Go for a walk. You know you always solve everything on your feet. I'll be here when you get back." He looked at her with that forlorn expression. "Oh, David, just look around! Compile a list of all the things that make you happy here, and all the things that make you unhappy about LA. You don't have to tell me what they are. I think then you'll know what to do."

Once outside the hotel in the street he stopped. "What the hell am I doing!" he muttered and turned to go back into the foyer, when there was a frantic hooting from the street. He turned quickly and saw a white minibus taxi swerving across the road straight towards him. For a moment David was frozen on his feet. Then as the taxi hooted again he managed to jump out of the way behind a lamp-post. A searing pain in the small of his back reminded him that he already had a problem and prayed he wouldn't break a leg before being run down. The taxi screeched to a halt in front of him and the side door rattled open. A full complement of passengers, white and black, stared out at him clutching the pole and shielding his body with it.

Then he heard a familiar voice. "Mr De Lange? Ms Nkotse here!" He peered into the mass of people, but couldn't see her among the shapes. Her clear voice belled out the information for everyone's benefit. "The Reverend has arranged a christening of the chocolate baby in the chapel of the hospital for next Tuesday at 10.00 a.m. Please be on time! He has physiotherapy at 11.30! On, driver, on!"

And with that the taxi with the name 'Zola Budd III' on its rump crunched off with a painful gear change, the door still open and arms waving out of the bus.

"Oh God," muttered David, "first Suzie, then Deli and now Joanie! Women?" He turned and strode up the pedestrian walkway that linked the Foreshore with the older part of the city. When the fat grey doves didn't even bother to move out of the way for him, he knew he was on home turf.

CHAPTER 20.

The grey squirrel sat on its hind legs and stared at him, first through one eye and then by cocking its head, through the other. It was a fat squirrel, used to begging, having its picture taken by gullible tourists and getting titbits from morning to night.

The man on the bench was not concentrating on it. He sat, legs stretched out in the gravel pathway, staring up at the mountain and tapping lightly on the armrest with a small stick.

The squirrel gave a lash with its magnificent tail, to attract the man's attention, but it didn't work. The squirrel looked around. The other humans were either walking up this avenue in the Public Gardens on their way home, or down to the city from where their trains would leave.

David watched the small creature out of the corner of his eye and was amused at the antics to attract his attention. He had nothing to give, as he'd said many times to the scores of grubby street children and derelicts that attached themselves to him with snotty-faced expressions of victimisation, pleading for alms in thin tearful voices, and when he declined, letting rip with a healthy volley of *"jou fokkin' ma se ou stinkpoes!"*, a Cape phrase that defied translation other than to indicate that the state of the most private parts of one's mother was loudly called into question. David felt the Cape hang on his shoulders like a familiar old coat, warm, slightly soiled and comfortable. The list he was making in his mind already seemed to spill over onto former blank areas, as he thought of Reverend Nkotse's deeply committed work among the people of the ghetto. He also saw Suzie Bernard try and sell the complexity of democracy in the simplest terms to those who had no idea what it entailed, other than being able to instantly move into a big house that belonged to whites, and to own a Mercedes Benz.

He thought of Judy and Hector and their smiling chocolate baby, happily expecting a good life with all the odds stacked against it. He remembered Sizwe's words in the parking garage, and the shock of seeing Henry's son sell what could only be drugs to clear-eyed youths willing to try anything to become men.

And he thought of Teema, holding her beating sick heart with one hand, straining to see through her thick lenses and handing out advice to others of her age, telling them not to lie down and wait to die, but to roll up their sleeves and help the children face the future by telling them the stories of the past.

The list of what was good here went on and on, and his name cropped up in each item. But it wasn't the name of David Clayton. It was Dawid de Lange. The other David was written in each line of the list of things he disliked about where he'd been for the last decades: the LA pollution, the violence that erupted from inequality, the mindless rat-race, the hopelessness of political change in a stagnant system, the lowest common denominator dictating the standards in the field of mass entertainment, the burden of investments, the chill of retirement and, above all, the constant reminder of youth not being his to spend.

Looking at the garden around him, David couldn't think of a better place to start again halfway through a life well lived. He got up and walked past the fed-up squirrel who clutched its tiny paws to its chest in affront when no gift of food was forthcoming. He walked along the small paths edged with indigenous flora, stepped under pergola of bougainvillaea and eventually left the Gardens through a small wrought-iron gate and found himself back in the city.

He was immediately struck by the sudden emptiness of the street. The business day had ended. Most of the cars had left and the usual bustle was down to a trickle of a few people hurrying toward the places where they could drop their daily armour and be themselves.

He put his hand deep into his pockets and walked up towards the slopes of Signal Hill. What Deli had said made sense. She always made sense and David knew he ignored her instinct at his peril. He had definite feelings beyond mere friendship for Suzie Bernard and didn't want to hurt Deli by lying to her. He would have to tell her and it would have to be tonight. He would also have to phone Suzie and explain. He would also have to contact Joanie and give her Ms Nkotse's message about the christening.

Suddenly a figure leapt out of nowhere and stood in front of him, a mass of rags and wearing a battered hat with a dove's tailfeather in it. David stopped abruptly, balling his fists instinctively and glad he didn't have any valuables on him.

The creature uttered a sound and David could make out a *bergie's* battered brown face under wisps of hessian that were stuffed under the hat.

"Evening, Master," said the beast and David saw a glint of toothless gum behind bared lips and sniffed an age of wine matured down the throat.

"Evening," David politely replied. He heard laughter to the side and looked into a small rubble-strewn plot where a building had been demolished. Against the grimy wall of the adjoining warehouse, a group of other *bergies* were clustered round a fire warming themselves and passing a large plastic chemicals bottle between them from which each took large swigs.

"Are they drinking meths?" asked David, hoping it was cooldrink, but knowing it wasn't.

"No, Master! It's nice wine. We pour it in that plastic jar and then we get a few cents back on the empty bottle to invest."

"Invest?"

"Ja, invest in more wine. Is Master lost?" God, did he still look like a tourist?

"Nee man, ek kom van die Kaap," David heard himself say in fluent Afrikaans and the *bergie* smiled a broad grin of brotherhood. Then he started jabbering away in his dialect, of which David could only catch a word here and there. He rambled on about his makeshift home in the mountain, where his wife was sick, and that he needed salt. He grinned and said something about a dog.

"You need salt for a dog?" asked David, reverting back to his American accent in the hope that more clarity would be forthcoming in English from the hessian heap.

"Ja, Master, my wife is sick and I need some salt because we eat a big roast tonight!" The pink gums glinted wickedly and his ripe whiff of life hit David in the nostrils.

"And the dog?"

"No," said the mountain man, shaking his head. "I never said we eat a dog. I said we eat a dinner! There." He pointed at the coven of fellow *bergies* who were dancing around the fire in happy abandon. Then David saw a taller figure leaning against a wall to one side and looked again. Wasn't that his blind beggar friend from the pavement?

He waved and called. "Phillip?"

The figure didn't react, but slowly turned away and seemed to melt into an opening in the walls and disappear.

"You know Phillip?" asked the *bergie*.

"Yes, Phillip the blind beggar?"

"Blind?" The *bergie* shook his head. "No, Phillip is our lawyer. Ja, he's got eyes in the back of his head." One of the gathered faithful gave a yelp and invited them to the fire.

"You want to come and join us, Master?"

David laughed and looked at his watch.

"Hell no, look, it's time to get back to the hotel," he said and saw the *bergie* appreciate his timepiece.

"Never mind the time, come and check what's for dinner!"

The creature shuffled off, stepping carefully over stones and boxes. He stopped and waved at David to follow. David looked around, but there was no one nearby. No cars in the street, no movement down the road. It was as if Cape Town had survived the final holocaust and he was left only with the underbelly of society as his civilised sounding-board. He stepped closer to the gathering.

There was a structure built over the fire, a mass of twisted wires and pieces of iron, and lying on a grid of sorts, he saw six chickens being fried on the flames. The chemical bottle seemed to have no bottom and did another round of the happy hawkers, who drank and sang and laughed as he got closer.

A few called out to him with a "Hello master" here and a "Hey welcome darling" there. Hessian Head spoke in Afrikaans and everyone nodded and seemed impressed. He sidled up to David. "I said you're a policeman off-duty who's just keeping an eye on us. Otherwise you'll be viewed with suspicion." David nodded while wondering why a policeman of all people would be acceptable to these vagrants.

David hurriedly refused a sip from the communal jar. He sat on a block of concrete, mesmerised by the energy and the fluctuating attitudes. Within a sentence some would turn viciously on others and a fight was always just a gulp away.

Then a police siren suddenly cleaved the air and everyone froze in their merriment. David got up and turned as a police car cruised by. The uniformed driver shouted something out at them and Hessian Head gave him a deep bow while letting off a loud fart. This in turn set everyone off farting and yelling obscenities which again centred round the private parts of the policeman's mother.

"I must go," said David eventually, starting to back away. Hessian Head looked hurt. "You don't want some of our food?"

"I'm not a great chicken eater," David lied rather weakly and they all laughed.

"Chicken? God, you reckon we eat chicken that's fed on all those chemicals and gives you cancer? No man, we eat pure city food."

And it was then that David counted the six rat tails dangling off the grid into the glowing embers.

"Yes well, have a nice time," he said taking another step back to the security of a deserted street. "Is it someone's birthday?" he added, wanting to fill the space with small talk till he could walk away without breaking his neck over rubble.

Hessian Head shook his body from side to side. "No Master man, it's our Christmas dinner!" Everyone hooted with laughter and danced in circles, the setting sun giving the party an eerie orange glow.

"But it's not Christmas!" David laughed.

The *bergie* threw his arms in the air and shouted to the darkening sky. "It's Cape Town! Here every day is Christmas!"

He stopped in the hotel foyer to put a call through to Suzie in Clifton, but had left the numbers up in his coat. As he passed reception the girl on duty called him. "Mr Clayton?" For a moment he didn't register, then looked at her waving at him. "Sir? Your wife left you a note."

David took the envelope wondering if this was the final note of his marriage. But Deli had only scribbled a few brief instructions.

He smiled. "Giselle?" he said and the girl at the desk nodded.

"Yes, Mrs Clayton asked for tickets to the ballet. She's taken hers and said she'd meet you there. You can take a taxi from here."

He looked at his watch; there was not much time. So he quickly showered and dressed, and put a call through to Joanie Craig who was delighted at the news of the christening and sounded a little drunk.

Suzie wasn't at the flat in Clifton.

"No," said the voice of the owner, "but she left a note for you. Do you want to come and collect it?"

"Could you read it to me?" he asked, preparing for an icy broad-side from the unpredictable Miss Bernard.

"Okay. Hang on." So Suzie'd gone back to Jo'burg. He'd now have to leave a message on her machine. "Eh … here it is: 'De Lange you shit. You'll leave one note too many one day and then no one will believe you when you call "Fire"! Leave a message on my machine. I want to meet the Delicatessen. Suzie.' That's it."

David thanked her and immediately phoned Suzie's flat in Johannesburg. He was relieved to hear the familiar recorded voice asking him to wait for the bleep. Then he left a silly message which he hoped said more than he dared, and then he took a cab to the Opera House on the Foreshore.

The ballet had started and he stood at the back until there was a suitable break in the concentration for him to take his seat. Of all the things to come to in Cape Town, he thought, as the music pulled him back into that spring in London in 1969 when he'd met Deli Hepburn on the set of a television film of the ballet *Giselle*.

She was an assistant dresser, meaning she had to be in ten places at the same time and do everything no one would deign to be seen doing. He was a runner, meaning he was illegally employed at a slave wage and was expected to be grateful for the abuse he suffered at the tongues of the old pros.

They wanted to call their first daughter Giselle, but luckily Deli's parents intervened and presented them with various ancestral alternatives.

But this music with its magnificent tale woven through the tragedy of sound and movement, always remained as the one thing Deli and David could call 'their song and dance'! He was eventually ushered down the aisle into a row and sat down next to Deli.

She nudged him with her elbow and pointed at the stage. "Hi! Isn't this a kick in the soft parts?" she hissed as the next act started with a graceful orchestral introduction.

The ballet was so familiar to them and yet each time the freshness of the emotion etched out a new scenario. He heard Deli sigh deeply a few times, always at the same place where she'd sighed deeply on the countless times they'd seen the ballet together during their marriage.

Then he leant towards her. She reciprocated and he felt her cold ear brush against his warm lips. "Have you found someone else?" he whispered.

She sat still for quite some time, looking at the movement on stage. "Yes," she eventually whispered back.

David wasn't sure what he felt. Part of him jolted in anger, while part of him was relieved that his later confession would not be so one-sided.

He stayed in his position and asked, "Younger?"

She didn't move, just took a deep breath and let it out slowly. "Yes."

He felt a smile play on his lips. "Sex?"

She nodded slightly and her hair tickled his mouth. "Yes."

298

The ballerina was lifted high by her partner and the music glided into a crescendo.

"Condoms?" whispered Mr Clayton.

"God, yes!" replied Mrs Clayton.

"Me too," he hissed and they both got the giggles. She slipped her hand in his and loved him more than ever before.

The heavy floral curtains had not been drawn and the first peep of the sun seemed to be straight into their bedroom. A blinding shaft of light shot into David's eyes as he screwed them up look out across the misty waking city towards the furthest mountains of the Hottentots Holland range, eating a jagged blue line on the horizon. He sat up in bed and lifted himself on his elbows as the sunshine blinded him to all detail. He felt Deli move beside him.

"Are you awake?" he whispered.

"No, just dreaming that I'm awake," she purred. He felt her mould her body up against his and creep her fingers across his chest. The sunbeam warmed his face and he smiled.

"So, how did you sleep?" he asked.

"Danced all night."

"And how was the you know what?"

She chuckled. "Great without the plastic-bag. One forgets what a human touch is like without gloves."

They'd come back from the ballet and ordered the special candlelight dinner for two through room service. A friendly black man in a scarlet uniform wheeled a table into the room which was laid with silver and crystal fit for a king. They ate at leisure and talked about small unimportant things like what they felt about jealousy and possessions and relationships and each other.

"We've past the halfway mark, David. I just can't summons those demons of mistrust and throw a wobbly because the man I love needs to exercise his sexual self. I just no longer see the act of sex on the same par with the doing of friendship. Do you expect me to be upset about Suzie?"

"No, and I don't suppose you expect me to be furious about the toyboy!" he said knowing how relieved he was and yet feeling slightly cheated. Deli chuckled at the word 'toyboy'. "I suppose if we were younger ..." David carried on but she stopped him. She sat on his lap and blocked the candlelight from his eyes. It gave her a glowing halo around her head.

"David, we're mature people. We've been through the audition, we've presented a full three-act performance, and now let's enjoy the applause … and the Stage-Door Johnnies!"

"Or Stage-Door Suzies?"

Now she swung her legs out of the bed and sat on the edge of it, stretching her arms and giving a creaky yawn. "Good morning, sunshine!" she sang.

"What do you want to do today?" he asked.

"I want you to show me where you lived," she said with a sudden energy. "And where you went to school, where you …" She stopped and let him bite her finger teasingly. "Where you so clumsily had your way with Joanie Craig."

"I didn't. I watched."

"Aha! I always wondered where you were trained, Dawid de Lange. So now show me the scenes of the crime."

He rang the estate agent whose name he had scribbled in his notebook. He couldn't remember why he'd done that, but was pleased he had. The old De Lange home was still in the market.

"Maybe you've thought of buying the house?" Deli suggested as they drove out to the oak trees of St Andrew's Road.

David shook his head. "No, I don't think that would be practical," he said.

"Well, I can't think of a nicer place to come for a dirty weekend. The world's so small now, and it's amazing what a Gold Card can do!" she laughed, patting her handbag.

A pale young man was waiting for them at the little gate. "My name is Mr Loft and I represent the agents," he said and shook their hands gravely.

Deli stood at the wooden gate and looked in to the garden. She gave a sigh of delight. "Oh, David! It's just like the jigsaw puzzle I had when I was a kid with the measles."

The house stood snug under sprawling oak trees, the small windows cheekily jutting out of the roof and a wildness of creepers trying to cover as much of the mottled cream walls as possible. The garden itself looked a little awry, with the grass too long and the shrubs spread helter-skelter across the path to the front door.

"Would you like to go inside?" asked young Mr Loft and led the way, the large latch-key poised in his hand. David suddenly felt a strange sense of dread as the door opened and he smelt the same mustiness that had been such a part of his life for so long.

"Is this the smell that gave you the asthma when you were

300

small?" Deli asked, sniffing the air and enjoying it. He just nodded. The house was quite devoid of any furniture, the dark wooden floor stretching from one room to the next, offset by similar dark wood beams in the ceilings on which the floor of the upstairs section of the house rested. The stone fireplace had been replaced with a more structured piece, set in with hand-painted tiles, but otherwise the living-room was the same.

David could see Renate sprawled on the carpet in front of the roaring fire doing her homework, with his mother sewing some torn school shirt and his father reading a book on travel, something he always wanted to do, but never allowed himself to enjoy.

"We used to sit here, just being together," David said, while feeling sad that it sounded so simplistic. "There was no TV, and radio was only allowed on special occasions. No pop music ..."

"God, how terrible!" Deli joked with wide eyes at Mr Loft who smiled honest agreement. "You had to talk to each other? And read? And listen to music?" She shook her head at the young man. "Can't imagine anything worse!"

"My little daughter is now five and she has her own TV-set and video machine," the estate agent said proudly.

Deli smiled sweetly. "Good for you, Mr Loft!" she congratulated, "Start them nice and young, I always say."

"So do I," said the young man and led them up the stairs. The one small room that so snugly fitted in under the slant of the roof had two windows, one looking out front to the street and the other across the side garden into the wooded edges of the property.

"This was my room," David said very quietly.

The young boy who'd spent so many years planning to conquer the world wasn't there anymore. The marks on the wall where his rugby heroes had been stuck were no longer there. The loose floorboard under which he had kept his love letters to Suzie, the ones he never had to guts to give her, was covered with a grey wall-to-wall carpet. There was a brown stain near the window.

Deli slipped her hand in his and squeezed. "Just as I imagined. It's like your den at home."

David looked at her amazed. "Is it? Really? I suppose you're right." His den had a slanting roof and two windows of a similar size and it had cost him a fortune to have it all specially built into the west wing of the house where he worked. "Yes," he smiled, "I suppose I rebuilt my old room in LA."

The rest of the bedrooms also brought back many memories.

Renate's little room was studied in silence. David had so much to say about her, but thought it not the place to start. The kitchen was completely rebuilt and there were a few more bathrooms added to the rooms upstairs, but otherwise the house in St Andrew's Road hadn't changed as much as the boy from St Andrew's Road.

"Where did Teema stay?" Deli asked, as they stood around the kitchen looking at the unimaginative structures that had been lifted from some interior design magazine.

David unlocked the back door and led them into the little courtyard, now anchored by a healthy lemon tree in its centre. Towards the back he saw the door to the room where Teema had spent the years of his youth.

She'd sit on a kitchen chair outside her room in the sun that baked into the concrete yard and encased everyone in a warm jacket. Teema loved summer and would bask in the heat of the day with complete abandon. The wet washing would flap heavily on the lines that were stretched in two rows across the courtyard from pole to pole.

"How can you just sit there in the sun like a big cow?" Dawid once asked her, not meaning it unkindly, but being reminded of a gentle beast of the field, as Teema sat arms folded in her lap, chewing at some bits of cold meat leftovers.

"Because I am a big cow," she said with eyes closed, "and the milk of my kindness is what will make you into a strong man one day." She rocked herself gently on the chair. "The sun gives me life and makes my battery full so that the lights in my eyes never go out." She opened them and gave him a wink. "You see, my child, if there is no more sun, your Teema will turn into a small dried-up stick and just break into dust like the vineyards after no rain."

David laughed at his recall and pointed at the door. "That's her room. God, I can see her sitting there …"

The door was closed. He tried the latch, but the wood seemed to be swollen with damp. Only after he and Mr Loft pushed at it heavily with their shoulders, did the door give way and open with a creak. The dinginess within gave very little indication of what the room looked like.

Mr Loft switched on the light. A naked bulb shot its illumination over what must've been a storage area. The room was a few square metres large. There was a chipped wash-basin in one corner and the marks on the cold cement floor showed where washing machines and other modern-age 'Teemamatics' had stood.

"This is where Teema lived?" echoed Deli with a grimace.

David's mouth was dry as he looked around the cell. Yes, this was the room where the woman who brought him up had lived, through winters on a concrete floor, through summers with a window no bigger than a large box of washing powder. Maybe there was another room? He didn't want to ask, in case it was smaller than this one.

"No," he said with a laugh, "this can't be it. Goodness no, this is a hovel! We'd never allow Teema to live like this ... No, I think Teema's room must've been demolished when they built onto the house." He waved vaguely at an area of the main house that looked as old as the rest. "Never mind," he said lightly. "It's not that important. Anyway, Teema spent most weekends with her family in Langa."

Mr Loft nodded and Mrs Clayton walked out. She'd heard of the abysmal state of the accommodation of some domestic workers in this country, but that little hole in the wall just made her sick. But her angry speech that she'd prepared in her head to make once Mr Loft had left evaporated, as she and David stood at the gate looking at the house again.

"It's so beautiful," he said wistfully.

"It's so cheap!" she said encouragingly. He looked at her and she showed him the amount Mr Loft had noted on his business card. "In dollars that's less than you'd pay for a new car-port."

They walked round the house once more, smelling the fresh odour of rotting leaves, watching the small birds bitch and warble and argue in a hibiscus bush. Through the trees the maternal limbs of the mountain seemed to open and admit them into her womb.

"You know, I wonder ..." he started.

"You could use this as a base for ... well, anything you like, David. Writing, setting up film production? I mean, just look at what you get for your money!" She waved around her at one of the most perfect film locations in the world. "And you could invite Teema to come and stay." David's face lit up. "Yes! She could have her own room upstairs! She could come for holidays ..." He laughed. "She can boss me around again."

Joanie Craig wasn't feeling great that morning. She'd had a rough night being sorry for herself and had polished off a bottle of wine she'd kept for a rainy day.

303

"Oh God, I feel like death," she mumbled.

"You look shitty, Ma," laughed Judy, holding her baby on her lap.

"Hector will collect us here in a moment and then you'll have this office all to yourself." She looked at the filing cabinet. "You might even have a sip of medicinal whisky from your medicine chest?"

Joanie looked shocked. "What are you suggesting? That I drink? On my own? God, since you've been with that boy, you've really become as cheeky as him and have no respect for your mother!"

"That's what black boys teach us white girls, Ma. You gotta be honest to have a chocolate baby in this goddamn town." She hugged the giggling bundle of laughs in her lap.

"And must you adopt his awful American accent? You're a South African and should be proud of the way you speak!" Joanie suddenly heard her own voice and it didn't sound so great either.

A soft knocking at the office door got her out of her chair and she opened it with the words: "Don't scratch, Hector, enter!"

The elegant woman in the passage gave a step back in reaction to Joanie's tone. "Oh," said Joanie apologetically. "Sorry, were you looking for me?"

"Joanie Craig?" the woman said in a real American accent. Joanie glanced back at Judy.

"Now this is not your mother-in-law, for sure." She smiled at her white visitor. "Come in." Deli Clayton entered the office and smiled at Judy. "What a cute little baby," she cooed.

"She's mine," Judy beamed. "Her father is black."

Joanie groaned and sat at her desk. Her daughter turned to her with a frown. "And don't keep doing that, Mummy! It's a fact and I'm proud of it!"

"And so you should be," Deli nodded and held her finger out at the little person who grabbed it for dear life with a gurgle and a burp. "So this is the little sweetie that dear Reverend Nkotse is to baptise next week?"

Judy stared at Deli, then looked at her mother for help. Joanie half rose to her feet. "How do you know, Mrs ..."

"Deli Clayton. Deli de Lange. I'm still not sure which works best here."

Joanie sat again with her mouth open, letting her eyes unashamedly travel over the smartness and delicacy of the woman that Dawid de Lange had married. "Well I'll be damned! Does Dawid know you're here?"

Deli laughed. "Yes, good grief, he gave me your address."

"Why, is there a problem?" Joanie glanced at her daughter, hoping the saga of the christening would not flare up again into a crisis.

"No," said Deli, "Frankly I just wanted to meet you. I'm leaving Cape Town tomorrow morning. David is taking me to visit the Kruger National Park and the Lost City at ... what is that place called?"

"Sun City," said Judy, bouncing her baby on her knee. "In the black homeland of Bophuthatswana."

"That's the name that escapes me," laughed Deli.

"My man ... her father came out to dance there, then he got a job here with the ballet," Judy said proudly.

"Oh? We saw *Giselle* last night. He's dancing in that?"

"You colour-blind, Deli?" asked Joanie wryly. "How many black swans can there be?"

"There are no swans in *Giselle*, Ma! That's *Swan Lake*."

Joanie Craig looked to the heavens and waved her hands in mock resignation. "Ballet! It's all the same to me. Anorexic girls with no tits and boys with big arses and ridiculous bulges!"

"Speak for yourself, mumsy dear!" A tall athletic black man slid into the room through the half-open door and covered Judy and the baby with warm kisses. "Hello women, how's tricks?" he laughed in his specific American way.

Joanie sighed at the tease. "I was actually talking about you, Hector ... careful the vase!" She rescued her flowers from being toppled off the desk.

Hector whooped and lifted his baby into the air. She greeted her father with a piercing shriek of delight. His teeth sparkled in his smile, as he nodded at Deli. "My lover's mother, it seems, has the hots for me. I think it's just her dormant Afrikaner prejudice coming out to bite a piece from the forbidden fruit!" Judy hooted with laughter and gave him a playful box on his thigh.

Joanie closed her eyes and pretended she was in Poland. "I'm not listening to this. Please, take my daughter and my grand ..." She swallowed the rest of the word.

"Say it, Ma!" demanded her daughter sternly.

Joanie opened her eyes and took a deep breath, forcing out the word painfully. "Granddaughter ... out of here and get them back before we close. I want to discuss the christening next week."

"Will you be coming with your husband?" Judy asked Deli.

"I won't sadly, but I'm sure David will be there." She went on to answer Joanie's unasked question. "He's decided to stay on here for a bit. In fact, he's at the estate agent right now, putting in a bid for their old house in St Andrew's Road."

"You don't say ..." murmured Joanie fascinated, while offering her cheek to be kissed first by the tall black man, then the petite white girl and finally smooched wetly by the laughing baby.

When they'd left, Joanie offered Deli the chair. "So you're Delicatessen." Joanie repeated and Deli laughed.

"Yes, I believe that's what you and Suzie Bernard call me. I look forward to meeting her too."

Joanie raised an eyebrow. "You know about Suzie?" she asked.

"I know all about you too, Miss Craig!" Deli twinkled.

"Jesus!" exploded Joanie. "What sort of marriage do you have?"

"A lasting one?" They both laughed.

Outside an ambulance howled past in the street below. Deli crossed her legs and sat back in the chair. She smiled at Joanie Craig, enjoying her perplexed look and thinking what fun she must be after a few drinks.

"Do we have some time?" she asked.

"Yes," announced Joanie generously. "What do we have in mind?" She glanced at her filing cabinet in anticipation. Deli Clayton leant forward and said softly.

"Tell me about Dawid de Lange."

And Joanie did, in detail and with great affection.

The subject of their gossip was signing the papers that would give him back his little room under the roof in St Andrew's Road.

"You say the bank-draft will be coming from America?" Mr Loft asked, delighted with his easy sale.

"Yes, my wife will organise all that from Los Angeles." He shook hands with a number of happy suited men and when he stood in the street outside the marble entrance to the office block, even the fumes from the cars at the traffic lights made him feel good.

Still a few things to do before he'd meet Deli at Joanie's office. He wondered how they were getting on, hoping that Joanie was in that morning, and not off sick nursing a 'cold'.

He started down the pavement, feeling the sunshine on his face and even sniffing a whiff of sea air. He looked up at the pert outline of Lion's Head and saw a fluffy cloud perched on its crown. That was a sure sign of coming rain, Teema had always told him.

He wanted Deli to meet Teema more than anyone else.

He bought an afternoon paper from the barefoot vendor on the corner and crossed the road to the next block. Then he stopped as he recognised his old friend, the Prince of the Pavement, holding court in his usual place.

Phillip was, as always, sitting with his back against the rough granite wall of the bank, wearing the same jeans and T-shirt all covered by the old grocer's overcoat, khaki-shaded and with the odd button missing. In front of him lay his wares carefully organised on a piece of cloth. The white stick gleamed on the sidewalk next to his hand and the roughly pencilled sign explained all:

> I AM BLIND AND CANNOT SEE
> LIKE YOU SO PLEASE HELP ME
> BUY A SOUVENIR!

David stepped closer to Phillip, looking at him carefully again. Was this the same figure he'd seen the day before without a white stick at the *bergie*'s last supper? Or were people of colour all tending to look alike to him, as many whites claimed? He stood next to the blind man and prodded him lightly with his foot.

"Hello, Your Highness?" he said and crouched down next to Phillip.

The unseeing eyes stared into nothing, but the mouth broke into a warm smile. "The American in Cape Town! Where have you been, my man? Life's been a drag without you!" Phillip's hands were again fluttering up and down on the pavement in front of him as if he was playing a piano concerto. "Tell me, did you find yourself?"

"Do I have a story for you …" David started, looking forward to telling someone of his plans for the future, but Phillip put a hand on his arm and stopped him mid-sentence.

"I'd love to hear, man, but I'm in terrible need."

David looked at the Prince of the Pavement concerned. He looked all right, considering. "What's the matter?" he asked.

"I have to go to the toilet!" Phillip said and pulled a face. "I can't see, but I still need to pee!" he added with a laugh.

David looked around wondering how this was to take place in a crowded main street.

"Where will you go?" he asked.

"I usually go round the corner to the coffee-shop," Phillip explained. "They let me use their facilities. I just need someone to

307

sit here with my wares and keep an eye on everything. Can you do that for me?"

David hesitated for a moment, then shrugged. "Sure, no problem."

Phillip hoisted himself up and stood holding his white stick horizontally at the wall. "I won't be long," he said, looking down with a smile and David could swear he winked straight at him. "Just enjoy the sun." And then tapped his way down the side of the bank and turned the corner.

David opened his newspaper and put it down on the pavement, sitting down on page one. He hadn't had a chance to glance at the headlines, one of which spread angrily across the page above a photograph of Sizwe Masekela and others, killed in a security-force swoop on known terrorists in 'an unrest-related incident' somewhere in the Midlands of Natal. David watched the cars cruise by, noticing the surface of the roads in urgent need of repair. It seemed, like New York, all cities were experiencing an abrupt change of life and a breakdown in the smoothness of local government that had so long been taken for granted.

He was suddenly aware of a woman standing in front of him, staring down angrily at his obvious eyesight. He glanced down the pencilled sign at his side and looked up at her with a smile.

"Are you really blind, my man?" she asked in a metallic tone. David quickly closed his eyes tightly, not wanting to destroy Phillip's credibility. He'd just sit like this till the Prince of the Pavement had finished his pee, and then he'd tell him what his plans were for the rest of his life.

Dawid de Lange smiled with excitement and was just about to start planning what he'd say to Suzie Bernard, when the first coin clunked into the empty blind man's cup in his hand.